Also by Susan Conley

The Foremost Good Fortune

Paris Was the Place

Paris Was the Place

SUSAN CONLEY

ALFRED A. KNOPF *New York* 2013

THIS IS A BORZOI BOOK
PUBLISHED BY ALFRED A. KNOPF

www.aaknopf.com

Knopf, Borzoi Books, and the colophon are registered trademarks
of Random House, Inc.

Grateful acknowledgment is made to the following for permission to
reprint previously published material:
A. S. Kline: Excerpt from "Requiem" by Ann Akhmatova, translated
by A. S. Kline, copyright © 2000–2013 by A. S. Klein. www.poetryin
translation.com. Used by permission of the translator.
Random House, Inc.: Excerpt from "Archaic Torso of Apollo," translated by Stephen Mitchell, copyright © 1982 by Stephen Mitchell, from
The Selected Poetry of Rainer Maria Rilke by Rainer Maria Rilke, translated by Stephen Mitchell. Used by permission of Random House, Inc.

Library of Congress Cataloging-in-Publication Data
Conley, Susan, 1967–
Paris was the place / by Susan Conley. — First edition.
     pages   cm
ISBN 978-0-307-59407-5 (hardback) 1. Women teachers—Fiction.
2. Americans—France—Paris—Fiction. 3. Immigrants—France—
Paris—Fiction. 4. Paris (France)—Social conditions—20th century—
Fiction. 5. Domestic fiction. I. Title.
PS3603.05365P37 2013
813'.6—dc23   2012050901

Jacket photograph © Jacinta Bernard Kellner/Arcangel Images
Jacket design by Kelly Blair

Manufactured in the United States of America
First Edition

To my husband, Tony,
and to my boys, Thorne and Aidan

And so when hats in Paris are lovely and french and everywhere then France is alright. So Paris was the place.

—GERTRUDE STEIN

Paris Was the Place

1

Family history: a shared story

I try taking Boulevard de Strasbourg away from the crowds at the St. Denis metro stop to find the girls. This isn't one of those gilded Paris streets heralding the end of a war or the launch of a new haute couture line. The sky's already turned gray again, but it's flanged lilac in places. The early dusk settles around the Beauty for You hair salon and a small pyramid of green-and-white shampoo bottles in the *pharmacie* window. I'm almost lost but not entirely, searching for an asylum center full of girls on Rue de Metz. Two mothers in saris pick over veggies while their toddlers jump in place on the sidewalk holding hands. A *tabac* sign yells LOTTERY FRANCE!

The sequencing of the neighborhoods here baffles me—arranged like the curvature of some terrestrial snail. I'm in the tenth arrondissement, anchored by two of Paris's great train stations, where the alleyways weave into mapless places. I'm not embarrassed to carry my *Michelin*. But it's colder here at four o'clock in January than I ever thought it could be, and three of my fingers have gone numb.

My lunatic father has spent his whole professional life drawing maps. He's older now. Where, I don't know exactly. But I feel him with me today while I walk. A high white cement wall runs along the start of Rue de Metz—a one-way alley off Boulevard de Strasbourg.

Four blue suns have been painted on the wall and the bodice of a woman's lime green dress. The end of the wall is a deeper cerulean, and the graffiti here looks done with chalk—spaceships and loopy sea creatures and messy stars.

Number 5 is a low, two-story brick interruption after the wall with an airport orange wooden door and a bronze plaque the size of an Etch A Sketch that reads ÉCOLE PRIMAIRE. Primary school. But this can't be a school anymore, can it? Unless I've been sent to the wrong place? Two bow windows sit on either side of the door like eyes on a face, and the door itself is like a mouth that might try and eat you.

A woman pulls it open, and the electric locks zing. She's got enormous black frizzed hair up in a scarf. "By the grace of God, you've come. We never know who will actually arrive. And this is not a tea party we are hosting here, you know? So we like it when people come who say they will come."

It's so good and unexpected to have someone waiting for me in this city. She says her name is Sophie. That she's here by way of Cairo. Her smile is a force field that pulls her to me. She takes me down the narrow hall, and her black tunic flutters behind her like a sail. Small pieces of kilims and Persians cover the walls of her windowless office. She says, "The girls here are desperate to get out, and they are oh so lonely for their mothers you cannot even know. But nothing is going to touch them while they are in here with me."

Then a man—early forties, gray crew cut, blank scrunched-up face—peeks his head inside and stares until I look away. He's in dark blue—shirt and trousers—with a gun in a black holster on his right hip. "You are new," he says in rapid-fire French. "New people sign in before they do anything else." What his gun does is take away my ability to use French. I follow him to an office at the start of the hall, where a small black-and-white television sits on a desk, playing a loop from surveillance cameras. There's the sidewalk outside and the bare poplar tree and the knees and shins of Parisians walking by.

"Visa number? Full name and place of residence?" He's got a green poster of the Paris metro system taped on his wall. I've taught classes in one language or another for almost a decade, but I'm jangly today. It has something to do with the locks and the surprise of that. But it's not the physical quality of being trapped, exactly. Or the lack of sunlight. It's that the locks are making me feel lonelier than I ever remember. People are living out their days inside here. So I call this man Truffaut in my mind, after the French movie director who made the new-wave film *The 400 Blows*. It helps to think I have a secret on him.

"Location of employment?"

I've studied French for years. Sometimes I'm lucky and dream in it. But I have to wait for my French to come back to me. My heart is beating fast—leaving in quick ascending scales and then coming back. Who is this man? It's the locks on the door again—the idea that no one in here can get out, and I always like to get out. To know the exits. All I manage is "The Academy of France. I'm a poetry professor there." These vowels are warm in my mouth and pleasing.

Truffaut laughs. *"La poésie."* He licks his lips and scratches under his nose. "How does poetry have anything to do with this place?" Everything, I want to say. My plan, though uncooked, is to teach the girls poetry. I know this sounds a little ridiculous. We're in a locked asylum center in the middle of Paris, and what the girls probably need most is a really good lawyer. But poetry is concise. It can hold enormous amounts of emotion. My friend Rajiv is the one who asked me to come here. He's an adviser to the center, and married to my best friend, Sara. Rajiv told me the girls' hearings would rest on wildly compelling, condensed versions of how each girl ended up in France and why they can't go back to their home countries. So they need poetry.

But I don't say a word of this to Truffaut. I've been in Paris almost five months, long enough to learn the part of the American *jeune fille*, even if, at thirty, I'm a little old for it. I smile and he takes my passport and job contract and holds the u.s.a. stamp close to his face. "Willow Pears. Poetry professor at the Academy of France. I suppose we should be lucky to have you here."

There's no good way to answer this. I'm not going to admit anything about the poetry. I'm afraid he'll make me leave if he finds out

I'm not trained in literacy or something else more helpful. I followed my older brother, Luke, to France. I would follow him anywhere. He is my lifeline. Applied for every single teaching job I could find in Paris and was so damn lucky to get the one at the academy. Truffaut slaps my passport down on the desk—which is steel, three drawers to a side, with black plastic pull handles. The sound is the thwap of a fly-swatter. It's been nine minutes on the industrial clock above Truffaut's door, but time crawls.

He finally hands the passport back and points me down the hall to Sophie's office. By now I'm one of those little children who used to come here every day for *école primaire*. Truffaut has shamed me. For what I don't know, but it's not surprising, this feeling of somehow not giving him what he wants. Of not performing correctly. The French enunciate the final syllable of the word "stupid" so it becomes *stu-peeede*. This is how Truffaut makes me feel.

Jazz plays from a radio on Sophie's desk. Reedy clarinets and the voice of one clear trumpet. She puts her hands on my shoulders and gently lowers me down to the wooden stool in her office and I'm grateful for that. For the simple connection. It brings me back to Rue de Metz and the girls. Where are the girls? I can't wait to meet them. "These are girls. In dangerous positions. They've left families. They've seen wars. They've known bad men. God wish it was not true." She's a large woman with smooth, brown skin and brown eyes that look wet and shiny. Her lips are the color of dark plums covered in gloss, and the tiny diamond chip on the left side of her nose doesn't move when she talks. Truffaut is scary. Hopefully Sophie's the sane one. There's always got to be at least one sane person. "I am Egyptian. Okay. So don't ever think I know what's going on with the French justice system. But I've been here three years, and I don't mind repeating myself." She speaks English with this high-pitched French-Egyptian accent, which makes her sound incredibly convincing. Then she does the French thing with her mouth where she makes a "poof" and shrugs like she's really exasperated. I pretend to listen, but I'm thinking, Don't let these girls down.

"A few girls already have English. But only French is allowed at the hearings, and they're never going to learn enough French by their court dates. So we teach English here. The international language. We get interpreters for the court. There is an organization called OFPRA. You must know about this, yes? The French Office for the Protection of Refugees and Stateless Persons. They run the asylum centers. There are about twelve girls here any given week. Many of them don't know how old they are."

"How could they not know?"

"They are girls. They are replaceable. Their parents didn't mark their birthdays. The French court's obsession is how the girls got into France in the first place. They want to catch the ones who came illegally. They want to trip them up in a lie or find them with fake papers long before the girls get to an actual hearing with a judge. The court never wants to listen to why the girls are really here. Are you following me okay?"

"But I didn't think it would be like a jail." I want to tell her that I might have screwed this up by coming—that I'm not good at incarceration. My heart is still racing. I'm embarrassed. It's the locks getting to me again. I wish I were good. I wish I were stronger.

"Ha!" Sophie lets out a belly laugh. "We are low-security! You think this is bad. You should see the big detention centers. You only get to stay in here if you've come in legally—a tourist visa or a short-time work permit. All my girls are on appeal. Only cases that have good evidence get appeals. But anyone can apply for asylum. It's a basic human right, okay? When they deport someone, they call it a 'voluntary return to country of origin,' but I've never seen a girl leave here voluntarily. Sedated, yes. Screaming, yes. But not voluntary. Sometimes the girls are here six months. Sometimes shorter. But 1989 is not a good time to be illegal in France. The far right is on the move. Our friend Le Pen is making it much harder for the girls. Maybe your new president, George Bush, can talk sense into him? Maybe not. But the economy is poor here, and this doesn't help. Your dollar is too strong. There is resentment. Identity checks. House searches."

———

SIX TEENAGE GIRLS COME to my class that night. They don't have to. The classes aren't mandatory. They walk into the common room with the dropped foam ceiling, and my stomach turns over. It's been a long time since I haven't known pretty much how a class will go, and tonight I've got no idea. The walls are white cinder block, with two narrow wooden windows at the end of the room that face the street. There's a nubby olive couch that I pushed closer to the chairs and the bench, and a black-and-orange flowered rug, but it feels bare in here. The plywood shelves are stacked with paperbacks: *Conversational English in Ten Basic Steps, Street Maps of Paris, Bangladeshi Cooking for the Novice.*

Two of the girls wear saris—fire red and the other green like a fake Arizona lawn. There's so much more fabric involved in a sari than I knew, and the moving around of the long piece that goes over their shoulders to get it right. Two girls wear stonewashed jeans, and the other two wear head scarves and embroidered tunics over pants. All of them seem quietly against me, which is partly a language deal and partly what always happens on the first day of any class, no matter how much the students want it to go well.

The girls sit very still on the furniture, so it's hard to tell if some are breathing. They look fragile. Breakable. They don't make eye contact except with one another. What I try to do is divorce them from their unspoken pact. "Hello," I say slowly and smile. "Greetings on this cold night in Paris. Welcome to our first workshop. My name is Willow. But everyone calls me Willie. Now could you each please say your own name out loud?"

The girl on my left has a round face and dark pond eyes. She sits rod straight, which is how I can tell she's paying attention. I'm getting more nervous. This doesn't usually happen. Usually I start to talk and I'm relieved by the sound of my voice and climb back into my body. But have I said that I don't have any literacy training? Or that I'm scattered tonight? "Yes. You. Could you start for us?" I turn to the girl on my left again with the big eyes and green sari.

Her hair's pulled back in a loose braid. She looks at me. "My name? My name will be meaning very little to you, but I will share it with you anyway in case it is useful. I am Gita Kapoor. I am asking you to help me so that I don't have to go back home to India."

I'm flooded by how quickly she's pushed things forward between us. There's an urgency now—a kind of chemical imbalance between what small things I can offer the girls and what they probably need. The battleship of a radiator clangs under the windows. Rajiv told me about the stream of caseworkers and lawyers who come in here to help. But I'm alone with the girls tonight. Maybe they have no use here for an American professor schooled in poetry.

The girl in the chair next to Gita says, "Long after the British tore us in two, I lived part of my life in one half of India and part in the other half. I am Moona." Her face is narrow, and she's got much wavier hair that Gita's, pulled back in a bun that puffs up at the front.

The girl next to Moona wears black Elvis Costello glasses and sequinned jeans held up by a belt with metal sprockets. "I am from Liberia. You can call me Precy."

Then the small girl at the far end of the couch says, "I am Esther." It's almost a whisper. "I am from the Congo."

The other two girls sit close together on the bench. One wears a blue tunic and pants and a red head scarf with glittery green and orange stripes. A black headpiece under the scarf completely covers her hair and neck. She stands up, embarrassed, and leans toward Moona and whispers. Then she looks at me. "Rateeka."

"She cannot understand your English very well or the Hindi," Moona says. "I learned Urdu in Kashmir. I will try to speak to them, but I only know a little."

The other girl on the bench just says, "Zeena," and waves. Her head scarf is bright purple, and she also has the black piece underneath so it looks like two head scarves, one on top of the other. "Zeena."

I reach for my bag on the floor and pass out pencils and small spiral notebooks covered in blue flowers that look like snowflakes. The pages inside are lined. "I'd like to start by doing a drawing. I'd like you to draw a picture of your old house with this pencil if you can. Could you do that?"

They stare down at their laps again like they're waiting for a secret sign to begin. "Could you try? I think it'll be good if you can. We'll use these houses for some practice talking in English. Why don't we start the drawing? Then maybe Rateeka and Zeena will understand once they see what we're doing."

More of the painful silence. No one says a word. A leftover alphabet is stenciled in blue on the wall above the windows, and I stare up at it and try not to panic. How are we going to get through the next hour if no one will draw? Each of the girls looks slightly bored. Their thin arms and legs disappear into the mouths of the upholstered furniture. But I think fear can look disarmingly close to boredom.

Then Gita says, "It is time for the class to begin. We must do what the teacher is asking if we are going to get any help inside this place." She smiles a perfect row of very small, square top teeth. Her bottom teeth are bigger and crowded to the front.

The class really only starts after Gita speaks, because they listen to her. We all listen to her. "You are asking us to draw our old houses on this paper? The houses we were living in before France?" She puts her hand over her mouth and smiles. "I do not know why you are asking us this when we are here in France. When we are trying to leave our old lives and our old families and our old countries behind." She looks back down at her lap. Her brown eyes take up half her face, which is a tougher face than I realized. Her body is thin but strong underneath the sari. She has a pendant on a chain that she keeps fingering with her right hand.

"Yes, Gita." I lean toward her and smile too quickly. "Yes, exactly." I want to be some kind of recording device that the girls can speak things into. I just want them to talk. Moona says something fast to Gita—in Hindi? Then she sizes me up. "We can probably do that." She's more wary than Gita. "We can try what you are asking."

They all draw in the spiral notebooks—rectangular shapes and thin, narrow buildings and short, round houses made with the outlines of brick. It's quiet, nervous work. When it seems like everyone's done, I hold up my drawing of three thin trees in front of a low, one-story house. I can't draw to save my life, but I've shaded in the bay below the house and the small view of the houseboats. "If you can try to form one sentence in your mind about your house, it would be good. Just one thing you'd like us to know about it. Please try to speak in English if you can."

Teaching can be a lightning-fast popularity contest with a very small population of voters. Your status rises and plummets in the course of one hour. It can also be like corralling students toward some unseen gate. Today I'm capable of more manipulation than usual. "This is my house in Sausalito, California, where I grew up. We were on the edge of the United States. My mother was a doctor. She worked at a hospital. My father was a mapmaker. He went into the desert to make maps that hung on the walls of my house. This is my family history. That's what I want to talk about today. Family and history. Together these two words are a huge part of the story you'll need to tell the judge at your hearing."

If the girls turn on me now—because of my old age or white skin, or the way I wear my red hair down past my shoulders with bangs that hide my eyes, or how I mispronounce their names—then the class is finished. How will I explain that to Rajiv?

There aren't any people in my drawing, but I know where my mother would stand, next to the biggest eucalyptus, if she were alive. My beautiful mother. There's an empty space in the drawing where she should be, and I miss her terribly in a way that's still mostly buried.

I look over at Gita and wait. I bet she isn't shy but has learned to bide her time. "Gita, could you do me a favor and go next?" She glances up and back down at her lap. There's this tension between her wanting to talk and a learned instinct to hold back and see. Then she raises her picture above her head defiantly, with both hands. "This is my house, near Jaipur in India. Two floors. One for the rice and hay. One for sleeping. Every day I was milking the cow and walking to school. I am not going back."

Tell me more, I want to say. Tell me everything. I'm hard to deny in the classroom. I have an eager face. I nod my head. I care about the details, so give them to me please. What I'd like is an invisible thread to connect me to each of them. It's not transparency I'm working toward. I can never fully know any of them. But as much as it's possible for a student to connect with a teacher—well, I want that inside here.

Moona goes next. She has a long, pointed nose and a small gold stud in each ear. Her picture is of a tall apartment building. "We were living in a slum outside Srinagar in Kashmir and I knew the Top Ten U.K. chart by heart." She walks in a small circle in front of the couch and points to the drawing in her hand. "But then the troubles were starting and we left because we are Hindu. We got two rooms on the sixth floor on a wide street in the south of Bombay. My father had to stay in Kashmir. This was before I began working at my uncle's shoe factory."

Moona is able to translate Rateeka and Zeena's descriptions of their small mud houses in a village outside Lahore. How have these two girls gotten from Pakistan to Paris alone? "They are Pashtun," Moona says. "The Punjabi army drove their families out. They have been living on the street in Paris for almost a year. I cannot believe they are still in one piece."

Then Precy says, "Hmmmmm. Hmmmm. Hmmm," and looks up at the ceiling. Her hair is in dozens of small braids. "We were very poor. Understand. I have six brothers and sisters in Monrovia." She looks down at her pencil scrawl, and I see tears on her face. Have we gotten ahead of ourselves tonight? This is another unspoken rule of teaching: I'll ask you to go further than you've ever gone with your story, but I won't abandon you in front of the class.

She smiles me away. There is a quiet fierceness to her. "The house was a plastic tarp with pieces of cardboard on the sides. Then my father got a job driving a bus. So we moved to a two-room apartment and I went to school. I was thirteen. There was a big rainstorm, and an orange van stopped on the road with the doors cut out. The war hadn't started, but my father talked of signing up with President Samuel Doe. It was raining hard. I found a place to stand inside the van, and I held on to the roof with one hand and we went to the river. That was my mistake. There were bad men in there, and it was the last day I saw my family." Precy's face clouds over.

She sits down and glares at me. "Why are you doing this? No, really, why are you helping us? What is in this for you?"

Part of me saw this question coming. But maybe not on the first night. "Being able to tell your story could be a way to save your life." I pause, because even though I believe what I said is true, the girls might think I'm crazy. Precy's about to be deported. She wants legal documents. Not stories. My face turns red. "There's nothing in this for me, Precy, but the chance to teach you. I'm a teacher. That's what I do." I'm not sure if she buys it.

I smile at Esther, and she looks away. Her hair is long and scraggly, her jeans baggier than Precy's. She's a little bird inside a black hoodie that has the words THE WHO in squiggly white capitals across the chest. The small bones in her arms move when she waves her hands. "We lived in the Congo, but I was very young when the men came and pushed us into Kenya. There was never electricity and bad things happened in the dark, but I cannot remember this to you. When we left that camp, we flew to a country called Sweden and we didn't have my mother anymore."

There's a softening. It started when the girls said their names out loud, and it ripples each time we drop down deeper into one of their stories. Who doesn't want to be seen or listened to? The girls' pasts feel so close they could get on and ride them back to their childhoods. They're better timekeepers than me, because when the white clock above the door says eight, they stand on cue and gather their notebooks and pencils, smile weakly, and leave.

Then Sophie pops her head in. She's almost ecstatic. "Gita was laughing for the first time she's been here! I could hear her in the hall, and this has got to be an act of God because nobody laughs much in here!" She helps me shove the couch against the wall with her hip.

"I asked the girls to draw houses, and they really tried. It's a great sign. Why do some of them have English?" I lean down to pick my bag up off the floor. I've got to go now. I've got to find my brother at our favorite Indian place for dinner.

"School is the magical potion that separates the girls from the girls." She clicks her tongue against the roof of her mouth and smiles. "Some of them got school and some of them didn't. Lord, it is good to have your new blood inside this place."

"How long has Gita been here?"

"Two weeks."

"Moona?"

"For Moona it's been close to two months."

"Moona has had bad luck."

Sophie stops me in the hall and puts her hand on my face. "You don't know good luck staring you in the face. You haven't been to the real detention centers in France. Five, ten, fifteen to a room and all waiting for a plane back to what? This here, my girl, is decent food and a bed and a chance in front of a judge." She steps into her office and waves me down the hall.

Will Truffaut let me out? Could he be on a coffee break? Then what? My heart beats faster again. How do you physically leave this building?

Then the door zings and a man with dark wet hair jumps in and moves to the side to make room. "Raining like a son of a bitch," he says in French and stomps his hiking boots so water that's pooled in the collar of his black raincoat slides down his pants and onto the floor. I pull up the hood on my own coat—the wool one with wooden toggle buttons. The man is sinewy in a navy suit, and has the start of a beard. His eyes are mapped with small creases that make them look kind, the blue porous, with small flecks of gray.

"I see that they've tricked one more sane person into teaching for us. I can tell by how scared you look. Shit," he says. "Shit, Shit." He paws through the saddlebag slung over his left shoulder, which is filled with manila files that have names written on them.

"You're a lawyer?" I say in French.

"So many girls here. Macon Ventri, pleased to meet you." He puts his hand out, and when I take it there's something gentle about the way he gives it to me. Then it's done, and he's on his way to Sophie's office. "You must wait here like a robot while the guard in the surveillance office decides whether to release the maddening locks and let you out or not. Gita Kapoor," he says, turning back. His eyes lock on mine. The fact that he doesn't know his eyes are sexy makes it so much better. "She is one of the girls who I'll see tonight."

Truffaut must be watching on his TV screen because the locks zing again, and I pull the heavy knob. It's a cold rain outside. "She is my student. Gita."

"Don't be fooled by her shyness. She will have her appeal hearing this summer. I'll know the actual date as we get closer," he adds in English. I hate when this happens—when Parisians switch languages on me as if I can't manage French verbs. He waves at me and turns back down the hall.

The door slams, and I jog in the rain down Rue de Metz, past the Saint Pierre Cosmétique shop with its poster of an African woman with straightened hair. The metro station is more menacing and smellier at night, so I stand close to the commuters on the platform—older women in saris and parkas and middle-aged African men in blazers and knit hats. I step onto the No. 4 and stare out the window into the dark. Our class meets for just three hours a week—such a short amount of time for the work in front of us.

2

Collusion: a secret agreement between
two or more persons; a conspiracy

I get off at the Gare du Nord—loud cavern of steel and glass—
and climb the stairs to Rue du Faubourg St. Denis, which runs
along the east side of the station. I'm late for dinner with Luke. The
sidewalks are even more crowded with shoppers. We're still in the
tenth but farther north. The train station shadows long banks of dove-
gray apartment buildings with wrought-iron balconies and cafés with
scalloped awnings. The rain's stopped but not before it froze on the icy
sidewalks, and the wind has only picked up. Dark limbs of chestnut
trees rock back and forth up near the highest apartments. And this
is a different Paris than even this afternoon. The city changes faces.

Teenagers sort through tape cassettes in the shops, and women
stop at the clothing store windows: New Madras. Saja Pathni. Then,
chatting, they move on, plastic bags of vegetables hanging off their
wrists. I take the mental notes of a foreigner: the strong smell of cooking oil in the air and the way the women lean their heads together
while they walk. For years I've been wanting to go to India. I read the
work of Tagore and Roy in grad school until the voices in those poems
were like kind, good people talking in my head.

Tiny white lights have been strung above the wooden door to
Ganges, a hopping Indian restaurant halfway down the block. They
blink on and off, and I can just make out the thin frame of Luke

walking toward me. The greatness of living in the same city with him hasn't worn off yet. He's got on a Russian hat made of beaver—the kind for hunting in Siberia with bow and arrow, and side flaps that button above his ears. I want to laugh at him except he looks so earnest in the hat. He kisses me on both cheeks and holds my hands. "Sister-love. Can we please talk about your cowboy boots?"

He's a tall, long-haired thirty-two-year-old with a pale V over his right brow from the fall he took off our refrigerator when he was five. Wanderer. Collector. He raised me. He studied engineering in college for one year but left in 1976 and reinvented himself in China. He lived in Beijing for seven years, teaching English in a state-sponsored job-training program and taking crash courses in Mandarin. But he's an engineer at heart, like our father, and wanted to get drinking water to the Chinese villages he'd fallen in love with. This became his passion, so he formed a collective of expats and local Chinese called the Water Trust that builds pipe systems into the villages.

"It's hard to do cowboy boots with a toggle coat, and I wish you'd called me first." He grins and opens the door to Ganges and moves us through the crowd waiting for tables. "I can take you shopping for real shoes tomorrow." By 1984, when I visited him in China, he was known at the Chaoyang flea market in Beijing as the crazy *laowai* who bought propaganda posters and silver cigarette cases with engravings of Mao—anything with a whiff of the Chinese Revolution. A movie designer approached him there one day about sourcing props—a Norwegian named Gaird, working on a Wu Tianming film called *Old Well*. When the filming was done, Gaird and Luke left China together and moved to Paris.

"But I don't want real shoes. I like my boots."

Even in Paris in 1989 it's the reign of Madonna—black lace shirts and shoulder pads and leggings. Levi's are also on the streets, but they hem them higher here, so you can see the equestrian boots the French women are wearing. No one seems to own cowboy boots. "You could wear more black at least. You could wear spandex. Everyone in Paris does when they're walking their dogs."

"But I don't have a dog."

The ceiling at Ganges is low and slanted, the walls painted with bright orange suns that yell out SAAG PANEER! and LAMB MASALA! Rajiv and Sara sit in a corner booth, their heads close together, talking. Rajiv stands and hugs me, and Sara jumps up. I've known her since our first day of college. Our school president said statistics showed that we might end up marrying the person next to us. The girl to my right seemed bored. She pulled a pair of aviator sunglasses down from her nest of crazy hair and said, "Sorry. I'm just not that attracted to you." Then she laughed out loud and grabbed my hand. "Sara's my name. We need to evacuate and go find some good marijuana."

Many years and several countries later, Sara and I hug in Ganges in Paris. "You smell so good, Sara, like verbena." I have to yell over the din of the sitar music and the voices of so many people eating food they love.

"I don't know my way from verbena to violets." She uses her whole broad face when she talks and crinkles the space between her eyebrows. She's four months pregnant, in a bright orange Marimekko tunic belted over a very small bump of a baby. "It's free sample cream I found inside a magazine." Tonight she's somewhere near the midpoint in the obstacle course that becoming a doctor in France entails, and the dark rings under her eyes prove it. "Now tell us! Tell us! Tell us about the center, Willie! How was your first night?"

"It's an amazing place."

"I told you." Rajiv nods. "Made more amazing by that force of nature named Sophie."

"The guard thinks he runs things, but it's really Sophie," I say. "She rules."

Rajiv's beaming. He's short and urgent, with a swoop of black hair, and runs food distribution for Oxfam. He orders everything. I never open a menu when I eat Indian with him. Sara leans back. "The food's so damn good here. Who has time to cook Indian anymore? Rajiv's mother tried to teach me. But who is home to rinse the beans? They don't let you sleep during residency."

She and Rajiv met in Advanced Biology the fall of our senior year—months when Sara and I played the song "It Ain't Me Babe" obsessively in our apartment and tried to figure out why we weren't having sex with sophomore boys. Rajiv came to dinner the Friday before Halloween, when the apartment was trashed: cereal bowls on the floor by the couch, the table covered in pumpkin intestines. We still hadn't bought a vacuum cleaner. He stood in our miniature kitchen while Sara and I raced to clean up, and he pretended to take interest in the bad wallpaper—rows of ornately painted artichokes and Meyer lemons next to their Latin roots in flowery script. Then he helped chop onions and ginger. I found plates in the sink and cleaned them with the sponge. Oil hissed in the wok. Sara and I sang, "It ain't me you're looking for, babe" while we cooked.

When the song was done, Rajiv leaned against the wooden counter and took Sara's hand. "But you are exactly who I'm looking for, Sara." I got out of that kitchen as fast as I could.

The food at Ganges comes on banged-up round metal plates— fried cabbage with peanuts and coconut, curried eggplant, spinach, mutton, and heaps of rice. I reach for the naan. "Where have you come from today, Rajiv?" He's always returning from regions in Asia I've never seen on a map. He lands in prop planes and takes jeeps to refugee camps that have swelled into what he calls small, volatile cities.

"Pakistan again. The North-West Frontier Province, around Peshawar. We've still got over three million Afghan war refugees there, and the drought is on. There are too many people. A camp built for fifty thousand now houses two hundred thousand." He hangs his khaki jacket on the back of his chair. He's as striking as Sara, with eyebrows like bushy commas that move as one while he talks.

"Two of the girls in my class on Rue de Metz are from Pakistan. I don't think they speak a word of English."

"They've probably never been allowed inside a school." He spoons more rice onto his plate. "The waves of foreign girls in France keep growing. African girls and Chinese and Pakistani and Bangladeshi and Indian. Imagine you are ten years old, living on the streets in Lyon or Toulouse or here in Paris." He points out the window.

"The girls in the center will love you." Sara looks at me.

"Truly, Willie, you will be like a mother to them." Luke takes a sip of water. "Or with your long red hair and cowboy boots, you'll be some scary apparition."

"No one knows what to do with teenage girls who can't go back to their home countries but don't have French passports." Rajiv throws his hands in the air and purses his lips. "The French government says that every child in France is redeemable, even the ones who come illegally. But then they lock them up." He hits the table with his hand, and I blush.

"All for want of a French passport!" Sara says.

"What I still don't understand," I say, "is where are these girls' parents?"

"Their families explode. Their only hope is asylum. They need teachers, Willie." Rajiv pokes at the red tablecloth with his pointer finger.

"Please stop poking." I smile.

"These enrichment programs are designed so the girls won't go mad. There is only so long you can be locked up with no future before you go cracker." Rajiv takes a bite of saag paneer. "The girls are not criminals. If you live in the ninth or tenth or eleventh or the thirteenth in Paris, then you know these girls."

I once taught a freshman writing class at the state university in San Diego, and there were high school valedictorians in there and gang members. A boy named Sean wanted to give himself over to my class. I knew this because every morning he'd ask me to define a new word for him. The first time he did this, I stood frozen at my desk. I'd met a soul mate in the shape of a small-boned African-American boy with the beginnings of an Afro.

Words have always attached themselves to me. They get inside the machinery of my head. There was a time in middle school when words appeared regularly and I had to define them. Now they just help connect me to the world.

"'Collusion,'" the boy named Sean had said before the rest of the class arrived. "Ms. Pears, can you please define 'collusion'?"

"'Collusion.'" I couldn't stop smiling at him. "A secret agreement between two or more persons. A conspiracy."

I eat my eggplant at Ganges, and can't help think that Sara and Luke and Rajiv have colluded. They keep trying to find ways to get me out of my apartment more. "I can't wait to continue with the girls. How could I not? I signed up for the semester. Sophie seems incredible, and so do the girls."

Three years ago, I had the luck to publish a small book about a French poet named Anne-Marie Albiach. It was my grad school dissertation, and what landed me the job at the academy and the lease on my apartment. Today I got a small research grant: two weeks of expenses to travel this summer to a Tibetan outpost in northern India, near the Chinese border, to look for the original manuscripts of an Indian poet named Sarojini Naidu. I smile at Rajiv. "My tongue's on fire. You're trying to burn it with this spice. I got the grant from the academy, so will someone please order wine!"

Sara reaches for the bowl of crushed chilies. "The grant! You got the grant!" She waves her hand in the air for the waitress. "We need wine. We need toasts!" She drops a handful of the chilies into the chicken curry. "This is brilliant!"

"I got the grant!" I yell back. "My college has deemed its new American poetry teacher worth sending to the hinterlands of India to write a book about a poet no one in France has even heard of. But it's a very small grant, Sara." Now I'm embarrassed. "Tiny. Very, very small. Please don't yell."

She raises her glass of water. "To India in July! To Sarojini Naidu!"

"To Willie and the poets of the world!" Luke yells. The way his eyes widen is my mother. Her chiseled face erupting into laughter while she tries to save someone. Save me. Where is my mother? Because my need for her—just to see her face—is elemental now. I crave her. I crave the way she could help me unlock my thoughts.

"You are going to India." Rajiv smiles. "You will not be sorry. Dharmsala is a place my mother often took me when I was a boy and the monsoons were on. Our mothers would flock to the mountains in droves, and the fathers would stay down in the sweltering heat of Delhi to work."

"I'm going to India." It feels more real to hear Rajiv talk about his childhood there. We pour the white wine and toast the grant. Then we toast the baby in Sara's belly, and the new movie Luke's working on. These people are my family. My mother's dead (my beautiful, willful mother), and my father drives like a madman to the desert and lives for months in a tent, so it's like he doesn't exist. It's late when we walk out to the sidewalk. I hug each of them good night and kiss their warm faces, feeling so grateful. Then I take Luke's arm while he flags me a cab. When I'm with my brother, my mother is sometimes with us too, and tonight it keeps working. So often the world isn't funny. It's sad and I'm not sure I ever know how to show real empathy. But then there's my brother. And the world becomes funny again. He loved my mother so much—more perfectly than me. When I long for her, like I do tonight, in a way that feels bottomless, Luke stops me from drowning. Because he's wearing his beaver hat again and laughing.

3

Heart: the emotional or moral, as distinguished from the intellectual, nature

I live on the fringe of the Latin Quarter, on a quiet, leafy street called Rue de la Clef peopled with Sorbonne students and young professionals and artists and would-be artists. The best way for me to get to the girls at the asylum center on Rue de Metz is to take the metro from Place Monge. It's the start of February, and a huge fog from the warm rains has tamped down the city. I never remember to bring an umbrella, and I walk north on Rue de la Clef in the steady drizzle. Walking is how I try to become more attached to these streets.

There's something unsettling about what's underneath Paris—tombs and catacombs and resting places of the great artists and politicians. I've heard the dirt was too soft when they built the first metro lines. The engineers had to stage tunnels as close to the surface as possible. Part of my dread comes from a fear that the dead are trapped too close to us while we wait in our trains down below. That they can hear us but we can't hear them, and they want to get out.

The numbering system of the neighborhoods goes from one to twenty on the map, following the snail's spiral shell, with the first arrondissement the start. I've thought a lot about this map. It's not like any other one I've studied. What a snail does is secrete its own shell, which hardens around it in deliberately ridged coils. This is what Paris seems to have done, spiraling out from the interior banks of the

Seine—the conical shrubbery of the Tuileries, with its immaculate gardens, leading to the Louvre on one side and the medieval Latin Quarter on the other, and onward and outward, winding and wending its way to the Bois de Boulogne and the farthest suburbs.

I think the twelfth arrondissement, in the southeast of the city, with Porte de Bercy on the surging Seine, would be the muscular foot of the snail. And the sixteenth, with its shining Arc de Triomphe and the bump at Parc des Princes near Porte de St. Cloud, would be the opening for the snail's tentacles and head. My instinct is for the linear—I can't undo what my father has taught me—and for the numbers of the neighborhoods to descend or ascend in order left to right or north to south. But this doesn't happen in Paris. To get to Rue de Metz, in the tenth, today, for example, I'll take a train that will pass me through the fourth arrondissement and finally into the first.

Each neighborhood has its own flavors—village within a village—but the more I walk, the more borders overlap and blur. Today it would take too long to get to the asylum center on foot. So I turn left on tiny Rue Dolomieu to Place Monge, where the metro station sits like an ancient crypt. The sign is Art Deco style, the word METRO painted in bright red letters on a piece of antique-looking glass. On either side of the sign, an arched doorway carved out of muzzy, moss-covered fieldstone leads to the underground.

It's ten minutes on the No. 7 to Châtelet, where I switch to the No. 4 to Strasbourg–St. Denis. I've got poetry planned for the second class with the girls tonight—pieces of poems by the Indian poets Tagore and Naidu. When the train car empties, the crowd carries me toward the dank stairwell in the far corner. I'm late, but in the crush of people, I can't get ahead—I move stride for stride behind a thin woman so close in front of me I could hold on to the nylon belt of her raincoat. Each time she places one of her high heels down it makes a pleasing, grinding sound on the concrete. How are the girls? What can I teach them that will help? How can I reach them? It's been a week. Too long for any rhythm in the classroom.

Our herd is almost to the top when someone taps me on the shoulder. Then a man's voice says, *"Excusez-moi, madame."* He touches me on the arm and I smile. He thinks I'm French, and I'm not immune to this kind of fantasy. He has a shiny, harmless face in wire-rimmed glasses under the fluorescent lights. But he's unbuttoned his pants. I repeat this to myself. They hang low in front so I can see the small wiry crop of dark hair and the sharp surprise of his penis. He tries to rub himself against the side of my coat. It's so disgusting. I push past the woman in heels out to the street. I'm furious at myself! Why couldn't I think of one single word in French to yell? I run then, which people don't ever seem to do in Paris, even if they're late.

Gita and Moona are already on the couch when I make it, breathless, to the center. They smile at me shyly while I take off my coat, wet with rain, heavy like a blanket. "Girls! You're more on time than I am. It's so good to see you!" They just open their notebooks and stare at the blank pages. Then the others walk in and find seats. It's so quiet in here it's like we've never met. I can hear the buzz saw of motorbike engines and Vespas outside. The ceiling lights can't cut through the gray of the afternoon rain. It will take time to find our rhythm again.

I stand up from the bench and read the Tagore: " 'When the heart is hard and parched up, come upon me with a shower of mercy. When grace is lost from life, come with a burst of song.' " Then I asked, "How are your hearts today?"

Moona laughs. "Can you read it again? I think my heart is like his heart. Hard."

" 'When the heart is hard and parched up,' " I repeat, " 'come upon me.' "

"Time away from your family does this to your heart," Moona says. "It has been three years since I saw my maa."

"It is not natural," Gita says. "To live apart like this. At India we slept together. My sister and me."

Precy nods. "I keep thinking," she says. "That if I can get legal, then I can go back and get my brothers and sisters. My mother and father. It's what I think about every day. I can bring them here. But first I have to get legal."

"Let's write. It's good to get ideas down on paper. Do you have the pencils? Let's write to the person you most want to talk to in your family. What would you say?"

Moona laughs again. "There is so much. I could start with winter. I could tell my father that it is too cold in France for his goats and honey mangoes." Then she speaks in fast Urdu for Rateeka and Zeena, who nod but don't write. I'm beginning to think that they can't write. Esther looks dazed. Precy chews on her pencil eraser.

"Let's go for five minutes. Say what's in your heart. Say the things you most want to say." Then I start writing too, because it helps when everyone's taking a small risk together. What kind of deranged creep pulls his pants down in the metro station? I write a list of English curses and French expletives that I wish I'd yelled at him. Then I feel better.

"Do we have to read these?" Esther asks.

I smile because I'm so glad she's speaking. "Even just your opening line would be good. It's great for you to hear your voice out loud before the hearing. We've got to get you comfortable with your story. I'll go first and make this easier. Because you'll see that I'm no poet."

"You didn't ask us to write poetry, did you?" Precy looks worried. "You said it was a letter."

"A letter. You're right. We've written letters tonight. Which sometimes sound like poems and sometimes don't. Here is mine: 'Dear Mom, I'm in France, teaching six girls how to tell the story of their lives. I'm so lucky to meet them. I wish you could know them, too.'" When I finish, my hand shakes. I'm not able to acknowledge it—this sadness for my mother that's so big sometimes it scares me.

"You wrote that for us, to make us feel better." Gita smiles. "Where is your mother? Why haven't you seen her?"

"My mother died last year. And it's okay. I'm okay. She was a funny woman. Go ahead, Gita. You read next."

"We are sorry." Gita looks at the other girls, who are all staring at me with wide eyes. "We are all so sorry for your loss, and you have to know that the gods wanted it this way. Vishnu will make peace for your mother."

"Thank you, Gita." I've messed things up. On the top of the list of what not to do when you're the teacher of emotionally vulnerable teenage girls locked in an asylum center in France is to talk about your dead mother. Why can't I just be quiet? I've surprised myself by offering up my mother. Sometimes I can wait. Days. Weeks. Months. Before I leverage something personal. But I want them to trust me completely. For that to happen I have to surrender something that matters to me.

"Really, it's okay." I try not to sound forced. "You go. We're listening."

Gita stands and adjusts the skirt of her sari. "Dear Pradeep. He is my brother. Dear Pradeep, I am still in France but you cannot know where. It is better for you with me gone. But you must go to school for me."

Precy says, "In my town we speak Bandi. I wrote to my father. I said thank you for also teaching me queen's English. It is why I have gotten this far."

Moona goes next. She's very mad at a man she refers to as "Uncle" in her letter. Then she calls him a rat and a snake. Her face is flushed when she finishes. I try to say something, but she leans over to Rateeka. Then she says, "Rateeka and Zeena can't write. But they say they lived on the same road in their village and their mothers were best friends and their fathers were farmers and tribal leaders. Then the army took their fathers away, so the mothers moved the children to Afghanistan. Zeena's mother was beaten there, and aid workers got them to Glasgow. They never went to school. Rateeka would tell her sister she wants to sleep together in their bed in Kabul. She says she wants to be young again."

Esther hands her notebook to me. The writing is in block print. "You read it, please. Just to yourself." I look down at the page. "Dear Mama in heaven. I am in a country called France now. They sent us here after the camp in Sweden. There are more white people here than I've ever seen in one place. Sometimes this is too scary. I hope it's not scary where you are."

I try not to cry. Esther thinks her mother can hear her. It's so enticing to imagine that all the dead mothers are listening. If I start to believe that I can really talk to my mom, then I'm afraid it will be like a drug and I won't be able to stop. I hand the book back to Esther. "It's beautiful writing, Esther. Strong sentences." She stares at her lap and can't meet my eyes.

"There is another poet that I'm going to read to you. An Indian woman named Sarojini Naidu. She wrote in English, but gave her poetry to the women in India like your mother."

Gita raises her hand. "But my mother is not able to read. It is one of the reasons I am not going back to my country, where the women are working in the fields and cooking outside over fire and not going to school."

"But your mother may have heard of Sarojini, Gita. People read Sarojini's poems out loud in India. Sarojini fought for women. She didn't believe in discrimination. She wrote that the only thing to do when your rights are being violated is to 'rise and say this shall cease.'" Gita looks at me like I'm crazy. Like she knows about struggle and that it's a much more practical thing than writing poems or small speeches about resistance. But I read a short stanza of the poem out loud anyway:

"Shall hope prevail where clamorous hate is rife,
Shall sweet love prosper or high dreams have place
Amid the tumult of reverberant strife."

The girls' faces are blank. The words in the poem are big and antiquated. "I want you to think about this thing Sarojini calls your 'high dreams.' She means what's important to you. The things that matter most. So if you can, please write about such a thing, in English or in your own language. Either would be fine. One thing that's important to you."

"Something that matters to us?" Gita asks.

"Yes, exactly."

Moona talks again in the language that must be Urdu, and it's enough to get the two Pakistani girls nodding.

"Gita," I say, when everyone seems done, "will you go first, please? Will you tell us your sentence?"

"I cannot." She looks down and stares straight ahead at the wall, as if she's coaxing herself to speak.

"Maybe Moona could go? Could you do that, Moona? Then Gita will follow along after you. It's hard, I know. It's scary. But we don't bite!" I look at each girl. "We are all here to learn with you."

Moona says, "My hair is important to me. My long, thick braid."

Gita goes next: "My necklace is important to me. Morone was giving it to me. My gold medallion of Krishna."

Moona translates for Rateeka and Zeena. Esther and Precy speak in English, and I write it all down. "Congratulations," I say. "You are all poets now." Gita and Moona look at each other and laugh. "We can call it the 'What Is Important Poem.' It goes like this:

"My long, thick braid.
My virginity.
Having babies and bathing them in the Ganges.
My mother.
The boy who will marry me someday.
My gold medallion of Krishna."

THE CLASS RUNS from five o'clock to eight, with breaks every hour. At seven we all stand, and Gita walks to the bathroom down the hall with the low toilets built for second graders. When she comes back, she stops at my chair and takes my wrist in her hand, the way you might reach for your mother when you want her attention in a crowd. It's a signal.

"We are glad you are back here with us tonight." She laughs. "We had bets on whether you would be returning for the teaching." Then she sits on the couch in her blue sari and fingers the pendant.

Moona comes back from the hall. "Tonight I will tell the story of my village in Kashmir before the war began and everything changed."

I try to hide my surprise. I can't believe she's going to do this on her own. "At first it was being a green place to live outside Srinagar. We had water. We had food. But then the drought came and the gods were angry. There was a statue of Vishnu in a pagoda. Bad people in the village smashed the statue because of a rumor that gold was buried underneath. They were so desperate for food that they destroyed the only hope we had. Kashmiris lived on one side of the river and Indians on the other. Kashmir was where I grew up, on the wrong side of the river when the water was low. The soldiers walked across together at night with loaded guns. The village is still green in my mind. But that village is now gone." She sits and the room goes silent.

"Thank you." I clap my hands. Then we all clap. It's an incredible thing Moona's done—trusting us with this story. "Gita," I say. She's fingering her necklace again. "Your necklace is lovely. Tell us about Krishna."

"Krishna." She speaks loudly, as if she's decided once and for all to no longer be the one who waits and watches. She holds the medallion and lowers her chin as far as she can to get a look at it. "My sister, Morone, gave me this when we got to Paris. One was for me and one was for my maa. They are from Manju's jewelry shop. What Krishna is doing on this necklace is playing music that is keeping people like me safe."

"Do you think Krishna is always benign?" I ask.

"What is 'benign'?" Moona asks.

"Harmless."

"But Krishna can also be fierce." Gita's voice rises. "His fierceness is forcing evil spirits away."

Moona leans forward. "I myself am loving Krishna. I would be marrying Krishna if I could. If I was ever going to be marrying, I would like to marry Krishna."

The girls seem relaxed. There's a softening again. "Krishna is kind." Gita sits up on the couch. "It started when Vishnu came down to earth as baby Krishna to save us. He was playing tricks! He climbed a tree with the milkmaids' clothes! He married a milkmaid. He put a blanket over his mother because he didn't want her to know he was a god."

"He just wanted a normal maa." Moona speaks slowly. "Who loved him and cooked dinner."

"He plays the flute, and all the animals come to listen," Gita says. "Humans, too. Everyone enjoys it. Especially the cows."

It's close to eight, and the girls look sleepy. Moona yawns. I stand up. "We're done for tonight. Great work. Go to sleep."

They file out of the room and I walk down the hall and run into Gita's lawyer again—the funny man with the hiking boots. My stomach does a flip. "Well, hello," he says, in French this time. "Gita has spoken highly to me about your class."

"She's a wonderful girl. How strong is her case? Do you think she'll get asylum?" Adrenaline courses through my legs and arms. Where did it come from?

He looks quickly at his watch and shrugs. Have I thrown him? Am I asking too many questions? *"Merde,"* he says to no one. *"Merde."*

"It's that bad? She's going to be denied?" I can't stop myself.

"No, no. I am late for a meeting with one of the girls in a very unusual case." His voice sounds scratchy, as if he used to smoke heavily but has given it up. "You are Ms. Pears, yes?"

"Please call me Willie." I blush. "No one calls me Ms. Pears."

"Okay, it's Willie then. What kinds of parents give a girl the name Willie?"

"A slew of parents in the United States named their children after seasons and bodies of water and trees in the 1960s. My brother changed my name from Willow to Willie. Can you tell me if you think Gita isn't going to make it?" I've never been good at flirting. "And how does a French boy in Paris end up with the name Macon?"

"By way of a French mother and an Estonian father who live in Canada and travel to a small town in Georgia and begin a love affair with the American South." He smiles. I can't stop staring at his lips while he talks. They're full and smooth, like a small, masculine flower. "We have a lot of work to build her case. I will press the judge and the representative from the office of the U.N. High Commissioner for Refugees. I will push them, but it's a challenging time."

"Because there's no clear reason she couldn't just be deported back to India?"

Another long silence. "I reserve comment." Where's his sense of impending crisis? His urgency? "Willie. Please do not misunderstand me. But I do not deal in speculation. I let the facts lead us to the court, and I let the facts tell their own stories to the judge. What I need from you are more of these facts. Building blocks. More specifically, I need you to help her write testimony. She needs a story that you believe is one hundred percent accurate that details her rape here in France. That explains why she can't go back to her family in Paris but also why she can't return to India, because there is no one there to care for her—a dead father, an arranged marriage with her rapist's brother, a man who also molested her. Her hearing is scheduled for June. France has a policy of not expelling unaccompanied minors. It is our law. But the only way she can stay in France is if I can find her foster care. The government will insist on family reunification. It is their goal with minors. They will try to reinstate her with her mother, or they will fly her to India if they can trace the grandmother."

"You need facts," I say in my best French. Gita's road sounds daunting. "I can help her with facts."

"Do that and I will look forward to reading it." His smile is big and infectious. I grin back. When? I want to say. When will you read it? When will I see you again? And even if you wanted to find me in this city, how would you do that? You don't know where I live.

Truffaut buzzes me out and the lawyer still doesn't come. It's dark out tonight. No stars. I turn at the end of Rue de Metz and pass the Restaurant de Chengdu with its black Chinese characters on the sign above the doorway. Macon Ventri. What kind of name is it? There's a dark green news kiosk on the corner with curved metal sides, not unlike the drawing Precy made of her house in Monrovia. From this distance the kiosk looks ornate—a street temple. Enchanted, even. A black placard on the back reads PRESSE. I climb down into the metro station and attach myself to the outer circle of a group of older African women until the No. 4 comes.

The foyer of my apartment building is lined with pieces of white-veined marble. There's a narrow elevator I don't trust, with collapsible brass doors and a wall of mirrors. To the left of the elevator are two rows of dark brass mailboxes. I'm No. 3. I hardly get mail in France, but I check it anyway. The carpet is thick and dark red with fading, light-colored roses. I follow the roses up to the third floor and find my keys in my bag.

Then I dial Luke from the kitchen and pour a glass of white wine. I hang up after the first ring. He lives in the grown-up part of Paris: gorgeous single-family stone town houses in the sixteenth where no one's on the sidewalks but older women in pencil skirts walking miniature poodles. We have a system, because he hates the phone. I dial again, and he answers right away. I can't help smiling. He's the reminder of the best part of our family. He's me and not me. Better than me, because he sees me from afar and still loves me in a way that I can't always love myself. And who can do that? Stop judging themselves? I felt my mother's judgment. She couldn't help it—the way she got mad at people at the hospital when they treated her patients unfairly. Roughly. Negligently. And then she'd get mad at me. At Dad. Hardly ever at Luke. I talk while, in bed, he watches a French game show involving plastic balls and trivia. He has a weakness for really bad TV. There wasn't any television when he lived in China, and he's making up for lost time.

"The girls talked about Vishnu and Krishna in class. None of them had heard about the poet Sarojini. But they have so many stories to tell. Gita got going about how Krishna came down to earth to save it. Moona wants to marry Krishna. She said Krishna changes back and forth from god to a human."

"And who is Vishnu?"

"Just the creator of the universe." The phone's quiet. "What are you doing? You're smoking, aren't you?" I hate it when he smokes.

"I'm relaxing. Before I begin my night job." During the day he helps Gaird design movies by scouring the Paris flea markets and building sets. But at night he works for his Water Trust, mostly trying to raise foreign money. He's the president of a small, active board that he's pulled together. My dad's on the board and two of his old colleagues from his time at U.C. Irvine. There's also a Chinese businessman who works in steel and a Taiwanese woman who runs foster care programs for orphans throughout northern China. Luke hasn't met anyone in China or France or anywhere else, for that matter, who thinks that getting clean drinking water to Chinese villagers is a bad idea. But he needs a great deal of money to make it happen. He's hired a full-time CEO—a Chinese foreign policy expert he met in Beijing when he taught the man English. But Luke raises most of the actual capital. He calls it flushing ducks. It involves a series of orchestrated dinners in Paris and Beijing and San Francisco, and lots of time on the dreaded phone.

"My book will be about how poetry and religion are woven together in India." I close my eyes. "I'm starting to run out of time."

"You got the grant. Don't worry."

"You're right. I got the grant." I'm not going to tell him about Macon Ventri. There's nothing to tell. And he will only make a joke, and whatever it is between Macon and me is too early. Too tender in my mind for Luke's jokes.

"I think you should book a plane ticket to Delhi."

I take a sip of wine. "Rajiv said I would be an English teacher at the asylum center. But it's more complicated than that. Why did I agree to teach there?"

"Because you are weak and Rajiv took advantage of you."

"I feel a little like a giant from outer space in that center."

"Normally you're graceful, and you are very, very short. You always pull the classroom stuff off. You're good at it. It's what you do. You certainly shouldn't have said no to Rajiv."

"How do you know anything you're talking about?"

"I don't."

"You've never seen me in the classroom."

"You're right, I haven't." Luke laughs. It's a low laugh. More throaty. Like my father's. When I think of my dad I'm filled with missing and white-hot anger. The longer I hold this anger the longer I hold my mother. Anger and love. Twins maybe.

"So, really, everything you've just said is guessing?"

"Exactly."

"There are no mothers and fathers. Can you believe that? They have no parents to help them in there."

"You're going to be good at this, Willie. Give it time. If they don't have mothers, then what an amazing thing that they'll have you as a short stand-in with flaming red hair that needs a trim. You must not quit, sweetness. You're not allowed to quit. Mom wouldn't want you to ever quit."

4

Fondue: a dish similar to a soufflé
usually made with cheese and bread crumbs

Our mother's name was Kate. She had long, dark hair parted in the middle, which she pinned up with two tortoiseshell combs. When I was five, I used to sit on her lap in the rocking chair in the kitchen and run my hands through that hair. I wanted to swim in it. It smelled elemental—like vanilla and her skin. Sweet and earthy. She spent the first ten years of her life in southern Thailand near the coast, where her Dutch father harvested rubber trees for export with a French lumber company. When she moved to Montana, my mother said, she was already an outsider.

When I was growing up in the sixties, she wore Thai sarongs like skirts over pants. She wasn't like other hippie mothers. She was sterner and more serious. She drank glass thimbles of espresso at lunch in our kitchen and swore out loud, and she was one of the first women psychologists in San Francisco. Her specialty was cognitive therapy, a type of psychotherapy developed by a doctor named Aaron Beck, who'd been my mother's teacher. For years she thought this brand of therapy would save even her most troubled patients. She believed it could change dysfunctional thinking and alter emotional reactions and transform entire belief systems.

Her standards for people were so extremely high. In her mind, personal change always lived just around the corner. So she was on alert for it. She'd stare at me when I stepped off the school bus and into our driveway, as if I was going to say something brilliant. Sometimes I was paralyzed by her, and I said banal things or, worse, I whined and knew I'd let her down. She was so intense. She held the world accountable. She believed that everyone she met was as devoted to their passion as she was. But she'd put her arms around me in the driveway and hold me. Sometimes she'd even cry standing there because, she said, she loved me so much.

She gave wild parties and took them almost as seriously as psychology. In 1970 she had a Halloween fondue party and asked everyone to come wearing a hat. Our house was a single-story redwood with skylights in the kitchen that Dad had put in himself. I got to greet people at the door. Luke took their coat in the hall if they had one. When the party was half full, Mr. Stevens, our neighbor, rang the bell. He was a neuroscientist at San Francisco State, and the only thing he had on was a blue beret. His genitals looked loose and ropy and scary, and I screamed for Mom. When she saw him, she laughed so hard she cried. Then she went upstairs to get him her kimono.

At the dinner table, everyone had to stab cornichons and little pieces of beef with skewers and dunk them in the bubbling cheese. My mother stood up in her felt cloche and said, "You can't drink the water tonight." I leaned against the dining room door and stared. Who was this woman in the exotic hat? Where was my mother? It was hot for October in Marin. The dimmer on the pewter chandelier was turned low, so the room took on the glow of Sterno cans under the fondue pots. "You can only drink white wine!" She raised her glass and took a sip to demonstrate. "Water will harden the cheese in your stomach like stone."

She played Joan Baez during the meal and smiled at her neighbors and friends, who slowly and systematically got lit. My dad liked it once my mother started things for him—the talking, the people, and the food. But he didn't seek people out the way she did. He didn't need people. He had his math and his desert and he had her. "The Weight" by The Band came on, and everyone jumped up from the table and ran to the sunken living room and sang "Take a load off Fanny." My mom had just painted the walls salmon the day before, and my father had hung his Indian weavings from Arizona.

My parents lifted their hands together like London Bridge Is Falling Down, and everyone went under their bridge. My mother closed her eyes and bounced on the balls of her feet. I was embarrassed for her intensity and enthralled by it. I couldn't look away. Luke came out from his bedroom down the hall and watched, too. "Why don't they let us sleep? They're not teenagers." But he was a teenager, and this meant he went back to bed. I couldn't stop staring. I was eleven. My parents had this whole other life.

The following January, my mother left on a trip to Greece with a group of intuitive healers from the Bay Area—seventeen of them on a 747 from the Oakland airport with a layover in Zurich and a visit to the Jungians there, then a tour bus in Crete. She was gone for thirty-one days. The longest month of my life. Sausalito got stuck in a wet fog, and she only called once from Athens. No telephone credit cards back then and it cost her a fortune. The line echoed so that she sounded underwater while she screamed into the receiver, "I'm coming home soon, Willow! But I'm testing the marriage theory I've been working on. I'm looking at the matrilineal bonds in generations of Greek families. The marriages are very strong. I'm doing interviews. It's so sunny here!"

She was supposed to stay in Greece for two weeks, and now she'd thrown our house off its axis. My brother cooked hamburgers for my dad and me every night while my mother was gone. You got to choose: burgers with a slice of American cheese on top or a bowl of cornflakes with milk. This was when Luke began to help raise me. He didn't say anything about it. He was just organized with the clothes washing and making sure I had food for lunch. Even then he carried my sadness for me.

The first night she was back, my mother unpacked the gifts at the kitchen table: a strong Greek liqueur called ouzo for Dad. A traditional black velvet vest for Luke; a white cotton dress with red embroidering for me. Her cheeks were flushed while she handed out the presents. Was she feeling guilt? Shame for leaving us? What I

remember is a mild defensiveness that flashed on her face if you ques-
tioned her too hard. I wanted to sit on her lap. I was too old for this,
but I did it anyway and stared and stared at her green eyes to see if
she'd changed. Then I buried my face in her chest. I didn't have words
for my longing for her. When she put me to bed that night, I asked
her why she'd gone. I couldn't not ask. I had to know. She said, "I just
needed a little break." Then she kissed me on the head like this was
normal—like mothers flew to Greece and took breathers all the time.
This wasn't the answer I needed. I wanted her to tell me her research
called to her. That it was vital work. I could understand that. Did
mothers really need breaks? This was different. Muddier. It made me
feel funny. Overlooked. Passed by.

Had she gotten bored with her marriage? Her spell in Crete was
nothing compared to running off with the artisanal cheesemaker on
Mount Tam like our neighbor Mrs. Gallant, three houses down, did.
The real problem was my father. I loved him entirely and he gave
hugs that involved spinning me on his back in a circle, but my father
was a mathematician. Yes, he listened to Jim Croce and smoked his
homegrown weed, but he was not a real hippie. He liked structure.
My mother had left and come back and my father was not done processing this information; there was more to come from him on the
subject.

It's not that he was anti-feminist or anti-women or anti-anything,
really. He just loved her with a mathematical conviction, and even
though he'd sanctioned Greece, he couldn't believe she'd actually
stayed away for so long. "One time," he said to my mom in the kitchen
the fourth night she was home. I could hear him from my bed. "I got
married one time. You're not going to leave me and make me do this
all over again with someone else, are you?"

I watched him out my bedroom window that night—a small man
with dark sideburns who threw one leg over the seat of his motorcycle
and kick-started it and drove away. He waited two more months to
actually leave my mother. Maybe her trip made him see how much
he loved her. Maybe he couldn't handle that kind of vulnerability. Or
maybe he was just too stubborn and proud. It was May 1971. A Mon-

day. One week before the end of seventh grade. He loved us, didn't he? He gave those hugs.

His leaving was the worst feeling I've ever known. He returned to the house on Thursday in his pickup to collect more of his maps— piles of old folded drawings and elevation charts and a pair of rare celestial globes by Vincenzo Coronelli. I found him in his basement office putting the globes in a blue plastic milk crate. I said, "You've ruined my life. I hate you with all my heart." I wanted to tackle him and hold him to the ground and make him stay.

This was the week in middle school when I began to spend a small part of third-period study hall reading the dictionary. Part of me felt like I was spinning off the flat surface of the earth. The words made my brain feel good. When I memorized definitions, it quieted my mind. Each dictionary entry was like an orderly, prescribed planet. How generous of the authors to give two or three alternative meanings and an archaic definition and to use the word in a sentence.

Luke was in *A Midsummer Night's Dream* that week. He came home from school on Friday to cook the hamburgers before the performance. He was nervous about the play. He made the burgers very thin, with Swiss cheese and onion. I sat at the table in the corner of the kitchen with the two windows behind me, and the word "divorce" appeared in my head. The letters were spelled on a small blackboard nailed to a white wall. It seemed pretty obvious why the word was there, even though I didn't know where the letters had come from. But I could define "divorce" and so I did, and the word went away and I had a bite of the hamburger. I thought maybe the word had just been a bad omen and I was done with it.

But the next word was "empty." An easy word. I defined it to myself while Luke poured us glasses of milk. Then it disappeared, just like "divorce." After that, things got a little out of control for a few minutes. Luke sat at the table next to me, and I thought he must know about the words in my mind because they were coming so fast. Maybe he was getting them, too? There was no reason for them and I still had to define them and I thought I was getting sick. He put ketchup on the inside of one of his hamburger buns and scraped around in the mustard jar with a knife and I decided he wasn't seeing the words.

It was hard to come up with definitions so quickly and eat the burger and it was close to time to leave for the play. I thought seeing these words in my head was worse than being sick and that I was crazy. My mother came downstairs in an Indian tunic dress and Greek leather sandals. "Let's go, my lovelies. Luke needs to get to school early. The play will be sublime." I didn't know what "sublime" meant. I hoped that word wouldn't come for me now, because what would I do when I didn't know a word?

"Please, Mom. Cut it out. No big words. This is serious." But I didn't tell her why. I kept the words to myself. I was scared. I didn't want her big words to come over to the blackboard in my mind and ask me to spell them. That would be more trouble than I could handle at the moment. The three of us walked out of the house and climbed into the Beetle. I think each of us thought Dad was going to surprise us by jumping out from behind a eucalyptus tree.

We drove to the play without him. I sat in my chair in the dark theater and clenched my hands in my lap and worried about Luke. Would he remember his lines? "Shakespeare" and "brother" came, and I defined them. Then the play started and Luke was Puck and he was so good up there on the stage. I relaxed and laughed out loud and cheered for my brother in my deepest of hearts.

I kept reading the dictionary—just ten minutes or so every day at school. I liked to do it. The words were like a nervous tic that lasted through eighth grade and on into the fall of ninth. They came only when I was rattled. I'd define them and they'd leave. I didn't usually mind them. They were almost a comfort, something I could count on, and they kept my mind busy.

After he left us, Dad became famous in the geology department at Irvine for the series of undergrad girls he brought to the desert with him. He lived in an old blue REI tent in the Sonoran Desert and kept a studio apartment near the university when he was back in town, and he sort of unraveled for a little while. He was thirty-five. Too old to be drafted for Vietnam, but he hung out with the anti-war protesters in the desert. There were many of them. And the girls at Irvine dared each other to go camping with him. He lived with one for a time in town, and Luke got to meet her. Dad wrote the girls great job recommendations and helped them get government grants. He was not unkind.

He moved back in with us after close to two years because a flash flood almost killed him. It was 1973. It wasn't the only reason he came back, I'm sure, but the flood changed everything. He started sleeping at the house again, and the words stopped appearing in my head as suddenly as they'd arrived. They'd been a phase, and now they were over. I didn't even need to read the dictionary at study hall anymore. Dad said the water had carried him downstream, but he'd kept his head up and looked for things to grab. He'd found a small tree in the middle of a basin and held on to it all night, and for the first time in his life, he began to talk to God.

Then he and my mother began doing what they called the big repairs on their marriage. He read the Bible every day and went to the church on Racino Drive—he knew someone there, a friend of a friend from the desert who was interested in space travel. He was calmer after this, too. But I've never been able to decide if the change in Dad was for the worse or the better. My mother forgave him. She told me it was because life is too short. "Life is fleeting, Willow." This was the first night after he'd come home. I was lying in her bed watching her get undressed, waiting for the quiet thrill of seeing her small pale breasts and her high-waisted underwear. She had such thin legs, like a deer. Flanks. Perfectly shaped. I was from that. From her. She was still my person even though she'd left me for Greece. Even though the passage of time haunted her and drove her away from psychology and sometimes even from us.

5

Testimony: a solemn declaration usually made orally by a witness under oath

Moona likes to smoke cheap American cigarettes—Pall Malls—and I don't know where she gets them, but I let her do it, even though it makes me nauseous. It's her nervous thing, and almost everyone else in France smokes, too. We can't find the ashtray at the start of the third class—the one with the black sketch of the Eiffel Tower on it. All the girls look under the couch and in between the cushions of the chairs. Precy finally locates it on a stack of books on the round ottoman by the window. Then we all take our seats. Moona's so grateful. She smiles and lights up right away and taps her foot on the floor while she smokes. She's got on thick brown wool socks under her sari today.

She's not the only one who seems stressed. It's been a week since I was last here. Tomorrow is Valentine's Day. Rateeka has this new, vacant look, as if the strain of staying in this place has become too much and she's already left us. Or is she on some new anxiety medication? Zeena has small, red burn marks dotting her forearm. Has she branded herself with a cigarette? Has someone else done this? Have the scars always been there and I just haven't noticed them until now? Precy can't stop touching her chapped lips with her thumbs. Esther chews the tips of her hair and hums quietly. Gita fingers the Krishna medallion.

The girls need to be able to tell the story of how they came to France. The judge will ask them this at the appeal hearing. They also need to write it down in a document for the judge called a testimonial. "Heart-wrenching," Sophie said to me today before class. "Make their stories so sad that there's not a dry eye in the house and even God's eyes are crying, yes."

I stand. "It's great to see you all again. So good to be back here with you. It's getting warmer outside." Then I regret saying this because no one in this class has left the center since I was last here. There's no going back. I screwed up, but we still have three hours together. "Tonight I want to talk about what the judge will ask you at the hearing and how you will answer. A lot depends on this. So think of one or two sentences in your mind that are the real reason you're here waiting on a hearing. Tell yourself this story. Then write it down or repeat it to yourself hundreds of times."

I plug a black tape recorder into the wall above the bookshelf while the girls write in their notebooks. I want them to read their sentences into the machine. Moona stands and walks over to me. "I'm done. I'm ready to tell my story now."

"Terrific." I can't wait for them to hear the sound of their own voices. I press Record. "Try to talk slowly and loudly."

She leans down close to the tape recorder and doesn't hesitate: "My uncle had a dark office near the bathroom stalls at his factory in Bombay. Every day he said, 'You look like a peacock in your sari. Where are your feathers?' I smiled at him because he was the boss but I was nervous because something was not right with the way he was talking to me. He told me to follow him into his office one night and close the door. It was loud in that place with the machinery and I could not be heard when I yelled out and he was unwrapping my sari and unbuttoning my choli and this is when the new troubles began."

She finishes. "Oh Moona," I say. "I'm so glad you're safe in Paris. I'm so sorry. You said much more than two sentences. You said so much."

"But I am not being safe here. What is this you are saying?" She pauses on her way back to the couch. "I am not safe here because they will not let me stay. They will send me back, I am sure of it, because I had a dream in which this is true."

Gita stands, puts her hand on Moona's shoulder, and lowers her head. I have no idea what they say, but their lips almost touch while they whisper. When they're done, Moona wipes the tears on her face and Gita joins me at the tape recorder.

The first thing she does is bend down and whisper, "My name is Gita Kapoor."

"Gita, you don't have to get quite so close to the machine. Can you step back and try to speak louder so the machine can hear you?"

She raises her voice, and I can't ever tell if Truffaut's watching us on the surveillance cameras in his office or not, but if he is then he should be ashamed. "In my story Manju is taking us to the department store. The big one. I needed a coat because the winter is coming. We all are purchasing the coats. Maa, Pradeep, Morone, and me. Mamie and me practice in the long mirror of the store, tucking the sari up under the coat, but we stop because that is not working. That is the week Manju presses into me where the coats hang in the back hall of the apartment and says that he will tell his wife—my sister, Morone—if I yell. Every morning he unties his pajamas and says the part about telling Morone. So I am not yelling. He is making red dots on my neck where he presses with his fingers and thumbs. He is almost strangling me sometimes. Then he turns back down the hall and I put on my coat that hangs behind me and I go down the stairs to my job at Shalimar in Brady Passage opening the restaurant."

Gita closes her eyes and pauses. Then she opens them and says, "I am not going back." This time I know she doesn't just mean India, but also her family's apartment in Paris. In a way she's asking for asylum from both homes—the one she'd grown up in and the one she'd left India for. I'm afraid what she wants is impossible. "I am not going back to Maa or to India," Gita continues. "If I go back to India, Manju has arranged for me to marry his younger brother Daaruk. He owns many acres of land near Jodhpur. It is all prepared, Willow. Daaruk already had me in the back of Manju's shop in Jaipur. I don't want this to happen again."

"Willie. You can call me Willie. I'm so incredibly sorry for what you've been through."

"But why would I call you the name of a boy," Gita asks, "when the name your maa gave you is being much more beautiful?" She smiles that big, open smile. "Willow is sounding better."

AFTER THE GIRLS have gone to their bedrooms, I find Sophie in her office writing notes on a pad of white paper as fast as she can, the black phone receiver propped in the folds of her neck. I stare at the corkboard of photographs above her desk—Polaroids of every girl who's ever come to the center, no matter how short or long a stay. A record of who was here. She swallows a big sip of tea, and it burns her mouth. She rolls her eyes at me and waves her hand in front of her face. Then she says, *"Oui, oui, oui. Merci. Merci beaucoup!"* And hangs up. "Ow. Ow. So hot! So darn hot! More girls coming tonight. Two from Algeria." She puts her fingers on her lips. "Ow." Then she looks at me. "How are things, my dear girl?"

"Moona? She tells me she's been raped by her uncle in a shoe factory in Bombay."

Sophie shakes her head from side to side. "Many of the girls here have been raped. You have no idea the number caught in human trafficking rings. You have no idea the number of children. It is the most appalling thing of all." She says Moona's father had been an Indian soldier in Kashmir for ten years. He later became a clothing importer, buying kurtas and saris directly from wholesalers there. When tensions began rising in 1987, he was stuck on the Pakistani side of the border. There was no work for him there, so he spent most of his time hiding in the house of a distant cousin.

I play Sophie Moona's tape recording. She closes her eyes and puts her hands together under her chin like she's praying. Then I play Gita's recording. Sophie doesn't seem surprised by this story, either. "A baby was lost. God's will. Amen."

"What do you mean, 'lost'?"

"Gita got pregnant, God save her." Sophie stacks papers on her desk. "For a Hindu girl like Gita, having an illegitimate child is grounds to be thrown out of the family. Disgrace. If Manju convinced Morone that Gita seduced him, Gita might have been killed. So God granted Gita safety here. It is a sad thing to be locked in so your own family can't get you."

"Oh no."

"Serious business." Sophie crosses her arms over her large chest, and the silver bracelets clink on her wrist. "We each asked Gita about the baby—Sylvie, the nurse at the hospital, and Roselle, the government's visiting nurse here. We had to know, of course. It's part of our work to track the born and unborn."

"These girls are so young to be having babies."

"She'd done a bad job trying to abort." Sophie takes a purple scarf off the back of her chair and ties her hair up with it. "They told me there was a lot of blood by the time she got to the hospital. We asked Gita, 'Does the father know about the baby?' The social worker asked first in English at the hospital. Then in French, Hindi, Urdu, and Farsi—all from a translation chart. I asked her all over again when they got her here. But Gita never answered. She was so slight. She slept the first week. Day and night, as if she hadn't known sleep in months. Roselle offered her pills to calm her because she thought Gita was in a state of shock. She thought Gita would remain one of the speechless ones—one of the girls here who never speak."

"But she has so much to say, Sophie."

"This is not something you need to tell me, my friend." She smiles. "Don't ever forget that the girls teach us just as much as we teach them. Now go home, will you?"

6

Story: a tale, either true or not, that is designed
to instruct or entertain the listener

On Saturday morning I take Rue Lacépède until I reach Rue
de l'Estrapade, then I walk south of the Pantheon past the
tip of the Sorbonne, where the blue sky sits above the tallest buildings
like a circus tent. I'm meeting Sara on the river. We do this on weekends. Talk and run and I feel intact again. Not the outsider who's
working, always working in my mind on my French. Boulevard St.
Michel is filled with places to eat—food stands and small shops selling
baguettes and cheese and crêpes. Everywhere crêpes. I don't think I'll
ever get tired of them. I stop at a *crêperie* at the corner of Boulevard St.
Germain and Rue St. Jacques and order one with lemon and butter
and sugar and eat it while I walk.

Students have infiltrated most of the cafés and ethnic restaurants
that dot the labyrinth of tiny streets in the fifth and sixth arrondisse-
ments. Passels of girls walk past me on the sidewalk wearing pom-
pom hats and wool scarves and waxed parkas. Two young women
in black leather bomber jackets sit at a brass table outside Café de
Flore in the cold. The woman with hair to her waist pulls a package
of Gauloises out of her coat. The box is shiny and red, like candy,
with white lettering. She takes a metal lighter and flips it open with
her thumb, then reaches for her friend's cigarette. She lights her own
afterward, and it's as if they're eating a meal. They lean back and

inhale and enjoy the cigarettes so much that for a moment it looks like a real pleasure.

Sometimes I find myself trying to list these pleasures in my mind here—maybe too often asking myself if I'm happy, and if I'll find a way to make this city my home. A waft of their cigarette smoke waters my eyes. I walk down Boulevard St. Germain to Rue Dauphine and cross over the river at the Pont Neuf to Île de la Cité. The Palace of Justice sits several blocks from the tip of the island, gold and massive. Sara is on one of the granite benches to the left of the sidewalk, tying her sneaker. Seeing her pulls me out of my solitude, and I bend and kiss her on the cheek, so grateful that she lives here.

A small group of teenagers lean against the stone railing nearby, listening to a bearded man sing in French. We make our way past them to the start of the bridge, where narrow stairs lead down to a cobblestone pathway. It's so cold, I can see my breath. There's a parade of boats moored to the stone embankment down here. The Seine hasn't frozen completely, but the boats are beset in ice—heavy wooden sailboats tied to hydrant-like plugs embedded in the cement and white tour boats with flat hulls, and a series of small, brightly painted fishing skiffs. Sara's hair is in a giant ponytail that sticks straight up. I still can't believe she's pregnant. Does she need to sit? "Is jogging good for the baby?" I ask. "Is it okay?"

"I'm only five months pregnant, and the baby's head is the size of a tiny Indian chapati. I am fine, for God's sake." So we bend and touch our toes on the cobblestones. No one is down here except a few men tinkering with the boats. We stretch each leg out to the side, one at a time, until I feel the pull in my hamstring. "How are all those beautiful girls in your class at the center?" she asks.

"I wouldn't call it a class, Sara. It's a jail. People die in these places." She, more than almost anyone else, understands an asylum center. Sara's been inside more refugee camps in more remote places on earth than I can count. Before med school, she'd helped Rajiv do camp assessments for Oxfam. She's pregnant, and I'm deeply happy for her, and I cannot wait to be the auntie. But maybe I need to become an expert in something, too? Maybe an overnight expert in refugee girls?

"They've locked up teenage girls in there." I speak with a little too much intensity. "Girls who have faces I sometimes can't read."

Sara's kind enough to remain unfazed by my little outburst. She reaches both her arms up in the air and jumps in place. "I'm so sorry for those girls. So sorry that detention centers even exist." She stretches her arms above her head, then bends back toward the ground and reaches up again. "But you're good in there, I just know it. You are a walking dictionary, and you can talk straight with the girls about what they need. Now, are you ready to jog?"

We start off slowly. I keep thinking maybe it'll snow. Is it really okay for her to be jogging? Her father moved the whole family to Nigeria in 1971, when Sara was eleven, to open one of the first clinics for Doctors Without Borders. Six months later, his appendix burst and he died of septic shock. Her mother was a nurse who stayed on in the village and still lives in Lagos, her mind fogged with dementia. When Sara was sixteen, she grabbed a spot at a boarding school in Delhi that her uncle arranged for her.

"Does anyone in there speak a single word of English?" she asks as we run shoulder to shoulder along the cobblestones.

"We sort of work through that. A few of the girls can translate." My lips are numb and drool's frozen on my chin. "But they're shy sometimes. Especially at the start."

"So bring some snacks." She's on call at the hospital, and her black beeper sits clipped to the waistband of her red sweatpants. "I always bring snacks. If I have a really sick kid, I'll use them."

"You mean you bribe them? And can you slow down, please? How is it that the pregnant woman is in better shape than the non-pregnant one?"

"Let's say I need to care for a kid who's on morphine because his leg is atrophying. The metal screws of his fixator stick out of his thigh-bone to hold it together. It's a very painful surgery." She catches her breath. "I clear it with his parents, and I bring him a lollipop. The boy will let me examine the wound while he licks the lollipop."

She's always been a rescuer. Has always gotten herself into jams with her quick tongue but found a way out. "Snacks." I say the word out loud. "I haven't used snacks since freshman composition class in grad school, when I just wanted the kids to like me."

"You really need these girls to like you now. Bring lots of food. Think of the girls as patients. Think of the class like a hospital. Their wounds don't show, but you still have to go about bandaging them."

"But therapy was my mother's job."

My mom left the city hospital when I was twelve and began her own practice. Dad was gone, and working at home allowed Mom more time with Luke and me. Money was a nagging problem. In 1972, everyone in Sausalito talked about healing—healing from the ongoing war, healing from Watergate. My mother started calling herself an intuitive. She said it was still psychology, but now she put her actual hands on people. She had cold hands—good hands for touching, she said. And she listened to the blood rush through her patients' veins, and somehow this helped them.

We run under the arches of Paris's most spectacular bridges—Pont Neuf, St. Michel and Petit Pont, Pont au Double, Pont de l'Archevêché. "You're in there, asking them to tell you their stuff, for Christ's sake," Sara says. "Bring them mithai. Bring boondi and coconut burfi. My favorites. Bring them snacks and smile a lot and you'll be fine." We turn back at the Tournelle Bridge, which crosses over into the middle of Île St. Louis. Snacks. Why haven't I thought of snacks?

I BRING boondi and burfi to the fourth class. The girls sit in the common room and consider the platter of sweets. Such patience. Will anyone break down and eat? Moona finally leans forward and carefully, carefully picks up a saffron-colored sugar ball and nibbles it. These are the boondi—so delicious. The coconut burfi is cut like brownies and has the consistency of fudge. Zeena chooses a piece. Soon all the girls sit back on the furniture and eat their sweets. Then they're not shy at all, thank God, and talk openly with one another about how to trim the ends of their hair with nail clippers, and how to put on black kohl eyeliner by burning a match and letting it cool before applying it with one finger, and how to sleep at night in the asylum center when they're scared and don't know where their mother is or if they'll see their brothers and sisters again.

Mothering often feels like the first cousin of teaching. And I've learned to squelch most of the urges to mother my college students. But in the asylum center, the instinct is too strong. Do the girls have toothbrushes? Winter boots? Tights to wear under their saris? How will they stay warm in the Paris winter? How will they make it without their mothers?

There used to be a playground in Sausalito near the houseboat flotilla in the harbor, and my mother and I drove there a lot when I was five and Luke went to all-day school. There were cedar steps up to a metal slide. One day I climbed a knotted rope that hung beside the slide and jumped into the sand. My mother, in jeans, stood with the other moms over to the side. I loved these mornings because I got my mother to myself. But they were always filled with anticipation—the sweet wait for Luke to be home. I found her and leaned against her and ran my hand over her thigh, claiming her. Then she and I knelt in the sand and shaped a moat and a castle, using my green pail. She was like all the other mothers that day, or better even. She loved the sand. We worked on the castle until it was time for Luke to come home from school. Then we got in the car. I said I wished Luke had been there, because it was the best castle we'd done. Sometimes things weren't real until I shared them with him. It's still the same today.

I look at the girls. "You are all learning to live in this really hard limbo."

"Limbo?" Moona asks. "What is this limbo?"

"You are unsure if you will go home or if France is now your home. Limbo means things that are not certain."

"I am not liking this limbo." Gita crosses her legs and looks angry. "I am not thinking this limbo can last very much longer."

I urge them to ask for more help at the center—Band-Aids and aspirin from Roselle, the nurse who comes on Wednesdays, help filling out the asylum forms from the lawyers on Thursdays, instructions from caseworkers on Tuesdays. I say their caseworker can tell them what to do about visiting hours, because sometimes a family member shows up. Sophie told me this caused a problem last Friday. An uncle of Esther's arrived. Esther saw him in the hall talking with Truffaut, and began sobbing. No one's sure what this uncle means to her or why he was here.

"Gita," I say. She looks straight at me from her seat on the couch. "Your limbo is guaranteed to last until sometime in June. That's the month of your asylum hearing."

"June," she repeats.

"It would be great if you could practice your testimony every day."

She starts laughing and has to put her hand over her mouth to contain herself. Her laughter is uncontrollable—almost like a fit— she's got so much emotion inside her that she has to leave the room.

I ask the girls to write down the word "help." Moona explains it to Rateeka and Zeena. I say, "I want you to get comfortable with this word. It's a good one. Can you make sure you're asking your case-worker for enough help? And your lawyer and me? Ask me for help."

Gita comes back into the room. "Willow, I am sorry. I was laughing. Then I was crying and I couldn't make it stop."

She stays after class when the other girls leave for their rooms. "I understand help," she tells me. "I can ask for help in French and in English and in Hindi. But I am not asking my maa for help because I do not want to ruin things for her or Morone. This is why they do not know where I am. None of them know."

She flips the pages of her notebook until she finds the picture of her house in India she drew in our first class. "In Jaipur we were hav-ing the cow. Plus the long walk to school. But at night all the women in the village would come together in the yard where the fire was lit and we would pick the rice and I would be braiding Morone's hair or she would be doing mine. There were six families. We were all cook-ing over the fire. Meat almost always came on Saturdays. I will never go back, but I wanted you to know that about my country because it is good for friends to understand where each comes from and I hope you are my friend."

———

I TAKE the metro from St. Denis north to a stop called Barbès-Rochechouart, where I switch to the No. 2 line, which I take all the way to Victor Hugo. Luke and Gaird are giving a birthday dinner for their friend Andreas, a kind man who imports Scandinavian furniture to Paris and sings Broadway show tunes to himself. I get to their apartment at eight-thirty and let myself in with my key. I come here. A lot. My special place in Paris. Refuge. Gaird's in the middle of the living room belting out a song in Norwegian. I've never heard him sing before. Luke flashes me a secret look of mock horror from the arm of the couch. Is Gaird drunk? He has a low, lovely baritone that vibrates when he holds the notes too long. He's a tall man in a black suit with ruddy skin and one of the most coveted people in the French movie business. The apartment feels like a movie set, overflowing with settees and ottomans and pillows. There's a purple velvet couch and ornate gold wallpaper and a large mural of hound dogs going after a fox, because Gaird is obsessed with anything French that references Versailles.

Andreas is also on the couch with his partner, Tommy, smiling. There's a woman across from him, whom I've never met, wearing incredibly high wedge heels. The song sounds like a Pete Seeger melody. Andreas claps. He's also Norwegian. He must know what he's doing. Then we all clap. Gaird sings: "Oh, I know of a land far away in the north, with a shimmering strand . . ." Then he bows. "Happy birthday, Andreas!"

His scotch is on the top of the grand piano, and when he reaches for it, he sees me in the hall. "I am still having a love affair with my home country, Willie." He takes my hand and kisses it. "We have been waiting for you." He speaks English in a singsong accent that ends on a high note and leads me into the dining room. He and Luke have done a seating chart for dinner—they always do. Tonight they've placed me between Andreas and Tommy. I put out my hand and say hello to the woman in heels before I sit. Her name is Clarisse. She says she's a painter at the Sorbonne. I'm relieved not to have to talk to her during the meal and offer myself up to her explicitly.

Tonight I just want to listen. I talk all day in the classrooms.

Andreas has curly black hair like a mop on his head. He wears clear plastic glasses. One of his eyes is green and the other is pale blue. I try not to watch his eyes while he talks, because then I think too much about whether they'll ever turn the same color. And they never do. He asks me about the asylum center. For him I'll answer anything. He's one of those generous listeners who makes me feel like I'm sharing instead of burdening him. He's calm and self-composed and absorbs everything I say about Rajiv's connection to the center and the backlog at the immigration courts.

Luke pours red wine and Gaird brings out a white platter from the kitchen with something he calls *dyresteg* on it. "In English, please, Gaird?" I smile.

"Venison." Andreas pats my hand. "Roast venison with a goat cheese sauce."

"It is straight out of my mother's recipe book" Gaird says. His parents owned a commercial dock in Drammen Harbor in Norway. He left after high school and rarely went back. In 1986, he parachuted over the Torne River into Finland. Last December he invited Luke to sit in the plane's cockpit and watch him drop out over Lemvig and pass over the Danish fjords. Luke called me when he'd made it safely back to Paris. "I live with a man who likes to open the plane door at ten thousand feet and jump out. People who fly are crazy. Stay away from them." Then Luke got the flu.

The woman named Clarisse has a sweet, knowing smile and perfect jaw-length black hair. She says, "Thank God for meat. We used to eat venison growing up in Switzerland. Sometimes it was all we had on the farm to get us through winter."

"This reminds me," Luke says, "of the food in Innsbruck, where Gaird was foolish enough to try to ski on the full moon."

"First he had us cross entire glaciers in our sneakers," Andreas laughs.

"We'd taken a tram halfway up." Gaird waves his hand in the air dismissively. "Then we began the push through the new snow toward the hut."

"At one point I was hanging off a small precipice by my right hand," Luke says. "Nothing but glacier below me all the way down to my funeral in Innsbruck."

"I got complacent—that is the word, yes? I took a trail alone through the woods. We were skiing without a guide at night, which was wrong in the first place. The snow was heavier under the trees, and I found myself in a dead man's gulley. Jesus, I was dumb." Gaird laughs out loud at himself. It's not everyone who can stop taking himself so seriously.

"We thought," Luke says, looking at Andreas and Tommy, "that he was gone, didn't we? We sat at the big stone fireplace in the hut waiting for him, and I began to have this sick feeling that crept through every bone in my body. I would lose him, and I could never bear that."

"We had no way to trace him because the new snow kept covering up his tracks," Tommy says. He's a tall Malaysian yoga teacher with a gorgeous face. "We were sick with worry. I had the hut manager call for more guides, and all three of them went out an hour later with lanterns."

"They found me in my boots, snow up to my knees. Only three hundred yards from the hut, but I couldn't see in the snow. There was no way for me to tell how close I was." Gaird shakes his head.

"When we're done eating, Willie, ask him to show you his feet. Poor blackened toes. Two almost fell off." Luke reaches for Gaird's hand at the end of the table.

I stare at my brother while he talks, and I can't swallow because here is his relationship offered up. And it's so moving to me. A love I've never fully understood until now. Here it is out in the open and based—like all love is, maybe—on some amount of abiding affection and on some other amount of need.

7

Crisis: a condition of instability or danger

The Academy of France sits on Rue St. Sulpice at the corner of Rue Mabillon. It's an eighteenth-century stone building on a winding, one-lane street in the shadow of the moss-covered St. Sulpice Church, only three blocks from the buzz of St. Germain and five more long, magnificent blocks to the river. Its yellow stonework has mottled and faded to a pale pink that always makes me think of India. The stained wooden door faces a small plaza on the north side of the church. This is where the American students gather between classes—under the limbs of a bare beech tree—to smoke and talk in English. Inside the school, they're only allowed to speak French.

Me too. Only French at school. I minored in it in college and read it for whole years in graduate school. My French is, if anything, precise. My American accent comes through, but I gave up trying to speak perfectly years ago. Sometimes I think there's a contest for Americans in France to see who has the best French accent. It's a contest held during faculty meetings at the academy, where otherwise sane, funny American teachers go on in exaggerated French until I think they're vying for the award given to the most obnoxious. People lose their minds when they speak French. Foreigners, that is. They just do. They become other people. It's amazing to watch. The shapes of their mouths change. Their speech gets more clipped. They think their French should be spoken faster and faster and that this makes them appear smarter. Funnier. I can never understand why this is so. Other languages don't ask so much of people. Or call for this personality change.

At ten o'clock on a Monday morning in late February, I'm a quarter of the way through my semester-long list of poets for the International Women's Poetry seminar. I pass out a short section of a piece by Anne-Marie Albiach, and a junior named Virginie, born in Camembert but raised in Chatham, New Jersey, puts her hand up to read:

"Les formes
elles reviennent de leur
plus retenue
lenteur
s'appesantissent."

Some of the students, I know, translate the poem mentally:

The forms / recover from their / most circumspect / slowness / become heavy.

I walk around the circle of wooden chairs. "Why does Albiach use the word 'forms'?" I love seeing the students grapple and get lost in the words. Poetry allows us to do this in the light of day—to go deeper into what feels familiar and what feels terrifying.

Deals were struck on the first day of this class. I could tell even then how much each student was going to give me by whether or not they made eye contact that day. It will be a long semester—six months talking about poetry, which means talking about our search for love and if we're afraid of dying.

Good poetry is like a map of the heart, tracing questions about the afterlife and the death of God and love. Always love. Which draws me to certain poems over and over. For some of the students, this delving feels like a very good thing, and for others it's too scary or beside the point.

"Could this be a poem about attention?" I ask. "About 'recovery from the most circumspect slowness'?"

"I think it's about memory," a girl named Lara with a pixie hair-cut says. Her French isn't as good as Virginie's, and she blushes and pulls at her bangs until they almost cover her eyes. I don't want her to get hung up on pronunciation. It's the ideas that matter.

"Nice." I sit down. "You're closing in on intention. You're homing in on the story inside the story."

Then Luelle, the Belgian school secretary with the peroxide-dye bob, knocks on the door and swings into the classroom on the door-knob; she's wearing high black knee socks and Doc Martens, and reaches her free arm toward me with a note. "What's this?" I say in French, unfolding it. It's been transcribed in capitals:

PLEASE COME NOW YOU MUST. ST. LOUIS HOSPITAL.
LUCAS IN TROUBLE. GAIRD.

I read it again, and when I stand up, it feels for a few seconds like Gaird and I are incredibly close, both of us getting ourselves to an unknown French hospital in the northeast section of Paris as fast as we can on Monday morning—because we're connected to the same person. We both love the very same man.

Gaird's dramatic and grandiose, but he's also busy. He has no time to write exaggerated notes to his lover's sister while she's trying to teach a poetry class in French. I'm not hysterical. I say *"Au revoir"* to my students and give them an assignment to memorize three more Albiach poems for Wednesday morning at ten, when we'll meet again.

There's been some kind of accident, and I'm sure it's minor. I walk down the red carpet and out to Rue St. Sulpice, take a right and con-tinue to Rue de Condé. There are no taxis. Rue de Condé is too tiny for many cabs. It runs into Boulevard St. Germain at Rue de l'Odéon, and that's where I jump in with a chain-smoking driver who crosses the river at Pont St. Michel. I've never been in this part of the city, and I madly study the little blue-and-white street signs. Where are we going?

The cab races up Boulevard de Sébastopol until we reach a maze of one-block alleyways and find St. Louis Hospital, which looks like a huge black medieval convent. Haunted and tired. It isn't the hospital nearest to Avenue Victor Hugo, or the best, but it's the hospital where Sara is a resident. Luke must have planned it this way. Room numbers are etched in black on metal signs glued outside each door in the dark hallway. Groaning comes from inside one. I take a peek inside the open door, hoping for my brother. The old man on the bed has an unkempt beard and looks surprised, like he's been washed up on a foreign shore, pinned to his sheets, and would someone please help get him out of here?

Luke's room is in the new section, off the back. I get there by crossing a small, glass-enclosed causeway. It's a concrete addition that reminds me of the YMCA I swam at during middle school and smells like the chlorine used in that old pool. I make it to his bed and study the thin plastic ten-inch-long tube that comes out of Luke's chest. A catheter line feeds into a clear bag on the floor, where the smallest amount of dark brown urine has collected. The bag of pee looks very serious. So does the IV line that runs out of the top of his left hand, where a bandage has been taped. Purple bruising has started around the places where the IV line and the chest tube go into his body. He looks lost lying there—gone from us. What if I yank the line and pull on the tube in his chest and take him home with me?

A nurse steps in and peers at me over the top of her white face mask. She replaces the saline bag on the metal pole next to Luke's head. Why doesn't she talk? Why doesn't someone explain? The cement walls are pink, and a piece of waist-high, three-inch-wide white paneling wraps the room. A watercolor of the Seine bordered by fuzzy green trees hangs in the middle behind Luke's bed, near two stainless-steel electrical outlets with thick plugs for the different devices. It's the painting that makes me long for home. Like a punch in the stomach. It's a tourist poster—water glinting off the river and the trees too perfectly shaved and what are we doing here in this country? It's okay to be a foreigner until somebody gets sick. I'm homesick now. Not for our house but for the people who lived in it. Luke's face and arms twitch in his sleep. I take his hand.

"I'm here. Just sleep. There's explaining to do in the morning."

White metal tables flank the bed. The one nearer to me has a pink water pitcher on it. I pour Luke a glass for when he wakes up. Then I stand frozen like that until Gaird comes back from the bathroom and presses my right arm with his hand and walks to the other side of the bed.

Sara puts her head in twenty minutes later, and charges in and hugs me so hard I have to break away to get a breath. Then she stands inches from my face. "Willie. Willie Pears. You must try to listen to me."

"I don't want Luke to hear you," I whisper. I'm now convinced that there's something really wrong with him and that the tubes coming out of his body mean he's dying. So I'm kind of delusional.

"He's in a deep sleep, Will. But we've given him lots of delicious pain meds, and he's going to nap for a long time. He could barely breathe. But now he's happy. You must believe me, and you must pay attention. He's going to be fine."

I wipe some snot on the inside of my hand and study her lips while they move. "What's he got? What's made him so sick, Sara?"

"We'll know more in a few hours."

I can't stop crying. "But, I mean, why are we here?" I wipe my nose with the back of my hand this time.

"Well, for starters, he's got a collapsed lung, so he couldn't breathe by the time they got him here. A collapsed lung isn't fun for anyone." Sara looks at Luke. "We're running blood tests. We're looking at everything. He's got a high fever, that's for sure."

We're in some dark French indie film: Sara playing doctor and Luke playing patient. Soon they'll stand back and change roles. Luke's already had the flu twice since I moved to France. He works too hard. He works on movie sets, yes. But there are more Water Trust projects in China in the border regions along the Gobi Desert, where the drought is on, and a big new one in Sichuan Province and one in Guangdong. China is six hours ahead of France, so when Luke wants to catch his engineers and CEO at the start of the day, he stays up until three in the morning to make the calls.

Hours pass in the hospital. Luke sleeps. There's a small window on the right side of the room, darkened by tan venetian blinds, and I can just make out the streetlights outside. It must be after eight o'clock. Gaird and I camp out in reclining chairs on either side of Luke's bed. "He wasn't supposed to get sick again."

"I know it," Gaird says. "I am going to sleep so I can be of use to Luke in the morning." Then he pulls a blue blanket one of the nurses gave him up around his chin and closes his eyes.

I don't know if he really sleeps. I lie awake for hours. I forgot to eat anything all day and I'm thirsty, too. The fake leather squeaks whenever I move in the chair, and I'm afraid of waking Luke. So I sit very still and keep my eyes on him.

When he started making me the hamburgers, I'm not sure he believed Mom was ever coming back from Greece. He knew things about her I didn't know. He was adult like that, even when he was thirteen. He loved her in a way that forgave her the big things. For Greece. For the way she allowed her husband to live for a while with a blond undergrad who majored in river ecology. Luke didn't ask Mom the hard questions. Why she got so mad at Dad. At us. Why she railed against the hospital where she worked when they didn't have a bed for one of her patients. It was as if Luke already knew all the reasons. I must fall asleep at some point, but I don't know when. Then I'm up with the earliest nurse, who comes in at dawn to check Luke's vital signs. His fever broke during the night, and his breathing's almost normal now.

Later in the morning I lie on his bed with him, waiting for the bronchoscopy results to come back. Gaird stands at the end of the bed, reading the chart. Maybe Luke has cancer or maybe he has a bad cold with a horrible cough? Or maybe his lung collapsed in a freakish, singular cellular event because he's been working too hard? He wears thick, white circulation stockings, which poke out from the end of the bed and make his feet look like golf clubs.

"What's really going on? Do you think anyone has a handle on it?" Luke asks when he wakes up.

"Your poor lung collapsed. You couldn't breathe. That is why you felt so awful." I try to be light.

"I'd love to know what I have."

"We all would. Gaird and Sara and me. We would all like to know." I push the bed tray away on its wheels, and Gaird puts the chart down.

"You two cannot do this talking thing together when I am with you."

"Gaird," I say. "We are speaking English. It's a common language known throughout the world."

"No more jibber jabber. Enough." He raises his right arm in the air and waves it back and forth like he's tracking a fly. Then he leaves.

I make my eyes really big. "What just happened? I've never seen his temper before. His accent always makes it sound like he's having a great time."

"He's nervous. He needs to blow off steam."

I take Luke's hand. "Tell me you feel better." I wonder if I need to call my father, just to check in. He'll either be at home or in the desert. But this is when Dr. Picard walks in and explains that Luke has an interstitial lung infection. Picard's a short, heavy man who looks like he works all the time and never sees sunlight. He wears tortoiseshell bifocals and a blue oxford with a red-and-white-striped tie. The buttons on his lab coat strain at the midsection.

"This means the infection invades the interstices between the lung sacs."

"Then I cough too much." Luke leans over to spit into the kidney-shaped pan.

"Then you cough too much, and in some cases, like yours"—Picard pauses and offers a small grin—"a lung collapses."

After Picard leaves, I put a wet washcloth on Luke's forehead and try to emanate calm. Pulses of electricity shoot through my arms and legs whenever he starts hacking. Gaird comes back and apologizes profusely to Luke for his little fit and somehow manages to make no eye contact with me.

I go home to shower as quickly as I can and change into clean clothes. Then I take a cab back across the river to my chair in Room 129 and try to sleep.

On the morning of his third day, Luke eats part of a falafel sandwich I bring him. We all wait to see if it will go down. He naps, and when he wakes up, I ask him how he feels. "Falafel," he says.

"Falafel," I repeat. I hold his hand and tears come. "Falafel, Gaird. He wants falafel this morning." It's the first time I've laughed since I walked into the hospital on Monday.

Gaird rubs his eyes with his hands. "There you go again. Speaking another language with each other."

"It means he's hungry." I laugh out loud again. "He's ready to leave." How much can we ever really know someone? Really? But it feels like I know my brother entirely right now. Part of me realizes we can't really ever know. But I want to. Every day. I want to connect people's words to the longing in their brains. Falafel. If it's code, then I understand it entirely. I walk over to Gaird and squeeze his wrist, just like Gita did to me a couple of weeks ago. He looks down at my hand and raises his eyebrows at Luke, maybe to apologize again for his huff. Or to signal that I'm the crazy one and what are they going to do with me? I think of Macon Ventri then. I don't know why. There's something about him. I see his face and his smile lines.

At two o'clock the nurses let Luke go home without giving his illness a name. In the end they call it a bronchial virus. I hold my brother's arm while we move through the revolving glass doors toward the open lot. Gaird brings the car around to the front door of the hospital, and we climb in. He pulls out onto the Quai de Valmy and follows Canal St. Martin.

"You're doing that ethnic thing with the tunic, aren't you?" Luke says to me, leaning his head back slowly in the front seat.

"Okay. You shut up."

"No, it works, sweetness." Luke laughs and closes his eyes. "But you've got to get rid of the pumps. You can't wear black pumps with a red tunic." I watch as Quai de Valmy intersects with a street named Rue du Faubourg du Temple. Then we reach the vast Place de la République. This is a part of Paris I've been to. This I know.

"Just stop, okay?" I'm in the backseat, with my knees crammed into my stomach, which makes me feel even younger.

"Promise me."

"I wear the pumps so that I look like I have my act together." I can joke now. He's better. We are going home.

"You can't make me laugh. It hurts. You want to be taken seriously, sweetheart? You must not wear pumps with those balloon pants. You look a little like a clown, and that's an insult to me."

"Okay, Mister Hair Down to Your Knees."

Gaird drives through the middle of the square at République. This part of Paris is epic in scope. I came here once, on foot, during my first week because I wanted to see the sculpture of the famous woman in the plaza. Our car passes her; she's up on a high stone pedestal wearing heavy bronzed robes. She holds up a tree branch and has a wreath of wheat around her head. "What is that woman doing there?" Luke asks. "Alone in this sea of cars."

"She's meant to represent France," I say. "The entire country. Her name is Marianne."

"It is not," Luke says. "You're joking. Her name is not Marianne."

"No, I'm serious. I've read about this. I came here in September. Meet Marianne. She's the symbol of French hope after the revolution."

Gaird grips the steering wheel with both hands and says nothing. We gain speed on Boulevard St. Martin, which changes names so many times until it becomes Boulevard Haussmann and finally turns into Avenue de Friedland at the maddening traffic circle around the Arc de Triomphe. The arch is enormous and peopled by so many commuters and racing cars. A long French flag hangs down in the middle. We turn right onto a tree-lined stretch of Avenue Victor Hugo. Luke and I have been through worse things together than that hospital. We're hardy.

We've spent weeks in the Sonoran Desert with my taskmaster father, camping out in valleys and rationing our water until we became parched and it was hard to swallow. 1970. I was ten and Luke was twelve. Dad was doing field measurements for the U.S. Fish and Wildlife Service. "It's cartography, for God's sake, Kate," he said at the kitchen dinner table the night before we were all meant to leave for the desert. "A science. Have I ever not been safe?" He threw his hands up in the air and rolled his eyes.

The kitchen was made of wormwood beams Dad had rescued from a nineteenth-century farm in Petaluma. Then my mother had added her own touches: the bird mosaic over the stovetop and the wallpaper with orange finches. Slices of medium-well pot roast sat on white plates, sides of scalloped red potatoes, two full glasses of whole milk. Luke and I laughed. Laughing at Dad's jokes could make things better or worse, depending whose side you were on.

The next morning Mom put things in our food at breakfast: brewer's yeast and wheat germ. She was doing this a lot now, said we couldn't taste it, but I thought it made the oatmeal like newspaper. She didn't wear a bra either. Just the T-shirt she'd slept in. I could always tell, because her breasts were soft and jiggled and I was still fascinated by them. By her.

She'd begun raising chickens, and carried one like a house cat outside while she watched Dad pack the truck. "I'm not coming," she said. "It doesn't feel right."

I'd learned at school that chickens have very small brains, and it bothered me how much she adored them. I couldn't tell her, though. You couldn't tell my mom these kinds of things. She resented you for it. She called them petty criticisms that didn't help change the world. And that was what she wanted to do more than anything when I was growing up. Heal the mentally ill. Fix people. Her birds slept in a little shed attached to the back of the house by an internal door. They were always going for me, pecking at my feet and making a racket. I went back inside the house and upstairs to get my sleeping bag. Then Mom was downstairs, telling Luke that it wasn't safe to camp in the Sonoran Desert during flood season. "What is your father thinking? He wants me to let the chickens go. He thinks the chickens are more important to me than our marriage."

I froze on the stair landing. I'd never heard her use the word "marriage" that way—like it was something separate from our family, a word that didn't mean me or Luke or the house. Wet things hung from the banister where I stood: Luke's T-shirts and my striped underwear and a blue bedsheet. To conserve oil, Mom had unplugged the dryer that month and rolled it into the shed, where the chickens had begun to roost on it.

I ran downstairs and grabbed my jean jacket from the hook in the hall. Then the three of us backed down the driveway without Mom. It always felt like a bad idea to leave her. I was so tied to her. How would she manage alone without me? I waved at her on the porch the whole time Dad pulled away. "Jack!" she yelled. "People die in flash floods every year. They don't even hear the water coming! Think about this, Jack!"

My father didn't slow down. The Land Rover had a dented right front fender, and the navy paint was peeling along the grille. But there was a radio. Luke and I lay in the way back with the red five-gallon water jugs and tent stakes and tarp and pressed our ears to the speakers. I tried to forget my mother while Luke sang along to Paul Anka and Johnny Mathis and I just pretended, mouthing the words.

"When do we get to make the maps?" Luke asked.

"Luke!" Dad yelled from the front seat. The yelling worried me and I bit my nails. Dad always became a bigger version of himself on the camping trips, barking more orders. "Longitude and latitude, right?"

"Right!" My brother wore khaki shorts with a metal compass on a clip at his waist and an orange T-shirt with a chest pocket crowded with pens. "Vertical and horizontal."

"Two lines and a point." It was their game.

We drove over the Richmond Bridge, toward Oakland and San Jose. The hills were dry and russet-colored, with new subdivisions stretching as far as I could see toward Alameda. After two hours we hit I-5, which took us three hundred miles. We parked in a rest stop at noon to eat the tuna sandwiches Mom had made and to pee. I must have slept for a few hours after that. I woke up when Luke said, "Dad, I'm going to design a radical map of outer space that shows the way to navigate a rocket ship to Pluto."

"A radical map," I yelled. I spent a large portion of each day repeating everything my older brother said.

"NASA will use the map for space travel." Luke smiled out the window.

"Space travel," I said. We drove another hour, toward Pasadena and I-10. Then past San Bernardino and El Centro and across the Arizona border to Yuma. In the very last half hour I began the tricky business of climbing up to the front seat. "Dad, I need to pee."

"Give me eight minutes, miss." His beard hadn't turned white yet, and he wore his straw safari hat with a chin strap even in the car.

"Too long, Daddy. Eight minutes and I'll wet my pants."

He turned off the narrow tar onto the dirt. We were deep in Arizona, flat scrub as far as I could see, broken up by giant saguaros and brown shoulders of the Santa Catalina Mountains. Dad was there to do a revised map of the Sonoran Desert, detailed with water sources and elevation lines. His job was growing in importance, though I didn't realize then that water would become a commodity. "Don't think about peeing, or go in the way back and use the cup."

"I'm not using the cup. The cup's gross." My voice got louder. "The cup's for Luke when he can't hold it. Not for me!" We'd been driving since morning. I hadn't peed since the truck stop three hours ago. Dusk made the sky look bruised and dangerous. "You don't get it. You never get it. Call Mom. Mom knows you need to stop!" I screamed, and Dad slammed on the brakes.

"Don't you speak to me like that, Miss Willow!" His yelling always made me ashamed, though not for the things he accused me of. Why did he have to yell? He yelled at Mom for the chickens and for the intuitive healing she'd started doing. He yelled at me for forgetting long division with decimals. He didn't yell at Luke so much. Luke was on some sort of par with him. The older one. They included him in their circle of two so much more often than me. They appealed to his good judgment. His yelling hurt my ears, and it embarrassed me so much I usually forgot what he was yelling about. "For your information, we're miles into the desert. Not a pay phone in sight. Don't ever forget whom you're talking to. This is your father speaking!"

Ten minutes later, we came to a stop in the scrub. I climbed out of the car sobbing and ran behind a saguaro to pee. Luke dragged the metal cooler out of the back and handed me a root beer when I was done. This was his way of saying how much it sucked. Just pure sucked when Dad yelled. We sat and watched our father make an angry pile of tent stakes. It was July 6 and already 101 degrees.

I gulped the soda. "Dad breaks Mom's rules, doesn't he?"

Why hadn't she come? It was treachery that she'd stayed behind, without me. Maybe this was the start of a feeling I sometimes had later that I couldn't fully locate my mother in the world. She didn't quite fit.

"He doesn't break all of them," Luke said.

"The soda one and the holding-your-pee one and the sleeping-with-your-clothes-on one." Why was it so hot? Dry heat that made me breathe too fast until my throat hurt.

"I think Dad breaks rules you have to break when you're camping."

"I'm gonna tell Mom about the soda rule. I'm gonna tell her that he wouldn't stop to let me pee. I'm gonna call her."

"She knows about the soda, dingbat. He told her he was going to give us soda."

"The next time we're in town, I'll find a pay phone and call her." I felt like I'd been abducted. I missed her in a visceral way. Her skin and teeth and hair. She was still how I tried to translate the world. Through my brother through her.

Dad carried the telescope from the car and unfolded its legs, and focused the lens. "I can figure out the location of that rock without ever walking over there." He wrote some numbers down on the small pad he kept in his shirt pocket. "Remember when we talked about triangulation? Don't tell me you've forgotten. Both of you. Don't tell me that." He could be strict, or he could be the most fun you'd ever known. But when his voice rose, I got nervous. He might start yelling again. Luke and I stood close and nodded our heads so we wouldn't be accused of having spaced out. "Here it is," Dad said to himself while he looked through the lens. "Once I know one side and two angles." He stepped back and smiled. "The math is beautiful! The math figures out the rest."

GAIRD FINDS a parking spot on Victor Hugo and jogs around the car to open Luke's door and help him climb out. Then he turns and pulls Luke's duffel bag from the trunk. I go hold the wooden door to the apartment building open. "Let's get him inside, shall we?" Gaird takes Luke's arm, and they walk past me.

I leave them on the living room couch and call Sara from the kitchen, where I start making them mac and cheese. "We're here. Eagle landed. But Gaird's being sort of priggish. It's a side of him I've really never seen."

"You need to give him room—it's his apartment, after all. You're too close to it, Will. Don't say things you'll regret."

"You're right. He's a kind man, isn't he? How did you know that I'm about to say things to him that I'll regret?"

"Because I've lived through your worst love affairs."

"What I want to say is something about him not being generous. Then I'll weep."

"Of course you will."

"I always weep when I get mad, which makes it more pathetic." I stand at the counter with the phone deep in my neck and grate cheese with the metal grater I found in the drawer. Tears leak down my face. "My crying has nothing to do with Gaird."

"You're jealous."

"I'm jealous."

"You don't like sharing your brother."

"And I don't like it when he's sick." I circle the kitchen with the phone and reach for the whisk and add cheese to the milk and make a big mess of a knot with the cord behind me. "But the real problem is, Gaird loves differently."

"Like in a different language? Like Norwegian love? What are you talking about, Willie?"

"There are rules about shoes: none in the apartment. And no

street clothes on the bed—take them off and put a bathrobe on before you lie down. It's more than that, though. I have to go. I have to feed them."

When I bring in the plates, they're watching a black-and-white special on the Allied invasion at Normandy. "I don't care what you say, Luke." I put the food down. "You glow. You look healthy. Though why you're watching this war channel, I don't know."

"It's history," Luke says without looking up. Gaird pretends he hasn't heard me. "War history." Luke picks up the plate. "This looks delicious. You are a good person to cook for us. Gays, by the way, need to watch war movies. We need to bulk up on this artillery stuff." He reaches for his fork. The TV screen blinks, and the sun goes down behind the clean line of mansard roofs across the avenue. I stare at the two of them and secretly wish them a happy ending.

I TAKE a taxi home across the river—a luxury, but it's late and I feel like I've been gone from my apartment for weeks. The message light on my machine blinks. "Hello. Hello, yes, it's Macon Ventri. Gita Kapoor's lawyer. Yes. I was wondering if we could meet tomorrow at the center before your class? I will be there to interview Gita, and I believe that is when you teach." I smile at the machine. I can't help it. His English is so precise and grammatical. And he speaks in something that almost sounds like a British accent.

I change into sweatpants, pour a glass of wine, and sit on the rug to set up the VCR machine. My friend Polly, from the drama department at the academy, gave me a copy of *Hannah and Her Sisters*. She says I'll love it—Woody Allen follows the lives of three American sisters and their errant husbands as they fall in and out of love. I've spent the fall and winter in France putting on more lipstick than I've ever worn in my life, and still it hasn't happened. French men seem to live inside some impenetrable fortress.

I've always chosen men badly. It's become a joke with Luke. I'm not sure how to love. I meet men and swoon, and overanalyze them. Then I can't bring them home and they can never meet Luke. He would only find ways to make fun of them, because this is how he shows he cares. Then I regret what I've done until the men leave me out of confusion. But I watch the movie for two blissed-out hours, and I allow myself to go far away from the student papers on French symbolism I need to grade and the question of what's happened to Luke's lung. Macon Ventri has called me here at my apartment. He knows where I live. I pull up the blanket on the couch and I'm alone again in France, but not lonely.

8

Thanksgiving: public celebration
acknowledging divine favors

*D*uring our senior year of college, I'd driven Sara and Rajiv home for Thanksgiving in an old pickup truck I'd bought from a waitress at the Japanese restaurant where I worked in Palo Alto. The trip took much longer than it should have. The truck could only go fifty miles an hour—all of us mashed into the cab. Sara sat in the middle, listening to beginner French tapes. *Parlez-vous français?* She wanted to move to France even then. *Oui,* the three of us said in unison. *Je parle français.*

Luke had flown in from Beijing that morning, and he stood at the screen door waiting for us, big circles under his eyes like he hadn't slept in a week. My father was at the stove, chopping oysters and creminis for the stuffing. This was after he'd found God in the desert and become a born-again Christian, which is still the greatest surprise of my life and something that, a decade later, I haven't figured out how to assimilate.

Rajiv was forced to stand at the sink with a malfunctioning peeler (my mother didn't believe in peelers and I'd found this one under old chopsticks in the wax paper drawer) for hours: sweet potatoes, white potatoes, pearl onions, and carrots. Sara got caught up in the turkey work. She and my mother and father fretted over the bird all day. Basted it and took its temperature like it was a new pet.

Then the turkey sat on the cutting board in my parents' kitchen in its heat-spackled glory while we waited for it to cool. We were really going to eat it after all the pampering? Luke brought red maple leaves from China. Were there trees in Beijing? The leaves sat on the plates like small, veined hands. I assembled the salad and boiled cranberries for the sauce, and willed the boy named Ned, an ex–wide receiver for the University of Southern California I'd been sleeping with, to call me. The night before he'd phoned drunk from my friend Betsy's house and said he was going to sleep there that night. With Betsy. Ned liked to flex his biceps when he was naked, which sounds horrible, but back then it made me laugh. He'd taken me to nightclubs and liked to borrow things from me—my sandals, my French linen nightie. I thought he was flattering me by stealing.

Luke kept putting his hand on my wrist in the kitchen and taking my pulse to see how I was. "I'm fine," I said when he did it for the third time.

"You're not fine. You're wearing a nightgown."

"It's a tunic. I swear I didn't sleep in it."

"It is a potato sack." Then he got serious. "You're really okay? I'm here, you know. Breakups can be the worst." I smiled, but I'd never felt this flatness before. I'd always been the one to end things until now.

My mother took my hand and pulled me into the screened-in porch. It wasn't warm enough to eat out there. She wore one of my father's long navy Mister Rogers cardigans and sat me down on the bamboo couch. She'd left psychology and was studying the body on shakier ground by then. This meant she was an expert in things like chakras and energy points and nothing with a name that seemed to have anything to do with the actual, physical human anatomy. Patients came to the house so she could lay her hands on them. She was the real fixer. She did it for a living. That day her hair was up in a thick bun, held in place with two chopsticks. "Do you love this boy Ned?"

"I don't know." I'd never been in love before, so I wasn't sure.

She studied me. "Your third chakra is the nexus of self-esteem. It's blocked."

"Oh, Mom. Please stop." I couldn't tell what was worse—when I was little and she used psychology vocabulary way too big for me or this weirder talk about energy. "What language are you speaking? You've got to stop." I stood up. I wanted to be in love so badly then because I thought it would transform me, and that only once I was in love would my real life begin.

I was a serial monogamist in college. First I dated Brandon, a boy from Film 101: An Introduction Across Genres. We sat together during *The Deer Hunter* screening, and I had a small existential breakdown during the movie and became an instant Meryl Streep groupie. I reached for Brandon's hand the first time the war vets walked into the woods with guns. He whispered that it would be okay—that he'd already seen the film five times.

We had sex on the floor of his dorm room that night. Neither of us knew what we were doing. His clothing hung off the radiator: dirty athletic socks with black stripes at the top, grayish boxers. He lived in a suite—six white guys who shared a swamp of a living room having Freudian relationships with their bongs.

Then I dated Sam from Pittsburgh, who wrote love poems in the school newspaper. I ran into him at an off-campus hash party and he filled my wineglass. He said, "The girl in the straw hat in stanza three is you." Need he have said another word?

The poem was about taking a girl to a small lake and helping her walk out of the water. It had a proprietorship that doesn't sound very evolved now. But here is what I thought: finally someone other than my brother to take care of me.

Sam started making Jesus pictures in Magic Marker after we'd been together for two months—the bright blue robe, dark brown hair parted in the middle. Lots of pictures. It became an obsession. What he was really afraid of, he told me, was dying. I couldn't go to class without him worrying when I'd be back. He moved in with me and cooked Sara and me meals—hummus and thick vegetable stews. What was this trend of people I knew giving themselves over suddenly to God?

Sam graduated and moved to Nepal with the Foreign Service

and sent an airmail: "I want to marry you." I wrote back that a man should never wait for a girl who was still in college.

Now there was Ned. Had I made another bad choice? Did I do it on purpose? Sara thought I intentionally chose the wrong ones. The complicated boys. I didn't dare psychoanalyze myself. I followed my mother back to the kitchen and sat on the metal stool at the counter and waited for Ned to call. Or Betsy. I would take Betsy. I thought she and I had bonded that semester when we'd stayed up until three in the morning drinking Kahlúa and reading our sestinas out loud. But no one called.

After dinner I transferred the mashed potatoes into Tupperware. Sara poured me a big glass of chardonnay and said the words "lose him" to me. She was very over Ned by then, partly because I'd pined for him in the truck all morning when we weren't practicing our French verbs, and partly because she was pissed at him. Deep in the languor of turkey hangovers, we managed to eat pumpkin pie, propping ourselves up against the kitchen counter. Then Dad clapped his hands. "Into the living room. Everyone. You haven't seen my August slides of the desert. You haven't seen the water holes I found."

A group of men still lived off the land together out there in the Sonoran Desert—academic dropouts, environmentalists, leftover war protesters, gold miners, and people who just wanted off the grid. That was what Dad always called Sausalito and our house there: the Grid. He had one of the few actual paying jobs in the desert. He loved to catalog what he saw—red-spotted toads, kangaroo rats, desert tortoise, big-horned sheep, coyote. We followed him down the two steps, into the cantilevered living room. The walls were overcrowded with maps now and the Indian weavings. "Everyone thinks they know where the biggest water holes in the desert are. But how hard are they to get to? Extremely difficult, people. Very damn hard. So to find this water I had to follow my nose."

"Did you use the latest geologic survey?" Luke asked. He and Dad were working together on Water Trust projects by then. One small village project at a time. Sometimes it took Luke a year or more to make local connections that would allow pipes to go through the village. Sometimes he had to abandon projects because they couldn't get the local Communist Party's support.

"That last survey doesn't go as far in as I went last month." Dad smiled. "The elevation rises too fast, and the topography lines stop. They vanish into nothing. But I kept going, and that's why I found the secret trove of water. I understood the land. I understood the place. I say this all the time, people. You've always got to know your place. Where you've come from and where you're going. Always ask yourself, What are my coordinates? If you go off the grid, how can you get yourself back safely if you need to?"

Then he turned off the lights. I sat on the cold tiles next to Sara and Rajiv and watched the slides on a white bedsheet Dad had hung on the far wall. Landscape photos of the washed-out desert and the lusher canyons. I was back there with him, hiking for hours in the sun. Was that time really over? Were Luke and I really so far on our way to being adults? Was it normal to long for the past like this? To parse it and physically miss it in a way I didn't know I ever would? In the desert everything was distilled into a series of simple questions: Would we have enough water to make it back to the truck alive? Would we find new hidden sources?

Dad narrated the slides in the darkness and his voice came alive. The Sonoran Desert was the place he liked most in the world, perhaps besides my mother. And he didn't fight with the desert so it was easier maybe than living with my mother. He didn't try to change the desert. He accepted it on its own terms.

9

Guardian: one who has the care of a person or
the property of another; a superior at a Franciscan
monastery

*I*t's Thursday. Macon sits on the flowered couch in the common
room talking to Sophie. She's brought a pot of black Assam
and vanilla biscuits and a small white pitcher of cream. I squeeze past
her in the doorway and sink down into one of the blue chairs. "My
goodness." I smile. "No one asked you for tea service, Sophie. You
have enough to do in here already."

"It's Macon who does too much. I'll make him tea until God
decides to close this place from lack of need."

Macon blushes. "Sophie, you are killing me with kindness." He
flashes a huge grin. It's a real smile. Genuine. Sophie rolls her eyes at
him. There's good history here. Then she waves and leaves. His hair is
all messed up. He's wearing jeans and hiking boots and a loose turtle-
neck sweater. "Sophie is extraordinary." He keeps speaking English.
There's a picture of a bright red soccer ball on his mug. VIVA MÉXICO!
WORLD CUP 1986. He puts it down on the tray and bends his head to
study the file in his lap.

"Mr. Ventri."

"Please. There is no need for formalities. Please call me Macon.
No one calls me Mr. Ventri." He's inclined to precision. When he
smiles, he has surprisingly small, perfectly shaped teeth. The bones of
his face are delicate too, small hollows under the cheekbones, and then

the honey-colored beard. "Willow Pears, what do you do for a living when you are not with the girls here on Rue de Metz?" He closes the file and looks up.

"I teach. I've written a book about one of your French poets, and I'm about to start another. This one about an Indian poet." I've never kissed anyone with a beard before.

"The girls in your class are lucky to have someone with your background."

"What are any of their chances, really? What, for instance, are Gita's chances of getting asylum?"

"Well, we need to go about securing her the best chance she has." He reopens the file and reads in silence. We sit like that, while French motor scooters buzz past the window, a swarm of mutant mosquitoes. I don't think he notices the noise. He's weighing Gita's chances, as if he's the only one who can save the girl. He closes his eyes and rubs them with his hands. Then he opens them and leans forward on the couch so that he's as close as he can be to me without getting up. "This system is intricate. Elaborate. With politicians breathing down its neck of late. Thanks to Le Pen." He puts his hands back on the tops of his kneecaps like he might stand and leave any moment, and in this way he also reminds me of Gita—both of them with this urgency.

He's not wearing a wedding ring, but I already knew that. Today I just double-check. "Here's how it works. Most people awarded asylum are flown into France after they've already been designated. It is much harder to apply for asylum status once you're already inside the host country. Plus, the government doesn't give out as many asylums now, and the process is too quick for girls to get their feet on the ground and establish a good case here before they're sent back home. There's no quota in France for asylum seekers and no lottery for asylum, and there are tens of thousands of applicants. Gita hardly has a claim. There is no war in Jaipur that I am aware of. No famine."

"Sometimes there is famine." I don't know this to be a fact. "There is a man in India who's raped her and will hunt her down if she goes back."

"The one who brought her to Paris? But he is on this continent, and France is planning to send her back to the continent she came from."

"I am talking about a different man. Manju's brother. An arranged marriage has been planned."

"How do I convince the judge not to send her back? This is my question every day. There is an Air France flight to India that leaves Charles de Gaulle at four-fifteen." He begins putting his things back in his saddlebag—the file on Gita, two pens, a small pad of notepaper with a bright orange cover and doodles on it that look like they've been done by a small child.

"The brother-in-law is the reason she's here at the center." Maybe if I keep talking, he will stay. "Yes, he lives here. In Paris. But he has arranged for his own brother in Jaipur to marry Gita."

"That won't be sufficient grounds for asylum. I'm sorry." He isn't interested in making me feel good, and I respect and resent it. "Here is what I have." He reaches for his tea and seems to relax again and relish his work. "A girl who by all accounts is remarkably bright. With a broken family that is probably all in Paris illegally now—tourist visas that have each expired, except for the brother-in-law, who's on a work visa and comes and goes as he pleases with the jewelry. There is a grandmother we think might still be in India, but we are not sure if she is alive. This will be a sticking point. There is also a nasty arranged marriage waiting for her in Jaipur. Lastly, I want to point out a small passage in the French Asylum Long Brochure—"

"I know this clause. I've read this part!" My voice rises. I can't help it. "I've read the brochures! They say defendants can be protected by asylum from their own family members when those members mean to hurt them." I'm so sure this is the statute that will save Gita, because it clearly states that you can be awarded asylum if your family is a threat to you.

Macon raises his eyebrows at me. "You are shrewd to have already located the statute. But it won't work for Gita because the person who wants to hurt her is Manju, the brother-in-law, and he is with her in France. She is asking for asylum from India. She is arguing to stay here, in the country where the brother-in-law actually lives, and to not go back to her home country. It's contradictory."

"Yes, it's complicated." I lower my voice. "But there's danger in India for her."

"But can we prove it?" He smiles—a wry, tough smile. "What she needs is a court guardian who can vouch for her in court. This is a new tactic we are just trying. Some courtrooms are open to it. The child lives in foster care with a French family, but the court guardian helps manage the child's well-being through the hearing and is the court liaison through the foster care. That is the only way they may release her in France. I have been thinking about you."

I fear I turn completely red. He has no idea how much I've been thinking about him. Then he says, "I am wondering if you might consider being Gita's guardian. There's a lot of pro forma you'd have to do with the court."

Guardian? I'm stumbling my way through being her teacher. "Why do you think I'd have any chance of being appointed?"

"You are a great teacher, by all accounts. You aren't French, and this will be a problem, but you've got a work contract, so there might be some room here. You know the girl. I think she trusts you." He begins packing up again. "What do you think?"

"I think I could try." What am I doing? "What's the first step? Maybe I can try it and we'll see if this is the right fit?"

He smiles again. "Wonderful. Fantastic. This is great news. The first step is the written document Gita needs for court. She will hand it to the judge and she will be asked to read some of it out loud. We're never sure how it will go. But it's essential that she know her story well. I will help her with this. It's part of my job. But if you can do it too, then we might win. She will get about five minutes to speak. Put small things in that you've learned about Gita. Things she might not tell me. Please try to stay away from actual interpretations of the law and away from speculation. That's my job. I will do that. We can meet next week. If you are willing to see me again?" He looks me straight in the eyes.

I'm not imagining things, am I? "I am willing." My heart beats so hard I can hear it in my ears.

He stands and moves toward the door. "Thank you for meeting me, Willow. Thank you for working so hard on Gita's behalf." He smiles, then he's gone.

I finish my tea alone. Is he choosing me? Am I choosing him? What's happening? I feel like life's asking me to be more open in Paris than I've ever been before. And when I think I've opened enough, it's asking me to open even more. I hear Esther and Precy talking back and forth in their bedrooms down the hall. Precy's louder. I can hardly make out Esther because she's so quiet. "Who has my brush? Did anyone see my hairbrush?" Precy asks. "I need to brush my hair. I have been waiting to brush my hair."

Gita walks into the room first and takes my hand. "You are back. I never know if you will really be coming back."

"Gita. I've signed an agreement to teach classes here at the center on Thursdays through June. It's only late February. I so greatly enjoy teaching here with you. I keep my word."

She sits down on the couch and starts talking without any warning: "My maa and I were sharing a bed in our home in Paris. I cannot tell you where. I cannot have you go there. So I tell my mind to forget. Promise me. Do not make me go back there. I want to live in France. But not with Manju. My pitaa waited for us in India. My maa and I only came to France for a visit. We were not meant to be living here. Maa came because Morone and I talked her into it. I am guilty she is here in France. I am guilty Pitaa is dead. I love all of my family. My mother doesn't speak French or English. The first day she was here, she packed up the beans and rice and mutton and left the apartment to find a way to climb up to the roof to cook. Morone and I stopped her in the hall. We said, in Paris we use the kitchen stove."

"We are trying to fix things so you can stay in this country, Gita. I just had a meeting with your lawyer." Is she starting to lose her mind in here? She can't slow down. This is what I fear the most for the girls. That the locking up and the faceless days will cause them to vacate their minds. And then they will slowly come apart. It's what would happen to me quickly. But I'm weak like that. To lock me up would be how to unravel me. I'd crave the world outside.

"He is a good man, Mr. Ventri. I can feel this. But he is very busy with many cases. What I wonder about every day is if Manju slept in that hall of our apartment. Because I am still not sure how he was finding me there every day. I screamed in my head each time. I saw a hammer in my mind while he pulled me on top of him, and I hit him on the shoulder and there was blood. But in the real life I did nothing, because of my sister and my maa and my little brother, Pradeep. The gem shop is the only way for them. Manju and the gem shop."

"Oh, Gita. They wouldn't turn on you."

"They would not believe me, and so they would turn me out. My father is dead, Willow. I cannot go back to India because there is nothing waiting for me there but Manju's brother, who will be my husband. So I am keeping the blue papers and the pink papers I get from the law people. I am meeting with the lawyer and the caseworker. I am working on the story. I am practicing. I am not going back. Please don't make me go back."

"We are working so hard on it. There will be an end."

She brings out a photo from her notebook and hands it to me. She and Morone and their mother and a younger boy who must be their brother, Pradeep, and then Manju. He's a short, thick man with a blunt strip of bangs across a broad forehead. Gita points to her mother's lined face and rests her finger there and stares. The only photo Gita has of her mother also has her perpetrator in it. Then Moona and Rateeka come in and Gita takes the photo and slides it back in the notebook.

The common room fills with girls. "Let's start right away." I jump up. "What if the judge in the courtroom asks you to go back in your memory?"

"Chapati and potatoes," Moona says. "That is my memory of the food in Bombay. The same thing every day."

"The judge may ask you to tell the courtroom exactly how you left your country—on a train or in a car or in an airplane or on foot. This is when you will be glad you've memorized your story."

Gita says, "In my memory Manju came to our house in Jaipur and sat for the coulis and masala and said that he was moving Morone to France to work at the gem shop. Then he announced he was taking my maa and me with him to France. We were scared but also feeling the excitement."

"Is Pradeep still here in Paris?" I ask.

"He is in Paris, yes. My baby brother. The boy who I love so much. But I won't see him. None of them know where I am."

"That has to be so hard," I say.

"Yeah. Hard." Precy stares at Gita. "I don't know where my mother is, but you know where yours is. How do you not go back to her? I would go back."

"Precy," I say. "You've made your decision and Gita's made hers and both for different reasons. It's better to stick to your story and not worry about Gita's."

Gita's got her hand over her mouth, scowling. I need to be their teacher. They already have caseworkers. Sophie is Gita and Moona's. A nurse from Bangladesh named Mrs. Kader is the caseworker for Rateeka and Zeena. I haven't met Precy or Esther's caseworker yet, but I've heard she is a retired public schoolteacher. "We should do some writing now. Can you open to a blank page in your notebooks? Do you have pencils? Who needs a pencil?"

10

Saint: a person of great holiness, virtue, or benevolence

*W*inter unlocks its hold on the city. Days grow warmer in March. The daffodils get an early start in the Luxembourg Gardens, where I start taking my lunch at school. Buds on the cherry trees swell and bloom into pink gauze, and everywhere there's the yellow surprise of forsythia. "I'm not a saint, you know," Gaird says into the phone on a Friday. Sometimes I only detect his Norwegian accent at the end of his sentences, because they finish on high notes and confuse me with cheeriness. He pauses to inhale his cigarette. "How much longer do I have to wait?"

"What do you mean, 'wait'?" It's hard to take off my skirt and change into my sweatpants while I talk. I've just gotten home from office hours at the academy, and I'm trying to go for a run. Gaird never calls me. Why can't he say that he's worried about Luke? Then at least we'd have that connection. Because Luke still doesn't feel completely better two weeks out of the hospital.

"I wait for Luke to go back to the way he was before the hospital. I wait for him to get out of the bed on Saturdays and to cook his own eggs."

Is this how Gaird's mind works? I make careful use of pronouns, trying to bring him inside the conversation. "This is not the easy part.

But it will get better. We'll figure this out." Luke is improving. All Gaird needs to do is make sure Luke doesn't work too much.

"It is a complete disaster." The brushback. "At home and now also at work. Because he cannot work for very long." Gaird inhales again. "He comes here to the offices, but then he lies down on my sets. My God. I think, What in the name of my maker is happening? I have deadlines. I have a headache."

On Saturday morning I walk the two blocks to Place Monge and take the No. 7 pink line, which goes underneath the river to Châtelet–Les Halles, where I switch to the A line. The train is crowded with families going to the Bois de Boulogne or farther west into the suburbs for the weekend. French boys with cropped hair seeing how long they can stand in the aisle of the train without holding on to anything. I plan what I'll say to Gaird if he's there at the apartment. I set out at Charles de Gaulle–Étoile and the fluorescent lights give everyone's skin a greenish tone. The staircase straight ahead leads to the Arc de Triomphe. It's always a surprise—this huge arch in the middle of the working city. Almost two hundred feet high, it comes from another lifetime of war and generals who marched entire armies around it.

I walk farther through the trippy tunnel and come up on Rue de Presbourg, which forms a semicircle around the far side of the arch. A series of streets fan out from here. Victor Hugo is a busy coiffured avenue of upscale clothing stores, Guy Laroche and Céline farther down the street, and cafés and smaller boutiques and jewelry stores. The stone is paler here, and the sky is piercing blue today. A flock of pigeons swoop between the buildings, blotting out the sun. I cross the street named for Paul Valéry—champion of Rimbaud long after the poet's death. The pigeons' bellies hang below their little bald heads. They all land together in a patch of sun outside Café Le Victor Hugo near a tall horse chestnut tree whose buds begin to poke from its limbs.

Luke lives at the corner of Rue Georges-Ville. I want to do something to help him get better—something concrete. The string bags of oranges for sale at the corner market seem like a start, so I buy one and carry it in both arms like a toddler the rest of the way to his apartment.

"The juice lady *est arrivée*!" I yell, turning my key in Luke's door.

"I'm having a quiet moment!" he calls from his bedroom.

"Have many quiet moments. I'm making juice!" I stand in his white kitchen and slice a dozen oranges and pull a metal juice press out of the cupboard next to the stove.

"Take off your coat first!" Luke yells after I'm into the oranges. "Come and sit and talk!"

"*Attends! Attends*. First I make the juice."

I take a full glass into his bedroom—a long, narrow room with a king-sized canopy bed and three blue prints of Napoleon in oval frames along the street-side wall. His bureau sits low to the ground, a straw basket on top filled with clippings of good furniture and loose francs and cuff links. "The lead today," he says, "the boy who thinks he'll be the next Depardieu, stormed off the set because he couldn't get his lines right." Then he takes the juice and drinks it like he hasn't seen water in days. "God, that is tasty."

I try not to stare at his neck while he drinks. It's thinner since he left the hospital, even though he should be fattening up. Those were my instructions from Dr. Picard—to feed my brother—and I've been trying. Gaird and I have both been trying. So why can I see the rise and fall of his Adam's apple so easily? He's been healthy all his life. So happy to be in Paris—a place, he'd told me when I landed at Charles de Gaulle back in September, "invented for me! A city completely committed to smoking and red wine!"

"You nap, I'll cook." He tries to protest, but I go back to the kitchen and sauté a hanger steak and chop garlic and pull together a Caesar salad.

I carry the plates into his bedroom on a tray. "Let's eat." I lay the tray on his lap in the bed. "Any chance we could get you into that gray sweat suit you like? The velour one?"

"Please don't make me get up."

"You can change on the bed."

"Too hard. I hate being sick. I hate not being able to go out. I hate not working."

"It's getting better."

"It's not, really. Not if I'm honest. I feel like shit."

"Put the sweat suit on. Clean clothes will help."

"Not doing it." He closes his eyes and seems wiped. I don't get it. "You can't make me. Turn to Channel 27, please. *Dynasty* reruns." There's a small TV on a mahogany bench near the foot of the bed. I flip it on and crawl back next to Luke and stare at the screen. They're having a Halloween party at the mansion in Colorado. Joan Collins wears a mask covered in glitter. Luke never misses Halloween. None of us ever did.

In October of the year before she went to Greece, my mother found Dad's wet suit in the barn and wore it back into the kitchen. She couldn't stop laughing or tripping on the flippers. Dad was at the counter in a green wig, putting handfuls of M&M's into Ziploc bags. *Abbey Road* played on the turntable in the living room. It seemed like the sound track to our lives in 1970. All we ever listened to. "Backward!" Dad yelled. "You've got to walk backward in the flippers, Katie."

She did a one-eighty toward Luke, who stood near the front door in a black cape, face a painted white, waiting for his friends. Mom stretched her arms toward him. "I'm coming for you!" Then she looked at me sitting at the kitchen table—the ladybug in leotard and tights with a red-and-black shell I'd made from shoe boxes. "Neither of you can get away from me."

"Oh God, Mom." Luke laughed. "Every trick-or-treater is going to think we're wackos." He was thirteen then, too old for public hugging, so he tried to dodge her but not hard enough. She wrapped him in her arms and leaned her face down toward his in the glass mask. "Totally freaky bug eyes!" Then Luke ran to hide behind Dad over by the counter. "That wet suit smells. That thing hasn't been washed in, like, one hundred years."

"It's just," Mom said slowly, giggling, "that this mask is so tight I can't really breathe." That my parents wore costumes on Halloween was one of the greatest things in my life—better, maybe, even than Christmas. I loved it when my mother laughed like this. It made everything in the world make sense and I believed she'd never be sad or lonely again. Never misunderstand me or Dad or take to her bed.

"Mom," Luke said, "you don't breathe through your nose! Breathe through your mouth, Mom."

Then Dad put the candy down and pulled the mask up off Mom's forehead so that it sat on top of her head. He kissed her on the lips. "Let me fix it, my underwater creature. You have the mask on too tight."

Everyone goes to bed on *Dynasty*. Luke's asleep next to me. I turn off the television. Where's Gaird? It's too late. Why isn't he home? I take some toothpaste in their bathroom and rub my teeth with my finger. Then I walk into the little den off the kitchen. The room is like a French jewelry box—red high-gloss walls, an antique wrought-iron daybed smothered in velvet pillows. I lie down and try to go to sleep.

When I hear Gaird's key in the door, Luke and I are climbing through a rock canyon somewhere in the Pinaleno Mountains in southeast Arizona. Heat of the day and our little bodies are those of middle schoolers—faces still soft and round, waists not as defined. Luke's legs have begun to lengthen, but his arms are so thin. The sun burns through our long-sleeved T-shirts, scorching my upper back. Our dad has left us at the bottom of this granite face to go find more water. What we're meant to do is climb to the top of the rock—a grooved, speckled piece of pancaked granite that Luke carefully studies for handholds.

We're ten feet up. Now twenty feet above the grasslands. Sometimes I put my hand where Luke's foot is before he's even taken it off the rock and he has to remind me to wait until he's found the next crack to wedge his sneaker into. He's only calm with me. We have hours to climb—days, maybe—to make it to the top, which is still out of sight. And no matter how much we climb, we can never see the end. My arms feel heavy, deadened. I know I'll have to let go soon.

Tears slide into my mouth and mix with my saliva. Then I'm sobbing—the rock. Luke tells me to hold on. He tells me it's not much farther. That I can make it. I'm not sure which I'm sadder about—

the fact of my death or that in dying I'll have to leave my brother. It's such an awful, scoured-out feeling. Only blackness without him. The numbness of this begins to take over me as I fall.

I jolt up—hair and neck and face wet with sweat, the top sheet bunched around my waist like a toga. My heart's racing. I'm disconnected from my waking life, floating on a black current of anxiety. The bedside clock says one a.m. I hear Gaird take a glass from the cupboard and fill it with water but I can't translate this into words. Then he clears his throat. I feel in the dark to the tiny bathroom off the den and lap up water from my hand under the spigot. I drink three times, until the water begins to move through my chest and my pulse slows. I'm not falling. Dad hasn't left us. Luke's asleep in the next room.

In the morning Gaird's up early frying sausage and eggs, and the kitchen is steamy with the heat. I fill a glass of water at the sink and drink it silently. My dream's still with me. I'm so thirsty. I turn to Gaird and make myself smile, but I'm not ready for human contact. I want to stay in the blanket of the dream and understand it more. I feel more part of the world—the sidewalks and sparrows and poems. The future. The past. These are those fleeting moments before becoming fully lucid. My brain can hold all of it. All of life. There's none of that pressing-in I feel on other days. None of the stark questioning that can gnaw at me in the night.

I let go of some part of my other life every time I come to this apartment. My mind is more malleable, more open. I'm not a poetry professor or a teacher at a small asylum center on Rue de Metz. I'm a sister. A daughter. Sometimes this apartment feels more like home than my own flat on Rue de la Clef.

Gaird hands me a plate. I follow them both past the couches to the round table that sits in a pool of sun in the living room. The drapes have been pulled back so we can see the people walking their dogs and grabbing baguettes. The coffee wakes my mind and I stay until noon, sprawled on the couch with Luke, looking at the books of still photographs he and Gaird have amassed on the set of the 1920s period film they're finishing.

Then I leave them because I have a date with Madame Boudreaux, the widow who lives in the apartment below me. She's a French bond trader with a fondness for bloody beef. Once a month she invites me to Sunday supper, where we feast and drink too much cabernet.

One of her long-haired teens lets me into the apartment. He smiles vaguely; black Walkman headphones cover his ears. I wave at his brother, sprawled on the long couch, listening to his own headphones. He gives a half wave back. It's an apartment of understated luxury— muted taupes and grays in velvets and silks, the furniture low and sleek, with rounded arms and sloping backs. Madame Boudreaux is in the kitchen, which has been untouched for decades. White metal cabinets with China-blue knobs, a steel pot rack that hangs in a half rectangle above the stove. She has a white apron on over her tight wool skirt and black stockings.

The meal is always brisk. The boys and their mother cut the meat sharply, precisely, and take small bites, hardly stopping until the roast potatoes are gone and the baked fennel and the gravy. Then the boys clear the plates, and we eat the flan and drink white cups of coffee with cream. How I love this flan she makes—so smooth and rich. The boys get to retreat to their bedrooms after this. Then Madame Boudreaux smokes a single cigarette through a small crack in the dining room window and finally relaxes.

"I hope the guys won't smell it," she says in French. "They hate it when I smoke." Then she shrugs and inhales again. Her fingernails are painted the color of the wine. She kicks off her high heels and puts her stocking feet up on the chair next to her. This is the part I wait for, when she tells me about her life. "Would you be a darling and get us the chocolates?" She points to the wooden sideboard, and I stand and reach for the green tin. Then she pours us more wine.

She's been widowed for more than ten years and has lived in the building for twenty. She knows everyone in here. Some she's slept with. Others she's only considered. She's a striking, secure woman who knows her power and how she wants to be in the world. She's joyful about the men and modest and open. It's simply one thread of her life—the men. There are many threads, and she seems to have found a balance. This month, she says, it's one of the younger men on the trading floor whom she's letting court her.

When I leave, she kisses me four times, twice on either side of my face. I think we're a little drunk, and I let that warm fog carry me up the stairs to my apartment. When I get into bed, it's seven o'clock. On my lap I have a stack of students' papers on the French modernist movement that I need to grade. The phone rings.

Macon Ventri is speaking to me in English: "I am sorry it is so late. I am here at the office, working. I believe we need to discuss Gita's case further."

"On Sunday? You're working on Sunday?" I smile and put my head back against my pillow.

"It is my predilection. But it's bad, no? I shouldn't have called. Should I hang up?" He sighs into the phone like he's capitulating to something.

"No. No, it's good." I close my eyes then. I can't stop smiling. "I'd love to talk more about Gita."

"Okay then. I have an idea. Could we meet on the river on Monday? At lunchtime?"

"Tomorrow? Tomorrow afternoon is good." I try not to let my voice sound too excited. "I'm done at the academy by one. But where on the river? It's a big river."

"Let's meet in front of the Hôtel de Ville. Do you know this area? It is what you call your City Hall. In the fourth, near the Seine. The oldest square in this city. It is also the mayor's office and not far from Pompidou and Notre Dame, across the Pont d'Arcole. I have meetings there with the mayor's people, and it's close to my office in Les Halles. I will wait for you at the fountains."

"I can find it. I love searching for new places in the city. So that's great. So okay then."

"I will go home now."

"You should. Good night, Macon. Thank you for calling." I say this last part with a hint of irony—because I want to say more and I think he knows this.

"Good night, Willie. I hope you sleep very well tonight."

————

IN THE MORNING I wash my hair and wear it fastened at my neck. I find my favorite oatmeal scarf, more like a blanket, and wrap it twice around my neck. I teach the Women's Poetry class at the academy from ten to twelve. Then I have office hours until one. Two students come— boys from U. Penn, friends in the States, each writing semester-long papers on Neruda. I'm frank with them. I fear they'll collude without even meaning to. But they're passionate about poetry. One is writing about Neruda's political dissidence and his exile to a small Italian island. The other is focusing only on Neruda's odes—some of my very favorite poems—especially the ones to watermelon and hand-knit socks. It's hard to find poems that celebrate language this way—with delight and wild abandon. I ask the boys not to compare notes. Their earnestness moves me. Can I raise boys like this when I have them?

Then I lock the door to my office and take the stairs down Rue St. Sulpice to Rue de Tournon until it hits Boulevard St. Germain. It's two blocks to the metro at Odéon. Late March, and it feels like spring has fully arrived. Sudden and immediate. The wind is so warm there can be no turning back to the cold, and the birds seem to understand this. Out in numbers finally—sparrows trip from the trees and blackbirds sit on chimneys and call down. The buds on the chestnut trees and poplars and beeches seem to understand it, too, everything now in the act of blooming. And I'm going to meet Macon Ventri. In Paris. I'm walking to the Hôtel de Ville to find him. It's spring. It's spring and Macon's eyes have flecks of gray and it's not that big a deal really, but everything feels possible now because I'm meeting him.

The No. 4 line takes me back to Châtelet–Les Halles, where I walk four long blocks on Rue de Rivoli to the Hôtel de Ville. The buildings are cream-colored and regal and sit in stately rows that stretch for what seems like quarters of miles. Some of them triangulate at intersections like the noses of giant ships—ocean tankers anchored in the middle of Paris. I've never been on Rue de Rivoli before, so close to the heart of the French political machinery. Closer to the start of the snail's spiral shell on the Paris map in my mind.

The Hôtel de Ville is made from the same blond stone but is so ornate it reminds me of a grand cathedral or palace. It must be a palace. I stand in the courtyard by the street and stare at the thick baroque moldings and the dozens of carved statues lining the rooftop. Where is he? He must be here. Can he see me while I can't see him? The French motto LIBERTÉ, ÉGALITÉ, FRATERNITÉ is etched in the center molding, surrounded by more carved figures. I scan the courtyard for him again. This time I find him, sitting like he said he'd be, on the stone edge of one of the fountains. I can't swallow my smile. The wind is stronger and blows my scarf up behind my shoulder like a banner. I reach with my hand and pull it back.

Macon stands before I get to him. "You've found me. Thank you so much for coming." He smiles one of those small, polite Frenchmen smiles.

"It's beautiful here. The seat of political intrigue."

"Well, it's not quite so exotic inside the mayor's office. We may get to talk to Chirac in this famous building, but we still don't agree with his immigration numbers." He points to the river. "Shall we walk?" A small rectangular blue sign on the metal post at the corner reads QUAI DE GESVRES. We cross the Pont d'Arcole, a narrow two-laned bridge with black railings and slatted green benches. We say nothing. My mind can't stop circling us. And looking down at us from above as we make it on to Île de la Cité. We appear to be a man and woman with a small enough space between our bodies—our shoulders and arms— for one of us to reach out and touch the other easily. The water is the color of slate and frothy from the rains. We turn left on a small lane that follows the river.

"How is your teaching on Rue de Metz going? How are the girls holding up?"

Work. He's talking work. That's what we'll do. Of course. It's why we're here. "I see them for such a short time. They're amazing. Formidable. When I was their age, I was being driven to swim practice by my mom."

"Gita trusts you. If she tells me where her family lives here in Paris then we can push for reunification."

"Oh, she won't tell you or the court where the family lives." I look at his face to read him.

"They almost always tell." He stares down at the cobblestones.

"You know her better, but I don't think she'll tell. Have you forgotten the brother-in-law? The one who raped her in the hallway? You want to reunify her with him?" Two white birds land on the water—French geese? This isn't the walk I thought. This isn't about anything else but getting information out of me. Upon closer inspection the birds are seagulls, and more follow, squawking. "Sophie said Gita was dropped off at the hospital by a taxi with no one to help her, and that this man in Jaipur, Daaruk, will abduct her to the south."

"Gita has filled you in on many details. She is treating you more like a lawyer." He laughs. "I need these details. This is how I build a case. I wonder why she trusts you so much. I wonder what her plan is."

"What do you mean, 'plan'? She's my student. I'm her teacher."

He picks up a stone on the sidewalk and tosses it into the water. "But Gita is one step ahead of you. At least one. She's very likely going to be sent back to India, Willie. So she's more desperate than you think. She will try to influence things. This is how I will say it. She will try to manipulate the situation, because you are kind and she is at a great disadvantage. You need to understand. She is in a corner, and I am going to try to get her out. Reunification here would be a way to have her legally remain in Paris—that is, if any of her family is legal, which I doubt."

"I think she's a young girl and that she and I really connect."

He laughs. Not unkindly, I think. But a real laugh. "Of course you connect. That's because you're good at your job and she is anxious for someone to help her. Don't blame her for doing what you would do. It's survival. She's going to ask you for things. You'll have to decide how much to give."

"I'd give her everything I could."

"But the classroom isn't real life. Be careful. You can control things to some extent in the classroom, but not on the streets. Often I lose at court, but every now and then I win, and my wins feel very good and restore hope."

"I'll help her in any way I can." We walk side by side so our arms brush against each other. "Why have you chosen to work in Paris?"

He moves behind me so a group of joggers can pass and places his hand on my lower back. I have a difficult time concentrating after this—can't focus on putting one foot in front of the other. Blood rushes to my head because of his hand. He's got this confidence that's palpable but not remote. "It is my genetic makeup. My family history. We were the traveling Jews you hear about—generations moving around within Russia. Then my grandfather took the family from Estonia to Toronto. I've inherited a complex understanding of what gets lost in exile."

More runners gain on us. Macon stops and puts his hand on my left hip this time. He's going to speak, but then he doesn't. He keeps his hand on me after the runners fly by, and we solidify something. At least I think we do. I've just met him, really, but a part of me feels like I've known him all my life. We haven't used words to describe what we're doing. It's hard for me not to give it a name, but his hand is on my hip. We walk another hour to the tip of the island, and the street is quieter, the water glints in the sun. He doesn't touch me again, but the memory of his hand—the warm feel of it stays with me. An imprint. So it's as if he's still doing it, walking with his hand on my hip. Then we're behind Notre Dame, next to a courtyard thick with trees whose buds are all turning green. The cathedral looks like an ancient, intergalactic spaceship from here. Almost pretend. As if the whole ornate edifice might take off soon and ascend straight into the heavens. There's a conical spire made of black metal that also ascends toward some decisive point high in the sky. Macon and I stand and crane our necks looking up.

"It's like the church is calling to God," I say. "The spire's a radio tower. Dialing-in God's frequency."

"It is quite incredible, no? Talking to God here in the middle of Paris."

"My father's heard the message. He is one of the people listening."

"And you?" Macon puts his hand on my shoulder and casually, gently redirects me toward the sidewalk.

"I'm not sure I can hear the message. I'm not sure I'm able to listen."

We turn toward the bridge. Should I invite him to dinner at my apartment? *He's Gita's lawyer.* We cross to the Hôtel de Ville and take Rue de Rivoli until we get to the metro. "Thank you," I say disingenuously. I want him to reach for me again. "That was helpful—the walk and the information you shared."

He takes my hand. *"Au revoir.* I needed to see you. Do you understand? I couldn't tell if you were real inside the rooms on Rue de Metz." He tucks a piece of my hair behind my ear. "Yes. Real."

I turn toward the station, blushing, and he continues on Rue de Rivoli toward the legal center near Les Halles. If he stops and waves, then I'll know for certain he's a good lawyer for Gita—and a good man. But he doesn't. Just before I take the stairs down into the underground, I hear my name. "Willie. Of the willow tree." I look back toward Rue de Rivoli and he's standing there smiling at me, hands in his pockets. Then he turns and keeps walking.

11

Refugee: a person who flees for safety, especially to a foreign country

For the field trip I have to submit a detailed itinerary of how I'll take Gita from Rue de Metz to the Rodin Museum on Rue de Varenne. We're going to get her out of the primary school. We're going to see some sculptures.

Gita's early for our class each week, and punctual for her meetings with Macon and Sophie. She completes all of her kitchen work—prepping vegetables and the cleanup—and she keeps her own room clean. Because of her good behavior, I'm able to obtain the permissions necessary to escort the detainee out of the asylum center from ten o'clock in the morning on Friday, March 31, 1989, to four o'clock in the afternoon the same day. This gives us more than enough time to get to Rue de Varenne, see the sculptures, and hustle back.

Gita's been living on Rue de Metz for two and a half months. Much longer than any French government official would like. It's taking its toll. Today she looks pale and thin. Sophie stands at the front door with us and buttons the top of Gita's coat. Then Truffaut buzzes us out. It's as if we've stepped through time. Catapulted back to the future. She's out. And it was so easy. Here's Paris having its Friday morning just like it always does, while Gita's been waiting inside. There's so much cruelty involved in the mechanisms of being actually locked up that I don't think either of us can process it out here in the bright sunshine. We walk down Rue de Metz past the wall of graffiti and turn on Boulevard de Strasbourg past the *pharmacie* and the Chinese restaurant and the beauty salons. At first we're both very quiet. She studies the city—mothers pushing strollers, businessmen in dark suits, teenage boys outside the *tabac*.

There's a line at the ticket booth at St. Denis. I have to resist the strong urge to hold her hand down here. I don't want to lose her. It's like another city inside the station—warmer and louder, with so many people calling out to one another and speed-walking and jogging and waiting in the chaos of getting from one place to another. I decide we'll take the No. 8 train to a stop I've never been to called La Tour–Marbourg. Then it's only a five-minute walk through the Place des Invalides to the museum. This way we won't have to change trains. This way it won't be quite as overwhelming for Gita. The platform is packed with mothers with toddlers in their arms and men carrying briefcases and rolled newspapers. Teenagers, too, of all skin colors, and why aren't they in school at ten-thirty on Friday?

Most of us get on the No. 8. The train's hot and crowded, but we find seats in the middle that face the aisle. Two trench coats rub our knees. The men in the coats don't look down and don't see us. We don't speak. I don't want to ruin the spell I think she's in—free from the asylum center. I don't know how to access what she might be feeling. What she's translating in her mind. The asylum center's like a netherworld now that we're riding away from it on the metro. It's not a bad place, because of Sophie. And because it's so small. Its size means everything. I think nighttime has to be the hardest. How does Gita quell the longing and fear? I think she must have to turn off. The ride takes thirty minutes. Then we climb a set of long, dirty stairs.

The Place des Invalides is more imposing than I thought it would be—a hive of military museums and monuments. Napoleon's body is consecrated somewhere here. Gaird and Luke are fascinated with Bonaparte. They've waited in line at his tomb. White tour buses—

lots of them—turn through the stone gates up ahead like big, round-nosed belugas. Gita and I walk along Rue de Grenelle until I have to get out the map. Then we stop and I study it.

We make it to the actual Boulevard des Invalides, teeming with cars and motorcycles. "We're almost there." I fold the map up and she nods. Older, well-coiffed men and women pass us on the sidewalk in fur coats and leather shoes. "The museum is just down this street." The scope of the buildings at Invalides is just so big. I'm sweating. Why did I think it was a good idea to bring her here? We turn left on Varenne and walk inside an iron gate cut into a stone wall. Then things get very quiet.

There's the contrast between the buzz on the street and this green, landscaped oasis. We're on the grounds of the mansion where Auguste Rodin lived—a golden-colored stone building called the Hôtel Biron, with the world's most famous sculpture garden that unfolds in front.

Two gravel paths lead from the stairs toward a tall, wide green hedge. The sculptures seem as though they've always lived here. Among the rose gardens and all kinds of different shrubbery shaved into perfect cylinders and domes. We stand at the start of the path on the left, and I hand Gita a small black notebook and a pencil from my bag. "If you want to write about anything you see here, please go ahead. Or if you want to make sketches. Or ideas of sketches. Because the day is yours, and now you have a notepad to do the drawing in." I hope she doesn't balk or think I'm nuts for bringing her here. She has only six hours outside the center.

"Thank you, Willow." She doesn't take her eyes off the sculptures. People walk past us, circling the paths, murmuring to one another as they study the bronzes.

"Your drawing is coming along so nicely, Gita." For the last two weeks, she's been making drawings in her room of men and women from her village in India. Sophie has showed them to me. The faces come alive on the page—haunting sketches of women and men standing outside the shapes of houses.

"It is not anything. It is silly for Sophie to be showing you." She puts her head down as if she's shy. I haven't seen this side of her in several weeks—young and uncertain.

"How do you feel in here?"

"Feel? I am feeling small here. These statues are so big." She looks around uneasily again. Hordes of tourists now—a tour bus must have unloaded. A group mills at the entrance, and smaller trios and duos move around the paths. Gita walks toward the statue of the man resting his chin on his hand. She stands under the man's knee. "This artist is faithful to the nature of people's bodies. What I am meaning to say is that the bodies to me look very alive."

"Rodin is famous for that. This one is called *The Thinker.* It's incredibly well known." The stone has sinew and muscle and tendon. How can it be so realistic? The man's left arm sits on his left knee, right arm propping up his chin. Gita walks around him and comes back to her starting place. She opens the first page of the notepad and stops and puts her hand over her mouth and laughs. I don't laugh. It's okay to be serious and for her to feel something strange.

"There are so many people in here. So many in one place."

We walk up to each sculpture and she circles them on foot—*The Gates of Hell* and *Balzac* and all the others. There's a strong March wind and Gita's raincoat is thin, pulled from the boxes of donated clothes, with a braided belt and gold buckle. It stops short of her knees, so her sari hangs below the coat. After we've seen the garden, we walk inside the museum, where it's warmer. More sculptures here, including *The Kiss,* which a small group congregates around—two naked lovers, but the man and woman's lips don't actually touch. Somehow the marble is able to hold the tension of the kiss that hasn't come yet.

There's a room of the works of Rodin's student and lover, Camille Claudel. They had an affair for many years. She was abandoned by him in the end and institutionalized. She died alone. But here is her work, pulsing with life. Here is her famous *Bronze Waltz*—a couple holding each other tightly, delicately, as they dance. Gita and I walk through the building, and I'm haunted by Claudel's madness. The parquet floors seem to absorb the sounds of our shoes and hushed voices, but Gita and I hardly talk. She doesn't seem tired. But the museum feeling settles over me, and I get very sleepy.

There are the sculptures—the naked bodies so well-defined—and all of Rodin's passion and conviction and stubbornness that must have gone into making them. I can't reconcile the enormity of what Rodin was trying to do with the stone—capturing a life. I stay there for a while, in between those two worlds. The outside and the inside.

"They are being almost like real people," Gita says. "I am forgetting they will not be talking to us."

"Are you hungry?" Even though she shakes her head no, we walk back outside and down the path to a glass-enclosed café in the garden. I order milk tea and grilled cheeses for both of us from a young Middle Eastern girl. It turns out we're starving, because the food is gone in seconds. Then the girl offers us chocolate cake or flan for dessert.

"If there is chocolate," Gita says with a smile, "I would like to try it."

I wanted Gita to see the sculptures, but there's another reason I asked her to the museum. I never know who's listening to us at the center. I feel an urgency to connect with her. I'm afraid that I'm going to let her down—that I'm not going to be able to help her the way she wants me to. I have this uneasy feeling—like we've entered into an unspoken partnership where I'm culpable.

"Do you have any other family here, Gita?" I lean toward her at the table. Have we gone over every option? "In Paris? Do you have other family you could claim in your asylum application? Or in India? Do you have a grandmother? You're fifteen, Gita. So young. They won't expel you from France on your own, but they won't let you stay on your own either, so we have to find a solution."

She takes a small bite of the chocolate cake and chews very slowly. "My maa does not know where I am at the center. She thinks I left her. She thinks I wanted to leave her. This is what I cannot fix. Morone and Pradeep are like my arms and legs. My brother and sister, who I would die for."

"I am so very sorry." Does she have a grandmother in India or not?

"Maa cannot help me. I know this. Only you can help me. I will never go back to that apartment."

She's proud and she can talk in circles, but does she know that less than two percent of asylum applications are approved in France? I don't use numbers. "You may be asked to return to India, Gita. We both know that, yes?" She doesn't look at me. She stares down at what's left of the cake and the small dollop of fresh whipped cream and sprig of mint. Sun shines through the long panes of floor-to-ceiling windows and lights up the blue bowls of salt in the middle of each table.

"We don't know about your hearing, Gita. If the judge decides you should go back to Jaipur, then we will make that okay for you." There are also tables outside in the garden, where people have claimed spring by taking their coffees outside and sitting.

"I do not want that life." She looks up. "We were living on nothing. It is hard for you to understand. Now we will be having even less. My baap is dead. No one leaves our village. That is your whole life, there in the yard. Manju's brother will come for me, and we will be married the day I return. Then I will be taken to his land farther south."

"Gita, I am trying to tell you that the courts may send you back and you will have no choice."

"There are ways to get away from the center. What if with you there are ways?" She looks away and becomes shy again.

What have I done? I've brought her to a French museum filled with manicured men and women who can afford to pass an afternoon in the sunlit atrium café. There's a mother in a plum-colored wool skirt and matching jacket who sits with her legs crossed and listens to a younger version of herself—a twenty-something daughter in dark jeans and low-heeled boots, one of which she taps impatiently on the leg of the table. To our left are three more French women with lustrous blond hair and thick, ropy gold jewelry on their necks. They laugh and smoke cigarettes and call for more espresso.

"To leave the center, Willow. There are things people can do to make people disappear."

What is she talking about? This isn't a movie. Luke and Gaird are working on one right now about a French girl in Paris on the run. Gita speaks with force. "Manju can do what he likes with me, but I can't start my own life. If they force me to go back to Manju or if they make me go back to his brother in India, I will walk into a busy street where there are other Indian people dressed like me and I will disappear."

Why did I think it was smart to bring her here? Who do I think I am? She sleeps in a cell-like room. The café at the Rodin is like another planet. We stand and make our way through the tables and chairs to the front door, flooded in sunlight. Then we retrace our steps. First the walk across Invalides. Then the wait for the metro.

I try to talk about where she'll live in France if she's set free after the hearing—how she'll get a job painting people's portraits. I ask her if she likes to chat with the boy named Kirkit—the new cook in the center's kitchen. I've heard the girls joking with her about Kirkit before class.

On the train platform she says he's a nice boy. Indian. From Kerala, and that he asks her questions about Rajasthan. "I want to be in love like in Bollywood movies I have never seen. I want a boy to take me away from here." She's never talked so openly to me. We're co-conspirators.

"You will know great love in your life, Gita."

"But when, Willow? My maa can't help me. Don't you see why I can't go back to India? It will be like I am dead!"

The train comes and we get off at St. Denis. The late-afternoon light makes Paris feel like one of the only cities in the world to live in. The peeling wrought-iron stoops on Strasbourg look good in the light; so does a fruit stand on the corner of Rue de Metz, run by a woman wearing the red bindi on her forehead. "We should get fruit. What do you want? Pineapple? Mango?" I'll do anything to change the subject with her. I can't give her what she really wants.

"No thank you, Willow. I am not hungry." She scowls at the ground. And I don't blame her. How can I please her?

It's five after four when we arrive at the center. Truffaut buzzes us in, and Sophie meets us in the hall. "You are back in one piece. How were these sculptures, Gita?"

"They are pleasing me very much. It is a real museum, Sophie. With paintings also, and there is cake for dessert." She turns to me. "Good-bye, Willow. Thank you for our day. Thank you for what you are showing me."

I wave her down the hall and go inside Sophie's office and sit on the stool by the door. Sophie follows me, singing in French. "I have to get her out of here more, Sophie. Each week she needs to see the sun and trees and grass in the parks. She's impatient. She's getting a little desperate."

"God willing, they all need to get out. The only way short of an act of our Creator is to find her a job that OFPRA would approve of. They will only let the girls work if they are not getting paid."

"She's good at speaking English. She isn't shy, though she can act shy." I look at the photos above Sophie's desk—hundreds of Polaroids of girls, taken before their hearings. Some of them are smiling boldly. Most look wary or confused.

"Gita can come to my school, Sophie. What if I can convince them to let Gita answer phones at the academy?"

"In English?"

"I think they will do this for me—let the phones be answered one day a week in English. Let me ask and see."

"You do come up with ideas. If you call it temporary, unpaid work, then the powers that be might allow it. There will be forms to fill out. There will be paperwork."

"It wouldn't be France if there wasn't paperwork." I stand and smile and walk toward the front door.

12

Bikini: a piece of clothing in two parts for swimming or lying in the sun and that does not cover much of the body. First known use: 1947

*M*acon and I meet at a bar in the sixth that night on a one-block street called Rue Christine, between St. Germain and the Pont Neuf. It's a dark, warm cave with walls paneled in red velvet. An African woman sits on a stool under a light and sings jazz in a low, gravelly voice. It's been four days since he and I walked on the river. No open tables, so we stand in the back and drink small tumblers of whiskey. The songs are slow and sexy and soothing. I want to stay in the bar for as long as we can. Maybe forever. There have been times before when I thought I was falling in love and I didn't understand what I was supposed to do next. I think now that this wasn't really love.

Macon holds my hand. And this feels so entirely right that I don't need anything else from him. When the woman finishes her last set, we clap and some of the people whistle through their fingers. Then we walk out to the street, still holding hands. We don't let go. He stops on the corner of Rue Dauphine and brushes the bangs out of my eyes. I'm sure he's going to kiss me. Because until he kisses me, I won't know. The kissing tells so much.

He looks up at the blanket of stars. "Did you realize there are beaches in the south of France where the stars come out in a great spectacle. The sky is dark and the stars are illuminated." He turns and we walk until a cab slows for us. Or for me. Because he doesn't come with me. He doesn't even kiss me. He just touches my hair again and says good-bye and this is part of the tease. The cab drives off, leaving him in the road. I can wait to kiss him. To sleep with him. When I do, I want it to be for a very long time.

ON TUESDAY NIGHT we have dinner in a small African café in an alley off Rue de Bretagne called Chez Omar. There's a warm April wind tonight, and the door is propped open. The food comes in small wooden bowls. "Drive with me," Macon says and takes a bite of couscous.

"Drive where?" I put my wineglass down on the red tablecloth. Is he asking me to go away with him?

"Drive with me!" He grabs my right hand in both of his and leans forward in his chair so he looks like he's about to stand and make an announcement. "To a town called La Napoule on the southern coast. There's a beach I want us to sleep on. Matisse and Kandinsky paintings not far away in a medieval village called St. Paul de Vence." Pieces of his hair fall around his face. Then he lets go of my hand and tears off a hunk of bread and dips it in the roasted tomatoes. He doesn't take his eyes off my eyes. "So will you come with?"

"What's that you said? 'Come with'? I've never heard that before. You speak Canadian." I'm stalling. Not because I don't want to lie on the sand with him. I could leave tonight for the town called La Napoule. I stall because of my brother.

"I speak a common dialect called English. I believe it's been named the world's international language." He leans back in his chair.

"It's those rounded vowels with some sort of Slavic mixed in." Red votives burn on the six tables in the small dining room. "I forget this accent you have. I have work in Paris. You have work here."

"It is a weekend. That's all it is. I'm asking you to go away for the weekend. We could leave on Friday. Please. Do I have to beg?"

"I teach at the academy on Friday. It's a course on international poetry at nine in the morning." *Yes!* is what I want to yell to him. *Yes.*

"My brother's in Paris. He was sick and he's better now, but I shouldn't leave him."

"You can tell me about him next Friday, while you're driving with me to the beach."

This time he comes in the cab with me back to my apartment. We sit on the cement stairs on my stoop. The night is warm and the humidity feels like a damp blouse. He pulls me onto his lap sideways, so my knees hang over his left thigh. There's no one on Rue de la Clef except the cats, who skulk and freeze in the car headlights. "You will love the south of France. You won't be sorry you came."

"I'm never sorry for any of the time I spend with you."

"Did you know you are lovely in the light from the streetlamp?" Then he brushes my cheek with his lips. I'm looking down at the sidewalk. He brushes his mouth against my mouth. I feel the warmth between my legs and the blood in my face and neck. It's not really kissing, not exactly.

"You should come with me to the beach." He kisses me on my neck and on my mouth again. "I should go home now."

"Go where?"

"Home. Home to the suburbs. A town called Chantilly."

I have no idea where that is. We stand, and I put my hands around his waist and hold him for a minute. Then I let go and he jumps the last two steps to the sidewalk and walks away in the dark, hands in his jeans pockets.

My apartment is a little warren of books, and the air is cooler in here. I climb in bed and call Luke. It's ten o'clock at night. Then I hang up. When it rings again, he picks up. "Gita's lawyer at the asylum center asked me to go away with him."

"Dearheart, Gaird and I are going to watch Catherine Deneuve."

"On a date. He's asked me to go away."

"I'm sorry." He isn't listening. "I don't know who Gita's lawyer is, and where has he asked you to go, to another courthouse? A different asylum center?"

"He wants to drive to the south of France and sleep on the beach with me."

"Well!" Luke lets out a little shriek. "Well, if only you'd said so in the first place! Finally! We can finally move your love life beyond hippie college boys and leg hair."

"You were there, too, lighting incense."

"Yes, but you? You almost dropped out of school, for God's sake. Let's stick to the facts here. Shave your legs! Wear a bra."

"It was 1978."

"Uh-huh." He stops to cough. The fit is one of the longer ones.

"I don't need to wear a bra. I've never needed a bra."

"What I need to know is, does this Macon understand the music of Earth, Wind and Fire?"

"Not sure."

"You need to tell me every minuscule thing. Start at the top of his head and work your way down."

I lean back against the headboard. "I thought you had a movie."

"This is what we've been waiting for! You have a sex life!"

"I have the idea of a sex life."

"Tell me everything."

"He has a dimple on his right cheek when he smiles. He only drinks red wine. He speaks English well. He likes to go on at least four dates before making love."

"Which means you haven't yet?"

"Haven't gone on the dates?"

"Made love. What if he's really good in bed? I mean stupendously good."

"What a great thing for me, then."

"What if he's bad? You're camping on this beach? What if you wake up the next morning and want to run and can't find a taxi? What if there aren't any taxis?"

"This is so unhelpful. Thank you for this."

"I try."

"I think I'm going to get in a car with him on Friday morning and drive. I think I feel more connected to him than I have with any other man before."

"Do you own a bathing suit?"

"Oh, God. I don't think so."

"We'll meet after your school tomorrow and find you one. You can't go to the south of France with a lover and no bikini."

"God, I hate that word. It's ridiculous—'lover.'"

"You're going to be sleeping together on the beach. Call it what you want."

"I'm going now. I'll meet you tomorrow. I'm scared of where you're going to take me."

"I know a few shops."

"I'm hanging up. I don't have money for Norma Kamali bikinis."

"There's a foundation I've heard of that has funds for celibate American poetry teachers in France in need of bikinis."

"Hanging up now. I love you. Good-bye."

13

Pip: one of the spots on dice, playing cards, or dominoes; each of the small segments into which the surface of a pineapple is divided; slang for sickness

*M*acon pulls up to the curb outside my building on Friday in a small blue pickup truck, not a car. I walk into the street and lean my face through the driver's window. He smells of pears and white soap. "Good morning." Then I say it again. "Good morning." It's almost like tasting him to breathe him in like this. Nine o'clock in the morning and warmer than it's been all year. The poplars look like they're wearing green headdresses—full and leafy.

I pat the hood of the truck like it's a dog. "You got a nice, *petit, bébé* truck." It's a Renault with a square cab and round hubcaps, and some kind of plaid synthetic fabric over the bench seat.

"You like it?" He taps the dashboard with his fingers and grins that grin. "I borrowed it from a law student interning at the office. We're starting small. We wouldn't want a truck we couldn't handle."

I make myself walk slowly to the passenger side—walk, don't run—and hoist my tote bag up onto the floor. I'm nervous. "I've found a new word." I'm driving away from the city with Gita's lawyer, and no one at the center knows about it. I haven't left Paris since I got here in September. "I called the school last night." I try to slow myself down. "I told them I was coming down with the pip."

"You didn't." He raises his eyebrows. They're the same shade of brown as his eyelashes. Everything about him looks big for the small truck—his legs, his hands.

"I learned it from Polly. My British friend in the drama department. The pip is vague enough to cover lots of symptoms." I glance up once at my apartment. The iron balcony looks like cake decoration from down here, with thick florettes and black metal leaves.

"I know the pip." He clicks the left blinker and puts the truck in first gear. We head south to Rue Daubenton over a series of cobblestone blocks lined with leaking gutters and sagging electrical lines. I imagine my apartment then. I like that apartment. The balcony looked good enough to eat. Where are we going? And who is he? This man? A diesel bus grinds its gears and releases a blast of smoke and we're thrown back into the late twentieth century. Then we're on a wider avenue that runs along the front of the Jardin des Plantes. I think it's called St. Hilaire, or maybe that's just the last part; some of the street names here are so incredibly long. I try to stay hopeful. We're driving to the beach. Paris-the-movie unfolds while he drives us through the narrow streets. The city looks different to me already. It's the effect of being inside the truck with him. I belong here more now. In France. Simply because somebody wants to drive with me. It's small but it's also everything.

The gardens even look different. The plants are a study in the most beautiful greens, with high and low manicured shrubbery and small banks of hedges and rosebushes. Is it the idea of love that does this? Gives the city this backlighting and connects me to it? If I let myself believe I can love Macon, then everything else in my life seems possible. Completely surmountable. I decide then that the greatest thing in the world is to long for someone and then to get to sit next to them in a small French truck driving south toward Lyon.

"We had the pip in Toronto." Macon laughs this time. "American girls get colds. They get stuffy noses. Or the flu. Not the pip. Your school will know you made it up." I stare at him while he drives and wonder if I'll love him. Truly love him.

"No. No, they won't. Today marks the beginning of my life with the pip. What I want to know is if symptoms include the need to drive all day in a small truck down the center of France?"

"They often do." His fingers are tapered, with nails that could use attention.

"And camp on a beach with a man you don't know?"

"Very common."

We pass through the fifth on Avenue des Gobelins. The rattan chairs are filled with Parisians smoking cigarettes and reading *Le Monde* or *Le Figaro* and drinking coffee. The thirteenth sits directly under the fifth, and the buildings here are taller and modern. We crawl around a traffic circle at the Place d'Italie, where a small orchard of magnolia trees blooms pink in the middle. Farther into the thirteenth we pass a check-cashing center and a string of Asian restaurants and food stalls. Have we changed continents? Luke will sometimes come down here to Chinatown between Avenue d'Italie and Avenue de Choisy to shop. There's a spice in Sichuan cooking that he loves called *ma,* which makes my tongue go numb, and he can only get it here. Luke feels far away now, even though we're still in the city. So do my father and Sara. Everything's been reordered. I'm calling it *the truck of requited longing* in my head. It's Macon and me and my mother driving to the beach. She's still with me. Smiling. Watching. She's often with me. She doesn't obstruct, now that she's dead. She just helps me.

"Did you bring anything?" Macon nods toward the tape deck. The blue street sign at Porte d'Italie reads A6/LYON/BORDEAUX/NANTES/ AÉROPORT D'ORLY. "I remembered sleeping bags and wine. But I forgot music." He hunches forward until he's hugging the steering wheel with both arms. I have the urge to give away all my secrets to him. Right now. All of them. And to see if he receives them or turns away. This is the part of myself I'm trying to calibrate. He smiles. "How can there be a road trip through France without music?"

We pass the exit for Orly Airport and the parking garages off the highway. I peel a tangerine to calm down. "I have music." The rind piles in my lap. I paw through my bag again. The suburbs give way to small fields. There are goats in fenced-in plots and stone farmhouses so close to the city. "I have music if you like Rickie Lee Jones."

I put the tape in. The song's "Chuck E.'s in Love." When Sara and I weren't nurturing our Bob Dylan obsession, we were deep into Rickie Lee Jones. This meant we grew our hair long and wore hats and long silk scarves.

"What is this song?"

"This song"—I roll my window up halfway—"is so good that I spent whole days playing it in my bedroom in college. The singer is in a pool hall. The boy she loves goes after another girl."

I put my hand out so it cuts through the wall of wind, which whips my hair around my face and up above my head. Another hour passes. Paris feels far behind. The fields are bigger now. Each plowed into a different-sized rectangle and conjoined into a patchwork of light brown soil and darker soil and chartreuse leaves. It's just after eleven in the morning and the greenish-white tips of the trees sparkle in the sun and everything is within reach. Love. Sex. Belonging. It's all always just within reach. Loneliness is vanquished. The bass of the song travels to my stomach and feels so good. Exhilarating even. Gone is that feeling of being just a foreigner watching. Of one step removed. "Did you listen to music growing up in Canada?" I peel another tangerine.

"Estonian folk songs." He says this with a straight face.

"Hah."

"My mother played albums on a gramophone."

"How could you miss one of the most important women singers of the 1980s?"

"Willie. I think I am a lot older than you. Either that, or I'm too busy constructing court cases."

I put my bare feet up on the dashboard and press my knees together. "Do you think you've got a case built for Gita? Do you have enough material? Do you have enough facts?"

"That is work, and this trip is play. You are considerate to worry. But that is my job. I take it very seriously. I will do everything I can."

"Gita isn't work, Macon. Gita is our friend."

"Your friend. Your student. My client. Yes, of course I am work-ing on it." He can shut off like this and sit in the quiet. Me, I'm trained to fill empty spaces. Maybe Macon doesn't subscribe to small lies out of convenience to please people. My mother was like that, too. She didn't believe in half-truths. She would have never called Luelle at the academy to say she was coming down with the pip. She would have said she was going away to the beach. Who knows with my mother?

"God, I never knew how much farming went on in this small country." I stretch my arms out and almost touch his shoulder with my left hand.

"France is surprisingly self-sufficient and proud. Very proud. I love this country."

Every five miles or so there's a wooden farmhouse in between the fields and barns and equipment sheds. Then, every twenty miles, there's a village built from coffee-colored stone. Rows of leggy trees stand in a green boundary line at the town's edge before the fields begin again. From here the villages look happy to be left behind by the highway. The flat roofs create a line in the sky that remains in my mind long after we've passed by, asking, What would it be like to live here? What is your old life that you could leave it behind?

We drive south and slightly west so we miss Dijon. I nap sitting up, but I don't have any memory of napping. I look at my watch when I wake, and four hours have passed since we left Paris. My lips are chapped. There's that twang again of being the outsider. Just one string of it but it's there while I'm still half-asleep. We're far from Paris now. I hope it's good. The kissing. The beach. The fields give way to thick forests of pine trees and bigger towns way off in the distance, built along steep hills and ravines.

There are signs for Beaune. Then Chalon-sur-Saône. Newer towns appear, rippling in concentric circles from a center I can't see. I can only make out the farthest subdivisions—rows of small, square, stucco houses and red tin roofs. It feels like we're driving across the whole country in one day. The truck eats up the miles. "France is so small," I say. "So incredibly small." Everything in the truck now seems to be about the mediated space on the seat between us and the kissing and his collarbones. Where will we sleep? Am I crazed? Maybe I shouldn't have come. Talking helps, but he doesn't mind long silences, and I can only talk so much. It's ridiculous—driving away from my job. I like that job. I need it. I've worked there for six months almost to the day.

Five hours pass, and we get to a puzzle of off-ramps and small highways circling Lyon. It's a bigger, industrial city with snarls of traffic and long lines of French trucks with canvas tarps covering their loads. Then the road opens up again and winds through orchards and over small sloping hills. It's past two. I slip in a tape by Los Lobos and Macon puts his hand on my knee. I want to sing now but I don't know any of the words, so I hum, confined to body language. Willing his hand to stay on my knee where it is burning an imprint.

I'm ready for whatever happens between us. But how do I say this? He pulls me closer with his free arm. "Spanish lyrics." He laughs. "You're humming in Spanish." We come up quickly on a white Peugeot, and before we incorporate it into our grille, Macon takes his hand off my leg and pulls out to pass.

"That was close." I will the hand back. "Name two places in the world you most want to go."

"Tartu." He needs both hands on the steering wheel now.

"Tar—what?"

"In Estonia. Near the Baltic Sea. Tartu. It's the city my family comes from."

I cross one leg under the other. "Do they speak Russian? Estonian? Or what language there?"

"It's Russian, yes, and French." He passes a large black truck on the hill. "I'll get there. There's still a house my parents own." He's quiet now. "They had to leave quickly."

"Who did?" I know so little about him.

"The Jews in Tartu did. I started to tell you this the other night at the bar. The leaving of the house. The defining moment of the century for my family."

"Oh God, what year are we in now?"

"Nineteen forty-four. The story still goes that Stalin's tanks were on their way. For my father it's as if he left yesterday. He walked away from his bedroom and his model airplanes and his books about flight. He wanted to be a pilot."

"He's haunted?"

"It got decided quickly: either you were going or not. My grandfather was a scientist who figured out a way to process black-and-white film in a lab in Estonia. He took my grandmother and my father with him."

"So there's still a house?"

"That no one has seen in forty years. But yes, my family owns it."

"Your family has lost a house."

"We lost a house, but we re-created it in Toronto. Down to the brick walkway."

"So you and Gita are both exiles in Paris."

"I am French, Willie. My mother was born in Paris. Gita is from India, and it will be hard for her to make a life here. You know that, yes?"

"But even harder for her if she's forced to go back."

"I understand your willingness to help Gita. I've had that need, too. Then it settled down into a job that I do every day. You will settle, too. Not because you will stand for anything less than what's right, but because life is long and it's hard to keep up the energy you have now. It's impossible, for example, for me to form special ties with each of my clients." He pauses. "The second place I'd go if I could is Joshua Tree. In California."

"I think you are the most unsentimental person I know." I smile.

"Then you do not know me very well yet. I cry at the movies, even comedies. I am what you call a sap. I have fallen heedlessly for you. Don't you see that? It's perhaps the most sentimental thing I've ever done. I'm shamelessly courting you because I have a need to see your face every day and the mole above your lip and this hair, this long red hair." His face is very serious. Then he looks back at the road. "So have you been to this desert?"

The things he's said are symphonic in my head. They keep playing there. I hear myself say, "I've been to Joshua Tree. The trees look like old men. There are whole fields of them." Why did I wear these jeans? It's so warm now, and they stick to my legs. He has a need to see me every day. My face. My hair. "My brother and I camped there in college."

"My mother has always wanted to go to California."

"She's in France now?" Courting. "Courting" is a pleasing word when I say it to myself silently in the truck.

"She never left Canada after my father got her to stay. But she's never stopped being French. She lives too far away from me. Distance breeds worrying. I've been trying to convince them to move back to France. She says Romania is having a revolution and other countries will try to get rid of their dictators soon. She thinks this will be too complicated for Jews in Europe. She's hounded by the past. She thinks I live too close to war zones. I tell her we live in France, far away from Romania and Poland and Yugoslavia, and that nothing bad is going to happen here, but she won't believe me."

He rubs his eyes with his right hand while he drives and looks over at me. "But you are from this golden land called California." Another black truck filled with apples slows on the hill in front of us. Macon glances over his left shoulder and pulls out to pass. It's been almost two hours since Lyon, and I'm starving. I pull a baguette and a small jar of Nutella from my bag. "It's a circus act. What else are you hiding in that bag?"

I'm tired and hungry and overcome by this lassitude that the drive's brought on. A deep, physical sleepiness. My mind thick and dreamy and associative. I walked into the asylum center on Rue de Metz and I met six girls and a lawyer and everything began to change. When will we see the ocean? I can almost smell it now. Signs for Avignon. I long for the ocean like a person. Like my mother. The closer we get to the water, the deeper my longing is. My brother's probably taking a nap in his apartment, and I miss him. I'm almost asleep. Is there a way to find a pay phone to call Luke? He's my family. He's how I make sense of Paris and of moving away from my father and the open-ended sadness I felt in California after my mother died. I look out the window at the brown hills and the wiry trees—olive trees? My mother is gone. I feel quieter about her death here. In California all I wanted to do was yell. I'm grieving for her here in a way I couldn't before.

"Where are your parents now, Willie?"

"We lived on the coast in a town called Sausalito. My father's still there—at least, I think he is. I haven't talked to him since last spring."

"Do you mean your parents are divorced?"

I miss my mother so much then. It's a longing I can't speak of to him. "My mother is dead."

"Ouch. I'm so sorry."

"Right after my mother died, my father designed this bench for her in the cemetery. Granite. Way too shiny, because that's the only way he said they came. He asked me to help with the wording of the engraving on the bench. But I couldn't. It was too removed from her—a bench in a strange town in Montana where all her family was buried. She didn't know anyone in that state except her sisters and cousins. Her life condensed to a sentence."

Macon just nods and listens. He's good at listening. "Once"—I rip the bread into smaller pieces and prop the Nutella on my knees—"it was impossible to live without my dad. But then my mom died and it was crazy to try to live near him. He's still my connection to her, though. He's more than that. But it's better here without him."

I try to hand Macon bread dipped in chocolate but he opens his mouth, so I lean over and feed him and get Nutella on his chin. We laugh, and he wipes the chocolate with his thumb. "It's better that you're in Paris. Better that I met you. But I am sorry. Sorry it has come at the price of your mother." An hour after Avignon we pull into a service station in a town called Aix-en-Provence. It's a one-story blue concrete shop with a concrete parking lot. Two red gas pumps sit out front in the bright sun. Macon pulls up to the first one. I get a metal key on a dirty string from a teenage boy in a mechanic's suit and find a smelly bathroom behind.

When I step back into the sun, a huge flock of birds is passing over—thousands of them. The sky darkens with birds until it looks like rain. I jog back to the truck and jump in. Macon bangs the gas nozzle down and slides in beside me. The birds turn the inside of the cab darker too, so that it feels almost like night. He takes my hand and kisses it quickly. The birds fly hard, as if they're straining to pull something—a black blanket?—over the sky.

When the sun reappears, I'm on Macon's lap, one leg wrapped around either side of him. We make out in the truck—small kisses over each other's faces and mouths, laughing. We kiss and kiss and the kissing is good and I'm connected to the truck and the birds and the green trees that flank the sides of the gas station driveway. It's not often we receive what we want. Now he's kissing my mouth harder. I want to bite his lower lip. To taste it. He kisses between my collarbones—that private hollow. Then down the center of my breastbone. He cups each of my breasts in his hands and I close my eyes. We stop kissing only because a car pulls in behind us.

Then we have to disentangle, and I'm laughing again. He puts the truck in first and second and third gear and accelerates onto the highway. I have this sense that everything is in reach—the drive, Luke's health, the beach where we'll camp.

The sign on the highway reads CANNES 140 KM. I place my head under the steering wheel on his thigh. I'm still sleepy, but it's a warm, delicious tired now. "My mother was a psychologist. But then she closed her practice and became a different kind of therapist. My father's a mapmaker. He started in the sixties, before computers. They bought a redwood house for nothing thirty years ago." I close my eyes. "You would have liked it, I think—the houses are stacked on the hill with redwoods and eucalyptuses and open stretches down to the bay."

After Aix-en-Provence the view widens again into dry fields and rows of the red poppies I've been hoping for. The air is salty now. The ocean must be close. "You haven't named two places yet."

"Game's over."

"No, really, Willie, where would you go if you could?"

"I'm not telling. Remember, you hardly know me."

"Oh, but I do know you." He traces the long creases that run across my forehead.

"I would go to India. In fact, I'm going to India. I got a research grant from the school where I teach. Two weeks in the northern mountains in July, tracking down the daughter of an Indian poet. I can't wait."

"That's incredible."

"You have to tell me if you think Gita will be awarded asylum and what tricks you've planned for the court."

"No tricks. Only facts strung together to make a story."

The *Graceland* album is playing when I wake up. I lift one sticky leg off the seat, then the other, trying to stretch the cramps in my calves. I finger a string bracelet on Macon's wrist. "Pablo made it." He looks down at me while he drives.

"Made what?" I squint in the light.

"The bracelet. Pablo beaded it."

"Pablo who?" I hold Macon's arm close to my face with both hands and look at the beads closely.

"Pablo Ventri."

"Ventri. Your name, Ventri?"

"Pablo my son."

"Your son." Now I sit up.

"He made it in school."

Something stings. I can hear Luke inside the truck: *Don't over-react. Don't panic. You never know how he might explain it.* But I always grow attached to people too quickly. I do this over and over. I've given Macon pieces of myself. Why did I do this? Why did I tell him about my mother? Why do I offer my parents up as if they're only what they appear to be on the surface?

"How old?" I study the toenails on my left foot and force myself to sound casual. "How old is your son?"

"He is four. *Merde*. He is already four."

"He lives where?"

"He lives with Delphine north of Paris, in a town called Chantilly. We all live there right now in an old stucco house I own." He slows onto a narrower road and yields to an orange VW van.

"Delphine." I repeat the name slowly and look out my window and try not to blink the tears.

"Delphine, my ex-wife."

"Ex-wife?"

"Delphine, the woman I once was married to."

"You have an ex-wife and a son." I thought he was opening his life to me.

"I do."

I sit on top of my hands. Luke will love this. He had no idea there would be drama. *Go slow*, Luke would say. *Do not pass Go. Do not collect two hundred dollars.* He and I went through a heavy Monopoly phase in middle school.

"Chantilly is the best thing for Pablo right now, and it's a way for us both to live with him. I've been divorced for two years."

I pretend to be busy finding lip balm in my bag. Then I redo the elastic in my hair. "It's hot in here." I turn the fan up on the dashboard and roll the window down. Then I move as close as possible to the passenger-side door. Whenever I choose badly in love, I only blame myself. I sit and stare out the window, and that familiar sense of disappointment creeps in.

"Have I lost you to the scenery?"

"I'm thinking about how much I don't know you."

"But also how much you want to kiss me." He reaches far over and puts his right hand around my neck and massages it. I feel a tingling in my thighs again, which I can't believe.

"That may be true." But it's more complicated now.

"The fact that you still want to kiss me makes everything easier."

"You have a son."

"I have a son." Macon doesn't seem put off by my logic, or the next long silence that follows. Ladysmith Black Mambazo sings along with Paul Simon. There's a smell of gasoline and sweat in the cab.

"Why are we even camping on the beach? Is it allowed?" The son and the ex-wife rain in my head.

"Because I want you to see the mountains from the beach at night." Is he crazy? Is he just stringing lies? The beach at night? I want him to stop the truck. I want to get out. I should go home. I should call Luke and go home.

We come down to the coastline in Fréjus on a narrow winding

stretch just above St. Raphaël. There's no music because Paul Simon shut off north of Cuers—just the whir of the truck's engine when Macon downshifts. In St. Raphaël, he turns east toward La Napoule and there's the click of the blinker and I still feel unsure. Why hasn't he mentioned his wife before? Why hasn't he mentioned his son? The road tightens through a small range of dry, brown mountains, which mark the final descent to the beach.

We pass through Miramar, then Théoule-sur-Mer, then finally La Napoule. Each mile feels excruciating. All the silence. All the deceit. It's a small village with flat-roofed stone houses built into the side of the mountain, overlooking the sea. Cafés line the main street, with steel chairs and round tables scattered in front. The edges of the awnings flap in the wind. It's almost six-thirty now. The sky is purple, with stitches of darker purple on the horizon, where a round tangerine sun sinks over the ocean. But I can hardly see it, I'm so caught up in myself.

"Why are you hiding them from me?" I can't stop myself. "You have a son. You have a wife."

"I'm not hiding." He looks straight ahead. "I wanted to tell you about my family but I haven't had enough time to properly introduce myself."

We don't know the most important things about each other. Am I deranged? I've always thought if you found the person you wanted to have babies with, then you didn't leave. You didn't take off for the French coast with a woman you'd known for three months. You didn't go to Greece on an airplane when your children were twelve and fourteen and stay away for a month. You didn't head out on your motorcycle for the Sonoran Desert for the better part of two years. You just didn't. Or you shouldn't. These are children we're talking about.

I'm foolish. I thought his heart was available. He finds a small road that runs parallel to the beach and parks between two Citroëns. We get out and I slam my door a little too hard and take the flight of wide cement steps to the sand, a rolled sleeping bag under each arm. I can't find anything to say. Macon has a knapsack with wine and a flashlight in it, plus a paper bag with some food in it that I hadn't seen before. When we get closer to the water, I sit down in the sand. It's childish, but I make a vow to myself not to move.

"If we sleep here, we'll get wet." Macon says it slowly. Patiently.

"I'm tired." The kissing at the gas station was too much. The news about Delphine makes me want to find a place to lie down and go to sleep. I think I'm going to cry. I don't want to be with him if he is with her.

"I've tried to sleep here before. It won't work." He pulls on my arm and walks me back toward the rocks until we're five feet from the seawall below the road. Part of me feels sorry for myself, which seems pathetic. We've come all this way. I've never been to the south of France. I drop the sleeping bags and walk to Macon and put my hands around his back.

I start kissing his neck. I kiss the side of his mouth, lightly, quickly, and pull back. Then I kiss it again, willing myself to get over it. He laughs, but not like he's surprised, and turns to face me. He unbuttons my jeans and tugs at them until I bend and step out of them. He unzips one of the sleeping bags and kisses my shoulders. It's only just dark.

We lie down by the rocks, and he kisses my collarbone and along my ribs. He kisses my breasts and puts each nipple in his mouth. Then he unfastens his belt and grins while he takes his own jeans off. It's wordless, our lovemaking, the very best kind of wordlessness. I've never learned to speak during sex. It's been pointed out to me that I'm unwilling to name what I like. But it's the surprise I crave. Loss of language. Afterward, he traces a circle on my stomach with his thumb in the dark.

"So you liked it? You didn't say you liked it."

"That's because you don't have to say anything." I close my eyes. "This is the great thing about sex."

"But you have to say something."

"We're sleeping together on the beach in France. What if we just say I liked all of it?"

"Which parts, exactly?" He kisses me hard on the mouth, roughly, different from his earlier kisses.

"Your lips, for example. I like your lips. You said you wanted to take me to the beach. You said nothing about this part."

"What part?"

"The part where I moan in the sand."

"I've been waiting for this part."

We sit and drink wine in little paper cups he's brought. We're alone on the beach. The small crash of each wave gives me this great, unequivocal joy, and Macon amplifies everything. Maybe he's the cause of the joy; I can't separate it. I hear the waves and car doors closing up on the road—all part of it—this surge of hope. I'm not sure I've ever felt so alive—like my life has been cracked open.

AT DAWN MY teeth taste fishy and I'm embarrassed. I can't find my underwear. I reach for my jeans and stand and hop into one leg, then the other. The beach sits like a half-moon in the cove with piles of rocks that form the seawall behind us. The sand is the color of honey and textured, not fine. Wide-hulled sailboats float near white mooring balls in the harbor. The water is a shocking, pure blue, with turquoise streaks closer to the shore. Two women swim back and forth from the cove to the boats. Their heads are shiny and smooth in black rubber swim caps that remind me of seals.

Bells ring out in a church in the town, and Macon rolls over and puts his hand in front of his eyes to block the light. The sun rises slowly far to the right, which must be northeast. The sky over the mountains is dark cayenne, infused from the sun, which defines the ridgeline so it appears to have been drawn in ink. I've lost my sense of direction. But that's got to be north.

"Are you real?" Macon wraps his arm around my calf and presses his face into my knee. "It's you. It wasn't a dream." He pulls me down on top of him in the sand, and I laugh out loud.

"There are people swimming now. They look like seals. The water must be warm."

"I want to make love to you again."

"Not here. Not on this beach." My knees are pressed into his shoulders.

"Then where?"

"I think I'm stoned on all the driving. And on not enough sleep."

"You need food." He stands and jumps into his jeans. Then we carry everything back to the truck. On the walk into town he stops on the side of the road and pushes the bangs out of my eyes again intently, like this is a small chore he must take care of regularly. The cafés spill onto the cobblestone sidewalk, which is more like a plaza that looks down on the train station in the middle of town, blocked off by black wooden fencing. We sit outside at a round table. It's maybe sixty-five degrees. There are more coves that dot the coastline down below, and tiny inlets set off from each other by juts of smooth rock. We order *pain au chocolat* and *michette* with melted cheese and tomato. I also ask for two eggs, poached, and café au lait.

"Why did you learn French? Why not Spanish or Italian?"

"It was the thing to do in 1978. To speak French and study Sartre and smoke cigarettes. Except I always threw up when I smoked."

"I like it when you speak French. I like it when you speak anything."

I blush and take a sip of coffee. The eggs come, and after I eat them the fog in my brain clears.

We leave francs on the metal table and climb the road behind the plaza until we get to an inn. I can make out the low shoulders of mountains in Théoule from the patio and all the way down in the other direction to the crowded marinas in Cannes. Small swells crest ten feet offshore and break lazy against the beaches. I feel very small, but in a good way—not distanced at all from Macon. A man finds us on the patio and asks us if we'd like a room. We would. Macon pays for everything inside with a credit card from Banque Populaire. Then a teenage boy walks us up the wooden stairs, which have been painted white. I stand on the landing and hold on to the banister while the boy gives Macon a skeleton key on a piece of red ribbon. We have no bags.

Macon carries me into the room. It's tiny and decorated like a ship's cabin with robin's-egg-blue walls and white wooden furniture. "No one's ever done that before."

He puts me down on a brass bed, also painted white. "Gotten you a room at a hotel?" He locks the door and pulls the curtains closed.

This time our sex is slower. I can't separate myself or watch him watching me like I did last time. The sex connects me to him in a way I wasn't sure was possible. Then he stops. I don't understand. He moves down my stomach, until he finds the place between my legs with his tongue. Then he's back inside me, kissing my face and neck. We fall asleep together after that, at ten in the morning while sunlight streams through the white curtains.

"You told me about a museum in Vence," I say hours later.

"I did, didn't I?" He rolls onto his side. "We can drive there later. There are more Kandinsky paintings than I've ever seen in one place. And Matisse." The sun has passed over, and the indirect light is warm and soft. There's no space to be scared of everything that could go wrong between us. He kisses me. "I promise we will go to Vence. Just later."

BEFORE WE DRIVE BACK to Paris on Sunday, we walk down to the cove again. French women in black one-pieces with tan, supple legs come and go from the shoreline carrying naked toddlers. Fathers in postage-stamp Speedos lose swimming races with older children. I'm wearing the green bikini Luke helped me find, grateful that I actually have a bathing suit. Macon and I dive under a wave before it breaks on our stomachs. There's the shock of the water, and I brace for the cold as it travels my body. It's elemental, the way water works on my mind and distills my life down to a simple question of how to swim.

We make it to the sailboats and float our way slowly back to shore, talking and not talking. I love this feeling of weightlessness. I close my eyes and listen to the sounds of the water. We used to do this some-times in the desert—float in water holes in the canyons that looked like pools of thick black glass. Luke and my father and I would slide in. The water was so clean that I could see my legs and arms in great detail underneath me. It was like looking at myself through some liquid magnifying glass. I didn't fully know myself like this. Or know my body. I was some kind of water creature, but I loved it. Every time we found one of these pockets it felt like we'd discovered something primordial. Something secret. And I thought the three of us were immortal while we swam. It hadn't occurred to me yet that anyone in my family would ever really die. Ever. These were some of the best moments I had with my father. Time stopped. He'd taken Luke and me so far off the grid. My dad floated in the water so close to me that we could hold hands and then we did.

Macon and I swim in until the water's too shallow. Then we have to stand and walk in the sand. We dry off on the beach with towels Macon grabbed from the truck. I lie down and close my eyes. I want to memorize everything. The sand. The rocks. The cement steps. I can share it with all these people. But I'll keep my claim on it in my heart. This is the place where I broke through something with Macon. Broke through something in myself—some harder casing around my heart. There's the plain view of the mountains. The rhythmic, percussive waves. The smell of salt and pine needles. I stand and put my T-shirt on and wrap the towel around my waist like a skirt. Macon does the same thing, and we walk to the truck.

On the drive back to Paris, we listen to the Rickie Lee Jones again and Paul Simon and Los Lobos and an Edith Piaf tape I find in the bottom of my bag. There are more loud diesels in Lyon and sedans full of families returning home from weekends in Provence. I roll my window up to block the noise of the traffic, and it gets warm in the truck. I start thinking about Gita again. "They lock girls up in France for too long."

"They lock girls up all over the world, Willie. At least the incarceration gives the people called lawyers time to build a case for the girls. I need time. That is something in itself, and you must see this. Some of the girls are denied summarily." His nose is thin and angular and perfect. I watch his eyes while he talks. Then his lovely mouth.

"It is still too long to wait. There's a girl named Moona, older than

Gita, and smart, and her hearing is in one week. I'm worried about her."

"You're right to worry. It's not a fair fight. The girls had no idea what political sand they were stepping in when they applied for asylum here. Things are changing fast in France in 1989. The far right has more influence. We've gone from a country that welcomed people from all over the world to one that erects barriers."

"I don't think there's enough evidence for Moona to prove what her uncle did to her in Bombay. Or what you call corroborating testimony."

"They are crucial. I could never begin to recount all my cases to you. So whatever Moona's uncle did to her, I'm sure it is unspeakable. But sexual predation is part of the vernacular inside the court. It's what we bargain in. Rape. Torture. Sexual slavery. By whom? I have to ask my clients. And how often did it occur? I have to explain it graphically so it has more impact. Sometimes, when I ask the girls to tell me about the violence in all its specificity, I feel like I'm the predator."

"How do you find evidence of a crime done against you in a factory your uncle owns back in a country you've fled? You're in a French jail where you know no one, and the crime was a whole season of rape, which the uncle is never going to admit to."

"This is what my job is, Willie. We have outreach teams. We have ongoing investigations." We're closer to Paris, and the cagelike frame of the Eiffel Tower marks the way. "This is my job," he repeats. "Please don't mix the two yet. It is still technically the weekend. You teach poetry, and I don't tell you how to do that. You are not a lawyer. There is a system, and it begins again on Monday, not today."

"But the girls are more than students for me."

"This girl Moona is someone you need to prepare yourself never to see again. Don't get sentimental on me." He takes my hand. "What is most likely is that she will be denied and she will have a month, give or take, to leave this country to go back to India. The same will most likely happen to Gita. Unless the court accepts my foster care idea. Thousands and thousands of girls are migrating across Europe as we speak."

"If Gita's forced to go back, then I'll follow her. She'll be kidnapped by Manju's brother. He has land. Acres near Jodhpur, apparently."

"What are you saying? Where will you follow her?"

"To India, when I go in July."

"If you could fly there this week, you could see whether or not Gita's grandmother is really alive in Jaipur. Then I would feel better about sending Gita back."

"Better? She is going to have to marry a man who's already raped her."

"We will try for foster care with you as court guardian. You will help her get ready for court, yes?"

"Surely." I have no idea what I'm really agreeing to.

"But you can't rescue Gita. That's not our job. You're a teacher. I am a lawyer."

"If there's a grandmother in India, she'll be an eighty-year-old woman who may or may not be living in a small house in Jaipur and won't be able to protect Gita. I want to come to the hearing."

"You have to come. But you need to sit in the benches, and you cannot speak."

"I won't. I'll just listen."

It's eight o'clock when we cross back into Paris at the Porte d'Italie. Macon double-parks on Rue de la Clef. Then I get out and stand in the street with my arm on the roof of the truck, listening to him through the driver's window. I don't want to leave him. The truck's been like a home to me. A time capsule. It's possible that I'll never see him again or never see him like this. It happens all the time. People get scared and change their minds. He's going back to a house he lives in with his ex-wife and their son.

"What's he like? Your son? I bet he's very beautiful."

"I'm afraid he has my nose." Macon laughs. His hands are on either side of the steering wheel. "He's a good boy. He lives for Lego right now."

I make myself step away from the truck. "You and your ex-wife must be very good parents." I don't know what I mean by this. If it's a compliment, then it's double-edged, because it's also a signal. I'm paying attention. I haven't forgotten the woman named Delphine. He doesn't seem deceitful. God, I hope he's not still sleeping with her.

"Pablo will want to meet you."

I walk toward my apartment and this is enough for me, so I smile.

14

Pablo: a Latin baby name meaning little; small

*L*ast summer before I moved in, some generous person converted the bathtub in my apartment into a shower by hooking a blue plastic curtain onto a rod fixed to the ceiling, and attaching one of those handheld nozzles. When I get inside, I go straight into the bathroom and peel off the shirt and jeans I'd changed into in the gas station in Arbois. I stand under the hot water for a long time. There's sand pressed into the skin on my left breast like a birthmark. Sand in my hair and stuck like glitter on my stomach. It's between my legs, where it feels like sandpaper. When I try to wash it off, the sand makes the bar of soap gritty like pumice.

There's still sand between my toes when I get under the sheets—proof that the trip to the beach really happened. I try not to think of Macon pulling up to his house in Chantilly in the truck. Our truck. And opening the door and calling for Delphine and Pablo. Once I start, I can't stop. I want to call Luke, but it's late and I bet he and Gaird are already asleep. I'd call Sara but she's incubating. Whenever she's not working she's asleep. It takes me a long time to close my eyes.

On Monday I teach at the academy all morning. After my office hours I take the metro to Châtelet and switch to the A line and get off at Charles de Gaulle–Étoile. Two o'clock in the afternoon, and Luke is lying on the couch eating a croissant smothered in melted Swiss.

He swallows his bite and smiles. Then he yells, "You're back from *la plage*! Tell me everything. Tell me how the bikini worked. Don't skip a single word."

His face is too thin and I try to adjust to this in my mind. The thinness makes him look even younger with his long brown hair. How is it that seeing him makes me laugh? And makes me long for some life I'm not even sure we ever really led but that I've created and hold on to in my mind. "We ate red pears in a nice hotel and drank port in bed."

"Truly, do you really think I give a damn about what you ate? Can you please stop?"

"The best part might have been the drive. We stopped at a gas station, and this enormous flock of birds flew over our heads."

"I'm dying and you ditched me for a French lawyer you've just met."

"You're not dying. They were starlings, it turns out. Detouring from Rome." I sit down on one end of the couch and take a bite of his croissant. "I love it when it's chewy like this." I lean over and put my hand on his forehead. "You feel fine, right?"

Is he keeping things from me? He better not be. I can't get inside his mind. Our mother died of heart disease that her doctor said would never kill her. Did she hide her symptoms, too? Did she know she was worse off than we thought?

"I feel almost back to normal, thank you."

"Almost." This means not really. He's not gaining any weight.

"Almost means very close to the way I was before my lung collapsed. You left me."

"I drove to the coast for three days."

"How does he kiss?"

"If you mean Macon, then I'm not answering. I know this is hard for you, but there are things that remain private." I look around. "Where is Gaird, anyway?"

"He went to London Saturday morning to scout out a special crane we need here for the set. He'll be home tonight."

"You've been alone for two days? Damnit. I'll speak to Gaird."

"Please don't." Luke laughs. "Gaird is still a little jealous of you."

I laugh and take a sip of water and snort a little of it out my nose. "Besides, he's never available. God, I'm full. Gross. I ate too much. Why did you let me eat the whole thing?" He looks at his watch. "I want to hear more about the Canadian lover. What did Macon wear to the beach?" He closes his eyes. "Tell me all the details!"

"Clothes. He wore clothes."

"When can I meet him?"

"He asked the same thing about you." The nature of our telepathy is that sometimes Luke and I have to say very little. This is why he's like home to me. If I'm going to love Macon, then Luke has to at least like him.

"He asked about my clothes?"

"No. He wants to meet you."

"You are moving *très* fast."

"You worked with Gaird in China for three months before you moved to Paris with him. Three months." I stand and walk toward the kitchen. "What are you cooking for dinner?"

"I'm just having breakfast. I need to meet him. Where does he live?"

"He and his ex-wife share a house in Chantilly."

"Jesus, that sounds complicated."

"It's a way for him to see his son more." I don't sound convincing. I lean against the kitchen door and close my eyes.

"His son."

"His son, Pablo. Macon and his ex-wife have been divorced two years, but Macon lives in the guest room to help raise the boy."

"And I thought Gaird was a reclamation project!"

"It's all okay, Luke. But how are you really?"

"I'm a little tired. That's all. I have a dinner tonight with people from the French embassy in Beijing who may support a new water system in Shunyi with us."

"Right now you rest. You sleep. What time will Gaird be back?"

"His train comes in at seven. Please go home and do some work. I know you have papers to grade."

I stay with him all afternoon and we order Indian food for dinner from a place near the Bois de Boulogne that delivers. We eat at the round table in front of the windows again. Avenue Victor Hugo gets quiet once the shops close, and becomes a Paris still-life—tall elm trees like border guards and the lavish pots of geraniums on the clean stoops. Gaird returns as we're finishing. He's full of ideas about how to get this crane—Chinese and operated from the ground without any-one in it—from London to Paris next week. He's buzzing from the high of travel and so am I still sort of, and the three of us have a glass of wine. I leave them after nine, when we're all sleepy, and I splurge on a cab to get myself home.

On Tuesday we start in on Gertrude Stein at the academy. She lived in France most of her life, writing stream-of-consciousness experiments she called rhythmical essays. She said they were meant to conjure "the excitingness of pure being." Critics called her work a literary response to the trove of cubist paintings she collected. Her book *Tender Buttons* is organized into three simple sections: Objects. Food. Rooms. We start with Objects. A prose poem called "A Box." I ask the students to try to translate it into French for me:

> Out of kindness comes redness and out of rudeness comes rapid
> same question, out of an eye comes research, out of selection
> comes painful cattle. So then the order is that a white way of
> being round is something suggesting a pin and is it disappointing

The students have to guess at what she means and talk about their own inner lives in response to her. There's no logical order or way to get around her language. They have to dig in. Nothing's pinned down. Language for the sake of language. I can't stop smiling while the class tries to parse meaning. Then I read another poem out loud in English called "The Daughter":

> Let me tell you a story. A painter loved a woman. A musician
> did not sing. A South African loved books. An American was a

woman and needed help. Are Americans the same as incubators. But this is the rest of the story. He became an authority.

This time I ask the students to translate the words into French out loud. There's physicality to Stein's taut lines. Something muscular that sends an electrical charge through the class. Some of the students think she's nuts. Others say she's a genius. None of them can follow completely. I love their confusion and the way they can't stop guessing and talking about Stein's intentions. As if the author's intention was always everything and that a deeper subconscious muscle wasn't ever at work. The class wants to find a narrative thread in Stein and hold on to it until everything in the poem and in life is tidy and solved. But Stein doesn't make it that easy.

The week goes by. No phone call from Macon. On Friday I finally call him because I'm wilting. Delphine answers. What was I expecting? It's her house. "Hello," I say in English like a schoolgirl. "I'm wondering if Macon is there? Macon Ventri?" Wife. Ex-wife. The distinction means nothing to me now.

She takes a loud breath—the kind of "poof" that Macon makes several times a day. She must also be shrugging her shoulders, so I try to imagine them—perfect sculpted French shoulders in some tiny pastel cashmere cardigan. Then she says in very fast, crisp French, "Macon is not here. Macon is out with his son. And who are you?"

"Willow." I can speak in French. Let me show her my French. "Willow Pears from the asylum center on Rue de Metz." What am I doing? Giving her my résumé? I'm unnerved by how lonely I am without him. It's only been five days. He's probably gotten back together with her. I see the end of us—a slow, horrible petering out into a series of awkward, guilt-ridden phone calls.

"I do not know when he is coming back." Delphine hangs up.

I stand at the counter in my dark kitchen because I forgot to turn the light on and the sun set while I was on the phone. I stare down at the black receiver. Delphine has managed to draw blood through the phone line. How has she done this? I can't move. Sara and I ate a picnic lunch yesterday near the Canal St. Martin—halfway between

Rue de Metz and her hospital. She told me she was afraid I was falling in love with Macon.

"No," I'd said. "Not after one weekend away together. It's not possible."

But I call her at home now and the phone in their apartment rings and rings. Maybe Sara was right. I pick up a file of poems on the floor next to the couch and carry them to my bed. They're all poems by Sarojini. I lie under the comforter and try to inhabit precolonial India and to forget Macon and Delphine ever existed. How stupid was I, to get inside the truck.

He finally calls on Saturday afternoon. Talks in a whisper. Says he wants to go to the zoo.

"Are you out of your mind? You haven't phoned since we got back to Paris. And why are you whispering? Why does it feel like we're hiding from someone?"

"Because we are." He laughs. "I knew you would be piqued. But my ex-wife doesn't understand why I want to bring Pablo to meet you. You don't know how much I've missed you. Craved you. I've been working on her all week. I didn't want to call until I had a plan."

"A quick hello would have been okay. A little 'how are you?' These are pleasantries we use in the country I come from. We don't let whole weeks go by after we've seduced someone on an old sleeping bag in the south of France on a public beach." I can't believe I'm laughing. It means I'm going to forgive him.

He tries to shush me, but I can't be sure because there's static. "I want to start with animals."

"Start where? What are you talking about?"

"I want you to meet us at the zoo. Animals are Pablo's favorite. He's more tuned in to elephants right now than humans. Can you come with us to the Bois de Vincennes tomorrow?"

"You're serious?"

"Zoos are very serious places for four-year-old boys."

THE BOIS DE VINCENNES is a wooded area in the eastern part of Paris. There's a castle and a botanical garden called Parc Floral and a lake with boats and the zoo, which has taken me longer to find than I thought it would. I see them before they see me: a tall man in faded jeans with a boy in a black karate uniform outside the stucco gates of the Parc Zoologique. Macon grabs Pablo's shoulders and laughs and says something in his ear, and the boy turns and waves at me.

It's the middle of April now, and the green beech trees stand several feet taller than the red gates. Their new leaves rustle in the wind. *"Bonjour, Willie,"* the boy says. He's got longish dark hair that hangs in his eyes, and he's beautiful like his father but more so. His face is smooth and perfectly proportioned in miniature. His eyes are also blue, and he holds on to a small plastic orange giraffe.

"Pablo," I answer back in French, "I'm so excited to see the animals with you." I put my hand out but quickly see it's not the thing to do with little boys. You don't shake hands. You kneel down on the ground and meet them at eye level, which is what I do next.

"I know," he says in English. He looks at me for a moment and then off somewhere over my left shoulder. Macon must speak English with him at home. Then Pablo dials back in to me. "I know. I know. I'm excited, too! This is a giraffe." He puts the animal very close in front of my face. "They cannot run as fast as cheetahs. There will be cheetahs here today."

"What's your favorite animal, Pablo?" I'm happy to speak in any language with him.

"Cheetah or tiger, I'm not sure. Who do you think would win in a race?"

"I don't think the tiger can catch the cheetah."

"I think you're right." He looks up at the trees that creak in the wind. "The trees have arms here."

"It looks like that, doesn't it?"

We walk to a white ticket booth tattooed with animal prints. Macon guides me through the metal turnstile, his hand on my lower back. We start with peacocks. This is one of those zoos without gates, just rock barriers and open moats that sit between the animal enclosures and the people. There's a very good gathering of lemurs next to the peacocks. Then we walk to the giraffes and spend some significant time here, while Pablo stares at the real ones and then back at his toy. After the sea lions, we walk counterclockwise along the perimeter, veering to the left around the elephants. The chimpanzees are hidden in a forest, and they're really hard to see. Some of them jump out and hang off the trees and holler at us over by the moat. I can't believe we keep any of these animals locked up. They seem way too smart for that.

"Do you know why I never want people in any of my stories at bed, just animals?" Pablo asks. I can't tell if I'm supposed to laugh. "I only want animals in the stories because I don't want anything scary to happen to people I know."

"I think you're smart to do it that way."

"Very smart," Macon repeats as we walk toward the cheetahs.

"Did you know I learned to blow air up my nose with my mouth?"

"Oh, Pablo," Macon says.

"I can do it! I can do it! Watch me."

The cheetah enclosure is bigger than anything the poor peacocks could dream of, with low-limbed scrub and river rocks to bask on in the sun. But even this feels too small. A cheetah needs open plains and rivers and miles to roam. Pablo stands as close as he can to the moat and stares at a cheetah, and the cheetah stares back.

"The cat's not moving," Macon says. "It's made of stone. It can't be real."

"It freezes," Pablo says without looking up at his father. "Until it sees prey, and then it pounces." The big cat leaps to a rock above the moat like it's trying to attack something up there—a piece of wood or the fake rabbit. It's so close now we can read its spots.

"That's it!" Pablo yells. "That's how he gets his prey!"

"He's beautiful," I say.

"Every cheetah has different spots," Pablo says. "There aren't any cheetahs with the same pattern."

"How far can a cheetah jump, Pablo?" I ask.

"Very, very far," he says with certainty.

Has one ever tried to jump this moat? Because it looks so easy to escape. I turn to Macon and whisper, "I wish they were all in the wild, where they belong." Macon smiles, and I want just one quick kiss.

Pablo runs ahead of us around a small hill inhabited by birds. We catch up with him at a sign that reads MOUFLONS, MARKHORS, ET VULTURES. Then we head to the snack bar. "He's pretty amazing," I say.

"Yeah." Macon smiles. "It's a weird thing to have people tell me about my child. I wish I could take credit. I wish I could say every bit of him is my DNA. But I'd be lying."

"And you never lie."

"I don't."

"He is so together."

"You mean even though Delphine and I have done our best to screw him up by divorcing and living together, he seems okay?"

"Exactly."

"It's luck. Or maybe a great deal more of parenting than I ever knew is just about showing love. Delphine doesn't approve of us, you know. I told her she could go fuck herself and her boyfriend, Gabriel, too." He smiles.

"You could have said something nicer."

"I've tried nice with her. She thinks we are moving too fast. I've thought about it. I think fast is okay, if you agree. I am unwilling to lie to make her feel better. There's too much to be done in a day and not enough time to lie."

"Fast is good if you make sure to call the other person every few days. Because last week we were two people who'd made love in La Napoule more times than I could count who were then separated by a very long phone line." I'm trying to trust him. Trying to stay at the zoo with him and not go far away in my mind.

We catch up to Pablo at a small crowd of kids watching a mime twist balloons into animal shapes. The man hands Pablo a miniature blue dachshund. He brings it to me. "Daddy told me you woke up in California once and a mountain lion was eating your dog."

"Daddy told you this?" I forgot I'd told Macon this story. "It's true. It was horrible."

The story goes that my father brought a cocker spaniel puppy with him when he moved back in with us. Luke and I left the dog outside by accident when we went to town on our bikes. We rode into the yard an hour later, and there was blood and most of the head was gone, but you could make out the puppy's spine. Mom sat on the steps with her face in her hands and cried. Dad yelled at everyone. Then he cried, too.

I cried for the puppy, but first I cried for my mother, because I knew how much she'd missed Dad when he was gone and how she'd worked to keep things together at the house. I thought I knew what the puppy meant for her—some kind of symbol of Dad's return. I hadn't separated from her yet. I still believed she and I swam in the same water. I thought I felt all the things that she felt.

Pablo and Macon and I eat hot dogs at the snack bar and drink warm Coke from paper cups filled with crushed ice. Then we head out of the gates toward the metro station. "What I really want to do," Pablo says, "is count to infinity."

"You're getting smart on me." Macon squeezes Pablo's hand tighter.

"I've been practicing." He counts out loud while we walk past the lake toward Porte Dorée. It takes him longer than I thought it would to get to one hundred, and he skips ninety-nine. I want to hug him when he finishes, or hug Macon and say, Look at us! We're talking about infinity on our way out of the zoo—can you believe this? A portal into the world of children. It's been here all along, but I've never had access.

Pablo reminds me of Luke when he was a little boy—his upturned nose, the smooth skin under his eyes. We stand outside the station and the good-byes come fast. It's quicker for me to walk home than to take a train. So I'll head to the river on the Quai de Bercy, past the park there. But I want more time with both of them, more assurance from Macon about what we're doing. I kneel and say good-bye to Pablo and get a quick hug, which he gives so naturally—arms open wide, as if we've always hugged and known each other like this. Then that's it. That's all. Pablo jumps into his father's arms, and they wave at me. Macon turns and walks down the stairs into the metro station, and they're gone.

HE CALLS the next morning. "Where can I find you tonight? When can I see you?"

"This is what I was talking about." I smile. "This invention known as the telephone. This is progress."

He's outside my building at four o'clock. I run down and let him in. He presses me against the mirror at the back of the elevator and kisses my neck and eyelids. We get inside the apartment before he lifts my T-shirt over my head and unzips my jeans. My clothes are off before we make it to the bedroom, where we stay for hours.

It's important to have him here, where I live, where I'm most myself. It makes what's between us real. I don't want to know what time he has to be home. I can't figure out how the operation works over there in Chantilly. I'm so hungry I finally sit up in bed.

"I'm starving." It's way past dinnertime.

"Tell me what you have in the fridge." He kisses me and stands.

"Very little. But wait, there's chicken. I was supposed to be roasting a chicken today."

"Where there's chicken, there's often potato." He steps into his jeans.

"And I may even have spinach."

"I'll conduct an investigation."

"I didn't know you cooked."

"There are many things you don't know about me."

"More wives? More children?"

"Not funny."

When I walk into the kitchen, he's leaning against the counter barefoot, chopping garlic. He kisses me on the mouth. "We're going to make my grandfather's chicken-potato stew. Do you have nutmeg and tomato?"

I reach for the bowl of cherry tomatoes by the sink. "Tomatoes." I find nutmeg in the narrow cupboard next to the oven. He cleans the bird and dresses it, then heats the skillet and throws the garlic and potatoes and tomatoes in. When they've stewed he spreads it all over the chicken and places the casserole in the oven.

"It's a dish they ate all the time in Estonia." He opens the cupboard and pulls down two white bowls. "Do you believe in love?"

I've lived alone in Paris for over seven months, and no one except Sara and Luke has ever cooked a meal with me in this kitchen. I'm trying to keep up with how fast Macon's moving. I'm sort of delirious. "My greatest surprise," he says, "is that my marriage dissolved. And that I didn't have the strength to fight for it."

I don't want to talk about his marriage. I want to eat dinner and make love again. I smile at him and nod and go take a shower. Then I put on my mother's kimono. When I come back into the kitchen, he's peeking into the oven.

"It's ready. Bubbling." He reaches in with the oven mitts and pulls out the casserole. "It's very hard to explain divorce to Pablo."

"I wish people married for life. I really do. But I'm glad you didn't." I lean over his shoulder. He spoons stew into each bowl.

"I never considered divorce until the very end," he says. "I'm not how I appear. I'm serious about the vows. I'm serious about you."

I smile. I can't help it. What he says makes me very happy. He follows me to the couch. "The only thing this stew is missing is anchovies. My grandfather used to fish them an hour north of Tartu. Big schools of them. Sometimes you could grab them with your hand. When he was tired of catching them, he would drive home and chop them and add them to my grandmother's chicken."

We drink red wine, and the meat is tender and falls away from my fork. There's a warm trace of nutmeg. The potatoes are brown and slightly crispy on the outside. My mother's kimono is one of the few things I have of hers. After she died, my father let the church-women come and clean out her closets. I haven't been able to forgive my dad for this. I was lucky I already had the kimono on permanent loan in Oakland, pink with bright tangerines and deep blues running

through the lighter-blue origami flowers. It smells like my mother—
like green grass and lemon—and also a little like a woman in Japan
we'll never know.

"You're not wearing any clothes underneath."

"This is true." I touch his forehead with my hand. Then I bend
toward him and he opens the kimono and places his hand gently on
my stomach. He reaches to kiss me on the mouth.

But then he leans back against the couch. "Is this crazy for me to
be here? What am I doing?"

I wrap the blanket around myself. "It's too difficult?" He's not
going to turn back now? "Should you go? Tell me this is okay?"

"It's simple when I'm here. It's so easy to be with you. But it's hard
to explain to Pablo where I go. I'm abandoning him."

"I know what it's like to have a father who left, so I can't tell you
anything about it that will make you feel better. I hated it when my
father was gone."

"Pablo says he won't go to sleep until I tuck him in every night.
We have songs we sing in a certain order. There is a way he likes to
have his back rubbed."

"Right now he would probably like his back rubbed."

"Right now."

"You should go."

"No, I should stay. Delphine is there." He takes the blanket off me
and smiles. "I needed to hear myself say what Pablo wants from me.
Now you know."

We make love on the couch, and afterward we lie in the dark.
Each time a car passes by on the street, the windows pulse with
refracted light. "You know, I think about Pablo, too. I want to make
this okay for him."

"I am trying to figure out how to tell him where I go when I come
here."

"Tell Pablo you go to the house of your friend from the zoo."

15

Flan: from the Old French *flaon*, "flat cake"; a custard baked with caramel glaze

*E*veryone wants to meet Macon then. Sara is adamant. She won't give up. And Luke is beside himself. I hold them off until Saturday night. Which is why Macon stands in the kitchen wearing my long green apron tied around his waist like a skirt.

"Should I be nervous?" he asks.

I open the wines. He adds sea salt to the tomato sauce. Then I put my arms around his neck and kiss him on the cheek. "Don't be nervous. Luke doesn't bite. He's very, very kind. But Gaird I can't speak for entirely. He will grow on you. Sara and Rajiv are two of the nicest people you'll meet in your life."

I climb up on the counter and pull down Fiesta Ware plates from the highest shelf. Luke found these for me at the Clignancourt flea market. They're almost identical to ones we had growing up. "Though a little bit of suspicion is warranted." I hand Macon the plates. "I never know exactly what any of them will say."

Then someone's banging at the door like they're trying to break it down. I open it, and Luke's standing there, bottle of red wine in one hand, yellow baking dish covered in tinfoil in the other. He's about to ram the door again with his shoulder. Gaird waits behind him, his face hidden by a huge bunch of red tulips.

"It smells so good in here." Luke walks right past me. "Where is he? Where is this man who's become your personal cook?"

Gaird steps inside and kisses me on both cheeks and hands me the flowers. "Dutch." Then he loosens his thin black tie.

"Thank you so much, Gaird. They're very beautiful."

"Ah, Willie, it's my pleasure to make you smile." He winks at me.

Macon comes out of the kitchen and Luke lifts him off the ground in a hug. "He feels solid." Luke smiles at me. "He's got a nice build, and he's not afraid of a little physical contact. What could you possibly be cooking that smells so delicious?"

We all follow Macon into the kitchen. "It's chicken Marseille, right?" I ask.

"It's called Everything We Needed to Use Before It Spoiled." Macon smiles.

Luke frowns. He can be a cooking snob. I want Macon to explain how much time he's put into the sauce and to show Luke and Gaird that the meal matters to him. I want more than anything for them to like each other.

"Where do we smoke?" Luke asks. "This has been horribly nerve-racking. Bathing. Dressing. Meeting Macon. I need to go up on the roof."

I have a skylight in my apartment that opens to the roof. What someone has done—the landlord? a previous renter?—is nail a ladder to the wall outside my bedroom so I can climb up and push a spring-loaded lever, which causes the skylight to open slowly. There are two wooden benches up there and a round metal table.

"Go." Macon waves us away. "I need ten more minutes with the sauce."

But there's more banging on the door. Sara and Rajiv stand with their arms interlaced in the hall. She's almost all stomach. A big, round belly on her tall, thin frame. It's a fantastic thing to behold and I swear she's glowing. Beaming. I double-kiss them both. Then Rajiv moves toward Gaird with his hand outstretched. I take Sara's arm and walk her slowly toward the kitchen.

"Where is this person I've been waiting to meet? Where is he?

I need to get my hands on him." I present her to Macon with a bow. "Oh, for Christ's sake, let me at you!" She hugs him hard next to the stove, and what I love about him is that he hugs her right back.

Luke comes down from the roof and distributes more big hugs. "How can I help?"

"Can you taste the vinaigrette and tell me if it's okay?"

He puts his finger in the jelly jar on the counter. "Too much lemon." I frown, and he says, "Hey, your brow furrows when you get stern like that. You shouldn't frown. Those are wrinkles that will stick. All I have to do is add sugar and more oil."

Macon holds out a spoonful of the chicken sauce for me to taste. "It's perfect!" I say. "Sublime." I can never use this word and not think of my mother and the day when the words crowded into my head for the first time before Luke's play.

I was a girl with words on a chalkboard inside my brain. Sometimes, when it became too much and I wanted the words to stop, I went to my mother and asked her for help. She said we can't fight our brains. That they're bigger than we are. All we can do is try to divert them.

Sara and I bring the plates to the table, and everyone sits. "This is beyond delectable," she says after the first bite. "Tell us your favorite food, Macon."

"The next time, I'll make you my grandfather's stew. It's not so different from this."

"Your father lived where?" Rajiv reaches for the wine.

"My father began in Estonia. He migrated with other Jews to Canada. 'Fled' is the word I should use."

"This is during the Second World War?" Gaird asks.

Macon nods. "The moment of truth for my family."

"I'm not Jewish," Gaird says, "but my parents had Jewish friends in town. The number of Jews was small—in the hundreds—but the Nazis found them, and this was horrible."

"Macon, how old was your father when he arrived in Toronto?" Rajiv asks. "Did he get sent to a refugee camp first?"

"No camp. There was a boat to North America. Then a long trip up the St. Lawrence River. He was twelve. He didn't speak the language." I reach for Macon's hand under the table. Rajiv and Sara and Luke are conducting a silent test of him. I know this. But I've already chosen Macon. There's a humming sound inside my head because of how happy this makes me.

"Rajiv," Gaird says, "how did you ever find your way to Oxfam?"

"It's quite simple." Rajiv carefully wipes his mouth with his napkin. "I grew up in a country where people were starving every day. I was lucky. I was sent from India to a college in the United States with a campus so beautiful it was what I'd heard Disneyland looked like. Privilege like this can alter you. After that, my path was clear. But you, Macon—how did you end up here?"

Macon smiles. "My mother was a visiting student from Paris in Toronto. I think my father had an awkward, eighteen-year-old-boy crush. She was dark-haired and striking. Everyone in my family says this. He walked her home after a chemistry class. They both wanted to be scientists. He played a very good accordion. Maybe this was it. They married. But my mother never stopped talking about Paris. Or how I had to live in the greatest city in the world. So I came for law school."

Rajiv nods. "Why immigration law?"

"I needed money, frankly, and there was a posting at school for a job at the Legal Aid Center. They paid me a small wage to be a legal assistant for refugee boys from the centers. That's when I learned that the centers were like jails and that children aren't supposed to be imprisoned, according to French law."

Rajiv bangs the table. "I get mad when I think about this."

"I was enraged," Macon says. "When my father landed in Canada, he couldn't pronounce the name of the country properly, but he had a much better chance there than these kids do in Paris. I began working at the courts. I graduated. I took the law exam and did a tour of every single asylum center in France."

"Wow," Sara says. "That's dedication."

"When these kids talk to a lawyer or speak in front of a judge, they gain social capital if nothing else. There's some power in getting to tell your story. Maybe you see that your life is not determined just by stars or fate. Because life is short, no?" We all raise our wineglasses. "I made Willie's favorite for dessert," Macon adds.

"You made flan?" I ask.

"On the top shelf of the fridge, behind the butter."

"You live with a man who makes dessert?" Luke laughs. "I can't get over your good luck."

"I love flan!" Sara says.

"She could eat it at every meal," Rajiv says.

"That's because I made it for her in college all the time." I go and find the flan and bring it back to the table. The candles taper down so we can hardly see our bowls, but the flan is perfect.

Gaird takes a bite, and his face changes. "You have made something delightful. I can taste the fresh eggs."

"Four," Macon says. "From the market at Gracieuse."

I'm not going to worry about any of them getting along anymore. They've already found something that connects them, and it's food.

16

Family: a group of people living under one roof

Then it's Tuesday morning and I'm bringing Gita to the Academy of France for the first time. I get to Rue de Metz and there's a thin Indian boy slumped in one of the chairs in the common room. Who's he? He's wearing a wrinkled white button-down shirt and black trousers, and he stares at Gita while she cries into her hand. Sophie keeps making this "tsk tsk" sound and passing Gita tissues on the couch. I stand in the doorway staring, until Sophie motions me in with her free hand. The boy and Gita appear to be having a fight in a foreign language that I can only guess is Hindi or some cousin of Hindi. He looks about twelve.

"Pradeep!" Gita stands up. Then she sits back down and begins with another torrent of the language I can't understand. "Pradeep!" Maybe this is the boy's name. Her brother? Pradeep. She's written about him in class. She puts her hand over her mouth again and talks through it. The boy has her black hair cut high around his little ears and her same huge eyes. He looks away while she yells at him.

Then she stops and he fires back, talking just as loudly and quickly as she did. They volley like this until Pradeep stands and hands Gita an orange tin of what looks like dried fruit. She bursts into tears when she takes the gift. Then she reaches for her brother and holds him tightly. Pradeep sobs uncontrollably now. He doesn't try to contain it. Gita makes a high-pitched shrieking sound until Sophie untangles them and takes Gita by the arm and walks her out the door.

In the hallway Gita yells, "Willow, please tell my brother he is wasting his time by coming here. Tell him he needs to be in school. Tell him he must never let my maa come here to see me." She keeps calling out to me down the hall. "Willow, please." The boy sits back on the couch and rubs his eyes. He looks much younger now. How do I talk to him? What can I say that he'll understand?

Then I hear him say, "I want her to come back very much." In perfect English.

"She can't right now, Pradeep. I'm her teacher, and we're trying to get her moved out of this center. Then you'll be able to see her. There are problems in your apartment, Pradeep. Gita can never live there again with Manju. I'm not sure you know why this is."

"I have been thinking it but not saying it out loud. I want to talk to my sister again. Please can I see her again before I leave? I have not told her that Maa will not cook. I need to tell Gita that."

I reach out my hand, and he clasps it in both of his. I say, "Thank you for coming. I'll take your phone number. I'll call you after Gita's trip to the court. It won't work to try to see her anymore while she's here, Pradeep. But as soon as she's out, you can." The boy bows his head. Then we walk down the hall to the front door and I wait for Truffaut to let him out.

Then I go find Gita. She's sitting on the stool in Sophie's office with her eyes closed. It's taken four forms in triplicate and several weeks, but today she can leave this building with me and begin an actual job at the academy. That is, if she's able. Because her face looks so sad. "Are you sure you want to go today?" I ask her.

"I want very much to go to your school. I am ready."

She smiles when Truffaut buzzes us out. Then we turn right on Rue de Metz and walk toward Boulevard de Strasbourg. "I am pretending," she says, "that I am not coming back here anymore. I am pretending I am leaving the center forever."

We take the No. 4 line to Rue St. Sulpice and we're at the academy by nine forty-five. "Luelle," I say when we get to the office. "Meet Gita, your new receptionist."

"I am so glad to make your acquaintance, Gita." Luelle speaks formal English with a Belgian accent. "I will have you help me sort through the invoices. We will do the unpaid and the paid piles. I will also ask you to answer the phone. In English, of course."

"Thank you, Luelle," I say. "Thank you so very much. You did not have to be so helpful."

Then I walk to my office at the end of the hall and get ready for the ten-thirty class. Today we're reading Anaïs Nin. Part of a poem called "Risk." I start class by asking the girl named Virginie to read:

"Et le jour est venu
quand le risque à rester fortement dans un bourgeon
était plus douloureux que le risque qu'il a pris à la fleur."

Then I ask a boy named John with perfect French grammar to translate it into English, which he does slowly, steadily: *And then the day came, when the risk to remain tight in a bud was more painful than the risk it took to blossom.*

This is the type of short narrative that the students love because they can attach themselves to the extended metaphors. Some of the kids compare the story of the blossom to risks in their own lives and how they dared come to France on their own. Some equate it with trying to write their own poetry.

The class finishes at twelve-thirty, and I look in on Gita. Two wooden desks form an L against the back wall of the office. Luelle is typing on a gray Olivetti. Gita speaks into a black phone receiver. They both smile at me. "It's going okay?" I ask.

"It's going very well," Luelle says. Her hands don't stop flying over the typewriter keys.

"Lunch?"

"I take lunch now," Luelle says. "We close the office down for an hour. So please, Gita," she says, nodding, "you can eat at your desk or outside in the park. There are also several good cafés."

"Follow me," I say to Gita and smile. "We can go find food." We walk down St. Sulpice to a small market on the corner of Rue de Tournon. I buy Brie and apples. There is a *boulangerie* next door where I get us a baguette. Then we take the long block all the way into the Luxembourg Gardens. The plane trees here are getting full and green, and the gardeners have cropped off their tops so the trees are flat and sculpted. We walk on the gravel esplanade toward the palace. There's a row of slatted green metal chairs to our left overlooking the grass. The garden is full of red geraniums and bright-colored tulips and a flowerless plant with pointed dark green leaves that I don't know the name of. I pull two chairs close together. Then I put the cheese and apples on the paper bag in my lap and break off a piece of baguette for Gita. "Is it okay in the office? It's not too much?"

"I am learning." She takes the bread and eats it without cheese. "Luelle is very helpful. It is nice of her to let me answer the phones in English. I hope I am good enough. I am grateful for the people who call and wait for me to speak my slow English."

It almost feels normal to have a picnic with Gita in the garden. So hard to believe this is only the second time she's left the center since I've known her, and that some of the girls haven't even left once.

In the afternoon I teach a seminar on Rainer Maria Rilke, a German poet who lived for a time in France and wrote one of the greatest last lines of poetry ever written. It comes at the end of the poem called "Archaic Torso of Apollo."

A girl named Hannah from Colorado reads the poem out loud in French. I tell the students nothing is superfluous with Rilke. Every line matters. Each word serves the next and moves the poem forward. "For a while," I say, "Rilke worked for the sculptor Auguste Rodin. He wanted his poems to have the same muscularity that Rodin's carvings did. He wanted to describe the statue of Apollo with sensory details that mirrored what a sculptor would do with a chisel."

I hand out the English translation and ask Hannah to read the last two stanzas. I want to spend the rest of the class dissecting the French words and comparing their meaning to the English.

> *Otherwise this stone would seem defaced*
> *beneath the translucent cascade of the shoulders*
> *and would not glisten like a wild beast's fur:*
>
> *would not, from all the borders of itself,*
> *burst like a star: for here there is no place*
> *that does not see you. You must change your life.*

Every time I come to that last line, the hair on my arms stands up. The imperative voice at the end changes everything. The reader is implicated. You. You out there. You must change your life. I've never read a better closing line.

A boy named Tyler, who rarely speaks, says, "This poem is an anthem. It's a call to action. It's about what a short amount of time we have here on earth. And how fleeting life is."

Virginie nods at him. "And there's immediacy. There's this incredible culmination. I think it's about how to live without pretense." We're equal parts poets and philosophers.

When class is over, I walk back down the stairs to the office to get Gita. "The Academy of France is happy to be sending you the information," she says into the receiver and smiles. "I am Indian. It is an Indian accent, yes, good-bye and have a nice day."

Her accent is strong, and she lifts her sentences up at the end, so the tone sometimes implies a question when it doesn't mean to. She keeps using passive verb construction, even though we've talked about using the simple tense. But she's answering the phones well. I wait for her to finish the last call. Then she stands up from her chair. "It is time to be going back already?"

"You've done great work in here today."

Luelle takes a pencil from between her teeth and taps the side of her typewriter with it. "You did a good job, Gita. Very well done. We will see you next Tuesday."

Gita nods and says in a formal tone, "Good-bye, Luelle. Thank you very much for all of your assistance."

We walk through the hall past the bronze bust of Balzac on the marble table by the front door. Students lean against the walls and call out to one another. It wouldn't be so difficult to think that Gita was one of them—an undergraduate in a sari perfecting her French during a semester in Paris.

I hold her arm out on the street. "You did it! You were wonderful! You have a job now at a college in Paris!"

"It is almost true, isn't it?" We go left down St. Sulpice toward Rue de Rennes and the metro. Her eyes take in everything: chestnut vendors with metal carts near the stone walls of the cathedral, cafés that line Rue Bonaparte, filled with young women and men talking earnestly while they drink coffee, crowds milling outside the doors to the metro station. It all seems part of a crueler story now that we're on our way back.

A teenage girl and boy hold hands next to us on the train platform and kiss tenderly. "They are in love, aren't they?" Gita stares at them brazenly. "They are kind to one another. I hope I know love before I die."

"What are you talking about? You're so young. You'll know love. Just not yet."

"I want to know what it's like to have someone care about me."

"That will come. You are only fifteen."

"But when, Willow, will it come? I am going to be sent back to India. I know I am. Even if we try to prepare for the court hearing. I will move to Jodhpur with Daaruk and have his children. I will love these babies even though they will have come at a price. I will commit to loving them. I have seen this kind of marriage very often in India."

We climb on the No. 4 and find two seats next to each other facing backward. "Gita. First, you don't know what you're talking about. You're not going to be sent back to Jaipur. Mr. Ventri has a plan. He's asked me to be your guardian for the courts. He thinks the judge will release you into foster care if I take on this role and help. Then we will figure out the rest." What am I saying? Macon's not sure this will work.

"You will do this for me? You will give your word to the judge about me?"

The car is full and people crowd around us, holding on to the metal ceiling bar. "I will do this." But I've got to talk to Macon first. What does guardianship really mean?

We get off at St. Denis and make our way up the cement stairs to the street. Groups of teenagers let out from school hang around the station, talking and laughing. "This boy in the kitchen named Kirkit. How old is he?"

"I think he's nineteen. Kirkit is very nice. He is making the kitchen work fun for me."

"He's much older than you."

"The man I will marry in India is thirty-eight. Kirkit is kind. He says he wants to have me home to meet his aunt. Why wouldn't you want happiness for me? I don't understand why I can't choose something I want." She's almost yelling as we turn down Rue de Metz.

The graffiti is still there. Every day I look to see that the sea creatures and blue suns and white stars haven't been painted over. And every day they're still there. I want to offer Gita something. All I ever have for her is words. "You are not going to have to marry Daaruk in India." I press the buzzer next to the door. "It's not going to happen."

Four-thirty—plenty of time for Gita to report for kitchen duty. Sophie hears us in the hall and comes out of her office. "Gita, you will be able to keep this job every week if your work here at the center is done and if you're on time. You must always be on time like today."

"Good-bye, Willow," Gita says flatly. I think she's lost somewhere in the gap between the outside world—the couple kissing and nuzzling on the train platform—and the fluorescent lights in the cramped hall of the asylum center. It's too big a distance. "Thank you for the day."

She turns and walks toward her bedroom and I follow Sophie into her office. The radio is tuned to an international station again playing the high-pitched, melodic music—Egyptian? Harps and flutes and clarinets. "Can I go down to the kitchen, Sophie? I've never been there. I want to see this boy Kirkit."

"Because you're worried he's after Gita?"

"She likes him."

"There's a lot to like. He is hardworking and responsible. He makes a variety of good dishes. He's on time and polite. You are welcome to go there." She turns to her desk. "But don't get caught up in these things. What's between Gita and Kirkit isn't something you need to concern yourself with. I will monitor it."

The basement is a storage area converted into a small, overheated cafeteria. It smells like cooked meat and onions. There's a soapstone counter that runs along the far wall, interrupted by a deep sink where Gita stands washing white potatoes. She's got a flowered apron tied over her sari. Three feet or so away from her, at an industrial-sized black stovetop, a young man stirs pots. A potato slips out of Gita's hands and drops on the floor, and the man's face broadens into a smile.

This must be Kirkit. Gita says something to him in what sounds like Hindi, laughing. She seems so relaxed down here. I've never seen her like this, her face pliant and smiling. He points to the cutting boards lined up on the counter next to three metal bowls of chopped onions. She nods and sits on a metal stool and begins slicing her potatoes.

"Kirkit." I say this with a question mark at the end. He turns toward me. He has a thick neck and a dark crew cut. "Kirkit." I put my hand out. "I'm Willie, a teacher at the center. I've heard about your new menu and that you're making good food down here."

"It is a pleasure to meet you. We have a lot of mouths to feed, but we have good job rotation and I think the girls like the food. So thank you for coming."

Does he know I'm the one who took Gita to the job at the academy today? How much do they talk? The raw onions make my nose begin to drip. "Where did you learn to cook so well?"

"I grew up with my mother and grandmother in Kerala. They both worked at the canteen my grandfather owned. They were much better cooks than me."

I look him in the eyes, and he doesn't look away. "I must be going now," I say. "Gita. Have a good meal." She blushes and keeps slicing potatoes as if her life depends on it. She knows I'm here to meet the boy named Kirkit. The pots on the stove boil away with their soups and stews. "Kirkit. It's been good to meet you. I wish you luck." It comes out more formally than I intended and I feel silly, but by the time I get to the front door, I'm glad I've spoken to him. He can't be bad for her. His whole face lit up when he saw her bend to pick the potato off the floor.

17

*M*ay comes to Paris in a spray of lilac blossoms. Their smell is of dried roses and something almond and lush. Macon and I take Pablo to the sailing pond at the Luxembourg Gardens on Saturday. Children stand next to the stone ledge and reach with wooden sticks, prodding, nudging the miniature boats. The wisteria in the park has also bloomed, with feathery purple-and-white stalks. Afterward we eat *croque-monsieurs* at a café on Boulevard St. Germain. The melted cheese oozes out of the sides of my bread. Pablo eats his whole sandwich.

Then we walk to the Pont Neuf. It feels like everyone in Paris is on the bridge today, leaning against the railing, taking in the bright sun. Tour boats slide under the bridge like lazy, low-riding convertibles. Pablo wants to get on one. "Please, Daddy. Let's go down to the water. Please." Macon says something about Pablo's birthday—that the boat ride will be an early present.

We cross the bridge back to the Left Bank and climb down the stairs to a stone plaza on the river. The words BATEAUX MOUCHES are painted in red letters on the boat's low, wide white hull. It's flat-bowed and sits heavy in the water like a barge. Macon buys three tickets at a portable steel booth next to the boat and gives one to each of us. "Happy early birthday, Pablo," he says, smiling.

Pablo's ticket flies out of his fist, and I let out a small yelp and watch it sail away. "Grab it. Grab it!" I run until I can't reach it without jumping into the river.

"Pablo." Macon's voice is stern. "Now we can't get you on the boat."

He goes to wait in line again, and Pablo starts to cry. I take his hand. "This is not a problem, Pablo. We can get you on the boat. It's only a ticket, and it's not worth crying about. Do you understand, sweets? Not worth crying about." I've never seen him cry before and I'd forgotten it was even possible.

Maybe the whole thing is too much—taking the train into the city, leaving his mother for the day. Meeting me again. Who am I, anyway? This woman with his father? He's got to be so confused—and lonely even, standing with me while we wait for Macon to come back. "Let's take a picture of you on the river for your mother." I walk up the cement stairs, back toward the street. When I turn around, he's gone.

I walk back down to the river. The water looks green and sloshes against the boat's hull and the long stone embankment. I go three minutes in either direction and don't see him. Nothing. I stare blankly at the boat. Where is he? A narrow dock is lowered down by pulleys between the side of the boat and the river walk. The engine sputters in the water. Maybe he's run under the barrier rope and gotten on already?

Small whitecaps roll on top of one another in the deeper water. People around me don't know that he's missing, but that doesn't mean he isn't missing. I can't find him. The little boy. Macon's boy. How could he disappear so quickly? My panic spreads like a rash—until my arms and legs are shaking. It's happened incredibly fast. He was with me. Then he wasn't. The boat fills up with tourists. Macon comes down from the ticket booth; he looks calm and slightly distracted by the sound of the horn of a larger barge passing us.

I yell, "The boy! *S'il vous plaît! Le petit garçon. Il a quatre ans! L'avez-vous vu?*" Then, in English: "Have you seen the boy?"

Macon's face changes into a look of cruel surprise. What is it that I'm yelling? Some of the people left on the walkway fan out in different directions, looking for Pablo. Others turn to each other and try to make sense of what I've said. Macon's eyes ask the question. "I've lost him," I say. "He's gone."

"He can't be gone. There hasn't been enough time for him to be gone. Think clearly, Willie." He holds my shoulders. "Where did you last see him? You must think."

"Right where you're standing." I step back. "Right here. When I went to take the picture, he was gone."

"We can't stay here. I'll go farther down the river. Oh Christ, Willie. Oh God, where is he?"

I walk and swear at myself out loud. I take the stairs back up to the street and jog in either direction. Then I cross the Pont Neuf over to Île de la Cité, but Pablo wouldn't have done this. He wouldn't have come all this way up here, would he? I go back down to the boat. I can't see Pablo or Macon. How does a boy vanish? Then Macon crosses the wooden ramp to the boat. He speaks with a sailor in a white military-looking uniform, gesturing with his hands toward the bow. Then he jogs all the way around the perimeter of the rows of seats. I'm frozen on the cobblestones, thinking about the water, feeling a terrible mix of fear and guilt.

We should be looking there—in the roiling water. But that's the worst possible ending. Macon goes below the deck. Once his head disappears and I can't see him anymore, I move behind the metal ticket booth. I've circled it once already, but now I look more carefully at the trees that stand like sentries along the stone wall. Everything slows. The world feels savage without Pablo. There's no other way to say this. A little boy. Such a little boy. I can see his smooth face.

The biggest surprise is that there's no in-between. He's either found or lost. Alive or dead. Safe or not safe. I see the bright red with the white swoosh of his sneakers. He's lying on his stomach under a small linden tree talking to—who? It looks like he's speaking to the dirt. Relief floods me. It enters my bloodstream. I scream his name and hug him, but my legs are still shaking. I have to check myself from squeezing his arm too tightly. Why did he walk away like that? Why did I turn my back? He's only four. Children like him disappear all the time. He says there were two ants following each other on the pathway. I yell for Macon. He doesn't come. I stand up and yell again. I don't know what to do now. I can't leave Pablo, not for a second. I vow to never let him out of my sight again. I yell another time, and Macon finally comes running.

He picks Pablo up in his arms. "Why did you walk away? That's not okay. We were worried. Do you understand, Pablo? We were very worried."

Pablo nods and gets maybe some part of the seriousness. We stand in the shade of the tree, and I can't speak. Relief is still moving through me. I'm correcting for the rational world, as if I hadn't once thought Pablo might have drowned. The boat blasts its horn three times. Final call to climb on board. We find three empty chairs on the bow. Some of the tourists stare at us and whisper and smile. There's a knee-high white handrail that runs along the edge—the kind a small boy could climb over with one quick move and fall into the river. So Macon keeps his hand on Pablo's neck. "What were you doing again?" he asks me. "How did he get away?"

"I wanted to take a picture of him. He was sad. I thought it would distract him. You got mad at him when he lost his ticket."

"I wasn't mad. I just didn't want to go back in the ticket line."

"You were mad. He was crying."

"I know what I was, Willie. I know my son. He doesn't cry over things like that." There's a tenseness to Macon's face that I haven't seen before.

I speak clearly and slowly: "He was crying. I took his photo. Or I tried to take his photo. Dumb idea. I'm sorry. I'm so sorry."

"Four-year-olds are in motion all the time. It's incredible. It's maddening." He pauses and looks out at the river. "*Merde*, I let my mind go to a very dark place when I couldn't find him."

"So did I. To such a dark place."

"It's my fault. I shouldn't have left you with him." One of the sailors pulls the bowline in, coils it, and stows it below the railing. The boat sets off slowly, churning through the water. "Remind me what Pablo was doing under that tree?"

I'm implicated. I'm still feeling guilty. Horrible. What would I have done if we couldn't find him? "He said that ants had carried a piece of popcorn on their backs together and he was watching them."

Macon's quiet for a long time after that. "Delphine would kill herself if anything bad ever happened to him. And I believe this. But he's fine. I shouldn't have left you. You had no idea he was prone to walk off. We are good. He's okay. Are you okay?"

"Okay." And I try to ease into the sound of his words and the simple fact of the three of us on the boat together. The sun shines on the Eiffel Tower. It looks like the long bodice of a woman's dress today and more beautiful than I remember. Macon pulls Pablo onto his lap and kisses his hair. We go under a bridge. Then another. Macon takes my hand, and Paris passes by us on either side.

A WEEK GOES by. Luke says he feels good. Steady. He doesn't complain of breathing problems. He and Gaird begin working on an independent French film about a bank heist by a director from Brittany. Then, in the middle of May, Luke actually flies to Beijing to meet with his board of directors—expats and Chinese nationals he's brought in over the years. I can't believe he goes, but Dr. Picard says his lung is fine. My academy students chat about the Eurail passes they want to buy in June and the trains they'll ride all summer, looking for love and history, looking for some photo they carry in their minds of Europe.

The girls at the asylum center are diligent about finishing their testimonies. Moona's court hearing has been postponed. I've gotten an Urdu translator for Rateeka and Zeena, who's come in twice, and it's helped enormously. All of them have finished a draft, and we practice reading the stories out loud, one by one, in the common room.

On Saturday morning the buzzer rings at my apartment. Macon has been busy in the courts. I haven't seen him since Tuesday. I go downstairs and open the front door and he's standing there with a knapsack strapped to his back. "You're finally going hiking. The moment I met you, I knew you would leave me for the Appalachian Trail."

He shakes his head. "I don't know this trail you're talking about. I'm moving in with you, if it's okay." He smiles.

"You're staying? For more than one night?" I pull him into the front hall. The backpack makes him wobbly. "You're moving in? You could have told me something before!"

"You said you want this. I want this too, so I've brought my things. I want to wake up with you and go to sleep with you every night. Tell me the truth. Tell me if you want this."

He stops talking, and I press him into the wall by the mailboxes. It's very quiet in my foyer on Saturday morning at nine. Quiet out on the street. Paris is just getting started again. We stand there silently, looking at each other. I kiss the sides of his mouth. Then his top and bottom lip. Gently. Lightly. And we walk toward the elevator holding hands.

He opens the door to my apartment. "This is what me moving in looks like." Then he grins. "You're getting a smelly man with an old backpack from college in Montreal who is humbled by his longing for you."

The apartment is one open room that fits the dining table and chairs by the windows and the oatmeal couch closer to the bedroom. Luke and I bought the couch last September with half of my first check from the academy. The bedroom sits off the far end, the small kitchen on the other end. Books lie everywhere—on shelves behind the couch, in tall stacks at the unused end of the table, in piles next to my bed. "Are you hungry? I can make crêpes. I've got mushrooms and Gruyère."

"That sounds good. I'll stow the pack." He goes into my bedroom, and I stir the flour into the milk and crack the eggs and sing to myself. When the crêpes are ready, I find Macon hanging his wrinkled suit in my closet. He pulls more things from the pack: a book of poetry by Wallace Stevens—the one with my favorite poem about oranges on Sunday morning with a cockatoo (I can't believe he has this book)— and a set of keys on a metal carabiner, dress shirts, and a framed black-and-white of Pablo on a pony in a ring.

He puts the stuff on top of my bureau and surveys it. "I've managed to leave my son entirely." It's an uneasy smile. "God, what have I done. What am I doing?"

"You can bring him here. We'll make a place for him. There are a lot of you in that house in Chantilly. Delphine and this man you say she's with now, Gabriel, plus you and Pablo. That's a lot. But you haven't brought very many things with you." I kiss him on the forehead.

"I've left Delphine in my house with my son. She has the dishwasher and the car and most of my belongings. I'd like to see how little I can live on. I've been waiting to do this for years."

"Why are you giving it all away?" I sit on the bed. Something warm moves slowly through my arms and legs. Jealousy. "Tell me about when you and Delphine had Pablo."

"Do I have to?"

"Please tell me why you split up." I wasn't intending to ask, but this question has been sitting underneath everything since I met him—why he left his wife.

"Pablo was born unable to rotate his left hip. When he was an infant it hurt, and he cried a lot. None of us slept. She was the first one to realize his leg wouldn't straighten. She'd made the discovery and the fact that I hadn't even noticed the problem yet—though I surely would have soon—made her distrust me. She got him a metal brace. But something hardened between us. I don't think we were ever able to get back to the kindness we knew with each other before the baby was born."

"Did the brace hurt him?"

"Once we got it on, it didn't hurt him, but Delphine fell apart over it. Music was her world until she met me, and there is such rigidity in that life: the practicing and performances. The competition. She was concertmaster in the Paris Philharmonic. She dropped out. She refused any child care or help, even from her mother. I'm not sure I can explain. Pablo became her compulsion. Delphine is nothing if not monogamous in her passion. First she was in love with the violin. Then she was in love with me. Then Pablo. She is still in love with Pablo, but Gabriel is who she sleeps with now."

"And Gabriel?"

"He plays the cello."

"Oh, God."

"She didn't want me touching the baby or the brace. She didn't let me pick the baby up. She had rules. First she was breast-feeding, so I gave her that whole year, but then in the high chair only she could feed him. She kept the house dark."

"What do you mean, 'dark'? Were there lights?"

"Dark. Later, the psychiatrist taught us about postpartum depression and how common it is."

"It's better now?"

"I told her to get help or I'd take Pablo."

"It was bad?"

"It was that bad."

I stare at him. I've never really considered how my own mother might have been sinking in our house. I always thought it was Luke and me trying to swim in Sausalito while my father was gone. But my mother was raising us alone. She'd often go to bed during the day on weekends. I never really knew why. But she'd go to sleep at two in the afternoon while Dad lived apart from us. Then Luke would make dinner. Sometimes she'd get up and eat with us. Sometimes she'd stay in bed. Then it would pass, like a small surprise storm, and she'd be back in her office at the hospital, fighting with the administration about the rights of her patients. She wanted private rooms. She wanted more cognitive therapy and fewer meds. She wanted all these things to happen that weren't happening fast enough. "It's better," he says. "She thinks I left her. Even though she's the one who stopped loving me. I believe she loved me once, but when things got hard I wasn't someone she was able to trust anymore, and I don't understand that. She still wants to hold on to everything she touches, houses, cars, clothes, and me. But I need very little. Pablo, you, maybe some heirloom tomatoes."

I pull him down on top of me and put my arms around him and breathe him in. "All we can do is try this, right?" I ask. "All we can do is try."

––––––––––

LUKE CALLS while we're standing eating the crêpes in the kitchen. He's just back from China. "You're back!" I scream into the phone. "How was it?"

"Fantastic. Come for dinner and I'll tell you about it. Gaird is cooking something exotic."

"Can I bring a date? Macon's here. He's just moved in." I watch Macon eat a second crêpe and I smile into the phone because I know this news will get a rise out of my brother.

"I'll set another place at the table. You two just go back to bed now."

It rains on and off all afternoon, and a light fog settles over the Latin Quarter. It's not cold, though, just wet like some essence of spring. We walk on Rue Monge holding hands until a cab slows for us. Luke's asleep on the living room couch when we walk in. I sit down on top of his feet to wake him up. "Ouch!" he yells.

"Your toes are cold. Why don't you have any socks on? Ice cold. And you must be so jet-lagged."

"I'm used to jet lag. But truly I am always cold. I've told you that." He smiles. "How are you? Let me see you. You're glowing. Macon's moved in with you, and you're glowing." Then he stands and gives Macon a bear hug.

Gaird walks in from the kitchen and the white door swings behind him on its brass hinges. The furniture and paintings look even more opulent and serious in the gray weather. Gaird doesn't say hello. "We have to be thinking about how to make Luke warmer, Willie. He complains he is cold and I keep the heat on high in here in May, and it's not working. So we have to figure out a better plan. He has a hacking cough from China." Gaird seems distracted. Shrill even. "I don't like it."

"Maybe you need to go see the specialist again," Macon says from the arm of a gray velvet chair.

Gaird claps. "Good idea! We need someone like you, Macon, with real ideas, because I'm only learning now that these two are crazy people!"

Luke blows Gaird a kiss from where he's sat up on the couch. "I'm going to help with dinner," I say, and follow Gaird into the kitchen. "Luke looks pale today. Is he fighting a cold or something?"

"I have lost track of how he looks." Gaird hasn't shaved or combed his hair, and he seems exhausted, too. He pulls a blue-and-white-flecked baking dish out of the oven. "I told him not to go to China." Then he nudges the kitchen door open with one knee and leans his head out. "I'm pleased to announce that dinner is served!"

We sit at the counter in the kitchen and eat fried potatoes and pickled herring. "It is delicious, Gaird," Macon says. "I haven't had this fish in years."

Luke tells us about the Beijing man he hired to run the Water Trust. He says the city is crazy right now with the protests in Tiananmen Square. He couldn't get cabs through the center of the city because so many students blocked the square. "There's something surreal about watching the protests on French TV," I say. "It all looks like make-believe." But Luke warns it will end badly if hard-liners in the Chinese government prevail.

I tell Gaird that the fish is mouthwateringly good. I didn't realize how hungry I was. "Thank you," he says and stands. "Now I must pack and get myself to Amsterdam for a meeting with a tugboat captain."

"The herring is good," Luke says. "But I'm still starving. God, I'd love a grilled cheese sandwich."

"Amsterdam?" Macon says. "It sounds lovely."

"I am taking the TGV." Gaird writes down a number on the pad by the black phone next to the fridge. "I will be at the Hotel Estheréa."

"The tugboat?" I laugh.

"I've met a Dutch sea captain," Gaird says, "who'll steer the boat down around Le Havre next month and then into the mouth of the Seine."

"You're joking?" I say. "You're commissioning boats now? This is getting out of hand. What do you know about tugboats, Gaird?"

"Very little. That is not the point. I don't need to know anything about tugboats except if they float and what the asking price is." He smiles. "I happen to know I can get one on the cheap. We will moor it here in Paris for a month. Two of the actors will jump from the bow in the movie's final scene. This will be something to see. Now I need to leave. Be good. Be good to each other, all of you." He reaches for a black roller bag he's parked in the corner of the kitchen.

"We always are, Gaird." Luke smiles. "You be good."

"My train departs the Gare du Nord at eight."

"The tugboat could be amazing," Luke says and takes a bite of my herring. "You are amazing." Then Gaird kisses him once on the cheek and runs downstairs to flag a cab.

18

Receptionist: a person employed to greet
telephone callers or guests

*D*id I bring a tie?" Macon asks on a Monday morning. "*Merde,*
I hope I brought a tie. Here is the suit and here is the shirt
and where is the tie, Willie? I have to be in court."

Seven o'clock and only a few cars move on Rue de la Clef. Laughter floats up through the open windows. French laughter? Do people
laugh in their native language? "I haven't seen a tie." I'm on the couch
reading papers on Rimbaud. How long will Macon stay with me? He
has so few things. He could be gone in a matter of minutes. "Do you
own more than just one?"

The papers are typed on thin sheets of onionskin. I give the first
one a B. It tries too hard to make the connection between Rimbaud's
poems and his drugs and sex life, culminating with a lurid description
of the time Rimbaud's lover, Verlaine, shot him with a gun. But the
paper forgets to look at the actual language of the poems.

"Aha." Macon is still searching in his backpack in the bedroom.
"My tie." He stares at it gravely for a second, checking for stains.
"I need this tie, Willie. It means something in the courtroom." He
stands and walks to the bathroom and makes a perfect knot with it
at his throat. Then he comes to the couch and kisses me on the lips.

"Kiss me again so I'm sure I'm not dreaming you."

"I won't be able to stop if I do that. So I'm leaving now."

"You know, there are stores. Places where you can buy more ties, so you could have two or three ties and worry less. You could have two suits. You could have two pairs of pants."

He walks to the door. "That would mean I would have to get to the store. If you think I'm doing that, then you don't know me very well."

"I don't know you at all." I smile.

"I'm leaving now. I'm forcing my brain into believing I have a job because what I want to do is stay here with you all day."

"Go. But come back soon. Always come back."

The second Rimbaud paper is written by a senior named Amanda with straight blond hair. She examines the tension of the line breaks and the tautness of the prose structure. She pulls apart Rimbaud's words for their symbolism and gets an A–. I fall asleep for a few minutes after that, which I never used to do, but I've never lived with a man before who likes to make love in the middle of the night, half-asleep.

When I wake up, the apartment is quiet and warm. The spring heat pushes past the stone roofs and the carapaces of the bridges until it comes fully down the Seine. It can't come fast enough for me. I love the heat like my mother did. There's a pile of folders on the floor next to the couch with all the Sarojini poems I've been able to locate. Indian poems posing as simple British verse. The language almost tricks the reader—rhyming couplets in the tradition of famous Victorians like Tennyson. What did the British education system do to the imaginations of Indian schoolgirls like Sarojini?

When I wrote my book on Albiach, she and I began this long, odd phone relationship. We talked dozens of times. It was like I was courting her. This culminated in her inviting me to lunch in Paris. The flight cost tons of money, and I had school loans, but Albiach told me she would be on the corner of Boulevard St. Germain and Boulevard Raspail at one o'clock on a Thursday in October 1985. I wanted to know every detail about her life: when she wrote and where and what she ate while she wrote and what kind of pens she used. I was trying to get inside her head.

I took a red-eye from Oakland. I'd never been to France before, and I stood on the street corner, out of my mind with excitement and dread. Would she dismiss me once she saw how young I was? Blow me off when she saw how crazy my hair was after the flight? Would she guess that I'd never been to Paris before? Or that I was incredibly naïve? But I was in Paris. On a mission. She looked exactly like the photograph on the back of her book except stouter—with long black hair streaked gray and darker eyes and silver hoop earrings. She reached for my hand when she found me. I felt very young, and so relieved that she was warm and teacherly.

We sat at one of the outdoor café tables crowded with students. The city felt so alive. The trees hadn't slipped their leaves yet, and the sun dappled everything in cognac. Who were these young people eating flan and drinking wine in the middle of the day? What was this city? I knew I wanted to live there. Anne-Marie ordered us mushroom omelettes and champagne and didn't talk about her past or about the new book she was working on. She spoke about her lover, an older German novelist she lived with, and how he wanted her to bring him raspberry pastry when she returned to their apartment.

She was elusive. "I am a skeptic," she said after her second flute. "So I'm doubtful about your project. But I wouldn't be a poet unless I had hope."

I flew home and finished my dissertation. A good university press—Michigan—bought the manuscript for a small amount of money. I mailed her a copy of the book a year later, and she sent me a postcard in Oakland with Salvador Dalí's face on it. It said, "It's a good book. You have absolved me of many of my worst writerly sins. Thank you. I'm still embarrassed to read about myself. Anne-Marie."

I won't get to have champagne with Sarojini Naidu. She died in 1949. But I've tracked down a woman named Padmaja, and I've begun calling her phone number in Dharmsala, in northern India, hoping she is Sarojini's daughter. The phone rings and rings on the other side of the world. If she ever answers, I don't know whether she'll agree to let a foreigner look at her mother's papers. I go to the kitchen now and dial this number again. It's seven o'clock at night in India. I let it ring until it's useless to keep trying. Then I put the receiver down and make a bowl of oatmeal with bananas.

There aren't any clouds today. Sunlight has made its way over the highest buildings on the street and floods my windows. I can hear Madame Boudreaux and one of her boys talking on the stairs. We both still think the elevator is unreliable, even though the landlord had men with tools in this week to fix it. The next Rimbaud paper is laid out on the table next to my oatmeal. But Luke calls.

He says, "I don't feel well today." My heart skips. "Truly, it's nothing. But I seem to be having trouble breathing again. It feels like there's a lead weight on my chest."

Shit. I take off my pajama bottoms in the kitchen while I talk. "Let's go to the hospital. This is going to be fine. I'll call Sara. I'll call Dr. Picard. I'll be there in thirty-five minutes. Can you wait that long? Should I call an ambulance? Have you called Gaird? Please don't try to be a hero. Please tell me how you are? Please don't try to be strong."

"If you could calm down, that would be great. Then you could just come and get me. Gaird's in Amsterdam till tonight, remember? It'll be so much easier if I'm with you and not alone."

I run into the bedroom and pull on jeans and a black T-shirt and go down to the street to find a taxi. When I get to his apartment, Luke's standing in front, holding the keys out for me. He says, "Poincaré."

I grab the keys without saying a word and run to find the car on Avenue Raymond Poincaré. Then I squeal back to him in the car and he climbs in. "God, you're fast." He coughs.

"Can you make it? Does it hurt? Where does it hurt, exactly?"

"It feels like there's a gallon of milk sitting over my heart."

"That's got to be your lung again." I don't know where I'm going. East. I need to go east. I drive around the traffic circle at the arch and on impulse turn right down Avenue de Friedland. Then the streets blend together. I just keep going straight on Boulevard Haussmann and the names change, but I know the streets are moving me closer to the tenth.

"I hate that I've made you come out like this. You have classes, don't you?"

"Which can be canceled with a simple phone call. I hate that you're not doing well. Concentrate on breathing." I'm trying to find that boulevard called Magenta. The traffic is horrible, and the wait at the lights feels excruciating. "God, I hate the traffic here."

"It's bad today."

"How long has your chest felt weird?"

"It started yesterday."

"You have to tell me next time. The minute it starts. It's what you pay me and Gaird for." Then we're on Boulevard Magenta, and I go north until we hit a little grid of one-lane streets. I get glimpses of the hospital's black mansard roof, but I can't seem to get the car close to it. "Is there a map in this car?" I'm losing my mind here. "There's got to be a map. Are you breathing? Tell me you're breathing?"

Luke's eyes are closed. He doesn't hear me. I finally find a one-way lane that takes me through to the hospital gates. I double-park outside the door to the emergency room, which is all the way around the back. Then I jump out and help walk Luke inside.

The nurses are on him in seconds with lots of questions in French. "I can't breathe very well," he says in English, and I translate his words into French in case anyone has missed the import. But the nurses take the breathing thing very seriously, and within minutes he's wheeled behind a door that I'm not allowed to go through. Oh, God. Please don't let him stop breathing. Don't let his lung collapse again.

It's very quiet in the hospital lobby. What should I do with his car? I run outside with the keys and move it to a spot in a lot across from the emergency entrance. Then I jog back in and sit in one of the bucket seats bolted to the cement floor. It's like an airport lobby from the 1960s in here. Seat colors alternate yolky yellow and robin's-egg blue. I have the feeling that we're not really at a hospital but at a departure terminal at Charles de Gaulle, and this carries me for a few minutes.

Then a nurse takes me behind the check-in station, down a brightly lit hall to a small examining room where Luke lies on a gurney in a blue johnny. The neckline hangs low in front so I can see how his clavicles jut out. The depression above each of those bones is so deep you could spoon water in there. We aren't doing a very good job of helping him gain weight.

"What's happening?" I say. "Can you breathe? I'm so sorry if it hurts."

"I'm better." His eyes and closed. "They gave me oxygen. Now they want to take blood, and I want a witness."

"A witness?"

"I want you to distract me from the needle."

"Of course! Of course I will." He's always been afraid of needles. He used to cry on the way to Dr. Burden's when we got vaccinations. My mother bribed him with new books. Mysteries were best. I take his hand. "We can get a new Hardy Boys."

"I've read them all."

"Squeeze my fingers as hard as you can." He winces when the needle slides in. He's thin, yes, but that's not new. It's the color of his skin that's changed—paler now. Grayer. There's tired skin under his eyes, and the bones of his face are also too defined. I can make out the sharp line of his jaw too clearly under the skin and the mechanism that opens and shuts his mouth. I hate seeing him like this. He has always been the strong one.

"Where is Dr. Picard? Where is your doctor? We need X-rays. We need chest scans. You couldn't breathe. Where is Sara? I've got to find Sara." I go out into the hall and find another nurse at the check-in desk; she says she'll have Sara paged and that Picard's at a conference at the Pasteur Institute with Dr. Montagnier.

"He is the doctor who discovered the HIV virus. All the leading SIDA doctors from around the world have come to France this week." The nurse calls AIDS by its French name, SIDA, and I nod. It makes sense—Picard's the doctor in charge of infectious diseases at St. Louis.

We see the attending, instead of Picard, whose name I instantly forget, much younger than Picard, with wavy brown hair over his ears and a wiry body like a marathoner. He says he's worried about white blood cells.

A different nurse comes in to take more blood then. She has a short, copper-tinged perm, and mumbles something to herself.

"What are we looking for with the blood?" I ask in French while she fills the second vial. I'm on alert now. I'm speeding up.

"Screening for viruses, madame," she says in English with a heavy French accent. Then she eases the needle out, places a square piece of gauze on Luke's wrist, and puts a round Band-Aid over the gauze. Luke falls asleep instantly, which surprises me. How did he get so exhausted? The nurse hands me a small bottle. "There is Valium inside."

"Valium?"

She nods. "The doctor thinks your brother's having anxiety. Which may be why he couldn't breathe."

"Anxiety? His lung collapsed once. It was three months ago. I didn't know this was about anxiety?" I think Luke's been living alone too much. He hasn't said anything to me about stress. But I've been so caught up in Macon. I've been selfish. How do I track down Sara?

He sleeps for another half hour, and I sit on the black stool with wheels next to his bed and watch him breathe. Then Sara bursts in. "My God. What's going on with him now?"

"You found us!" I hug her. "It's not so good, Sara." Then I start to cry, which surprises me. I didn't realize I was holding it in.

"Oh, Christ."

"He felt like he couldn't breathe."

"I haven't seen the report or the labs. I don't know anything yet."

Luke wakes up then and smiles. "I needed a good nap. I feel fine now."

"Sleep as long as you want," I say. "They've given me drugs that you're going to like."

"What flavor?" He looks too much like a really sick person lying on the bed. I'm desperate to get him up and home.

Sara reaches for his arm. "She's not telling you until we get you home."

"Let's go, Luke. Let's take you back. We have work to do. People to see." I don't look at Sara while we help him get dressed because I'm afraid I'll start crying again. How did this happen? He's so tired that he doesn't protest when I help him with his socks and his sneakers.

We walk into the hall, and Sara hugs him. Then she pulls me close and whispers, "I'll call you the minute the labs are ready. Could be days, though."

"The second they're ready."

There's a light rain falling outside, and the sky has turned pewter. On the drive home the pink hydrangea in the parks look gaudy. Luke would like a coffee. He says he feels better. I don't believe him. He insists, so I find a spot on Victor Hugo and we walk to Madeleine's on Avenue Raymond Poincaré. It's his favorite café. I get a table away from the draft.

It's timeless inside—dark wooden chairs and round tables. Jazz. A black granite bar. The service is good and slightly formal. Our espressos come quickly on miniature saucers. Was the attending doctor really worried or only a little worried? Is Luke breathing okay now? Is there a pain in his chest, or is he having an anxiety attack? How have I not seen any of this coming?

"It's a tea party for dolls in here," Luke says, stirring his coffee with the tiny spoon.

I drop two sugar cubes in my cup. "You need to call Gaird. He's got to come home."

"He's supposed to be gone one night. I'm going to be fine. I'll call him this afternoon. But I bet he's already on his way home."

"Would you like me to cook for you tonight?"

"You don't cook."

"I cook."

"You make instant oatmeal."

"You need help. You're not staying alone."

"I talked to Dad last Thursday."

"Oh really." I lean forward. "And why?"

"I do every week." He turns back to the window. "You know this. Or at least I thought you knew this. We talk water. We talk engineering and if I've hired the right guy to run things. Dad wants a real engineer in there instead of the policy guy I picked. He asks about

you." He reaches for his coffee. "He says God's watching out for us."
Now he unwraps his black scarf from his neck. "He said he's praying
for us."

My mother died in her bed on March 8, 1988. My father lay next
to her. He said she moved her arm as if she was going to roll over, but
then she couldn't. She was only sixty-one. Dad made Luke and me
fly to Hardin, Montana, afterward to bury her in her family's plot.
The three days before our flight Dad badgered me about words for
that bench he was having made. He was furious because I couldn't
think of what to write. He didn't speak to us the whole flight to Boze-
man. We landed in a blinding snowstorm and made our way outside
the terminal to Avis. Then Luke drove us slowly, very slowly, to the
church in Hardin, where Mom's younger sister, Happy, still lives on
a sheep farm. It was like we'd landed on the moon—the wide-open
swales next to the road blanketed in deep pillows of snow, and the low
arms of the trees. Luke hardly spoke. He was so focused on getting us
through the storm.

Aunt Happy belonged to a white Congregational chapel with
a steep, pitched roof and a musty alcove. Dad's two older brothers
flew in with their girlfriends and kids from their first marriages. Dad
didn't speak during the funeral. He just cried and hugged people. His
grief was too big to allow him to do anything else. I could almost pretend none of it was happening—that we hadn't just flown from San
Francisco and driven three hours in a Montana whiteout. Luke took
me aside in the church and said, "I don't want to spend my afterlife
buried in the ground in Hardin. Don't ever let this happen to me."

After the ceremony, Aunt Happy served fruit punch in a glass
bowl in the alcove with star-shaped shortbread cookies on dark
wooden trays. Then there was a caravan to the graveyard and more
talking and hugging outside in the snow. The minister, a tall, gray-
haired man in bifocals, gave a brief sermon. None of it was happening to me. I was outside my body—up above the cemetery watching
with my mother. We were accomplices. She and I. The heavy piece of
orange equipment needed to cut through the frozen ground sat one
hundred yards away next to a wooden shed. It looked like a tractor

or a monster, depending on your mood. The minister spoke about the generations of Mom's family who'd been buried at the plot. Their surname was Alder. And Alders had been buried in that ground since Alders began coming to Montana from Holland.

Everyone else drove back to Aunt Happy's in a snaking line of four-wheel-drive vehicles. Then it was just Dad and Luke and me. The hole they'd dug in the ground was very deep for the casket. How had that monster machine done this with all the snow? Dad knelt on the ground next to Mom's casket and started rubbing his hands together. Why was there a casket? I didn't think Mom would like that. I've always been afraid of caskets. Scared of them the way I'm scared of elevators and of being stuck underground in the Paris metro—a fear of being closed in that I inherited from my mother. Why were we even at a graveyard?

I needed something from Dad. Anything. There were rows and rows of gravestones. They looked like round loaves of bread. Dizzying. The light never rose above muted. Some people welcome the introversion of gray, but my mother built a life in California based on the sun. Yellows and ochers and oranges—brightly striped scarves that she wore over her braid and tied at the nape of her neck. At night she'd take her scarf off in the kitchen and unwind her hair until it fell in her face. I was eight and nine and ten, and I'd sit in her lap on the rocking chair in the corner by the door and brush her hair back from her eyes with my hands until she began to look like my mother again.

I hated it when she got haircuts because she wasn't familiar to me in the first days afterward. I never wanted to be without her back then. When I told her this one night in the rocking chair, she said, "And so you won't be. I'll always be with you. You'll always be able to feel me." I put my face close to hers and we kissed once, twice, three times, and one more kiss on my nose. I wanted to sit in the rocking chair with her for hours, because I couldn't always get my hands on her like this. She was beautiful. It was a beauty that wasn't mediated by anything. Just simple.

"Why are we here, Dad?" I said in the snow at the cemetery. "She wouldn't have wanted to be here."

"You two don't understand." Then he sobbed. I'd never seen him cry like this before. It should have brought us closer, but instead it served to heighten some impasse. "I know what she wanted. Family meant everything to her. She wanted to be buried near family."

"It's too cold here for her. What have you done to her?" I needed him to be strong like he was in the desert. I was yelling now. "Why did you leave us? Why did you ever go away?"

I've always been able to become the most upset around my family. Luke took my arm and pulled me back toward the rented Honda. Dad never looked up at us. He shut me out. What I didn't say then was that I'd missed him more than he ever knew when he was gone. I haven't spoken to him since the funeral.

Luke takes a sip from his espresso cup. "We're in Dad's prayers."

"Even the gay son?" Luke is beyond grudges. He's the oldest. The fixer, just like Mom was, which always makes him more evolved than me. He and Dad have done so much work together on the Water Trust projects. There were very few foreigners in China in the early eighties, when Dad started going there. He was zealous about his religion and wary about being in a country where Christianity was all but banned. But he and Luke worked all day in desert towns. Dad didn't speak Mandarin and Luke didn't speak the Bible, and they got along fine. They enjoyed it. I think it was exhilarating for them—building something that had purpose. Dad believed in the importance of water almost as much as he believed in my mother and in God and in math.

Luke reaches for his cigarettes in his coat. "You're sick," I say. "You can't smoke."

"You're furrowing your brow again. It's nice that Dad calls me. I like it."

"Just be careful."

"You're edgy. Dad screwed up at the funeral. Get over it. You're too old to hold on to it."

He clasps his hands in his lap and looks monkish, like our father. I stand and grab his scarf off the back of his chair and put it around his neck. We walk out of Madeleine's and make our way to his apartment. He lies down in bed, and I give him the phone receiver and the remote control and one of the Valiums. Then I bring the note from the kitchen that has Gaird's hotel on it. "Call him," I say, handing it to Luke. "Now, please. So he can come home."

Luke turns the TV to some French talk show. Then he takes the Valium with a sip of water from the glass on the bedside table and dials the Hotel Estheréa. "Brekken," he says loudly. "B-R-E-K-K-E-N. Gaird. One night. I don't know the room number." Then he waits. I think it rings and rings but no one answers in Gaird's room because then Luke hands the phone back to me. "Not there. I didn't think he'd be in the room right now. He would have checked out already."

He settles into watching French TV—I'm not sure how much of the shows he even understands, but he laughs from time to time and I go into the kitchen and call Macon. "Are you missing me?" he asks. "I've got salmon I'll grill on the roof."

"I'm missing you more than you even know. Luke isn't feeling well. It's his lung. He's had breathing trouble. I think I should sleep over."

"Oh, Christ. Is he okay?"

"We've been to the hospital. We've seen a new doctor. They talked about anxiety, and they're running blood tests. It could be mono, I bet. Or hepatitis."

"Why didn't you call me earlier? I'm so sorry."

"I tried you at the legal center twice, but then I gave up. Sara says to give the lab a full week. I'm going to need to be sedated to wait that long. Maybe I should take one of his Valiums."

"Go to sleep now."

"I'll try. I miss you. Did I already say that?"

I LEAVE LUKE's early Tuesday morning and get Gita at the asylum center. Then we both take the train to the academy. When I come back in the afternoon, Luke's in the den on the phone to China. He hangs up and says he feels fully recovered. I think it's the Valium. I make asparagus soup.

"Leave." He almost kicks me out after dinner. "I'm fine. Go back to your French lover. Go live your life!" I make him dial Gaird at the hotel again so we can both ask him to come home, but he's not there. I take a cab home, but it's painful to leave my brother alone in his apartment, and my resentment for Gaird grows. Why doesn't he call Luke? Why isn't he home?

When I get back to the apartment, there's a note from Macon saying that he's in Chantilly with Pablo. He returns after I've fallen asleep. On Thursday morning I get to have coffee and oatmeal with him before he leaves for the courtroom. Then I teach on Rue St. Sulpice and leave the academy for the asylum center at three.

Sophie lets me in. But she doesn't smile. "What's wrong? Tell me what's wrong."

She puts a long, pink-manicured finger to her lips to shush me. Then she takes my arm and walks me down to her office and closes the door. "Moona has been taken away."

I don't hear what she's saying at first. "What do you mean, 'taken away'?"

"She was deported yesterday. They changed the date of the hearing at the last minute, and her lawyer didn't get the paperwork. The hearing was last Friday. She and her lawyer believed it was meant to be yesterday. If you miss your court hearing, you're automatically denied. The officers came for her after breakfast."

"You're joking. You're not serious."

"This often happens. They had a seat on a charter plane leaving for Bombay. I tried to reach you, but you never answered the phone at your home. They are calling it a voluntary reunification with Moona's aunt."

"The wife of the uncle who raped her? How could they send her back?"

"The girls cannot be expelled on their own, because they are only children. But they can be reunited with family. You know this."

"Oh, Sophie." I sit down on the stool with my bag in my lap.

"Gita won't get out of the bed. She saw them take Moona out to the van. Then she screamed and ran into her room, and she won't move. She skipped kitchen duty. If she isn't up by the time she's meant to work there again, then I will call Roselle and try to get her a medical excuse."

"Or the guard will report her?"

Sophie stands up. "He will report that she is uncooperative if he knows that Gita is in bed, but he won't find out if I can help it. Today is the working of a mysterious God." She looks up at the ceiling and raises her eyebrows like she's frustrated with her God today and why can't he just give her a little help?

I look down at my watch. It's four o'clock. "Can I stay? Can I see her?"

"Dear girl. You can sit in my office all night if you like. I will be acting like this is just another day in the asylum world, because that is what it is, so help us God, and we will wait for Gita to wake up."

I sit in the chair and stare at the little rugs on the wall. Where has she gotten all these kilims? Every ten minutes or so I lean my head out into the hall to see what's going on. I keep seeing Moona's face—an older face than Gita's, with wise, dark eyes. Gita gets up twenty minutes later to go to the bathroom, and Sophie and I follow her back into her bedroom. It's a small, makeshift space with a plywood bureau that has decals of Winnie the Pooh stuck to the second and third drawers. Nothing on top of the bureau. The bed is the only thing in the room that feels permanent. An island. Safe zone. I lean against the radiator, and she sits on top of the blue polyester quilt. Her feet are side by side in small black sneakers on the floor. The skin under her eyes has gotten darker in the two days I haven't seen her. Tears slip down her face and onto her hands, which she's folded in her lap.

"I'm not being strong today." She cries harder and puts her hand over her mouth.

"Oh, Gita, no one said you had to be strong. This is a bad day. This is a very bad day." I can't even say Moona's name out loud. It's like she's died. It's got to be so damn scary to get taken to an airport and put on a plane and flown to a city that could be days away from your real home. You don't know anyone and you have very little money, maybe enough for a meal. How is this meant to be reunification?

"Moona was not thinking far enough ahead when they came for

her," Gita says. "She was not fully expecting it, and now she is gone and we will never be seeing her again."

"Gita, I'm so sorry. I know you loved her. We all loved her."

"I have great respect for you, Willow, but I loved Moona like a sister. You do not know her the way that I was knowing her." Gita looks stronger. Blood returns to her cheeks now that she's a little angry with me.

"You're right. But your hearing in court will give you the chance to get out of this place legally. Just think of the life you could have in France."

"Kirkit is legal."

"You still think of him often?"

Gita gives me a very small smile. "He is my friend. I want a friend like him." She looks away. Sophie just smiles.

I moved toward the door. "It's time for class, Gita. Let's go down the hall and get set up."

"Thank you, Willow." She smiles. "Thank you, Sophie. I will be in class in a few minutes if that is okay." Then she lies down on her bed with her sneakers still on and puts her hands over her face. She looks too young for any of this to be happening.

"The system is making this girl crazy, so help me God," Sophie whispers in the hall.

"The hearing has to work. That's it. It's just got to. We can't let what happened to Moona happen to Gita." I'm full of self-righteousness and false conviction. Macon will fix everything. The good side will win because we have more heart.

Precy and Esther are already on the couch when I walk into the common room. Then Rateeka and Zeena. Gita is last. I've brought maps for class, and I spread the one of Africa out on the floor so we can all circle around it on our knees.

Precy points to Liberia. "My brothers and sisters are going to bed there now. Look how close they are to the war. How close. I am praying they are okay."

Esther traces the African coast with her finger. "It's a long way from France to the Congo." She doesn't smile. She just stares at the map. "One day, when the camp was flooded again, my uncle sharp-ened a piece of wood and took me up to a lake. We caught three fish for dinner, which was good because sometimes my mother would cry when there was no food."

I unroll a map of Asia and put it down on the rug next to Africa. Rateeka and Zeena and Gita begin talking all at once. We don't have Moona to translate, though. There's such a hole where she used to be. Delhi sits close to the center of India, and Pakistan sits on India's left shoulder. Gita says, "Where is Bombay? Where? Where is it?" I point to the city. "I wonder if Moona can hear us there now? Where is Jaipur?" I point again, and Gita gets quiet. She puts her finger on the Arabian Sea. "That is the ocean? I have always wondered where it was. Our country looks so small here. I thought it was a bigger place than this."

"Everything is smaller on the map. Here." I point. "This is Jaipur."

"Where is the national palace where my baap was working?"

"The map is too big to include the palace."

"Where is Swam Singa Road, where my house is standing?"

"I will look for it when I'm there." I stand up. "I'm going to India this summer. I have a book to research there in July."

"India," Gita says like she can't believe it. "You are going to India?"

"I'm going. I'm so lucky to get to see your country."

"It will be hot in the summer months. Very hot. Watch out for the rickshaw drivers because they will want to take your money. Remem-ber, many of the people do not speak English like you." She smiles. "You are going to India. I will write you a letter for Moona and a letter for my grandmother. I don't know if she's still alive. The last time I saw her she was very sick and sleeping."

The girls each stand and find seats. "Can you try to tell me one thing you're afraid of about living in France?" I ask. "Just one sen-tence. I'll go first." I pause for a second. I'm trying to get them used to talking about the stories they carry in their heads. I say, "I am afraid that my brother will not get better." I wish I could take my words back the minute I say them. The girls have enough fears without adding my brother to their list.

"Brahma has made the universe as it is for a reason," Gita says slowly. "I know you are sad, Willow, but you should not have fear. Brahma is wishing it to be, and your brother will find peace."

I've bungled class for the night. There's another awkward silence. Then Precy says, "You have told us something that matters to you. We each need to go now. I will start. I am afraid of men. All men. Beginning with the men that were in the van that took me away from my family. And the man in the kitchen who cooks for us and the man who is the guard here." She finishes and looks down at the rug.

"Thank you, Precy," I say.

Gita says, "I am afraid that my family will find me here and take me back with them and I will have to live with Manju again. I must write the letters for Moona and my grandmother." She pulls a piece of paper from her notebook. "You must go to India and give them my letters."

Esther says, "I am afraid there is no one to marry me in my lifetime."

"The army," Zeena says. She understands more English than she can speak. Rateeka just smiles and moves her hand back and forth in front of her face to signal no. The sky darkens outside on the street.

"Speaking to the judge in the courtroom will be much less scary than the things that happened to you before you got here. But you have to be willing to tell your whole story." I've become fixated on the court testimonials. I want to cram them with as much detail as possible.

When the girls stand to leave, Gita hands me the letters she's been furiously writing. "Sometimes," Gita says, "if I closed my eyes in Brady Passage and listened to the Hindi and smelled the chapatis, I was back in Jaipur."

The lights are on in my apartment when I get home. I'm so grateful for that and for the man sautéing a steak at the stove. I kiss him on his face and make a salad with arugula. "Moona's gone."

"Moona who?"

"Moona on Rue de Metz. My student. Gita's friend. They came and deported her yesterday with no warning."

"Oh, God."

"How can they do that? How can they just take her? I can't believe the system works like this."

"Did she miss her hearing?"

"Apparently."

"They do that. They change the dates and catch you on the mistake."

"God, it's a cruel system." Then I tell him about the letters Gita wrote in class today.

"Well, now we know that the grandmother is alive. We know that Gita's got family in Jaipur."

"We're not sure she's really alive, are we? She was an old woman. Gita thinks she's probably dead. So the fact that I just told you Gita wrote a letter to her grandmother will hurt her case?"

"The court always wants reunification with family, Willie. The girl is only fifteen."

"But you said you'd make me her guardian."

"For the courts. You guide her through the preparation for the hearing, along with me. But the only way she gets to stay here alone is in foster care, and it's very unlikely. Here." He passes me a plate. "The steak is done."

"I don't want to lose this appeal." I stand in the kitchen holding the plate and stare at him.

He considers me for a moment. Then he takes the plate back and puts it on the counter and pulls me toward him. "I'm on your side. I'm her lawyer, remember? I'm the one working for her. Me."

"You?"

"Yes. Me." He kisses me on the forehead and on each cheek. "Do you understand now?"

"I'm too wrapped up in it."

"Yeah, you're wrapped up." We sit side by side at the table, and I pour red wine. The candles burn down while we eat.

I call Sara after we're finished. "What is the news on Luke's lab report?"

"It's Thursday," she says. "We took the blood Monday. We won't hear anything until tomorrow at the earliest. But plan on next Monday. Things work even more slowly in the lab on the weekends."

"This is cruel."

"This isn't cruel. It's science."

"It's France is what it is. Painfully slow. What are we looking for? Are we looking for mono? Hepatitis?"

"You can't think about these things now. It's late. Go to bed."

"Sara, you're the one who must be exhausted. How do you feel?"

"Bigger than a truck and lobotomized. I can't remember anything and I weep constantly. Yesterday I forgot where I parked the car. Today I forgot where I put my keys. Rajiv found me tonight crying in the kitchen, but I'd forgotten who he was. The love of my life—can you imagine? But other than that, I'm doing well."

"You're going to be the most incredible mother ever. I love you. Go to sleep."

"To sleep."

"Right to sleep." Then I hang up.

19

Jell-O: a brand name for a dessert made from a mixture of gelatin, sugar, and fruit flavoring

On Friday Delphine gives in and allows Pablo to sleep at my apartment. It's taken her most of the spring to agree. June and the horse chestnuts on my street are in their glory, with shiny leaves and white flowers that have begun to drop on the streets and turn yellow. There's a boy I know walking toward me hand in hand with his father. I run and pick Pablo up. "I've missed this boy!" I give him a kiss on the face and he laughs.

We head to the market on Rue Gracieuse to buy things Pablo will eat for dinner—potatoes that I'm going to mash with butter, carrots, white onions, beef in wax paper, and peaches and ice cream. We appear to be a small family. A simple construct. But no family is simple. Not mine. Not Macon's. We're always more complicated than we look. Our history complicates us. Our longing. Macon holds on to Pablo's hand, and every few minutes Pablo reaches for me and asks us both in French to lift him off the ground.

When we get back to my apartment, he circles the living room twice and stares at the furniture. Then he looks over at his father, who stands in the kitchen doorway watching. I've made the couch up with blue sheets and bought two Matchbox cars and a plastic bag of Legos and left it all on the trunk by the couch. Pablo picks up the cars first and drives them over the trunk and drops them off the edge. "There is a roof," Macon says and sits on the floor with him and puts the cars through a series of races. "There is a roof and a ladder that we can climb up to see the city."

"Where will I sleep?" Pablo's mind must be working hard to fit these new pieces together.

I stand next to the couch. "Here is your bed, Pablo. Your very own bed."

I can't tell if he approves. He says, "Where is the roof, Daddy? Let's go up there now."

Macon puts him on the third rung of the ladder and climbs behind him, lifting him in his right arm rung by rung. I stay in the kitchen and finish the pot roast my father used to make, with the white pearl onions and potatoes and little slices of carrots in a brown sauce with the meat. During dinner we run out of milk. Macon says, "Pablo is a muesli man in the morning. Muesli and bananas. I should go to the store." He runs down to the street.

"You are doing such a good job of eating, Pablo," I say in French. I hope he won't cry while his father's gone. But it's entirely possible that he will, and I'm ready for it.

"Thank you, Willie," he says in English and smiles. Has Delphine coached him to speak only English with me? Does she know I can speak French? "I am eating to get strong."

"What is your favorite food, Pablo?" I say in English. "I want to cook that for you tomorrow night. What do you like the very best?"

"Jell-O. Orange Jell-O is best."

I've been expecting a child—someone to tend to—but he's a sweet little person. Macon walks in and does a small kick in the air with the milk jug in his hand. Then he goes to the kitchen to pour Pablo a glass. Pablo eats everything and starts to rub his eyes at the table. I get the dishes in the sink while Macon carries Pablo to the couch and pulls the blankets up under his chin.

Then I kneel next to them on the floor. "Good night, Pablo," I say. I imagine Macon and Delphine tucking him into his bed in Chantilly all those other nights, and another wave of jealousy comes over me. Macon kisses his son ten times on the cheek.

"What should I dream about?"

"Flying horses." Macon smiles. "And red kites."

"Where will you be, Daddy, if I need you? Where will you sleep?"

Macon rises and stands in the door of our bedroom, just behind the couch. Pablo can see him without turning his head. And he can see our bed inside the doorway. "Right here," Macon says. "I will be sleeping so close to you. I can hear anything you say."

"Leave the door open," Pablo says. "And my covers on. Half of my body always has to be covered up. Then the bad guys can't see me."

"I won't ever shut the door. But there are no bad guys here. Only Willie and me. Sweet dreams, Pablo. See you in the morning."

I follow Macon into the bedroom. "I hope I can learn to speak the language of four-year-olds," I whisper, taking off my shirt and jeans. "It's so good to have him here."

"He is away from Delphine for the first overnight. You have to understand how close he and his mother are."

"Tell me what you mean."

"She's getting better. It helped when I told her that if she didn't let him come, I'd go back to the judge and bring Pablo here on weekends without asking. I didn't want to have to do that. She's been good about this trip. There has been very little yelling."

"She used to yell?"

"I would like us to not ever yell. Do you think that's possible?"

"I think anything is possible. You are here in my bed, and Pablo is sleeping out there on the couch. I didn't even know you four months ago." We lie in bed holding hands and I try to listen for the sound of Pablo sleeping, but it melds with the sound of his father sleeping next to me.

IN THE MORNING Pablo crawls into bed with us, and it's so surprising—so thrilling—that I lie very still under the sheets while he climbs up on my back. "I'm hungry, guys." Then he crawls over to Macon's back. "When are we having breakfast? When are we eating?"

"There's only one rule in Willie's house," Macon says. "It's serious.

It's called the Don't Laugh Rule. I'll explain it to you, and it's important you follow along. Do you understand?"

"Do it! Do it!" Pablo yells.

"But do you understand? The rule is, you must not laugh."

"I'm ready. I won't laugh!"

Macon tickles Pablo under his chin and down the sides of his stomach until he screams and laughs and can't stop.

The two of them go out for croissants once the sun is up. I sit at the kitchen counter with my coffee and call Sara. "It's been more than three days. Where's the lab report?"

"It's Saturday at nine o'clock in the morning, and I told you to plan on Monday."

"Monday is a horrible idea. Pablo's here, and he's terrific. Macon's taken him out to get chocolate croissants. What if Luke is really sick?" The idea of waiting until Monday exhausts me.

"You've got to stop thinking like that. We're going to make this okay. We don't know anything yet. It's fantastic that Pablo's actually getting to stay with you."

"Pablo is sweet. Very sweet."

"He'll love you. Just make sure you're fun, Will."

"When am I not fun?" I yell into the phone.

"No, really. You have to be willing to get down on the floor with him and play. You need to build things with him."

Macon's key is in the lock. "Since when are you the expert in child rearing?"

"Since I devoured every book on parenting I could get my hands on."

"I love you, and I'm hanging up."

"I love you, too."

Pablo runs into the kitchen with a white paper bag in his hand. "Willie, they had the chocolate ones!"

I put the croissants on a plate and slice a melon. Then the three of us sit at the table and eat. "Yum." I smile.

"Chocolate is my best one." Pablo takes little nibbles of his croissant.

The phone rings after I've taken a big bite of melon. Luke says, "Is the sleepover going well?"

"My mouth is full of cantaloupe."

"I can't understand you. You're talking with your mouth full."

I swallow. "I wish they had your blood results this morning. Sara says it will be Monday now."

"You're worrying. You're not supposed to be worrying. I'm good. I feel much, much better. How is Pablo? Are you having the most wonderful time?"

"He's a funny boy. You'll like him. Have you talked to Gaird yet?"

"Yesterday. I finally reached him. He says he's been crazed with the logistics of the tugboat. It's much more involved than he ever imagined."

"And did you tell him to get himself home? It's been a week now. Did you say that your lung is acting up again? That you need him? Did you ask him why the hell he hasn't been calling you?"

"I did. Maybe I didn't use those exact words. But I did ask him. He says he's got to go out on the boat now, so I won't hear from him."

"He's not coming home?"

"Not yet. I'm fine, Willie. He's got a job, you know."

"I'm not impressed. And I'm baking a fish and I want you to come over." I cut the other half of the cantaloupe in pieces with the phone stuck deep in the crook of my neck. I don't like Luke spending so much time alone. "I'm going to keep the head of the fish on, Chinese-style. I do this maybe once a year if you're lucky. It's my tradition."

"Oh, I'm feeling lucky. Truly lucky, let me tell you. Beijing is going to explode. They've brought tanks into the city. Thousands of people are going to die if the army opens fire. And you don't have any baked fish traditions that I'm aware of."

"I have the Chinese cookbook you gave me. You can't miss it."

"But I can. I can miss it." He laughs. "You don't get enough practice cooking."

"I do good fish. You have to come."

———

"CAN YOU TELL ME again how old Luke is?" Pablo asks from the arm of the couch while we wait for my brother to arrive.

"He's thirty-two, and I'm thirty."

"How many years older does he have than you?"

"Two years." I smile.

Macon calls Pablo from the kitchen: "Come help me crack eggs for custard."

Luke knocks four times on my door. I open it, and he kisses me on both cheeks. "Do you know how expensive, how *très, très chères framboises* are in Paris, sister of mine?" He goes into the kitchen, gives Macon a quick hug, and opens the freezer. "Burn. A great deal of burn in here," he yells, trying to find a place for the sorbet he's brought. "You are both aware of it, I trust? Freezer burn, Will? You've heard of it? And of defrost? And of getting rid of these dead things that live here? These plastic baggies of unidentified brown meat?"

He stands up. He looks fine. He doesn't have any secret disease. I can rule it out. "The Chinese government has enforced a curfew. You know that, right? They've got the tanks there, and no one is allowed out on the streets."

"French TV has been following it around the clock," Macon says.

"It's getting tense. I don't like the way it looks. God, I was just there in May. The sun was shining on Mao's tomb. I would have never predicted this. But it's going to get bad. How can it not?"

I light the white tapers on the table. Paul Simon's on, and the bass line moves through the apartment: *My traveling companion is nine years old. He is the child of my first marriage.* Pablo runs laps around the couch—three times and then a jump, four times and then a jump. Luke catches him on the sixth round and hands him a black pirate hat he's brought in a paper shopping bag.

"Shiver me be!" Luke yells, and Pablo runs to the kitchen to show Macon.

Then we sit down at the table to eat. "To the men in my life." I raise my glass of Bordeaux and look to Macon and Pablo and Luke.

"The Father, Son, and Holy Ghost," Luke says. "If only Dad were here to appreciate this."

We look for bones in the fish. When I'm happy like this, it's unfettered—as if I'll never feel removed from life again. Why doesn't anything achieve this lightness on other days—not even Macon, not even Luke singing over the telephone? I want to remember this night when I'm not longing for anything and not mourning anyone's absence.

After dinner, the men take on the dishes. I play a Joan Baez album, and Pablo lets me rub his back on the couch. "How do you make hair, Willie?" I'm half-listening to Macon and Luke talk about their favorite ways to braise calf livers. "Hair," Pablo says. "How do you make it?"

"You don't, my friend. It grows. From the time we are born, hair grows."

"Like corn? Grows like strawberries?"

"Exactly. Hair's alive."

The song "Kumbaya" comes on. Luke and I always make fun of it because our parents used to sing all the verses out loud in the car. The needle crackles, and Pablo listens closely: *Someone's singing, Lord, Kumbaya. Someone's singing, Lord, Kumbaya.* "Willie," he asks without looking up, "can the people in the music hear us talking right now like we can hear them?"

"No, sweets." I finger his hair. "They can't."

Luke pokes his head out of the kitchen and sings the last line falsetto: "Someone's singing, Lord, Kumbaya, Oh Lord, Kumbaya." He looks hollowed out around his eyes, but healthy. I bury my worry. I've been overreacting. The lab results will be fine.

VERY EARLY the next morning, even before the pigeons have stirred in the gutters outside the bedroom window, Pablo climbs into our bed again. He's got Lego pieces in his hands. Macon says, "We need to sleep more, Pablo. Either you lie here and get quiet, or go back to your bed."

He chooses to lie down between us and pulls most of the top sheet and quilt off me. "Hey," I say. "It's cold. Blankets, please. Can someone give them back?"

Macon wrestles some of the sheet away for me. Then Pablo stands up so his little toes are very near my face. He says, "I need to get my astronaut hat for flight."

"No flights this morning," Macon announces. "The airport is closed for sleeping."

I'm in a deep REM cycle when the phone rings. I pick up the receiver in a dream. "I went down to the lab last night before I went home," Sara says. "It was one a.m. Too late to call. But it's not good, Willie. It's not what we wanted. His T cells are off."

"Where are you? Why are you calling me in the middle of the night? Are you crazy?" I can smell coffee in the kitchen. Macon's moving dishes around in there, while Pablo chatters away to him.

"It's six in the morning, Willie. Wake up. Wake up, my friend. I have bad news."

I feel calm and very still, as if Sara will now give me the information I've been waiting for—the precise answer to why Luke can't kick his perennial cold or all his fatigue—and using this, we will fix everything. "Tell me." The only sign of panic is that my arms are prickly.

"It's his T cells. They're bad."

"I know all about T cells." I still sound calm. "Do you understand how many of Luke's friends have died in the last five years? Why didn't you say you were looking at his T cells?"

"I thought you knew. I thought you understood we were looking at everything, and that the blood would tell us about his immune system."

"You never said that."

"Did I really need to say it?"

"I thought you were going to tell me he has hepatitis."

"He may."

"Or mono. I thought you were testing for mono."

"That and a host of other things. HIV looks a lot like mono at first and a lot like the flu. It's been really hard to diagnose him."

"HIV." I've circled it in my mind in the darkest, most private moments but only at peril to my sanity. And I've been able to banish these thoughts. No one I know with HIV—not one person that Luke or Gaird or I know—is getting better from the disease. All I see are people getting worse. People dying.

"That's what we're talking about, Willie. I'm so, so damn sorry."

"Tell me his number." I'm crying, but she can't hear it yet because the sobs start so far down inside my body. I open my mouth to let the sounds out, but nothing comes.

"His T cells are becoming more damaged, which weakens his immune system and leaves him at risk for other infections besides the lung. The higher the number, the stronger he is."

"Tell me, Sara. Please just tell me." Tears start streaming down my face. I'm cold now. Shivering.

"Five hundred. He's at five hundred, which we're considering normal for someone infected by the HIV virus."

I close my eyes and put the phone down beside me on the bed. Then big, loud, racking sobs rise up, and the snot and tears run together down into my neck. "For someone infected by the HIV virus." Oh, fuck. Oh, God. My poor brother. Oh, what are we going to do? I pick up the phone and listen to her—she's still talking—but I can't speak. I must let out some kind of sound; I'm not sure. But Macon hears something and comes running in from the kitchen and sits on the bed.

"Willie, I know you're there," Sara yells into her end of the phone. "It's 1989, Will. Not 1985. We will have new drugs. We have AZT. I'm following this closely. Picard is one of the best in the world. He consults with the Pasteur people every week. They're the ones who discovered the disease, for God's sake. AZT. It's a good drug, Willie. We can fight this. I'm going to help you fight this. Don't go away on me. Don't go away on him."

I hold the phone to my ear so I can feel her there, and she waits. A few minutes go by like this—with me panting into the phone and Sara silent. "What's a normal count, Sara?" I finally ask. "What's normal?"

"You and I have seven hundred to one thousand T cells in a drop of blood the size of a pea." She's almost whispering now. "If the number drops below two hundred, we classify it as AIDS. Or if, God forbid, he gets some opportunistic infection."

"So we are three hundred T cells away from AIDS?" I force myself to keep talking. I have only a dispassionate interest anymore in what she's saying. My mind's fogged. I can't process the numbers. I could hang up and this would all be over. I could try doing it—hanging up. Just to see what would happen. Pablo yells from somewhere in the apartment, and Macon goes looking for him.

"Let's not look at it that way. It's a continuum. It moves around." Sara's crying now, too. "Oh, sweets, don't do this to yourself. Don't cry like this." But she can't stop either. "We're going to get him through this. There are good protocols now. The prognosis isn't as bad as it used to be. You need to call him and tell him."

"I'm not." I snap out of my haze. "I'm not doing that. He's been at Andreas and Tommy's house in Neuilly all weekend. He's happy right now. Gaird is a fucking deserter."

"It's really bad," I say to Macon and put the phone down again when he comes back to the bedroom. "Luke's sick. It's HIV." He grabs the phone and I roll over on the bed. I can tell it's going to be one of those fucking heartbreakingly beautiful June days in Paris. A milk-blue sky washes over the faces of the apartments across the street, and the sun shines down on the wrought-iron balconies, munificent. God-like.

"Sara. It's Macon now. Can you tell me about the lab report? What the numbers are?" He nods and rubs my back with his free hand. "Oh, *merde*. Okay. Okay, you're right. All right, we'll talk later." He hangs up the phone and climbs onto the bed so he's lying on top of me. Then he puts his arms around my shoulders and holds me. We lie like that for what feels like a very long time. Where is Pablo? I have no idea what Macon has him doing. Neither of us talks. And the bad news takes shape in my head. I'm trying to find a place to put it.

HIV is everywhere in the news. There have been days I thought Luke fit the description, but every time I got to that point I turned back. I couldn't even try the word on. I hid from it. I don't know how long we lie there. Everything's different now. The line between Luke having HIV and not having it is everything. If it were a mark in the desert, I'd get down off my camel and rub it with my hand. Because I want something I can touch. Demarcation. Proof.

"Willow Pears, this is Macon speaking." His mouth is directly over my ear like a megaphone. "Where have you gone in your mind? You've left me. I'm calling you back. Come back to us. You need to get up. You need to get dressed. I've got really good coffee in the kitchen. Pablo is drawing you a picture of a giraffe. Can you smell the coffee? Luke isn't dying."

I open my eyes and look at him. "How do you know he isn't dying?" I feel primitive. Reduced to whether Luke will or will not die. I only want this one question answered. "How do you know if he'll live?"

"Because people live with HIV for many years. Sara is going to make this happen. She'll get you another appointment with Picard. You're going to talk to a leading doctor soon."

"When? I want to talk to him today. Right now. I want to know everything there is to know about HIV. What does HIV even stand for? Is it really even a word?" I know from my mother that the brain is chemically wired to hear bad news and think of it only as a threat. And that's all I see. Threat.

"You'll get to talk to him soon. In the meantime, there is a girl in the center on Rue de Metz who's got a hearing next week. You're her court guardian. She needs you to go there today and help her get ready."

GITA IS THE only reason I get up. I told her I'd be there today, on Sunday, to listen to the full testimonial we've been working on. I put on clothes without thinking and drink the coffee standing up in the kitchen. Then Macon and Pablo walk me down Rue Monge to the metro station. I take the train to Châtelet and switch to the No. 4 line and get off at St. Denis. Nothing on Boulevard de Strasbourg looks beautiful in the glaring sunlight, not the green ivy growing on the side of the gray bank or the chestnut trees so thick and full of leaves they remind me of drawings of the tree of life. Paris has closed in on itself today. It feels too insular in my grief. I want my home language. I want home. I'm homesick. Sick for home. But I'm not keening for the house. It's for all of us together. My mother and father and Luke and me. Halloween. *Abbey Road.* The longing is acidic in my mouth. Dizzying. Why do we live here, so far away from Dad? Far away from the good hospitals? Shouldn't we be in San Francisco?

Truffaut buzzes me in. I sit with Gita in the common room and try to stay focused. HIV. HIV. I've got to go find Luke. It's quiet at nine in the morning on Sunday at the center. Most of the girls are working in the kitchen or in their rooms. Gita stands in front of the couch and smiles shyly. She's holding the typed pages of what we've written. "Speak as loudly as you can," I say. "Look the judge in the eye, if possible. Look the attorneys in the eye. We need to make them realize how believable you are."

"Speak the truth," Sophie says from the door. "Only the truth. They know lies when they hear them."

Gita repeats the story five times. She keeps standing up and sitting down and pacing to the windows. "I will not do it well. I am too nervous. I will forget what to say."

"But that's okay," I say. "The judge and Mr. Ventri will have the written version—copies of this very one we've typed on paper, Gita. Mr. Ventri can help you if you lose your way."

Sophie smiles. "You have everything you need right there on the paper."

"I am not sure I can do this," Gita says again. "Mr. Ventri said I will need to stand in the courtroom and that I will be doing a lot of talking, and I cannot talk for very long without becoming nervous." She starts to cry.

Oh, God. We are all falling apart today. "You came to France legally," I say. "This is going to be okay, Gita. This is going to be good. Please don't cry. You are great at talking, Gita. Talking isn't a weakness of yours. Mr. Ventri will hand the judge a copy of your story.

Then you get to recite it out loud. This is your chance to tell them. You've been waiting so long to explain."

"I think you should go take a break now," Sophie says. "I think you're tired, Gita."

We work through her testimony two more times. Her story sounds convincing and true. Because it is true. I stand up from the couch. I've got to go find Luke before the hospital calls him. "You are good." I smile at her. "You are so good at speaking this." No one will be able to deny her asylum. Her story is irreproachable.

She reaches for my wrist. "Do you mean that? Do you really mean what you say?"

"I wouldn't say it if I didn't believe it, Gita. Go rest now. Go have lunch. I've got to go see my brother."

"He is unwell?"

"He is sick today, yes. He is not good today."

She widens her eyes. "I am so sorry to know this. You must go to him. You must go now."

ON MY WAY DOWN Boulevard de Strasbourg, I pass the market on the corner and buy broccoli. Luke will have an onion in the drawer below the toaster, and milk and butter and cheese in the refrigerator. The sun is still high and bright and menacing. It follows me when I get into the cab. Sometimes my mother made soup when Luke didn't get a part he wanted in a school play or when I was going to be up late writing a paper. She'd leave it warming on the stove for us when she went to bed. Cream of mushroom. Clam chowder. Cream of broccoli. I loved her soups. I want to make one for Luke. It will help us. We need help.

I get to his apartment, let myself in, and yell, "Hallooooo!" He doesn't yell anything back. I tiptoe into the bedroom. He's asleep. This is good. This means no one at the hospital has called him yet. I go back to the kitchen and cut the broccoli and wash it and slice the onion and grate the cheese. I don't think of anything except how to make the soup.

When the soup's done, I get the ladle out of the drawer and fill two bowls and walk them into my brother's room on a tray.

"You knew all along, didn't you?" he yells at me. What's he talking about? There's spit in the corners of his mouth. His nose is red and swollen from where he's pressed it against his hands. "I keep calling Gaird in Amsterdam, and he doesn't answer. I think he's moved there. He's left me and you're just not brave enough to tell me!" He rolls from side to side on the bed, banging his head against the headboard and scraping the skin on his scalp with his fingernails.

I stand frozen on the rug. Is he losing his mind? Is this dementia? How have we gotten to this place so quickly? He's unhinging. Jesus, what do I do? I have no idea where Gaird is. Why isn't he calling? Where the hell is he? Luke screams again, and I can see the tendons strain in his neck. "You just let me think he'd come home!" He punches his pillow. "All those kids in Tiananmen Square are about to be dead. What government would do such a thing?"

"A depraved government." It's the only question I can accurately answer.

"And I'm alone now. Don't you see? Don't you even begin to understand?"

"You're not alone." I mean it as much as it's possible to mean anything I say. Even when words feel insufficient, I still believe they matter. They save lives. Offer a rope. A foothold.

"You can't save me. I know what's wrong with me, Willie." His sobs shake his whole body and come from his chest, not his throat. I sit down on the bed and rub his back. I want him to feel my hand on him. I can't bear that he's so alone. "They called with the lab results this morning. It's HIV. It's fucking HIV." He starts to sob again.

Shit. "You're not alone," I whisper again. It's all I can think of to say. Why did they fucking call him? Why didn't I come sooner? "I'm right here, and Gaird hasn't left you. He's just slow coming home."

"It's AIDS, Willie. I have AIDS. You have to see that." He can hardly speak, he's crying so hard. "I've dreaded it and now it's here."

"Oh, Luke, hang on. Hang on. Please. Slow. Slow down if you can. You don't have AIDS."

His best friend in high school was a boy named Roger, who came to our house to draw cartoons with Luke almost every day. They made really good graphic novels at our kitchen table about space travel and life on the moon. Roger got sick five years ago in San Francisco. The doctors called it pneumonia. It happened quickly. That was the most terrifying part. I went with my brother to see him over Thanksgiving, when Luke was back from Beijing. We drove to Noe Valley and walked up the hill to Roger's apartment in the morning fog. He'd set up his life on the pullout couch in his small living room because he was too weak to make it upstairs. It was dark inside the apartment. Any kind of light hurt his eyes.

This was 1984. They didn't have the name for it yet, so they kept using the word "pneumonia." It was shocking to see how sick Roger was. Luke's dear friend. The gorgeous boy from high school, skeletal and going blind. His eyes swam in his thin face. He looked mournful, too, like a child but with the wisdom of a very old man.

I start crying in Luke's bedroom. "I'm listening," I say. "I'm right here." We are just the two of us, away from our home. My mind moves to doctors' appointments and hospital visits and how is Luke going to manage?

"Gaird's always come back to me. But it's been more than a week. I only got to talk to him the one time. He didn't sound like himself. He sounded guilty, Willie. Like someone who was leaving without saying good-bye. It was his idea to live here in Paris. God, I truly hate this apartment now. His clothes are in that dresser, and his reading glasses are on the sink in the bathroom, where he forgot them. How could he just leave me?"

I rub Luke's neck and between his shoulder blades, and the muscles in his back. He stays quiet while I do this. My mother would have been calm. She would have told Luke that he wasn't going to die, and he would have believed her. He made her laugh in a way that no one else did, and he understood her sarcasm and her curiosity and how she was a mix of those two things.

My mother was attracted to urgent people. She would have liked Gita because of this. What would she have made of Gaird? Is he really on a tugboat somewhere near Holland? Can that be? Who will love Luke the way Gaird loved him? It's the middle of the afternoon now and the sun is thankfully gone, replaced by a gray rain that a new batch of wind has brought in.

Luke falls asleep on the bed, and I begin all over again in my mind: Where's my mother? What would she say to Luke? What would she say to Gita? I finally get up and call Macon at the apartment. "I'm here with him."

"How is he?"

"Over the edge. He thinks Gaird's left him for good. He thinks he's dying."

"It's too much."

"I'm sleeping here. I'll take him to the hospital in the morning."

"Should I meet you there? Do you want me to come?"

"I think I'm okay. I have to be okay, right? This is just the start."

THE CHINESE ARMY opened fire on the protesters in the square last night, and Luke screams about this the whole ride to the hospital. He was on the phone at dawn, talking to his people there. This time the nurse takes us down a different hall. She's the same woman with the copper-colored perm who took Luke's blood last week. She wears a blue face mask and has on purple latex gloves. I can tell by the way her eyes widen that she recognizes us. And that she's scared. HIV. We're put in the old part of the hospital, where it feels almost deserted. Almost quarantine. The room is cold and ancient. The concrete walls are a dirty cream color and bare. The gray stone floor looks cold, which is how I imagine all the floors in medieval convents must look. A wooden desk sits in the corner next to a black metal scale.

She hands Luke a blue cotton robe. I can't stop staring at her and her face mask. I can't tell what her mouth is doing. Is she smiling, even faintly? Frowning at us? Disapproving? I've heard of doctors who've gotten the virus from their infected patients. But they've been surgeons. Dentists. I understand the fear. But the mask heightens things. There's something about it that screams emergency. We Have An

Emergency. When really we don't. We just have Luke. Sitting quietly up on the high examining table covered in crinkly white paper. And me. His neurotic sister perched on the metal chair next to him.

"My name is Joséphine." This time she speaks in French. "I'll be back to do more blood work while we wait for Dr. Picard."

Luke takes off his shirt. There are two red sores under his right collarbone the size of quarters, scabbed and inflamed. I try not to show my shock. The sores are terrifying. Roger had those sores.

Joséphine scans Luke's arms for good veins and slides the needle in, saying "I don't mean to hurt you" through the face mask. She takes two vials of his blood.

Dr. Picard walks in while she's putting on the Band-Aid. He's got the lab coat, unbuttoned over a blue-and-white thinly striped shirt. The tie is polka-dotted. His hair is in a short bowl cut that makes his face look wider and rounder than it really is. He doesn't sport the face mask. But he's wearing the gloves. His are the pale skin-colored ones I'm used to from the States. He shakes Luke's hand. "Hallo, hallo," he says in English with his thick French accent. "I am disappointed in your labs. We didn't want the T cell count to plummet."

"The numbers aren't so good, are they?" Luke smiles, but I see tears pooling in the corners of his eyes.

"The numbers will vacillate. But you have the immune system of a very compromised person now. You must take every precaution. Do you know what that means?"

"I've had friends die of AIDS, Dr. Picard. Good friends. They were alone at the end of their lives because their families worried that the disease was contagious. Please don't sentence me to that kind of death."

"Luke," I say. "Stop. You're not dying." I sound strong and convincing. It's all show for him. The disease scares me completely.

"Your sister is right." Picard puts down the file he's been holding. "You will be pleased to know that I want you surrounded by as many friends and as much family as you can stomach. You have a lot of living left to do. We are not talking about dying today. We are talking about how to lengthen your life. But HIV is very contagious in certain bodily fluids. Not saliva, for example. But blood, yes. Start by using clean needles if you take intravenous drugs."

"I don't ever."

"Use condoms whenever you have sex. Do not practice unsafe sex no matter who your partner is."

"I do practice safe sex, and I only have one partner."

"He should be checked right away."

"I would tell him that if I knew where he was. He left me."

Picard nods as if he hasn't understood. "Please step on the scale." It seems too much for any of us in this starkly lit room to acknowledge that this man, my brother, who has so much fighting to do, will have to do it alone without the person he thought loved him most.

Luke gets down off the examining table carefully, slowly. The scale is one of the old ones with the sliding metal arrow and numbers etched in ascending order by fives. "Just what I suspected," the doctor says. "One hundred and fifty pounds for someone your height isn't what we like to see." He turns to me then. "His weight has fallen. *C'est mauvais,*" he adds in French for emphasis. "This isn't what we want." He asks Luke to open up his robe so he can listen to his chest with the stethoscope. The scabs look awful. Picard circles the area around each of them with his finger and bends to examine them more closely. "These sores are called Kaposi's sarcomas," he says matter-of-factly while he studies them. "They are a form of fairly benign cancer."

"I thought so." Luke closes his eyes. "Oh God, that's just what I thought."

"That's what Roger had," I say out loud. Then I look at Dr. Picard. "Luke's best friend from high school." No one I've known who's had AIDS has lived long with it. Not my gay Chaucer professor from college, who got sick in 1987, or my grad school friend Blake, who fell in love with the man who ran a bike shop in Berkeley. They ended up ghosts of themselves. One with colon cancer. One with the scariest neurological disease I've ever heard of.

I want to take Luke's hand and run. Where are we, really? Why France? Where is our father? I need to call him. I need to call Dad.

"Is Kaposi's a sign of more aggressive cancers we can't see?" I ask, trying to keep myself together. I need to be the strong one here.

"We are monitoring everything. His T cell count is at five hundred. If we can keep him there, then we will ward off other opportunistic infections. We will be looking at his kidneys and liver. Luke has to gain more weight. It is one of the ways the body can fight off infections."

"We're all trying to get him more calories." I look over at my brother. "Sometimes he doesn't want to eat. Sometimes he can't eat because he's constipated or has diarrhea. Other days it goes well. I'm not sure where the food goes, though."

"Well. He is certainly not gaining weight." Picard pushes his bifocals up on his nose and takes in Luke's thin face.

"If you had any suggestions for weight gain?" What I want to say is, give us some good news—some breakthrough, or something we can leave here with today.

Picard writes down the name of what he calls a high-calorie French vanilla drink. "You are to buy this at the pharmacy. It comes in cans by the case." Then he closes Luke's file. "Eat all the foods you ever wanted to eat, and then eat more. We will start AZT in a week or so once we have run our full battery of tests on the blood. AZT has shown some very good results in patients at slowing the disease."

That's it? That's fucking it? A vanilla drink? I don't want Luke or Picard to see my tears. I brush them off with my sleeve, and they slide down the sides of my face and under my ears. Luke changes out of the robe. Then I take my brother's elbow. We walk down the hall to the elevator, then through the bright lobby with the colored seats and out to the parking lot—all without speaking. There's nothing funny to say today.

Luke keeps his eyes closed in the car on the way home. He's in pain. But I'm not sure exactly where it comes from. The sores on his chest? His lung? There's a Nina Simone song in French on the radio that my mom used to play when Luke and I were young. "Music for lonely people," I say out loud in the car.

Sometimes Mom would go to bed the morning after Dad left for a map trip. She didn't like him to leave her. She fed off people. Luke and I were supposed to play outside on those bad days. If we went inside, we had to whisper. Her bed looked out over the front yard and the eucalyptus tree and the gravel and a slice of the bay. We couldn't go into her room, and I hated that separation from her. I hated that in missing Dad, she couldn't receive me. I had so much to give her. I'd peek on my way to the bathroom and see her under a pile of blankets, and it was confusing. I wanted to help her brush her hair.

I turn down Boulevard Haussmann and drive toward Avenue Victor Hugo in the drizzle. Luke says, "I want to go to church." I can't look at him because there's too much traffic. "I want to go to Chartres on the train. The famous cathedral."

"Do you for some reason think I live in a small hole in the ground and don't know what Chartres is?"

"I want to see the stained-glass windows. I've lived in France for five years, and I've never been to Chartres. How did I let that happen?"

"We can go. We can get you to Chartres. It won't be a problem." My hands are sweaty on the steering wheel. My heart's beating faster again. He's thinking about dying. How do I distract him?

"I'm going to throw up."

"Hold on. Almost home. I'm so sorry, Luke. I'm so, so sorry."

The trick at the Arc de Triomphe is to stay in the outer ring of cars around the first half and then veer off quickly—as if shot from a cannon—over to the wide start of Victor Hugo. Luke stares through the windshield. His eyes are blank. I park two blocks from his apartment.

"Custard," he says. "Let's get custard at Madeleine's."

"You really want to do that?"

"I'm starving, and it's delicious." He climbs out of the car and waits for me to lock up. It's crowded inside the café. But we find a table in the back corner. The custards come in small, ridged, blue bowls. Creamier than flan. I eat all of mine. Luke has two bites. "I think I'm too nauseous." He puts his head down on the table. "I'm

glad you'll take me to Chartres soon. We got terrible news today, Willie. What are we going to do?"

He's sentimental and broody, and I'm afraid he's going to completely lose it in the café.

"I'll take you to Chartres. I'll take you anywhere you want. It's
going to be okay."

One Easter Mom forced us to drive to the Congregational chapel
on Sycamore in dress-up clothes. She was trying to find a church that
fit us. Dad stayed home. I sat in the pew between my mother and
brother. I was ten, and I knew church was supposed to feel good.
The people sitting closer to the preacher were smiling, but I had this
numbness in my arms and legs, as if I swam above my body. I wanted
to pick the scabs on my knees—anything to connect my head back
to my body. But my legs felt too far away. I think I was too young to
understand prayer.

There's a part of me now that wishes I had some ritual. It would
be so nice. As much as I can tell Luke that I'm with him, I also know
that he's alone. I can't change places. I can't even find words to tell him
how afraid I am for him. My words would only scare him. So when
he needs me to be the most honest with him that I've ever been, I'm
hiding things. And it distances us—just when Luke needs closeness.

"We should go back to the apartment now," he says. "I have to lie
down." He reaches for his raincoat.

Why did I think it was a good idea to bring him to the café? He
needs bed. When I motion to the waiter for the check, I see a blond
man walking in the door. "Oh, God."

Luke is staring out the window, so at first he doesn't see who's
making his way to us. Then his face turns and registers the surprise
of it.

"I knew I would find you here chatting. You two are always talking." Gaird reaches out both hands to me.

Luke looks down at the floor and begins to weep. It's just too
much for him. I want to scream at Gaird. I want to hit him. But I
stand and give him two polite kisses on each cheek. It's so crowded at
Madeleine's that there's hardly any room next to our table. Luke won't

look at him. Gaird finally says, "Can I sit, or are you going to make me take my inquisition standing?" Luke points to an empty chair two tables over.

Gaird weaves through the people and grabs the chair and carries it back over his head. "I want," Gaird says slowly as he sits down, "to explain." Luke stares at some place behind Gaird's right shoulder, tears spilling down his cheeks. "I want to say that I did get stuck in Amsterdam. The boat was a fucking disaster. Bad engine. Captain with an expired license. Leaking hull. I thought it was better not to call. I did not have the intention to stay away, at least at first. Then I decided it was easier for you to live without me because you have your sister here and your language and I was a fumbling idiot. I was not seeing it clearly."

"I'm HIV positive, Gaird," Luke says and sobs.

Gaird runs his hands through his hair and reaches for Luke's shoulder. "Oh, Luke," he says. "I've been so goddamned afraid of this. I'm so scared."

"But you didn't say anything? And you left me? How could you?"

"I was a coward. I was seeing it too clearly—too far to the end. I see the whole movie. This is the way I think. I see the entire film. You were sick, and I was unable to fix you. I decided that maybe you have another lover in Paris and that this is how you'd gotten sick. Because I can't understand how else it happened."

"But that's just not true, Gaird. There's no other man. And there are so many ways to get HIV. It could have happened long before I met you." He starts crying again. "They need to check you. You've got to get checked."

"I know. I know. And I was weak. I was very weak. It is what they say in France, bad wine. Would you like to go home and have some lunch with me?"

There's a minute while Gaird's apology settles into the space around Luke and makes its way under the black scarf wrapped around his neck and inside the lining of his raincoat. Gaird left us, and I understand why more now. My own mother left us for a while.

It took an act of God to bring my father back after he left. Life is long.
Luke and Gaird are doing the best they can. We need Gaird now.

Luke says, "Soon I'll be a heap in the bed. In fact, I'm falling
asleep right now, and truly you are a dream. You're a sad, sad dream
of mine. How could you? How could you? Now take me home."

20

Palace of Justice: built on the site of the former
royal palace of Saint Louis; justice of the state has
been dispensed at this site since medieval times

The courtroom sits inside the Palace of Justice, which looks like
a small city within a city—an ornate masterpiece of yellow
stone at the end of a packed street of shops and cafés on Île de la Cité.
The cab drops me off where three sides of the palace open up to a
large courtyard cordoned off by a tall, black iron gate. It's Monday
afternoon in Paris. One week since Luke's diagnosis. I taught at the
academy this morning, and now I'm filled with unexpected grief as I
climb out of the car. Grief for Luke and for Gita. Guilt, too. That I'm
not sick. That I'm free to leave the palace later and go to my apartment
with my new lover, who I cannot get enough of. This is what makes
me feel very guilty.

I enter through a huge wooden door on the side of the palace
and walk down a wide, polished stone hallway where portraits of
French justices hang in gold frames. Courtrooms peel off on either
side, wooden benches outside the rooms begin to fill with families—
mothers, fathers, sisters, brothers, husbands, older children, babies,
and toddlers, who run back and forth through the people and yell.
Everyone's waiting for the lawyers.

When I find Gita's courtroom, I feel so much relief. At least there's
a room now—a place where the hearing will really happen. The walls
inside are painted slate blue. The blue, white, and red French flag

hangs on a metal pole in the corner. A giant clock ticks on the wall above the flag. A court stenographer with dyed auburn hair sits in a chair underneath the judge's platform rifling through her purse. I perch on a bench behind Macon at the lawyers' table. It's finally happening. He looks older. Last night we made love silently, both willing away the fears we have about today.

A police officer walks in with one hand on Gita's shoulder. She's wearing a blue sari and handcuffs. Her face is pointed down to the ground. She looks young and shy, and I want to yell to Macon about the handcuffs. She isn't a criminal. I stand up from the bench, but Macon turns halfway toward me while he waits for Gita, and he catches my eye. I sit back down. I promised to be quiet. I gave him my word.

I look to my right and there's Pradeep, two rows back. What's he doing here? He gives me an enormous smile and I smile back, but my heart sinks. He'll only make Gita more nervous. How did he find us? The judge walks in then, a tall, heavy woman in her forties with a brown pageboy, black pumps peeking under her robe. She has the frame of someone who takes thin for granted and can't account for a recent thickening.

The representative from the United Nations refugee agency is next. He doesn't wear a robe and sits to the right of the judge, up above the stenographer, in a gray pin-striped suit. Macon told me the representative is weak and always votes with the judge. The man from the French government walks in last and sits to the left of the judge; an older man in his sixties, with a beaklike nose, who keeps shuffling files.

How could anyone listen to Gita's story and not be swayed? There's a big French coat of arms or something hung on the wall above the judge. The judge smiles at Gita and asks her kindly to come forward. Good. The judge is nice. Gita stands slowly and looks at Macon and back at me for the first time, and I nod to her. This is when she sees Pradeep. Pradeep waves, but she doesn't wave back or smile at him. She glares at him. I want to get up and say, *Leave, Pradeep. Go back to school. This is not the place for you.*

Gita walks around the lawyers' table until she's below the wooden platform where the judge sits. "Please say your name out loud to the court," the judge says in French.

A translator stands a few feet from Gita's right shoulder—a college-age woman who'll turn all our English sentences into French and the French ones back into English. "Gita Kapoor," Gita says quietly in English.

The judge asks, "Why do you think you should be granted asylum status in the state of France?"

Gita will get exactly five minutes to tell the story we've practiced. Gita nods and looks down at her black sneakers. Her only shoes. I should have bought her better ones, because the sneakers make her look even younger in her sari. I'm afraid she won't dare tell the whole story about Manju because Pradeep is here. She smiles one of her nervous smiles and puts her hand to her neck and finds the Krishna medallion. "I love the country of India. I was born there. My memory is of my pitaa and maa and my brother and sister in our house in Jaipur, eating lamb biriyani. This is a good memory. But my sister, Morone, married Manju, and he had work here in France in the stores he owns. Gem stores. I came to France on a tourist visa and I planned to go back to India when it ran out, but then my pitaa died. We received a letter from his employer at the palace in Jaipur. He died of a disease called malaria, while we were in France."

Things are going well. The judge says, "Gita, please tell us why the French government should grant you asylum in France. Tell us exactly what dangers await you if you return to India."

"Because my pitaa is dead, there is nothing for me in India. I am not safe with my own family there. Manju has harmed me. He has arranged for his brother Daaruk to marry me in Jaipur. Daaruk has already hurt me." She looks down at the tile floor again, deciding whether to say anything more. "Please do not send me to India, where there is no one but a man twenty-three years older than me who my brother-in-law is forcing me to marry. I will be a good French citizen. I have already found a job at the Academy of France. I already know how to speak some French."

Now she needs to explain exactly what Manju did to her in the apartment and how often. We've practiced it many times. But why is she stopping? "Please, Your Honor," she says. "Please believe me." She hasn't even used the full five minutes, but she's done. Maybe it's because Pradeep is there. Or maybe it's because there are so many strangers in the courtroom. But I don't think her testimony has made anyone cry or want to change their life to save her, except maybe me.

The judge says, "Thank you, Gita. Now the lawyers may want to ask you some questions."

Macon stands and smiles warmly at her. Then he says in English, so she can understand him, "It must not have been easy to tell the story you just told. Thank you, Gita. You've known a lot of struggle in your life. You never meant to live in France, did you?" The translator spins his words back into French.

"No. I just came here to visit."

"This man, Manju—he raped you in your apartment in Paris, yes?"

"Yes," Gita whispers and looks ashamed.

"Did his brother Daaruk also rape you before you came to France, Gita?"

"Once," she says with her eyes on the floor. "One time in the shop where he keeps the gems. It was very soon before we came to France to visit. He said it would make me remember him while I was here. He said I was going to be his wife."

"I think you're remarkable for what you've been through. Are you scared by the prospect of living in France in the foster care system?"

"I will be very good. I will do work and help cook."

"I have no further questions, Your Honor. We have here a very talented, bright girl who's been preyed on in India by a man who would marry her against her will if she returns and who's been preyed on here in Paris by that man's brother. The only reasonable thing to do is to grant her asylum by way of the persecution clause. We seek foster care for three years, until the girl is eighteen. Thank you, Your Honor."

The OFPRA lawyer stands up from the table across the aisle from

Macon. He is short and stocky, with the jowly face of a bulldog. He says, "Thank you for your testimony, Gita. Tell us about the tourist visa. When did it run out?"

"I can't remember exactly. I think back in October maybe." She's begun shifting her weight from leg to leg, and I can tell she's getting tired. There must come a point where you just want to sit down and hear the decision.

"So you were living on an expired visa for eight months in France?"

"We had no way to get home. My pitaa died and we had no way to live in India any longer. We couldn't leave Paris."

"I see. Is Daaruk the only person waiting for you in India? Isn't there a grandmother who would take you in?"

She looks surprised by this last question. "I don't know if my grandmother is alive."

"But you think she might be? Because she was alive when you left, and you've only been gone a little under a year. So there's a good chance she's at your old house, where you left her?"

"It's possible," Gita says. "She was very old and sick."

"Anything is possible," Macon calls out in French.

"Quiet from the defense," the judge says, also in French. The practical parts of the hearing are so confusing. Why can't Macon talk more now? Why can't he interject? What are the rules of who goes when and who gets to say what?

"But, Your Honor," Macon argues, "the prosecution is working off a hypothesis. The defendant will not be any safer from the man named Daaruk if she's housed with her eighty-year-old grandmother."

"If I need analysis of the prosecution's argument, I'll ask for it," the judge says quickly. Then she looks at the opposing attorney. "Please continue."

"We seek reunification with the defendant's grandmother in India. OFPRA has a history and a preference for family reunification. The girl won't be safe in Paris on her own. She's only fifteen. I don't think her case warrants foster care. I would like to approach the bench, Your Honor."

"Request granted," the judge says.

The attorney walks over to the judge, and they confer in whispers for several minutes. Then the lawyer goes back to his table and says, "We rest our case."

Gita makes her way back to her chair. Macon leans over to her and smiles, but it's a forced grin. The judge asks Macon to approach. Now he and the judge have their own muffled conversation. When Macon goes back to his seat, he looks furious. The judge says in French, "We have been informed by the prosecution that the defendant's grand-mother is alive in India. She's been located at the defendant's family house. Were you aware of this fact before you came into my court-room today, Gita?"

The translator finishes and Gita's eyes widen with surprise. She stands at the table and speaks so quietly it's hard to hear her, but what I think she says is "No, ma'am."

The judge nods. Then she leans back in her chair and talks in hushed tones with the U.N. rep and French government rep. It's very quick. Next the judge leans forward. "It is deemed by the state of France that Gita Kapoor be voluntarily reunited with her grand-mother in her home country of India, in the city of Jaipur. Transport will be determined under the auspices of OFPRA and the asylum center at Rue de Metz."

Oh, God. Why didn't Macon say more? Why didn't he argue harder with the judge? He sits in his chair, making notes on one of Gita's forms. Then he stands and walks toward the judge with the form in his hand. The OFPRA lawyer rises too, and he and Macon begin arguing in French. I think they're arguing about Gita. Maybe there's still a chance she might win. I hear the word "deportation." It's over. No hope. Macon seems to be trying to secure Gita a bed at Rue de Metz until she's flown back.

The judge stands abruptly and walks out. Then everyone else stands. The representative from the U.N. leaves, and the stenographer and the translator and the government lawyer, until Gita's left at the table with Macon. She turns to me and puts her hand to her mouth as if she can't breathe. "Gita." I try to keep my voice steady. "Look at me." But she won't. I walk toward her. "Look at me." I don't let myself cry. "We will fix this."

The same police officer snaps the handcuffs back on her thin wrists. She starts sobbing while he leads her out. I wait for Macon to explain, but he gathers his papers up and puts them in his saddlebag and jogs to catch up with Gita, who's already out the door. I turn to find Pradeep, but he's vanished. The hall at the Palace of Justice is even more crowded now with families and lawyers and crying babies. And it's gotten hotter in here. Everyone's waiting for their allotted slot to meet the judge and tell their story. Nothing inside our courtroom went the way I thought it would. There was so little time to make a good case. I walk until I reach a wooden door with a metal push bar that opens to the inner square lined with steep flights of cement stairs. People sit on the steps and hug and cry. I lower myself down and put my hands over my face and sob. Where's Macon? No one on these steps seems to have good news. No one is laughing or celebrating the French summer. I've got to call Sara. I've got to talk to Sophie and Rajiv. Macon still doesn't come. It's starting to get dark, and the iron gate around the palace looks more forbidding. Finally, I wipe my face on my sleeve and walk down the steps to the street.

He's already at the apartment when I walk in. "How did you beat me?" I ask. "I waited for you in the courtyard."

"You waited? Oh, you shouldn't have. I'm so damn sorry for the way things went in that courtroom. I didn't tell you the lawyers leave through a back door."

"A back door." My hands are shaking. Gita's been denied. She could be sent to India any day.

"That judge is a hard one," he says. "It went very badly."

I'm so disappointed that I feel short of breath. There's no air in my lungs. My throat feels hot and scraped. In a way, my disappointment makes no sense. I knew Gita had a thin case, but I'd been able to trick myself into thinking that the system would pity her.

"Did the judge read the testimony? Did she read Gita's whole story? We worked so hard on it."

"The testimony is not why Gita didn't get her ruling today. The people at OFPRA made a verification that Gita's grandmother was alive. I didn't know this when the hearing started. But that was all the judge needed to send her back to India. I told you to prepare. The hearing was over before it started."

"I still don't understand. It doesn't make sense. Why is she any safer from Daaruk at her grandmother's?"

"This is the problem with the fucking system. You cannot understand it because it is cold and capricious and you are of the warm-hearted species."

"Gita has to marry her rapist? Because that's what's going to happen in Jaipur." My voice begins to rise. "They're going to fly her back and she's going to land in a random town they happen to have a seat on a plane to. Somehow she'll make it back to her house, where her grandmother may or may not be. Daaruk will be there within a day or so. She's better off dead." I'm screaming now.

"Stop what you're saying. She's not going to die."

"Don't you get it? She'd rather die than live with that man! Why didn't you fight harder for her? Why didn't you explain it more to the judge?"

"*Merde, Merde.* Willie, I am trying to make you understand. You act like this is the only case that was tried all day in the Paris immigration courts. There are hundreds. I've had twelve already this week. This is how it works. The judge looks for some way to comply with the laws, and when they find a living relative in the home country, it's finished. Gita didn't have a good case, can't you understand that? You are not a lawyer."

"But I was her guardian." I start crying again, only this time it's not those quiet sobs I could swallow in the courtyard at the palace.

"That doesn't mean you're a legal expert. Christ, Willie. You have to trust me. Don't you think I tried?"

"Why didn't you talk more about the rape!"

"They never want to hear about rape in court if they can avoid it. They want to talk about illegal entry into the country. You don't see it. Do you know how high the numbers of girls are who have been assaulted and raped? It's too much emotion in the court, so they avoid it. Don't you think I wish it had ended differently?"

"But did you want it for Gita?" I raise my voice again.

"I always work as hard as I can for my clients." His voice is very low, his face like a mask. Only his eyes move.

"You have no idea, really. You have no idea what it's like to be a woman and be raped." I start to cry again.

"Christ, Willie. Am I missing something here? Have you been raped?"

"I'm not saying that. I'm saying you don't know about Gita's fear. It's sick that the court is sending her back. I'm ashamed to be a part of the process. There's nothing fair about it. This is what you do for a living every day? Send people back to the places that almost destroyed them?"

"You need to go to sleep now. You're saying things you don't mean."

"But I do mean them." I sit on the floor by the door to the kitchen, and I let the tears come down.

"Then you're cruel. I don't want to be anywhere near you." He turns and walks past me. "I'm sleeping on the couch."

"Do that. Sleep there." I stand up and walk past him and slam the bedroom door. Then I lie on the bed and fall asleep with my clothes on.

21

Flight risk: someone with a likelihood of fleeing before a sentence can be carried out

I wake up in the middle of the night full of regret for what I've said to Macon. He didn't deserve it. I spend the rest of the night on an inventory of my weaknesses—why I led Gita to believe she might win asylum; how I didn't allow myself to see Luke's HIV so now we're caught on our heels, only waiting for more drugs. Macon's gone when I get up and walk into the kitchen. I don't call Luke to tell him about the disaster at the palace. He doesn't need any of my bad news. Let him sleep. Let him sleep as much as he can.

At eight I go down to the street and find a cab. I can't decide how far the hand of OFPRA reaches into France now that Gita's appeal has been denied. I don't know, for example, if she's technically allowed to leave the center with me today and go to the academy for her job. Maybe Truffaut will consider her a flight risk and refuse to let her. By the time my cab turns left on Rue de Metz and stops in front of the wall of graffiti, I've decided to try it. Maybe Gita and I will get at least one more trip across the city together. And I owe her an explanation.

There's a man waiting at the door in a blue nylon windbreaker. Kirkit. I can't believe how glad I am to see him. "Is that you, Kirkit? Do you remember me from the kitchen the other week? I'm one of Gita's teachers."

"How are you, Ms. Pears?" He smiles. I'm surprised he remembers my name.

"Well, I would be better if Gita had been granted asylum yesterday. I'm sure you've heard the news?"

"I waited here all day yesterday to find out, and I got to speak with her when she returned. It's not fair, what the court has decided. Gita isn't safe in India."

"It's hard news, Kirkit."

"What you don't know," he looks at me, "is that I intended to take care of Gita once she was released. I have an aunt here in the city. She is like a mother to me. I have told her about Gita, and she has made room in her apartment for one more person. Indians need to stick together in France."

"I knew you were friends. It's a very special thing, your friendship. I didn't know you had made plans."

"Yes. We share the same dreams. Do you know what I'm saying?" The buzzer zings, and I smile at Kirkit and say nothing. But I nod. And when I do this, he smiles back at me and holds the door open. Gita is standing inside the hall in her green sari. She gives Kirkit a small fierce look as he walks past her.

Sophie steps out of her office then and puts her hand on Gita's shoulder. "Good morning, Willie," Sophie says. "We have a girl here who is trying not to despair. I tell her that you never know what God has in store. I tell her that you always have to hope."

"Hope," I say. "It's true, Gita. Hope never stops." But I feel that distance again between the sound of my words and what I really want to say. I tell Sophie we'll be back by four-thirty. Then Truffaut buzzes us out from his command central. The locks release and Gita's in my custody again. Yesterday I couldn't touch her in the courtroom, much less get the handcuffs off. Today we walk slowly, freely through the city. We walk down Boulevard de Strasbourg, past Boulevard St. Denis, until it turns into Boulevard de Sébastopol. There's a luggage store called Amigo, with hard suitcases wrapped in clear plastic out on the street. The theater is showing a new Bollywood film.

We pick up the No. 4 line at a stop called Réaumur–Sébastopol.

The glass sign above the stairs is shaped like a scallop shell and spells out MÉTROPOLITAIN. Gita doesn't say anything. I don't want to talk to her about the hearing—it's too big a disappointment to try to put words to, but it sits between us on the train. "Gita," I finally say, "you've become so good at helping in the office at school."

"I saw the job of answering phones as something that would lead to something else." She speaks flatly and stares out the window.

"Maybe it will."

"Where, Willow?" She turns and looks at me fiercely. "Where will it lead in India? Do you think that I'll be offered a job in a school there? In an office? This is not true."

We get off the train at Rue St. Sulpice and walk past the dark shadow of the church to the academy. "Tell me about Jaipur," I say. "Tell me who you know there and where you could live so Daaruk won't find you." We have very little time to get her ready for India.

"I know many families in my neighborhood, and they all understand that Morone and I left with Manju. They know everything about my family and my engagement to Daaruk. They will think it's their job to reunite me with him. They won't know what he did to me. Or they won't believe me or they will think it's part of marriage. I cannot hide in my own city. The people I need to help me are the people who would also bring me to him. But you can help me if you are willing. You can take a risk."

The students come and go on Rue St. Sulpice, pushing the heavy door open and letting it slam behind them. "I'm trying to get you flown to a different city where you know someone. We can get you money. Enough to start a new life away from Daaruk."

"I want you to help me here in Paris, Willie. I am asking you to do this for me. I could walk and you could turn your head and pretend you didn't see me."

I stare at her. "The police will find you in a number of hours."

"I am nothing to them. They won't spend one day searching for me. There are so many Indian girls in the city who look enough like me."

"You need to do your job today for Luelle. Later we can talk about your flight back and about books and things like shoes. You need another pair of shoes."

"I need you to listen." She's gotten bold now.

"I know what you're asking, and I can't do it." My students are all gathered in the room upstairs by now, wondering where I am.

"Oh, Willie, you are so serious. You are so good at rules. Kirkit and I have made a plan for today, if you would just let us do it."

I'm the one who's gotten permission for her at the academy. I'm the one who helped her write her testimony. I don't say anything after that. My feelings are hurt, and I savor it—like I'm the one who's at a disadvantage.

I realize how cruel I'm being before I deliver her to Luelle. "Gita," I say when we're at the door to the main office. "I would do almost anything for you. You have to know that."

My FIRST CLASS is on the Russian poet Anna Akhmatova. We're reading her poem "Requiem," in which she waits outside a Leningrad prison for seventeen months to get one glimpse of her son. The government took Akhmatova's husband from her after they took her son. She risked execution to write about it. The government didn't kill her. But it killed the people she loved.

And somehow she distilled Stalin's reign down to five lines of poetry. I am still in awe of this every time. I ask Virginie to read a stanza out loud.

It isn't me, someone else is suffering. I couldn't.
Not like this. Everything that has happened,
Cover it with a black cloth,
Then let the torches be removed . . .
Night.

"Maybe this is all we really need to know to understand love," I say. "A mother who stood outside that prison every day in the freezing cold winter just to see her child's face."

"I think this poetry is all about death," a tall African-American boy named William says in French. "It's about hope, too." I nod from my seat, hoping he'll continue. "Or at least the human condition."

"In a way, perhaps." I stand and walk around the chairs. "Akhmatova says what is unsaid. She lets go of convention." I let this last sentence sink in. Several students smile. "So perhaps," I look at each face, "she's able to say things in poetry that can't be said any other way." I almost have them. Poetry. Transmitter of the inner life. Then it's twelve-thirty. Class is over.

They stand and wrestle with their notebooks and knapsacks. I go downstairs and wait for Gita. She puts the phone on the receiver and stands and pushes the chair away from her desk. Then she says good-bye to Luelle. Rue St. Sulpice is cramped with cars and Vespas. We move single file on the tight sidewalk and don't speak until we're past the church.

"I have an idea." I can't believe what I'm saying. "I talked to Kirkit this morning, so I know something about your plan."

"He is waiting for me. He is also hoping that you will do this for us. Please, Willow. Please." We keep walking, and I can't come up with any other way that she can be free. At some point Gita says, "There are not any Indian people on the street here, Willow."

"I know that." I'm tense and short with her now. Nervous. "There have never been Indian people on this street. You're only just now notic-ing it." Some internal switch has been flipped. It's the court hearing that's made me furious. It's Akhmatova's devotion. It's the state law-yer's unwillingness to talk about rape because it's too emotional. It's my remorse and my shame for trusting the system. For getting her hopes up. I haven't slept. "I'll go into the market on the corner of Rue de Tournon to get the apples, and you will walk away." Now it's decided.

This has been our routine whenever she's worked at the academy. The apples. The cheese. The bread. The chairs at Luxembourg Gar-dens. Then back to school, where I teach the second class and she transfers calls to the different department offices. We've been constant with the picnics. So no one will suspect us. "You will do this for me? I am beyond words to thank you with. I am crying inside."

All winter she's been asking me to help her. Guardianship for the court. Yes. I could do that. It was easy. Cost me nothing. Now Luke is dying. Who am I to say who gets to run away and who doesn't? We take a right on Rue de Tournon. The metal bins in front of the market on the corner are full of green apples and blood oranges. "There are not any Indian people here, so I will be sticking out. I will seem the odd one," Gita says then.

"We've gotten our lunch here before. It's going to be fine. It's going to be okay." I can't cry. I will myself not to cry. Am I ever going to see her again? I hand her all the money in my wallet, which isn't enough. Maybe a few days' worth of food. I rip a page out of the notebook in my bag and I write my phone number on it and I give that to her, too. "Call me. When you are in trouble, you must call me. Now walk away and keep walking to the metro."

We don't slow down on the sidewalk. I'm so worried now that my legs shake, even though this part where she leaves is really the easy part. And I know this while it's happening—that there will be bigger consequences. I just haven't thought through exactly which consequences will matter. I'm her teacher. What does that really mean?

"Do not stop when I turn and go into the market." How have we gotten here? I pretend that losing her to the street isn't a painful thing. I have to give her courage. Or maybe she's giving me courage. Maybe she's always been the stronger one. That's what I think. That she's the stronger one. "Just keep walking and get to the metro and find Kirkit. He better have more money. If your plan was to stay at his aunt's—well, you need to change it. Do not stay there. They'll come for you. Sophie can't lie, and they'll find out about Kirkit's aunt. Not even one hour at the aunt's. You go back to the metro and you take the train to Dijon and then you're gone. You need to be far from Paris by the time you sleep."

I don't give her time to speak because I'm worried that I'm going to start crying and that she'll be distracted by me. "Pretend you're interested in those red shoes in the store window across the street there."

"But I am not."

"It's just a way for you and me to separate. Don't you see? You go look at the shoes, and I'll go into the market. Don't turn back toward me once you cross the street. It's as if we don't know each other." I want to put my hand on hers so badly. But I don't. She's leaving without papers—completely illegal. I'm mad at the system again. There's the thin thread that's connected me to her until now. A kind of pliant filament. She steps off the curb and waits for a tiny black car to pass. "Good-bye, Gita. Be safe. Be very, very safe, my friend. My dear, dear student." Then she crosses Rue de Tournon and the filament snaps.

I go into the market and pick up a round of Camembert and stare at the ceramic bowls of cured olives. She's a child. Fifteen years old. What am I doing? She's taught me about resolve. The money I've given her won't last. Where will she and Kirkit live? I almost leave the cheese and the apples and the bar of chocolate on the counter by the register and run back to the street to look for her. The old woman tallies up my lunch. How is it that our most pressing moments pass invisible to people around us? Can anyone here in the store tell what I've just done? How is it we can feel so alone?

When I come out to the street after I've paid for the food, she's gone. I skip my afternoon class. I go back to my apartment and call Luelle and tell her I'm sick. Then I call Sophie on the phone, which is cowardly. I should go to the center and talk to her in person, but I don't because I can't imagine lying to her face. She answers the phone in her office. I say, "Sophie, it's Willie. Gita and I have been to the academy." I can see the rugs hanging on her wall. And her hair up in one of her scarves. The radio is playing Ethiopian clarinets on low, and she's probably sipping from her mug of vanilla tea.

"Of course you have, my friend. I just saw you four hours ago. You should be back soon."

"But that's why I am calling, Sophie. I wouldn't call if there wasn't a problem, but something's come up."

"Dear God, what's happened to you two? Was there an accident? Is Gita all right?"

"She's gone, Sophie. Gita is gone." There. I let it sit in the air between us. I have no idea what happens next, but at least I've said it.

"Gone? What do you mean, 'gone'? She can't be gone. It is a big city out there, Willie. Now tell me where she is."

"But I don't know the answer to that, Sophie." She can hear the lie in my voice. "I came out of the market near school where I often buy our lunch, and she wasn't standing by the door where I'd left her. I don't know where she's gone. I can't believe this." It's hard to muster fake outrage. I need to lie down on the floor. I've never told lies like this to anyone.

"You don't know?" Sophie makes the "tsk" sound with her voice. "Oh dear Lord above." This in a high-pitched singing voice. "I need to hang up now, Willie. You should wait by the phone for me to call you back. I need to call OFPRA, and they will start looking for Gita everywhere."

22

Custody: immediate charge or control
exercised by a person or authority

I make a carrot soup next because we happen to have two beat-up
bunches of carrots left over from Saturday's market. Also
heavy cream and one onion. Macon comes home at seven. "Hello, my
friend," he says and kisses me on the lips in the kitchen. I'm so happy
he's back that I start weeping.

"I was horrible last night, and I'm so sorry. I let everything get
away from me. I have no excuse."

"You do have an excuse. A couple of excuses, in fact, and they're
very good ones. But God, you can cut me with your words. You say
them like you mean them. Then I question my whole reason for
being—why I'm in the law at all. Why I run the legal center."

"I'm an idiot. I know nothing about French law. I talk too much,
too. You did everything you could in the courtroom."

"I wanted to win that case for her very badly." He kisses me again,
this time on my neck.

"I know you did." I lean into him, and we stand with our arms
around each other.

"Now let's eat," he says. "And you can tell me how Gita was today."

I bring the soup to the table with a warm baguette. I can only
swallow a few spoonfuls. What should I tell him that won't be a lie? I
talk about Luke instead. I worry out loud about AZT and whether it

will work. I say how very glad I am that Gaird's come back. We need Gaird. I don't mention Gita. Every minute that passes without me telling him that she's gone deepens the lie that's in the room with us.

He finishes the soup and stands up and reaches for my hand. "I am going to take you to the bathtub." It's easier to follow him than to tell the truth. He removes all my clothes on the bed. Then he kisses my breasts and I reach for his jeans and unbutton them. He picks me up, and I put my legs around his waist and hold on to his neck. We make love standing in the bedroom. I say his name over and over, which I've never done before, and I kiss him harder, rougher than I ever have. I don't want it to end. I don't want to believe that I've ruined everything there is between us.

He turns the water on in the bathtub afterward. I get in first. He climbs in behind me, and we lie in the dark. I imagine telling him the truth. I say the sentences in my mind. But if I tell him, then he'll make me call Sophie and confess. Then the police will question me, and I'll ruin things for Gita. So I say nothing.

We get into bed, and I hold his hand until he falls asleep. Then I stare at the place where the ceiling meets the wall and wait. I'm with Macon and also far away from him and what I can't understand is how it happened this way—that Gita's gone. Gone. Gone. Gone. And Macon will never love me again. The call comes at ten-thirty. I run and grab the phone in the kitchen. Then I pull the cord until I'm under the dining table and lie down there. Sophie sounds frantic. It's a voice I haven't heard before, wavering and breathy. "So when was the last time you saw Gita, exactly? She is really missing, Willie. The girl is missing, and we have a problem now."

"I know that, Sophie. That's why I called you. I went into the market on Rue de Tournon, like I always do to get our lunch. When I came out, she'd disappeared." Everything I say into the phone is a little bit of the truth. I almost convince myself that I'm telling the whole truth by parceling out these half-truths. But I don't think Sophie's really listening. She's onto me.

"So she disappeared at lunch."

"Before lunch. While I was getting lunch. She walked away."

"Lord help you if you have aided that child in her escape. You will take all of us down with you! She was in your custody. I put her in your care. She is fifteen years old, Willie!" Sophie's screaming now.

"She came to school with me, Sophie, like she always does on Tuesdays. Then we walked toward Luxembourg for lunch. On the way I went into the store and bought apples and cheese. I told her to wait outside under the awning, away from the hot sun. It was the last time I saw her."

"You did not call anyone? You did not report this right away? You are responsible for her! They can shut us down over something like this! These are hard times in France, Willie. People are looking for any reason they can find to make all of our girls go home. She was scheduled for deportation. It is the law! What in the good Lord's name have you done?"

"I called you as soon as I got home. I've never used the pay phones here." This is weak. Very weak. I had enough franc coins. I close my eyes and bite my lip.

"The police will be here in the morning and I will be here and you will be here and, dear God, let's hope Gita will be here."

I stand up and put the phone back on the wall in the kitchen. Then I lie down on the edge of the rug again so that my head's partly under the dining table. I bite my nails to the fingers, something I haven't done since I was ten and my father covered each of my fingertips in Band-Aids and told me I couldn't take them off. I'm there for maybe six hours. When Macon finds me, the light outside is just starting to turn. He sits on the rug by my head and scoops some of my hair up in his hands. "What are you doing down here? What's wrong?"

"I only did what she asked me to do."

"Who asked you to do what?"

"I haven't hurt anyone. She has a plan with Kirkit, the cook from the center. I think they were meeting at an apartment near Orly. I tried not to know too much. Then they were taking the train to Dijon and farther south."

"Oh, Jesus. What girl?"

"Gita."

I watch the shock move its way across his face. First his kind eyes grow hard and narrow. Then his mouth sets in a thin line. I've gone over it all night under the table—how Gita chose me, but how I also chose her. She and I understand each other. We fit. This doesn't happen very often in a life. I've deceived him. And "deceit" is another word for lying. So I've lied. "You didn't," he says.

"I did." I stare at him so he'll believe me.

"I don't want to hear a word." He lands on the syllables one at a time. His French accent makes them sound even more dramatic. "You are com-pli-cit. You have bro-ken the law." His words speed up and he begins to yell: "Because she was in your custody! The more I know, the more the police will implicate me!" He stands. "Willie, they could re-voke my li-cense to prac-tice law if they find out that I live here with you and they think we col-luded!"

"But you wanted to free her just like I did."

"By following the law, Willie!" Now he's furious. I've never heard his voice like this. "She ne-ver had a good case! *Merde!*" It's the first time I've seen his face contort. "You don't listen! I never said it would work! I never said that just because her family was a danger to her that she would be allowed to stay in France! She's a minor! She's fifteen. What are you thinking in that head of yours? We've landed so few asylums into foster care! You weren't supposed to go outside the system!" He keeps leaning toward me and then stepping back and pulling his hand compulsively through his hair. "Just because you taught her doesn't mean this was going to have a happy ending! The system is much bigger than that!"

"I just thought . . ." I say. What had I thought? I'm being honest. It seemed like the good thing to do. But I needed to have bigger thinking. I needed to be able to look ahead and I couldn't, and it's my failing. Gita is too young to know what the right thing to do was. "I thought she needed help. I thought I understood her."

"She wanted to leave the asylum center!" He's raving mad now. He won't stop yelling. It's like all his exhaustion—all his frustration at his job and at the legal system—is coming out at me. "But if she leaves, don't you see that it makes it harder for all the other girls to stay!"

"I owed it to her. I felt like I set her up for asylum and it wasn't coming."

"You don't get to please the people you want to please." His voice gets quiet. He's almost whispering, but it's more like hissing. "You don't get an award for running a workshop, or for understanding the girl. It goes with the job, Willie. Even when you're in the right. Even when you're doing work that is on the side of good. There is nothing that says you can break the law for one girl." Then he's loud again and getting louder: "Every girl is special, Willie. In this country, you just have to do the work and trust the mechanisms!"

"Now you're the one lying. Because all this time you've been talking about your challenges to the court and your challenges to the damn system, but when the moment comes you give in." I don't know him anymore. He's just a man I met in the hall of an asylum center five months ago—a lawyer who's sticking to the law in the most predictable ways. I'm too tired.

I sit up and put my face close to his. "You don't understand this because you're a man." I don't believe my words as soon as I say them, but they're my only line of defense left. It's still dark in the apartment, but the sky has gone from black to gray to the palest pink, and cars are starting to move on the street. "I could help her, and so I did. She asked me. She was like a daughter to me."

"She was your student, Willie! She was never your daughter!" His yelling has a bitterness. Has he been waiting to hurl these things at me? "There is a code of ethics. This is my profession, for God's sake! This is what I've staked everything on, and we're not in high school here, picking favorites and taking them on field trips!"

"I kept you out of it on purpose. Nothing bad will happen to you." Look at how worried he is about himself. "I think Gita has a shot at a better life in France and that I'll get to see her. Not anytime soon, but maybe in a year or more she'll surface."

Quiet again. He's almost subdued. He seems tired and resigned when he walks toward the bedroom. I'm waiting for it to be over. It's been worse in some ways than I'd thought it would be. But then, I hadn't really thought. He will have to forgive me. I don't know when. But slowly I will convince him to love me again. Right now I fight.

"You are out of your mind." He stops and throws his arms into the air once. "I wish I'd learned this much earlier about you. You create these fantasies. None of this is ever going to happen. All you can hope is that she doesn't end up dead. You didn't give her money, did you?" He's getting worked up again. His voice rises. "Tell me you didn't? That's a worse offense. They'll get you for it if you gave her money!"

I pretend I haven't heard his question. "So you don't get to stay here unless you have a war on your side? Or famine or religious persecution? She has a sister in France and a sweet-faced brother and a mother. She has nothing in Jaipur except an arranged marriage. Maybe she'll make contact with her family here again—not right away but soon enough. Maybe she and her mother and Pradeep can find a way to live together in France."

"You have been secretly planning this!" Macon yells.

"Not really. That is the weirdest part of this. I only decided at the last minute." I have no empathy for him, and it's such an unsettling sensation. To be that removed from him. All my feeling has transferred to Gita.

"We can save more girls if we follow the law, Willie. This is what you don't understand. It's my job!" He keeps yelling from the bedroom. "To follow the law! It does not mean I agree with the law or admire the law. But at least the court lets the girls speak. The girls see that there is a system. They see that their lives are not dictated by fate. This can be empowering. Just to know there are laws!"

"Try," I yell back, "telling that to Gita. Please, Macon. What part of Gita's hearing do you think was empowering for her?"

"They decided to have her fly safely back to her grandmother! Now she is a homeless teenager on the run in France! Jesus Christ! If the state censures me, then the other kids I represent in court will have no one, don't you see? One breach like yours and our little, wobbly system topples." He grabs his things and puts them in his backpack. It takes him only about four minutes to gather what he needs, which is about the amount of time I've always thought it would take him to leave me.

23

Leave-taking: a decamping, departure, or exit

I get dressed slowly after that. I'm not stalling; it's that my body's coursing with dread. This is Paris in the summer—windows open to the street and brown sparrows busy in the tops of the green elm trees. The wind blows the curtains out into the room and retracts them, so the pale linen presses flat against the glass. The apartment building across the street looks like a smaller ocean tanker. There are yellow awnings on the windows of the highest floor, and the front is like a rounded bow that wraps the street corner. Every morning I've woken up here this architecture has pleased me deep in my bones. Every morning until now it's inspired me.

I put on my jeans and a black T-shirt and pull my cowboy boots on by the door. Gita's out there somewhere in France with a boy she's known for only a few months from the kitchen at the asylum center. I take the elevator and flag a taxi outside the front door. It's still early—just after six-thirty. The flower markets that block the narrow streets along Boulevard St. Germain have been going for hours, and so has the fish market near Pont St. Michel. Maybe Gita got scared and came back to her bed on Rue de Metz last night. Maybe she's lying there now and we can forget this ever happened?

The taxi driver smokes a filterless cigarette that reeks. He says he's from Lebanon and talks to me in speed French about the abuses of Mitterrand. How the French president doesn't create enough new jobs for immigrants. How he himself sends money home to his wife and children in Beirut, but it's not enough. So why is he here? he asks. Away from the children he loves?

I feel too far apart from my brother. In the two days since I last talked to him, everything's changed. I've got to call him. There's no traffic on the streets, and the cab is outside the front door to the asylum center in ten minutes. Truffaut buzzes me in and motions me to his office with a flick of his finger. The room feels just like what it is: an almost empty old principal's office with a metal desk. The green poster of the metro system seems like a cruel joke to me now. How many of the girls in here ever get to ride the metro?

"You will stay," Truffaut says in his strong French accent. "We are waiting for the officials from OFPRA and the police and Sophie." He brings folding metal chairs from a closet next to his desk.

The OFPRA men arrive first, dressed in black jeans. The policemen are municipal, and come in full blue uniform. One has a shaved head and a brown goatee; the other has a crew cut like Truffaut's. Sophie's last, in a long, black caftan, which only adds to her gravity. Everyone speaks French. Truffaut is able to smoke two cigarettes in a row, mashing them in an ashtray in the shape of a soccer ball on his desk. The policemen write down what I say about Gita's face (round) and her hair (black) and her sari (green) and her sneakers (black). "We will all be looking for her," the one with the shaved head says. "Looking for a short, big-eyed Indian girl in a green sari."

Good luck, I want to say. Good luck with that. Everything heightens inside Truffaut's office. Everything is distilled. Gita knew how to name her affections. She thought she was being loyal to her sister by not saying anything about Manju. Loyal to her mother. To her brother. And to some complicated idea she had of what family is. She was fierce in her love for Pradeep. I saw it that day in here—how much she needed him to go to school. I want to stand and walk all the way to Luke's apartment. This is something else Gita taught me: how important it is to name our intentions.

"When did you last see her?"

"Outside the market on the corner of Rue de Tournon and Rue St. Sulpice."

"Did she tell you she was planning to escape?"

"No." This is a full and complete lie. I don't look at Sophie while I say it. She sits very close, staring at my face while I talk, willing me to break and tell her the truth. Instead I see the starlings at the gas station in Aix-en-Provence in my mind—how the flock of birds pulled a black blanket across the sky. I can't concentrate on what the police are saying. Macon gave me kisses on my face in the truck. Kisses on my neck. Where is he today?

"Did she tell you her final destination?" one of the policemen asks.

"No." I'm so glad I don't know this, because I'll never have to divulge it.

"Do you have any idea how much money she has on her?" the crew cut asks. "Plane tickets?"

"I have no idea of these things."

"Do you have her writings?"

"Some."

"Do you have any papers from your class that might indicate what her plans were? Did she reach out to family members about her intentions?"

"Not to my knowledge." The letter Gita wrote in class for her grandmother. What's in that letter? It must be in a file somewhere in my apartment. Maybe there's other stuff that will implicate me. Maybe they'll search and find a poem Gita wrote in class or a metro ticket stub, which will be enough to let them press charges. I want to get out of here and run home to search.

The police discuss the idea of surprising Gita at Kirkit's aunt's apartment somewhere near Orly. There's excitement in the room and the scraping of chairs and more cigarette smoke. Sophie gives them the address, and everyone leaves to go find Gita. Then Sophie and I wait in her office the rest of the day. Long hours pass. I sit on the stool and read *Le Monde* and try to make myself invisible while Sophie comes and goes and runs the center and pretends I don't exist. She seems to want me there so that she can ignore me.

Kirkit's supposed to report to his kitchen job at three, but he never shows. I'm not under arrest exactly, but the police won't let me go home and Sophie won't even look at me. Gita isn't at Kirkit's aunt's when the police get there. I try not to celebrate too loudly in my head. I'm afraid Sophie can read my mind and knows how I'm deceiving her. At five o'clock, when it's clear that there's no cook coming to make dinner, she says, "Willie, what did you and Gita think I was going to feed the girls tonight?" There's none of her softness.

I hadn't thought about dinner. I forgot there would be no cook. It's an embarrassment—the girls need food. "You are not working here anymore," Sophie says then. "Lord knows you did good here, but now you have done very bad. Go home, Willie, and wait for the police, because they will be coming for you."

I have to call Sara from Sophie's office so I wait for Sophie to go out into the hall. Then I reach for the phone. "You home? Can I come over?" It's six o'clock. Almost twelve hours since I got to the center. I can't cry. Don't cry. Don't you dare cry.

"I'm ordering Chinese takeout. Rajiv's away on a trip. What would you like, sweetness?"

"I'm not hungry." Sophie walks back in and scowls at me. I whisper, "There's been a problem here at the center."

"What's happened, Willie? Are the girls all right?"

"We'll talk more when I get there." But I don't go to Sara's. First I flag a cab out on Boulevard de Strasbourg and take it all the way home. Then I run up the stairs and unlock my door and fling it open and race into the bedroom. There's a stack of files on the wooden bench next to the bureau—files of the girls' poems. Drafts of testimonials. Writing prompts. Where's Gita's letter? I remember wanting to put it somewhere so I wouldn't forget it if I ever actually made it to India. Where did I stash it? Come on, Willie. Where?

I keep a brown leather case in the top drawer of my bureau under my lingerie. This is where I hide my passport. And this is where I find Gita's letters, the one to Moona and the one to her grandmother, written in a language I can't decipher. I have no idea what they say. But I've found them. That's what matters.

Then I run back out the open door to my apartment and down to the street and I find another taxi. Sara and Rajiv live in the fifteenth, on a wide residential street called Rue Lecourbe. They have the first floor of a three-story redbrick town house. I let myself in with a key I keep in my wallet. Sara sits on an overstuffed couch in the living room with her feet up on a camel cart. She's got on her batik bathrobe, which is tied in front of the beach ball that is her baby. I lean down, and she kisses both of my cheeks. The scene looks so incredibly hopeful. I almost can't believe it. "I'm not getting up," she says. "Don't ask me to get up. I'll never get back down."

I lie next to her on the couch and curl up my knees. "I've ruined everything. It's something stupid. Something that Rajiv is going to be very angry with me for. So angry for."

"Oh, boy. Tell me. Tell me what you've done." She puts her hand on my right thigh.

"I let one of the girls at the asylum center escape. Gita's gone."

"You have not." I look at her once. Her face has gotten red.

"No, I have, Sara, and she's gone and we may never see her again. People are very angry with me."

"People have every right to be mad at you, because what were you thinking? How is that girl going to last a night on the streets?"

I close my eyes. "You would have done it too, Sara. A boy from the kitchen at the center is helping her."

"But do you know anything about this boy and where his family is and how he's going to keep Gita safe? How old is this boy, anyway?"

In the sunlight, these questions had easy answers. But at night it seems much more unlikely that any of these things will work out the way Gita wants. "Nineteen. I think he's nineteen, and he must be responsible. He's a cook. He comes to work every day. I met him and liked him."

"So we have a fifteen-year-old girl on the loose with a nineteen-year-old and no one has any money or anywhere to live that we're aware of and you feel comfortable that everything's going to work out."

"Please don't be mean very much longer. I helped her go. She wanted to go. How much longer are you going to be mad at me?" I want to keep Gita's letters here at her apartment. I'll slip them into one of the books on the shelves above the couch.

"What does Macon say?"

"Macon took everything he owned in my apartment and walked. He thinks if anyone in his office finds out that he's been living with me, he'll lose his job." The starlings fly over the truck in Aix-en-Provence again. An orchestra of dark birds. The sound of so many flapping wings. We sit in the truck and we kiss. I'm completely over the top. I want to go back to Aix-en-Provence.

"Macon will come home."

"He's really incredibly furious at me."

"You love him."

"How do you know?"

"He'll be back."

"I'm supposed to go to India in a month, Sara. How can I do that? Gita is missing. Luke has a falling T cell count. Macon won't speak to me. Maybe I'll be arrested by then. I'd been trying to talk Macon into going with me. Now he'll never go. Now he won't even talk to me."

"India. I forgot India. Wow."

"Macon thinks I'm a liar." I've lost him. I let him walk out. I could have tried to stop him. What's wrong with me? I crave him. I crave looking at his face.

"I just don't get where you thought it would help the girl to let her loose in this city."

"They weren't staying in Paris. I knew the boy she left with—the cook at the center, Kirkit—I knew he had an aunt with an apartment outside the city."

"But doesn't everyone know that if you do?"

"I'm just telling you they had a plan to meet at that apartment to get some things together."

"Okay then." Sara looks away and raises her eyebrows like she's done with it. Like she can't believe me. "What time are you taking

Luke in tomorrow?" She's been following every step of Luke's treatment with Dr. Picard. The AZT injections start in the morning. Some doctors think the drug is almost as good as a cure.

"Nine."

"Why you and not Gaird?"

"Gaird has a huge day on the set, and Luke's okay with it. They talked, and they both want me to take him."

Sara nods. "The AZT will be good, but it's highly, highly toxic. I'm worried about whether he can tolerate it. He's so damn thin. If it goes well at the hospital, they should let you bring home a small supply. Then you or Gaird or I can do the injections at the apartment."

A dark-skinned boy delivers the Chinese food. When I ask, he says he's from Tibet and that he's eighteen, but he looks twelve. Just about Pradeep's age. I give him a wad of extra franc notes and he nods his head and leaves.

Sara opens the chow mein noodles on the camel cart. "Eat!" She waves her chopsticks at me.

"I'm not hungry. You haven't met Kirkit, Sara. He's a good boy. He'll take care of her."

Their apartment is full of black-and-white photos Rajiv has taken all over the world. Africa. India. Indonesia. Afghanistan. Some of the pictures are of Sara during the years they lived in London and worked at different refugee camps. My friend is tall and strong in every photo. I watch her eat and I try to siphon off a little of her strength. There's no one who understands me better in the world except Luke.

"But there's something I have to ask you, Sara." She looks at me over the big bite of noodles she's just wrestled from the carton. "Small favor. Gita wrote a letter. I don't know what it says. To her grandmother in India, who we now think is alive. I have a feeling this letter might say good-bye. It might explain that Gita was planning an escape."

"Where is it?" Sara talks with her mouth full. "The letter."

"Well, that's the thing. I have it with me. Two letters, actually. The other is to Gita's friend." I reach for the envelopes in my bag on the floor. "If I could just keep them here? Because I didn't ask her to write the letters. But it will look bad if this letter to her grandmother says what I think it says. And no one is really going to come looking for Gita. I mean the French police have much better things to do with their time."

"Give them to me." Sara puts her arm out. "Hand them over." I pass them to her. She reaches up to the wooden shelf above her right shoulder and takes down *A Bend in the River,* in hardcover, by Naipaul. She slides the envelopes inside the middle pages. Then she tries to stand up. "There. Done. We don't need to say another word about it. The baby and I are really tired." She puts her hand on her belly. Her anger has dissolved. It always does eventually, if I just wait long enough. I want to hug her for how much I love her. For how honest she always is. For how much she seems to love me. All of me. "We need to sleep. You need to go home and sleep, too. There's a lot more to talk about in the morning."

"But I can't. I didn't sleep at all last night."

"You have to try. You have to go home and lie down and try." She gets up from the couch slowly, very slowly, by leaning back and pushing up with her legs first. Then she takes my hand and I pull her to standing. "Your heart was in the right place, Willow Pears. But not your head. Go home and wait for that French man to come back to you. Then apologize. Get down on your knees and tell him you're sorry." I can't reach my arms around her belly so I hug her shoulders and press my face into her neck. A short, fierce hug. God I love her.

I walk out on Rue Lecourbe and flag another taxi and we drive east in the dark. I get back to Rue de la Clef and climb the three flights of stairs to my apartment and lie in my bed and miss Macon in a way that's bottomless and real. I've taken him for granted and I'm alone now. He's gone. I've taken him for granted. Why do I do this? I'm alone now in the apartment and there's nothing good about it. It's just lonely. I can't believe this is how we live sometimes. How I live. Waiting for the person I love to call me. To show some sign. And he doesn't. He won't. I breached something too big. His profession. His life calling.

24

Prayer: a spiritual communion with God or an object of worship, as in supplication, thanksgiving, adoration, or confession

*I*n the morning I have to stop at the long red light on Boulevard Haussmann. I adjust the rearview mirror. How does Luke see anything out of this tiny car? "Is your breathing okay today? Is there pain?"

"I'm good. Except for my throat. My throat hurts when I swallow."

"Okay. Your throat. That's odd. We can ask them to take a look." We idle and idle and then we're off again. First gear, second, and third. The stick shift feels miniature, almost pretend.

"Andreas called last night and gave me the numbers from some recent Norwegian AZT trial. Good numbers. He's doing all this research for me. The disease is a mind game. A horrid little private conversation I have every day with myself. I look forward to going to the hospital now. Isn't that sick? The trips consolidate. Organize all this fucking free-floating fear. Isn't that pathetic? That I like going to the hospital?"

"No. Not pathetic. Smart. Self-preservation. And I like going to the hospital with you. I get it. We learn things. We feel better at the hospital. At least I do."

"We're supposed to get answers there. So all week long I look forward to getting the answers."

"And medicine. We're going to get new medicine."

"I get lulled into thinking we're truly doing something every time we drive to St. Louis. It's like my life is sitting on the head of a fucking pin. I've waited all week for this drive. All week to see Dr. Picard. Do you see how pathetic my life has become?"

"Stop." I'm speeding along next to the canal and I glance quickly over at him. He has his eyes closed.

"God I don't want to talk about this anymore. So sorry I've droned on and on. I'm done now." He opens his eyes and sits up. "How's your student? How's Gita now that the hearing got so messed up?"

"She's gone." I turn onto Boulevard Magenta. I'm beginning to know my way to the hospital.

"Gone? Back to India gone?"

"No, I've done something stupid."

"What? What have you done?" He turns so he's fully facing me while I drive, and I can't avoid his eyes.

"Stop staring at me like that. I told you she was asking for my help." We wait in front of the Canal St. Martin while a band of little children in raincoats are led across the street. The lilacs are gone. They were my favorite. But the irises and clematises are out. So much more serious and stately than the lilacs.

"Where is Gita now, Willie?" He won't stop looking at me.

"She's missing." I look again in the rearview.

"Oh, man."

"It's a problem. I helped her walk away, and there have been problems."

"You know, I'm actually worried about you. This is too much."

"I made a mistake."

"Well, that's for sure." He lets out a long whistle.

"I think she's too young. She's with this boy who worked in the kitchen at the center. I should have tried to learn more about him. I never thought Gita would actually walk away. But then she did. I can't tell you how natural it felt. I was tired. Wasn't thinking. Was worried about you."

"Me? Don't pull me into this."

"Macon's moved out. Sophie, the woman who runs the center, never wants to see me again."

Luke bangs the back of his head lightly on the headrest over and over. I say, "They were going to send her back to a man in India who's already raped her. Do you know how many forced, arranged marriages there are in India between girls and men old enough to be their grandfathers?"

"But that's not your job, Willie. We can't have volunteer teachers escorting refugee students to the metro. The whole country will collapse."

"Oh, please." I pull into the hospital parking lot. "Not that. A bunch of detainees from the asylum center on Rue de Metz isn't going to disrupt the French political system." We climb out of the car and move through the revolving doors into the lobby. I don't know the nurse's name today. I think she's African. She speaks English with a slow lilt through her face mask. It's another one of the baby blue masks with the thin white elastic band over her ears and around the back of her head. I'm trying not to see the masks as some personal affront to Luke. I know very little about HIV, but everything I've read says you don't get the virus from breathing near someone who's got it. You don't get it from the air. Which means it isn't airborne. It seems vascular. Of the blood, is what Sara has tried to explain to me. So why on earth the face masks? The gloves I understand much more, and this nurse wears those too. Bright purple ones again.

She walks us back to the old wing. *The AIDS wing* is what I'm calling it in my mind now. "AZT today, yes? You might start feeling very sick a few hours after injection or you might not. You may be in bed for a day or a week. Some people throw up. Others just feel like throwing up and can't. Some people feel fine."

This time the room is a bad mustard color, and there's a spider plant hanging in the window inside a macramé planter. "I hope I'm one of the fine ones." Luke takes his shirt off and lies down on the table. There are more sores on his chest. They look so painful and remind me that the disease is working away on him—cracking the code of his immune system.

The nurse gives him a big shot of something she calls Bactrim, to stave off any more lung infections, and a smaller needle for anti-fungals, and a medium needle for the AZT. The French newspapers referred to it as a miracle drug this week. I don't want to get too excited. But AZT is the first thing I've read about that has a chance to help him. They're working hard on the vaccine in France and in the States. What Luke needs to do is stay healthy until they find it. That's all he needs to focus on: waiting for the vaccine.

Dr. Picard walks in and studies Luke's face. "You look pretty good, Luke. How are you feeling?" he asks in English.

Good? I think he looks like a shadow of himself. I think he looks horribly thin and that his face has become skeletal. I allow myself to think these terrible thoughts only in the safety of the hospital.

"I feel okay," Luke says.

"The breathing?" Picard asks.

"The breathing is steady."

"You're not too tired?"

"I need to lie down more. But I'm still cooking. I'm still getting around."

"Let's watch for the bad side effects of the AZT. We just have to wait and see."

"I'm prepared for that."

"This drug reduces the replication of the virus and can lead to immunologic improvements. I call it a DNA chain terminator. It gets immediately absorbed into the cells and runs interference with cell replication. Are you continuing to feel okay since we last met?"

"I feel the same. I'm tired and thirsty and I always have diarrhea and my throat hurts now. But otherwise good."

"Your throat hurts?" Dr. Picard takes the flashlight out of his pocket and shines it into Luke's mouth. "Probably candidiasis. Yeast. You call it thrush. It's nothing unless it's in the esophagus. Then it's defining for HIV. I want to stop it before it infects your bronchi, or your trachea or lungs. We'll take a swab today. Then I want you to go home and rest. I'll see you in a week." He taps his hand twice on the examining table.

Go home and rest? I want to beseech him. I want to say, *Help us, please. Look at us a little more closely.*

"Au revoir," Picard says to us by the door. *"Au revoir, mes amis."* Good-bye, my friends.

The carpet in the lobby of the old wing of the hospital is green and hard like turf, and Luke trips on the way out and falls. Then he cries. "I just like it here," he says when I kneel and try to pick him up. "I just want to stay alive a little longer."

"Of course. Of course you do." I pull him to standing. "Of course you want to stay." And I don't cry even though I want to stand there and sob with him. Or scream. I'd like to scream in this old, forgotten part of the hospital where they've stashed us and see what would happen. It's so quiet. I want to scream and see if someone would notice us.

On the drive home there's the slow letdown. Like I've been up too late on a boozy night and now there's the incipient hangover. Fighting this disease is starting to feel like an accumulation of trips to the doctor where nothing much happens. There's so much buildup. Yes, we got the AZT started, but what does that mean really? Everything is so much starker outside the hospital safe zone.

I space out and ram into a green Citroën at the intersection of Boulevard Haussmann and a street called Boulevard Malesherbes. I think I crack the other car's back fender and I scream. Luke puts his hands over his face, while an angry French woman in a tight black skirt suit raps on our car window. "Do I have to talk to her? Don't make me. You do it," I say.

"You have to open your door." Luke talks with his eyes closed. "Please make her go away."

I climb out and follow the woman to her car, which is double-parked in front of ours, hazards blinking, and I pretend to examine her fender. I nod and say in French, "Yes. I am so sorry. I'll pay for everything." I just want this over with. I'm tired. I've been driving impaired. The woman and I stand on the side of busy Boulevard

Haussmann while cars fly by, and wait for the police. After twenty minutes I climb back into the car. Luke's fallen asleep. When will the immigration officers find Gita? When will they come looking for me again? I want to get my brother home. The police finally come, and after they've taken my information and driven away, I climb back in and put my head on the steering wheel. Luke places his hand on the back of my leather jacket and tries to pat my back. His seat's almost fully reclined to take the pressure off his sitting bones.

"Is it impossible for you to drive?" I can't believe I ask him this.

"I have to pee is the thing," he says, his voice rising. He's wrapped the black scarf twice around his neck, even though it's mid-June, and this heightens his gauntness. "So drive on, *mon amie*! To the nearest leafy patch by the side of the road! Drive on!"

"You always have to pee!" I scream. I'm so grateful that he hasn't fallen apart. "What's wrong with you, anyway?"

"I know. I know. I may have a condition."

I pull out into the traffic, and we crawl home. I get Luke into the apartment and give him some orange juice from the supply I keep in his fridge. Then I call Gaird at the movie studio. "He fell," I say when Gaird answers. "Luke fell down."

"I will come home. I'm leaving now."

I run water in the tub in Luke's bathroom and climb in and wait for a headache that's coming. This feels new—like we've entered a different phase. Luke fell in the hospital. He never falls. I want to call Macon and tell him about the AZT. I want to say how sorry I am, and could he please come home now. I blew it and Gita's gone and everything's not what I thought it would be. Macon will say he isn't sure which is worse: that I knew what I was doing or that I was foolish enough not to think about what I was doing.

I can't call him. He wouldn't talk to me, anyway. And Delphine wouldn't let me through. I lie in the tub and look down at my breasts and my stomach and the V of lighter hair between my legs. My disconnect to my own body seems immense. My boyishness has given way to rounded hips. I think of Sara's pregnant belly. Tumescent. The word sounds like the roundness it describes. I can't imagine a pregnancy. Can't get my mind to hold the idea of it. And yet I want it too. The thickening. The life growing inside. I can hear jangling keys. Then the apartment door opens. Gaird yells, "Hallo?"

I sit up in the tub and pry at the rubber plug with my big toe. Thank God he's come home. And that there's someone else here with us. Thank God for Gaird and his world order.

THE POLICE ARE outside my apartment when I get back—same two from the center but not in uniform. They wear brown sports coats and flash badges at me. "We will need to search your rooms," the bald one says in French. Somehow this destabilizes my knees and I can't walk naturally. I'm not afraid of jail. I'll get out eventually. But I don't want to implicate Sophie or the asylum center. We climb up the stairs and into the apartment and my legs feel gelatinous. They pull open the silverware drawer and reach around in the cupboards. They take down the dried cherries. The salted almonds. The flour. Olive oil. Dark baking chocolate. Vanilla.

I boil water and make a cup of lemon tea and pretend I'm calm and that this is customary. But really, what the hell are they doing here? It seems sort of ridiculous. She's one girl. Who may or may not have been aided and abetted. They have time to send two men to my apartment? The kitchen feels so much smaller with all of us in it. Cramped. It's a room Macon and I have made meals in. Kissed in. It's the room I may have known him best. Where is he? Where is he? I know where he is. He can't be anywhere else but the house in Chantilly. "Would you like tea?" I ask. "Or coffee? I could make coffee very quickly."

They both decline with a wave of their hands and move on to my bedroom. I stand in the doorway and watch them pull out my top drawer and dump everything in it onto the bed—slips and bras and lace underwear and T-shirts. It was a one-time thing, I want to tell them. I broke the law by helping a girl. I won't do it again. Please. Could you just go now. What they don't know is that I've taken all the girls' writings from the class on Rue de Metz and stashed them at

Luke's, and Gita's letters are safe with Sara. There isn't anything left in my apartment that ties me to the girls.

But is Gita getting food? Does she have a place to sleep? I can't get her face out of my mind. I can see her sharp jawline and the soft shape of her mouth. I can make out a blurry smile but not her eyes. I can't see her eyes and they would tell me so much about her if I could. Maybe they'll put me in the city jail. That would be fair. City jail. I've probably compromised the center's funding. Probably made it so much harder for any girl to ever get out of there. An hour creeps by. The police rake through the bathroom drawers. Scan the piles of books in the living room. Then, without a word, they walk to the door and say, "*Merci*" and leave.

I never thought they would take it this far. I sit down on the floor in my bedroom and close my eyes. I think Gita's gotten away. Far away. I'm not crying. There's relief mixing in with my guilt. They've got nothing to go on. Gita's going to be okay. I haven't tried to pray in maybe twenty years, but I can see the face of Krishna on Gita's medallion. I sort of invoke him in my bedroom. It's not a real conversation—not the kind Moona or Gita would have with him. It's a self-conscious thing that I do in Gita's honor. But I say his name out loud, and it feels good. I say, *Thank you for letting her walk away,* and I don't say anything else after that.

It gets dark outside. All the windows are open in the apartment, so I can hear the rain on the street and the pattering on the roofs of cars. I pour a glass of wine in the kitchen and call Luke. "How do you feel? Are you throwing up? Are you nauseous?"

"It's all good. Gaird's here and he made chicken soup and I'm really tired but okay."

"That's fantastic. You're tolerating it. Hooray." I'm smiling at the phone. "I'm not going to French jail, by the way."

"Were you ever really?"

"The police were here. They actually took the time to come to my apartment."

"Don't they have better things to do?"

"They looked through my stuff, and I mean closely through my bras and my deodorant, and they didn't find anything. I think Gita's going to make it now. I think they're done with her."

"You have to hope that she's street-smart. She needs to choose the right people. It's all about the right people."

"I know." I don't say again how guilty I feel. I've set her up to be preyed upon, and why didn't I see all the dangers before I let her go?

"I have to go to bed now."

"Good night, Luke. Hanging up now."

"Hanging up."

25

Vaccine: any preparation used to confer immunity against a specific disease

Classes end at the academy. Another week passes. Then it's July. The delicious month. The heat is on full. I meet Sara at our spot below the Pont Neuf. She likes to walk in the early morning now, before the city gets too hot. The linden trees create a canopy of leaves, so we can walk in and out of their shade by the river. There's no breeze. The water is still and silky. "Luke's so much better," I say. "Your drug is working now. He isn't in pain. He's going to work every day, and he's eating. His numbers are way up."

"Picard is very pleased," Sara says. "I talked to him yesterday. There are patients like Luke who get second lives." She's like a small truck—front-heavy and moving slowly. So she's waddling really, and completely beautiful. The baby's due in two weeks. "Thank God Luke is one of them. Not all of them see their T cell count climb back into normal like his has. I'm calling this his summer reprieve."

"It's a miracle drug, Sara. It's unbelievable. He's gained weight. He's actually put pounds on."

"But AZT isn't a cure, remember. It just slows cell replication down."

"We're biding our time until the vaccine."

"The vaccine isn't anything to count on either, Willie. The vaccine is still far off. We've got to keep looking for other ideas. Other treatments."

"They've got to be close. Aren't doctors working around the clock in labs all over the world?"

"They're making progress. Dr. Picard will be one of the first to know. When is your ticket for Delhi?"

"In two weeks. Crazy, huh? I can't go. How can I go to India right now?"

"Go to India and do the book research."

"I can't leave Luke."

"He's got Gaird. He's got me. He's got Picard. He's healthier than you or I am, for God's sake, right now. His T cells are up around eight hundred. Willie, if you don't go, I will be so pissed off at you. You need to go for your book and your career and your sanity. For all of our sanities. You need to get out of Paris. Please. Please do this for me. You can't just hang around waiting for Macon to call you."

"If I go, I'll never see Macon again. What if he finally calls, and I'm out of the country? Then everything we had will be over."

"It will just be on pause. That's how I'm thinking of it—as a pause."

"A very long pause. I'm trying to give him up."

"Well, you can't do that until you talk to him. You've got to call him."

"He won't listen."

"How do you know unless you make the phone call and get him on the line and say your piece? Say what's in your heart? Maybe he's got pride. Maybe he's just waiting for you."

"Maybe he's beyond forgiveness."

"Go to India then and lose yourself in that."

"Will you be Luke's person if I go? Will you call him and call Gaird and visit?"

"Of course I will."

We walk for an hour. There are dark mallards on the river with black-oiled heads. Mallards in Paris? Theirs must be a long migration. I put Sara in a cab back up on the bridge and kiss her cheeks through the open window, both sides twice. "I love you." I'm so glad I remembered to actually say it. Maybe that's all there is in the end—the speaking of the love.

Her pregnancy and how big she is make her even more lovable. Vulnerable. Wise and powerful all at once. It raises things up—makes me want to hug her and tell her what an amazing mother she'll be. I tap the top of the cab as it pulls away. Then I start walking home.

What's Sophie doing at the center right now? Even if she never forgives me—even if I never see her again, I miss her. I cross over the bridge to the Right Bank and walk until I get to the shops around Les Halles and the enormous metro station. Then I take Boulevard de Sébastopol for another half hour to Rue de Metz. I stand across the street from the asylum center, inside the Syrian sandwich shop. There are two metal spits that spin meat by the door. I hope Esther's getting ready for her hearing. It would be great if she could practice speaking really loudly. Precy will be fine in the courtroom. But you can hardly hear Esther unless she speaks up. Zeena and Rateeka will need translators who are willing to show real emotion in front of the judge. What am I doing here? Is this my life? Underneath it all every day is this longing to hear Macon's voice. To have him move the bangs out of my eyes.

I walk across the alley to ring the buzzer and ask Sophie for forgiveness. All I have to do is tell her how sorry I am and say what's in my heart. I stand in front of the door and will something to happen—someone to come in or out. Someone to see me on the surveillance camera. Then I get scared. I feel foolish. What if Sophie won't even let me in? I turn around and I don't stop walking until I'm home. All that time I'm missing Macon. Angry at Macon. He left me. How could he just walk? But when I pick at it a little and stare it down, I know I'm really angry at my mother. Angry and so sad that she's gone and I'm here, making all these bad choices.

IN THE MORNING I make piles on the floor in my bedroom for India. I'm taking Sara's advice. Getting ready for my trip. It feels more satisfying than I thought—T-shirts and two pairs of wide cotton pants, plus a long, dark cotton skirt. It's Pablo's birthday today. I know this because weeks ago Macon drew a heart around July 2 on the calendar and wrote the words "Pablo's Day" in the small white square.

Rajiv calls at ten-thirty. Sara's in labor. They're on their way to a birthing center near the Bois de Boulogne. "Oh my God!" I yell into the phone on my bed. "She's early! She's early! How much is she dilated? Oh my God."

"We won't know until we're there," Rajiv says calmly. How can he be this contained? Where is his urgency?

"I'm not leaving the apartment until you call me back and say that you have a baby!"

"Of course. Of course we will call you." He's eerily calm. Then I realize maybe he's play-acting for Sara—that she's probably sitting next to him in the cab with her eyes closed. Maybe terrified. Except Sara doesn't really get terrified.

I hang up the phone. She's having a baby. I call Luke and he doesn't answer. I'm frantic but it's a good frantic. Euphoric even. A baby. I blast the *Graceland* album on the turntable and pack and repack the small pile of clothes in the backpack Macon surprised me with in May. Then I take on the books. Make preliminary piles of the ones I want to bring to India. Too many books. This will call for a whole other backpack. The music's so loud and I keep dancing in circles next to the couch and jumping. I add books to the pile and jump up and down and check the clock by the bed.

Then I can't stand it anymore, and I pick up the phone in the bedroom and call the legal center. He's not there. I don't leave a message.

People say love takes time. But I also think it can be something decisive at the start. A man walks into an asylum center. He has wet hair and wears dark green hiking boots. You don't know that you're going to end up sleeping on a beach with him. You just know you're open to it. What do you call this? Not love. But something foundational maybe, before love. It all looks better, sweeter now that the baby's coming. I feel reckless. Why haven't I called him until now?

What am I waiting for? It's not going to get better by waiting. I need to tell him how much he's meant to me. No matter what happens, I need to say it.

Another hour passes. No word from Rajiv. I call Macon at his house. Sara's having her baby. How can he not know? He's part of my family, even if I never see him again. Someone picks up on the second ring and I ask for Macon in French. "Willie?" Macon says. "It's me."

"Sara's in labor, Macon!" I talk loudly and fast. "She's having the baby! The baby's coming! Can you believe it?" I don't know if he'll even listen to me.

"That's great news," he says slowly and quietly. Then his voice brightens. "Well, over here we've eaten the cake and the ice cream and had the pony ride in the yard behind the house."

"You're talking to me." I try to make my voice sound loose. But my heart is in his hands. I don't want to sound hopeful. "I didn't know you were talking to me." I don't want my love to spill over and overwhelm him.

He ignores what I've said. "It's Pablo's birthday, and you must have known that. We've spent the week here in Chantilly with Delphine and Gabriel."

My heart's beating in my throat. "Happy birthday to Pablo." I almost cry but don't allow myself to because I'm afraid I'll throw Macon off. Please let me in, I want to say. Don't keep me out.

"My boy is five."

"He is a sweet boy. Tell him I said that." What I want to say is, When are you coming back? Are you ever coming back? "I screwed it up. I miss you, Macon. Can you forgive this? Can you let it go?"

"Merde," he says. "I didn't want to talk about this. I didn't want to talk to you. I still think what you did was stupid. But I won't waste my time on that right now. Because today is a good day."

"I'm so sorry." I say it again, and the words aren't enough. This is the thing about words. They fail. But you still have to use them. "I'm sorry that I lied. That I ruined things at work for you." I'm trying to tamp down my joy about the baby. Trying not to scare him.

"You did a good job of that. We've had so many damn meetings since you let your student fly away. How is your brother? I have been very concerned."

"He's steady. He's having what Sara calls a summer reprieve."

"More good news. That is tremendous. When will you know about Sara's baby?"

"As soon as Rajiv calls me back."

"Then you should probably get off the phone in case Rajiv's trying to reach you."

"You're trying to rid yourself of me?" I pretend to joke. But I feel sick. It's such a thin line connecting me to him.

"Call me. When the baby's born. Please call me."

"I will. I will do that," I say. I can't tell yet. I can't tell if he's really softening to me. But he hasn't hung up. He hasn't yelled.

"Good. I'll be waiting."

Then I pace my apartment. I reorganize all the books and notes for India. Maybe I'll hardly bring any books. Just notepaper and copies of Sarojini's papers, and some Tolstoy to read on the long train rides when I'm alone. I go into the kitchen and do a full assessment of the fridge. We have lots of tomatoes. We have onions. We have cheese. I make lasagna and place the glass dish in the oven. How many babies born two weeks early have complications? How long does the average labor last? Is she in extraordinary pain? For how long? How long?

The phone rings. I run from the dining table to the bedroom and do a full leap onto the bed to grab it. "Rajiv? Is it you?"

"Baby girl and mother are both doing very well."

"A girl! You have a girl!" I scream.

"She's a funny little girl. She didn't even cry at first." He's still so calm.

"Oh God, I'm so happy for you guys! You're a father, Rajiv."

"She studied us as if she'd been expecting to see us. Then she let out a battle cry that told us how hungry she was. Her name is Lily Rouse Amarnath."

"Two weeks early! How is Sara? Is she really okay?"

"Sara's sleeping, and so is the baby right now. Maybe I should try to sleep. We're going to be back in the apartment tonight."

"Tonight? So soon?"

"It's hallucinatory, I tell you. I've never done drugs, but I feel like I'm on something. We're going home because Sara's never wanted to sleep here. She wants us all to sleep in our own home."

I hang up and call Luke and scream when he answers. "Sara's had the baby! The baby's here! She's here!" Then he screams and I'm still screaming and I start to cry. Really cry. Because I'm happy. Finally some good news.

"Don't cry. You're supposed to be glad. You'll make me get weepy and I hate the mess of it."

"Tears of joy." I sniffle into the phone. "And I know you're crying too. It's a girl. Lily Amarnath."

"I love that name. When do we get to meet her?"

"Tonight. I'm going over to their place to hold the baby. I get to hold the baby! Come! You should come!"

"I'll try. I really want to. But that means I'd need to pull myself together. Kiss her for me if I don't make it. Give that baby a kiss for me."

I GET TO Rue Lecourbe at seven and knock on their door. It's as if time's stopped in their living room. Sara sits on the couch holding the baby, and I watch how she surrenders to the girl. Then she hands her to me. God, don't let me drop her. "Well, she's beautiful," I say. "She has black hair that sticks straight up from her head. Whose hair is that, Lily? Let's hope it's your mama's. I think you're perfect and that your parents should camp out in here with you and never go outside again."

"She's not kicking." Sara laughs. "That means she likes you."

I stare at Lily's tiny lips. Rajiv pokes his head in the living room and announces he's going for takeout. He waves at me. It's the most we've talked since I let Gita walk away. Sara told me he was so angry for a while that he couldn't speak to me.

"Mango chutney, please! Extra mango chutney!" Sara yells. "Money in my bag." Then Rajiv's gone in his sweatpants, and I walk the baby in circles in the dark kitchen.

"She's stronger than you think, Willie. When she latches onto my boob it's like she's never letting go."

"Watch your feet," I say and lower myself down next to Sara on the couch. "I don't want to hurt them." Then we both sit and stare at the baby's face. "She is you," I laugh. "Those are your eyes, Sara."

"You can't tell yet. For one, her eyes are always closed, and two, they change every few weeks, I think."

"It's the shape of the lids and underneath the eyes that's like you."

Rajiv comes home with the food, wet from the rain but smiling. He has an easiness about him that I haven't seen before, not in college in California, certainly not at his own formal, Indian wedding in London. "It's the baby, guys. It's Lily," I say while he unpacks the bags. "She's the first thing I've ever seen calm you both down. It's so peaceful here."

He gets out the bowls and forks and smiles, and I whisper things to the baby about how wonderful her parents are and how lucky she is to have them. No one talks about Gita or how mad Rajiv was when Sara told him what I'd done, and this is how I know I've been forgiven.

"You are going to Delhi! Delhi!" Sara says. "A great city! Curl up in some hotel and rest, Willie. Baby Lily and I both think you need to rest."

"I'm going to be on the move, Sara. No nice hotels. It's an austerity program. A research trip. It's all about how long my money can last."

"Well, don't expect for one second to see India as an Indian. I've been trying for ten years to do that. I see Rajiv's mother almost every day, and every day she makes it clear that I'm from away and they're from here—their French version of India."

The baby falls asleep in a basket on the dining table while we eat. Just the eating of the meal in their apartment feels sacred because there's a baby with us. A baby with a round, bald Buddha head. Before I leave, I walk over to the bookshelf by the couch and take down that

Naipaul novel. Then I quickly pull Gita's letters out and put them in my bag. No one says a word.

I don't get home until after ten. The phone rings once I'm in bed. Macon says, "You didn't phone back. Please tell me that the baby was born healthy? I've been worried."

I can't believe he's called me. It sounds like him again, not someone guarded and angry. "I didn't want to bother you all on Pablo's birthday. Lily Rouse Amarnath. She is perfect in every way." I smile into the phone. If he were here I would throw my arms around him.

"Well, that's a very impressive name."

"And a beautiful one." There's a long silence now. I don't know what else to say. I could gush. I could tell him how much I love him and then he might hang up.

"Would you meet me at the train station tomorrow if I came in?"

"I would do that." I remain restrained. But I allow myself another small, relieved smile. "You know I would do that."

I GET TO the Gare du Nord the next night at seven-thirty, five minutes before the commuter train from Chantilly arrives. Will he be on it? I hold my breath. He's been gone long enough for me to forget the exact shape of his face. Then he's moving down the platform with his beat-up backpack. He comes to me, and I put my arms around his neck. Then his hands reach for my waist and we stand together like that without saying anything.

When we get in the cab he says, "What I don't understand is why you planned it without telling anyone."

"But I didn't plan it. I'm not asking you to understand." I move closer to him on the seat. "I was trying to please her. I wanted to make her happy. It's my genetic predisposition. I'm not making excuses. But it's hard for me not to give people the things they say they want."

"I missed you. I missed holding you and listening to you, but that doesn't mean I forgive you. Are you wearing a dress?" He stares and takes me in. "I've never seen you in a dress."

He pays the driver at Rue de la Clef, and we climb out onto the sidewalk. I got the dress last year at a flea market in Neuilly with Luke—sleeveless and vintage and pink. Macon smiles. "Promise me you will wear this dress every time I have to leave you." I do a small twirl for him inside the elevator. "If you wear this dress every time I have to go away from you, I will undress you slowly with my eyes whenever I see you in it. Then I will take you home and ask you to stand very still so that I can unzip this silver zipper."

He pulls on the zipper inside my front door until the dress opens. Then he slides his hand down my back and slips each shoulder strap off and tugs at my hips until the dress is on the floor.

"I'll wear it," I whisper. "Will you always come back?"

He kisses me slowly on my face, and finally at the end, as if in answer, on my mouth. I take his hand and walk him to the bedroom. He steps out of his jeans and takes off his T-shirt and we lie down on the bed holding hands. "You're back."

"Tell me where it feels good," he whispers. Then he licks along the edge of my underwear.

"In words?" I don't want to say a single thing.

"In words, Willie. I'm going to keep this underwear on you." He kisses the inside of my thigh. "Until you tell me what you like." I keep my eyes closed. The underpants feel wet from where he's touched. "If you can't tell me, I'll stop." He sits up.

"But don't stop." I open my eyes. "I think that would be a very bad idea."

He brushes the inside of my thigh with his face. "So you like the kissing?" He looks up.

"I like it."

"I thought you did." He focuses on the small strip of silk between my legs.

"That's what I want." I smile.

"What do you want?"

"For you to do that."

"To do what, exactly?"

I blush. He keeps running his fingers over my underpants. "I want

you to take these off," I whisper. "I want you to take these off me."
And he does. I've never been able to say it out loud like this before. I've
never wanted to name these things, but he makes speaking them feel
right and natural.

A WEEK PASSES. Macon brings a few clothes over in his backpack.
I begin to trust that he's really staying. My piles for India grow taller.
Gaird takes Luke to Provence for a vacation. Luke calls me on Saturday and says, "We're staying in some stunning château where they
keep filling my champagne flute whenever it gets below the halfway
line." They mean to stay until Thursday.

"Do you love it there?" I'm in the kitchen watching Macon play
guitar on the couch. I've been waiting for him to say that he'll come
to Delhi. He's arranged for the days off at work. He's convinced Delphine. But he hasn't made peace with leaving Pablo.

My flight is on Wednesday night. The Air India ticket sits on
the counter under the phone like an ultimatum. Departure Date:
July 12, 11:00 p.m. What if something happens to Luke while I'm
gone? What if he comes back from Provence and falls down on the
sidewalk or something?

"There are lots of trees here," he says. "The willows look like they
have dreadlocks. Your namesake trees. I love trees, Willie. Have I ever
told you how much I love trees?"

Maybe he really is drunk. "It's so good you went," I say. "You
needed this." I can't hear any cough or shortness of breath. The virus
is going to be more complicated than we think. I know this. And it
will try new ways to reinvent itself. But right now he's in Provence.
This is more than any of us could have hoped for.

"You'll be all right while I'm gone, Luke? You'll do the injections
and take the medications and you'll eat? Promise me you'll eat."

"Gaird's become worse than you at forcing delicious food on me.
Truly I will be good. Go find the missing poetry. Go meet the crazy
daughter. I'll talk to you when you're in India."

"Have you called Dad, Luke? Have you told him anything?"

"Dad and I talk about the circumference of the pipes for the new Shaanxi project. We don't talk about my health."

"I'll be looking for phones in India. I'll be thinking about you. And if you're not feeling good, then I'll come home. It's only a seven-hour flight."

"Seven hours to India. Seven hours to a different world. I'm hanging up now. There's more champagne here."

"Hanging up now. I love you." I put the phone down and stretch my back.

"How is Provence?" Macon asks.

"He's drinking champagne."

"Then there is no excuse, is there?" He leans the guitar on the couch. "For you not to get on that plane." He walks into the kitchen and puts his arms around my waist and kisses me. Then he picks up my ticket on the counter and stares at it. "I don't have any excuse. Pablo says India has elephants. As long as we take pictures of elephants for him, he sanctions the trip."

"You're serious?" I don't believe him.

"I'm afraid I'm often much too serious."

"You're coming?" I take his face in my hands.

"I can't miss this."

"You're coming."

"I've got to get on the phone with the airlines. Delphine will be glad to have me out of the way."

"What about the hearings? What about the kids?"

"That is why I have colleagues." Macon smiles.

"You're coming!" I kiss him on the mouth and put my arms around his neck and squeeze him. "Thank you for this! You're going to love it. I'm scared to leave Luke, but I think this is going to be good. This is going to be okay."

"I hope you thank me when I get us lost in some Indian village. I'm not the best with directions."

"There are maps for that. I am very good at reading maps."

26

Aeroflot: a Russian airline

On the cheap Aeroflot flight we get an apple and a baked potato and a block of white cheese for dinner. No one stays in their seats after takeoff. Women in saris walk the aisle and share samosas and chapatis from plastic bags. Many men stand and smoke. Russians with Russians and Indians with Indians and plumes of cigarette smoke fill the cabin. The fire alarm goes off again and again and no one seems to care. We're in row 28, across from the bathrooms. I will the plane not to crash. I visualize the pilot in my mind and what he's had for breakfast and how he said good-bye to his daughters. Then I wish him good luck and ask him not to let us crash. I can't abandon Luke in that way. He's the one fighting for his life. I can't crash.

Before we left I made a list of the names of the towns we'll be in and the hotels we'll stay at. I gave a copy to Luke and one to Gaird and one to Sara. But there are going to be days out of reach on trains and buses. We'll be in villages without phone lines. How will anyone find me if something goes wrong?

I've written three letters to Dharmsala this month to an address I hope is Sarojini's daughter's house. She never replies. Then I made two phone calls there and an older woman answered and said she'd been expecting me. Her name was Padmaja, and she screamed into the phone: "Maybe I will let you see the manuscripts and maybe not! I won't know until I meet you!"

So we're on our way to meet Padmaja. I doze and wake up and read *War and Peace*. Then I make sure to wish the pilot more good luck. I will him not to fall asleep now. Not to get even a little bit tired. Not him. Not his copilot. Macon snores lightly for what seems like the whole flight. I can never really sleep on planes. Too much worrying to do. Too much piloting. We land in Delhi at dawn and haul our backpacks off the crowded luggage carousel. Then we walk outside the teeming terminal into a blast of sticky heat. The taxis are ancient— boxy yellow Ambassadors from the '50s. Everywhere I look men in white tunics push staggering stacks of luggage on metal carts.

"Do you feed them?" I ask the cabdriver after we slide inside his car.

"Who, madame?" He looks in his rearview mirror at me.

"The cows."

"Goodness no, madame. We are getting tired of the cows. We are wanting them to go away, but no one says so. They hurt business. But still we cannot get them into trucks and drive them. They have to go away on their own."

"No one gives them food? Someone must feed them."

"Tourists feed the cows. In the old city, madame. Yes, a shopkeeper, a Hindu, for example, will leave his garbage out from time to time for the cows when he closes. The cows are our mothers. The cows get fed, madame, this we know."

Macon smiles at me and goes back to gazing out his window. It's sweltering in the cab. He's got sweat on his upper lip and looks rumpled and exhausted. For the second time the driver gets out and claps at a stubborn cow, who hoists himself up. There's the idea of the book I want to write, yes, but this city with its cows and heat is so much wilder than I imagined. Why did we come, really? How did we get here?

The fields give way to cement shacks and one-room homes linked by corrugated roofs. We drive farther into the center. Women in saris walk in the ditches with iron pots on their heads. I've been in France too long. I should have come to India sooner.

We get a room on the second floor of a tiny hotel jammed in the middle of a block in the old city. Crowds of people shop the store-fronts and eat food from stalls set up next to the road. The walls inside the hotel room are pale violet. There's a wooden bed and a matching bench. A decrepit, peeling bathroom is attached with a hole in the floor for squatting. The tin can of water next to the hole is called the *lota*.

"I know this." I point to the can. "I researched this."

"You researched the can in the bathroom next to the toilet hole?" Macon smiles.

"It's the custom. It's meant for washing the wiping hand."

"What else did you research?" He takes me by the waist and pulls me down onto the bed and wraps his arms around me. We sleep the deep, drooling sleep of people who've been on an airplane for a long time.

Three hours later, a thin boy bangs on the door with his metal bucket. There's no lock. He walks in and flushes the toilet hole with cold water from his bucket and washes the stone floor on his knees. I can hear the cows and motorcycle rickshaws outside. It's not Paris. But what country are we in? India is only an idea in my hot sleep—a foreign land so far away from where I grew up in California that it seemed to be make-believe.

Then Luke's sickness catches up with me, the way it must with him every morning, and I'm wide awake. Gita's high-pitched laugh comes to me next. She told me I had to go to Jaipur. She was so direct. In this way she was unlike any student I've ever known. This is why I'm delivering her letter to her grandmother. It's the least I can do. The heat in Delhi is wet and everything in the hotel room feels damp because of the monsoons—the sheets, my clothes, my skin, and my sweaty hair.

The boy leaves us, and Macon rolls over in bed, mumbles, and goes back to sleep. I walk to the window. Groups of men smoke cigarettes and spit red juice through their teeth onto the street. Someone's hung green awnings over sections of the food market, and pieces have ripped away and hang down like wallpaper. I go lie on top of Macon's back and press my face into the side of his neck. "Wake up, my traveler." He speaks in his sleep in a language I don't understand. Estonian?

I walk into the bathroom. There's my round forehead in the mirror glued to the wall. Sometimes I've thought it would be easier if I got sick with Luke. Is this normal or some kind of pathology? Do other people feel like this, too? The creases in my face are deeper after heavy sleep. There's the dark mole on my chin. There's the turn at the end of my nose, like Luke's nose. Like my father's nose. I know that holding on to some of my anger at my dad also connects me to him in a strange way. A current between us—and it keeps my mother alive to me.

Macon's dressed when I come out. I pull on the black pants—wide and loose and made from some synthetic I don't know the name of. We take the narrow stairs down through the cramped lobby, where the TV plays for no one and two white cups of tea sit unfinished on a card table. There's a large color poster of the elephant god Ganesh above the television and a poster of Krishna on the opposite wall. Lots of black flies circle the tea.

We have one day in Delhi. We start out of the hotel on a road called Chandni Chowk, and pass more incense stalls than I've ever seen, and just as many shops selling saris. A small group of teenage girls pass us on the sidewalk, laughing. They remind me of Gita and Moona, or who Gita and Moona might have been if they'd stayed in India, born into different families. The distance between France and India feels huge. Insurmountable. The girls at the center have lived through long plane rides and train rides and buses and cars. They've journeyed so far to get to that place called France, where they were locked up.

A man wants to read my palm. Another wants to sell Macon a paper bag of lapis lazuli. "Come with me," he says. "I'll show you gems and electronics. I'll change money. Change dollars. Come."

Another boy wants to make a cobra rise up from a round basket he carries in his hands. "No," Macon says politely and smiles. "No thank you."

We walk faster, until we're away from the crowds and pass a garage where a car engine's spread out on the dirt like a banquet. Three lepers sit nearby in front of a wooden door. They have stumps where there should be hands, and they call to us and lean forward on the ground. An older boy in torn shorts pulls two small kids in a metal cart. The boy is three or four or ten years old; it's impossible to tell. He parks the cart on the sidewalk in front of Macon.

One of the children pulls on my elbow. Neither of them has legs. "Please. Madame. Please." The heat's concussive. The kids look tired and dirty and hungry. I press two rupees into each of their hands and put coins in the metal bowls in front of the lepers.

"Willie," Macon says, "I'm not sure it's the right thing to give them money."

"These children are hot. I want to give them something so they can eat." I don't know if I'm right. I don't care. I think of Precy, living in her room on Rue de Metz, and her fierce questions. Is she still there?

"Why," Precy asked me that first day of class, "are you helping us? What's in this for you?" I hadn't answered her honestly. Was I trying to prove something to Rajiv? That I could do it? That I could step outside my world of books and teach the girls? Gita told me I didn't know how to take a risk. What if I've made the girls' lives there worse by what I did? What if I've almost shut the center down?

"Do you see that food stand?" Macon points to a corner near the garage. "I'm hungry." We walk toward it and a teenage boy sells us bottles of orange Fanta with straws. It's the only thing he has to drink. We get potato samosas on cardboard plates and devour them—they're so good. Then we walk.

When we get back to the hotel, it's late in the afternoon and the sun has dipped behind filmy, striated clouds. The block outside is filled with men and women who hold big posters of the elephant god on wooden sticks. "All for the festival of Ganesh," the hotel owner says, and waves at us from his plastic chair in front of the blaring television. A half-eaten plate of chicken with some kind of brown sauce on it sits next to the TV.

We go up to our room to nap so we can stay awake for the festival. Macon turns the shower on. I take off my pants and T-shirt and lie on the bed in my underwear, listening to the water. Then he lies down next to me without drying off. The water on his legs feels so good against my legs. We fall asleep and miss the whole festival. At some point during the night, I move down to the floor to sleep, but I don't remember doing it.

"Where are you, Willie?" Macon says before there's a trace of light outside the window.

He climbs down to the floor next to me. "It's hot in this country. And I think India is a crueler place than I imagined," I say. The wooden ceiling fan whirs above us. "God, I'd love to go swimming now."

"Are there lakes in Delhi? We need to find a lake."

"When I was six, Dad taught us how to swim underwater in a lake near Mount Shasta. Luke got it right away and held his breath and glided back and forth around my ankles. I stood up to my waist, scared. In the car on the way, we'd sung this song, 'Shoo, Fly, Don't Bother Me,' over and over."

Macon says, "I'm starting to sweat down here. I think it's cooler up on the bed."

" 'Shoo, fly, don't bother me, / Shoo, fly, don't bother me, / Shoo, fly, don't bother me, / For I belong to somebody.' I don't know why we picked that song, really. Maybe we missed our mom. I know I did." Is it the jet lag? I can't stop talking. "I'm not sure where Mom was. Dad finally got me to put my whole face in the water and hold my breath, but I didn't like to get my hair wet. I wanted to get out. Then Luke shot up from the water and sang, 'Shoo, fly, don't bother me, / For I belong to somebody! I feel, I feel, I feel like a morning star!' It was our favorite line of the song and the whole reason we sang it. I held my nose and followed Luke down into the water. His eyes were big and surprised underwater. I'm sure mine were like that, too." I start crying on the floor in the hotel room. I don't know why.

"Willie, why are you crying? We're here. We're in India. You're going to get to do the research. You need to sleep more. We're both really tired. We're going to figure things out for Luke."

"You really believe that? Or are you doing what I do—saying things you think will make me feel better?"

"I think better treatments are coming." Then he kisses my hair and my neck. Maybe he's right. Better treatments. A vaccine even. It's all coming.

We make love on the hotel floor after that and sleep some more. But his black watch begins beeping at four, and we sit up and throw our stuff in our backpacks. The Delhi train station is stifling hot and moves to some great, unseen order. Men rush back and forth, yelling and pushing more towers of bags. There are lots of goats. Cows mill outside the open doors. The crowds and the din make it hard to think. A long time ago someone painted the steel girders on the ceiling the color of limes. I stare up and feel farther away from home than I ever have and this time it's a good thing. It's almost narcotic even to be in motion at the station. To be leaving one Indian city and going across the Rajasthani desert to another.

There are so many trains to choose from. Halfway down one of the platforms, Macon shows our tickets to a man in a uniform who points to the second car, where two porters haul a cardboard box up the stairs. We climb on behind them and find the twelfth compartment. It is five-thirty in the morning. Two Indian men in black pants and blazers sit in the opposite middle seats dozing. Nearer to the door are men on either side in saffron-colored turbans. The train is called the Shatabdi Express. It will carry us as far as Jaipur. Macon and I are by the window. I stand and try to open one of the metal casings, but they don't budge. He gets out a novel set in India called *Heat and Dusk* and starts to read. There's a loud, violent hissing when the train's brakes release. Then one big jolt. A pause. And we're off, in the pouring rain.

We gain speed and pass hundreds of small shacks, which must be the homes of the people who stand in the dirt lanes, getting wet. Gita took a train from Jaipur—she and her mother and sister and brother, following Manju to the airport. Or was it a bus? Or someone's borrowed car? The sprawl of Delhi slowly gives way to fields filled with pieces of metal plows and stacks of cement blocks, and a few half-built foundations. I never had any idea of the scale of this country. How big it feels. How wide and hot and long.

We ride for eight hours across the sand dunes, which look wind-beaten into hard clay for long stretches. Some of the land has been irrigated and farmed, with occasional clusters of desert trees, but mostly it's sand in large swales and scuds like hills. The train stops in Jodhpur. The rocking motion ends and I miss it. Because when the train's moving it seems to absolve me of important things—of any real decision-making whatsoever. I just give in to the lull of it, the rocking and the whooshing of air outside the window that sometimes turns into a high-pitched, very thin whistle. No one in our compartment gets off. There are mangoes for sale, and pineapple slices on wooden sticks, and sweetened rice balls in wax bags. Passengers slip rupee notes through the windows and reach for the food.

Then we start up again, passing smaller villages and rows of scrappy trees and endless fields of dry melon beds. I sink down low in my seat until I can see only the tops of the trees. I'm not exactly asleep, but I'm close. It's trancelike—India passes by, a series of sun-drenched Polaroids. It's as if the train erases our cares in the waking world. My stomach feels full, but I haven't felt like eating much today. Maybe it's the heat. I've missed my period, but I'm not concerned. My periods have always been a mystery to me. Never regular. They come and go with months in between. I close my eyes, and it's three in the afternoon when I wake up.

The train station at Jaipur is smaller and hotter than the one in Delhi, but the crowds seem just as large. The men wear colored turbans—pink and purple and pale green. "How is it," I ask Macon while we stand on the platform in the moving sea of people, "that the men in this part of the country get to wear something so beautiful on their heads? Luke would love it here."

He takes my arm. "Luke would wear a turban very well." Six-thirty at night now. Only a few hours before darkness. We need to find Gita's grandmother. The trick to tracking down her house will be locating a street called Swam Singa Road. How we will do this is unclear. We have a map, but no house number.

I want to try to finish this part of the story. I told Gita I would deliver her letter. At first Macon was suspicious of going. He thought it was a breach for him to go. But I've convinced him that no one will care and that Gita deserves to have the letter delivered.

In the cab outside the station I say, "Swam Singa Road," to the driver, trying to get each syllable right.

"Swam Singa!" he repeats. He's a tall man in a purple turban with a thick beard.

"Yes, Swam Singa! Do you know it?"

"I do not know it," he says happily and keeps driving.

"Where are we going then?" Macon asks under his breath.

"I think it's on the outside of the city," I say. "Near the edge."

The driver doesn't act like he's heard me. He speeds through two red lights and squeals up to an identical yellow cab at an intersection, where he leans across the passenger seat. Then he and the other driver yell back and forth through the open windows. Then our driver puts the car in first gear and guns it. He looks in his rearview mirror at me and says, "Swam Singa Road. Twenty minutes. It's very good."

We pass dirt roads lined with small wooden shacks. Dogs and chickens and goats stand in the yards. Any of these could be Gita's house. Then we take a sharp right onto an even narrower, rutted lane. The cabdriver says, "Swam Singa Road" and points out the wind-shield.

"Slow, please," Macon says. "Could you go very slowly, please." We creep over potholes and around the dogs that stand in the middle of the road barking blindly at the car. Then we pass a yard where an old woman with a long white braid stands petting a goat.

"Stop the car! Stop the car! It's got to be her!" I yell. The driver turns sharply to the left and pulls the emergency brake. I jump out with the letter in one hand and a Polaroid Sophie took of Gita in the other. This woman is even tinier than Gita—a little granny with black eyes in a nest of wrinkles. She holds my arm tightly and laughs whenever I say Gita's name out loud. This is how I know we've found the right house. Macon takes a picture of her and me standing in the yard together. He says he wants to give it to Gita. How will that ever happen?

Inside, Gita's granny takes the sunglasses off the top of my head, puts them on, then points at me and screams with laughter. She's a widow who lives alone, and her only son is dead. But she thinks everything about me is hilarious, and not just me. Macon, too. The camera. The sunglasses. All of it is comical. She keeps touching my hair, fingering it like it's a foreign substance she's never felt before. Then she laughs some more.

The whole time we stand in her dark house she wears my sunglasses, which makes it even darker for her. I laugh when she tries out a series of poses with the glasses—standing in profile and grinning and generally cracking herself up. I try to imagine Gita sleeping in this house. The first floor is more like a stable, with the kitchen and rooms for the animals. The smell of hay and dung overpowers everything else. Did Gita leave through the kitchen door and walk to school? The woman makes us tea and insists on pouring. She's so bossy that I stop worrying about how she lives on her own. We drink it on straw mats on the kitchen floor, and I remember what we've come for.

I hand Gita's letter to the old woman and say "Gita" again. "Gita. *Shukriya. Shukriya. Namaste.*" She waves the envelope in the air like a fan and laughs and wipes away tears in her eyes. But she doesn't show any interest in opening the envelope. How will she know what's inside? Can she read?

We walk back outside, and she still has my sunglasses on. She's holding my arm in her right hand and the envelope in her left. Maybe there's a message for her inside the letter. Maybe she'll open it later, when these strangers have left and she has privacy or can go find a friend to read it for her. The cabdriver has his engine running. I don't know how to say good-bye to this woman. It's almost like being with Gita again to see her. I wish I had some news about the girl—some word from the other side of the world. I have nothing except the letter and the sunglasses, and I leave her with both.

"*Namaste,*" I say, and she laughs. Is it my bad Hindi that's so funny? "*Namaste,*" I repeat, and she thinks that's even funnier. She pats my back like she's always known me. Like she understands everything. Then she pats Macon's back and lets him take another photograph of her wearing the sunglasses. I get in the cab. Macon gets in the cab. How are we leaving? She's my connection to Gita. But we back down the narrow street. Gita's grandmother is alone in the yard, waving Gita's letter.

27

Taj Mahal: a marble mausoleum located in Agra, built by Emperor Shah Jahan in memory of his third wife

That night we sleep in a pink stone hotel in the old part of Jaipur. There's a talking parrot in an orange tree down in the garden that I can hear under our mosquito netting. This distance from France is a gift. I promise myself to be more hopeful when we get back there. More patient with Luke's disease. Nothing feels as urgent in Jaipur. Or as stark as the old rooms in the back of the St. Louis Hospital.

In the morning we walk to a Hindu temple that sits behind a palace in the center of town on a quiet, narrow street. There's a pink stone wall that opens to a hard clay courtyard, which leads to the temple's entrance. To the right inside the wide doorway is a tall statue of Vishnu—almost life-sized. A stone altar stands at the front of the room, and coils of incense burn on the floor. Many people are on their knees praying. They've all taken off their shoes. Macon and I add our sandals to the jumble of flip-flops at the door. Then we kneel on the floor. It's cooler in here. Quiet. I think of Gita and hope that she's healthy. I make a wish for Luke's health. Then I stand and put rupees in a basket near Vishnu's feet, and Macon does the same.

We go back to the train station. Our compartment is smaller this time. Six brown leather seats and a metal luggage rack above on each side. An Indian woman with the red bindi on her forehead sits next to the window with her teenage boy beside her. They both fall asleep. I try on the idea that I might be pregnant. We've always used condoms, except for the very first time in the dark on the beach. We aren't kids. We aren't foolish. I keep the idea of the pregnancy to myself. I don't want Macon to think I'm crazy. It's too soon for a baby. I'm still not sure that he trusts me fully. I keep thinking, *Today I'll get my period. Today I'm sure I'll get my period.*

Halfway to Agra, I wake up from a dream of Pablo and Luke swimming in a pool in Arizona with my father. They were both young, and acted like brothers. Dad called them his little fish and laughed and threw them up in the air. The dream makes me miss both of them so much. Pablo and the little-boy version of Luke. Where did he go? And how did we get this old? I have to pee, so I hold on to the backs of the seats and open the sliding door to the hall.

Macon's got the Lonely Planet guidebook out when I come back. "The Taj Mahal is going to be amazing," he says. "I want to take photos for Pablo. It took twenty-two years and thousands of men to build. The whole thing is a statement of love." He squeezes my hand. "There are rare gems inlaid in the walkways."

I put my head on his shoulder and doze again. When we get to Agra, there's a small fight among some of the rickshaw drivers outside the station over who will take which tourists. A man pushes his bike to the front and yells at us in English to climb in. We sit and put our packs at our feet and he starts pedaling into the city. "Hello, my name is Abkar."

"Hello, Abkar," Macon says. "I am Macon, and this is Willie."

I lean toward Macon. "There's a small chance I might be pregnant." I can't keep it a secret anymore. No lies. That was the agreement when Macon decided to come with me. No lies or half lies. Only the truth.

He's examining a strap on his backpack that's begun to unravel. "Right now? Today? Pregnant?"

"Maybe pregnant. Not sure pregnant. Probably not. But maybe."

Then he laughs. "This is incredible. We're going to the Taj Mahal and you might be pregnant!" Which is the best thing he could possibly say, and I kiss him.

When we get to the front gates, Abkar stops pedaling and puts his feet on the ground. "I will wait there." He points to the other rickshaw drivers sitting on their heels in the dirt under an almond tree next to a long, white concrete wall.

Macon takes my hand, and we walk toward the ticket booth. "You can't write a book about poetry in India and not see the Taj Mahal."

He gets his camera ready inside the gates, but a man wearing a white turban approaches us. "Sir. Let me help, please." So I sit on a marble bench with Macon next to me and the man takes many pictures in which we're both laughing. Then we thank him and follow a long, rectangular pool of water until we get to the tomb. It's enormous and dome-shaped and built out of creamy white marble and precious stones with intricate paintings of lotus flowers.

Macon reads out loud again: "The false sarcophagi are in the main chamber. The actual graves of Shah Jahan and his third wife, Mumtaz Mahal, are at the lower level."

"This is raising the bar on how to honor the dead," I say. We spend hours walking through the different chambers of the tomb, and the whole time I feel slightly dizzy.

Then Abkar bikes us to the Hotel Rashmi. We get a small room with a double bed on a metal frame. There's a blue-tiled bathroom and a wicker chair near the foot of the bed. During the night, I get cramps. I hold my stomach with my hands and try to keep very still so the cramps will stop. But the bleeding starts in the morning.

"What's going on, Willie?" Macon says when he wakes up. "My God, there's blood here—where is it coming from?"

"It's okay," I whisper.

"We've got to get you to the hospital."

"Macon," I say slowly, "my love. Please promise me right now you won't take me to a hospital. I must have really been pregnant."

"But we should go to the doctor, shouldn't we?"

I lie back on the bed and start crying, and he tries to rub my arm. "If it doesn't get better in an hour, then maybe we'll go to the doctor's."

"But are you in pain? Are you in too much pain? I can't let you sleep on this sheet." He leaves the room for maybe five minutes and comes back with the woman who owns the hotel, who I met when we checked in. She and her husband have a young boy, maybe two years old, who played with a red truck on the floor by the front desk. "Willie," Macon says, "this is Kaela. She and I are going to help you get to the doctor."

"Oh, Macon, no," I say. "Please."

"We've got to make sure. Just let me do this, okay?"

He helps me stand. Then he takes me into the bathroom, and Kaela hands me several maxi pads that are like small hand towels, they're so big. "Thank you so much," I say. "I'm so sorry about this." She just smiles and nods and closes the door. I put on my long skirt and place a pad in a pair of clean underwear. I feel nauseous and heavy and sluggish, like I'm walking in water.

The three of us make it down the stairs and into a car waiting outside the hotel. Kaela gets in the front seat and instructs the driver. Macon sits in the back with me, and I put my head on his lap. We go to an international clinic attached to a big hotel in the new part of Agra. Kaela organizes everything there. She speaks to the office receptionist, and I'm taken into a small, unfinished doctor's office with a wooden examining table in the corner. Macon helps me up on the table, and I close my eyes and doze until a woman in jeans and running sneakers walks in.

"I'm Dr. Pellman," she says. "By way of Canada and Nepal. Willie, it's nice to meet you. Let's find out what's going on here." She takes my temperature with a glass thermometer. "Have you ever miscarried before?"

"I've never been pregnant."

"The thermometer says you have a slight fever. One hundred and one. That's consistent with a miscarriage. How are the cramps? Are they easing at all?"

"Not yet," I say, wincing. "They're the worst cramps I've ever had."

"That sounds about right. I'm very sorry. Unfortunately, miscarriage is the most common type of pregnancy loss. Do you think your bleeding is still as heavy?"

"I don't think it's let up."

"The main goal of treatment is to prevent hemorrhaging and infection. This pregnancy, by all counts, was a very early one. The earlier you are, the more likely that your body will expel all the fetal tissue by itself."

"So I won't have to stay here overnight?"

"I am not ruling it out, but I don't think you're going to require further medical procedures. If your body doesn't expel all the tissue, the most common procedure would be to scrape the uterine wall, but I honestly don't see any need for that yet. We're going to let you sleep now."

She leaves, and I have a dream that I'm dying and that Macon's dying and also Luke. When I wake up I feel so tired I can't imagine ever standing again, or washing my face, or putting on a shirt, or leaving the clinic. I will live here forever. Where's my father? My mother? It's so hot. They would want to be here with me. I fall back asleep, and in this dream the baby's born on different days, in different hospitals, but it's always unrecognizable. "I'm having some sort of breakdown," I say to Macon when I open my eyes again. He's sitting on a wooden chair by the table. "I dreamt the baby was a monster."

"You had a nightmare."

"I can't ever leave this room."

"Okay. We can stay here as long as you want. Have I told you that I love you very much?"

I've been waiting to hear this almost since the first time I met him on Rue de Metz, and I try to store his words away for later because I wasn't expecting them today. I can't take in his kindness fully. Even though it's what I'm most hoping for. "But I can't leave the clinic ever."

"Not even once you are better?"

"Not ever. And please don't bury me. I don't want to be down there in a tomb."

Macon looks at me with such concern on his face. Then I don't feel so alone. "I will never bury you. We will lie here in this clinic for the rest of our lives together. I'll rub your back and maybe later, in a few hours, you'll feel like getting up and having a shower."

I take one in the afternoon and wrap myself in a blue towel the nurse gives me afterward. Macon says, "I'm going to go back to the Hotel Rashmi with Kaela now and gather up our things."

"Kaela is still here? She waited all this time?"

"She was very worried about you. She and I have figured out a plan. You and I are going to take the four o'clock train to Chandigarh. Then we'll go to Shimla and sleep. If you're feeling strong enough in the morning, we'll go farther north and take a final bus to Dharmsala. Or we'll stay put. It all depends on how you feel."

"I don't care where we go as long as we go."

"There's so much good stuff to come on this trip, Willie. You are going to be okay. We haven't even gotten to Dharmsala yet."

28

War and Peace: a famously long Russian novel
by Leo Tolstoy

We're the only two people inside the compartment on the train
to Shimla. The seats are made of old red vinyl. Dirty, cream-
colored vinyl curtains hang in three-inch strips across the windows. I
pull them to the side and button them to a matching sash. Then I open
War and Peace and read for hours. I learn that Napoleon extended too
far into Moscow and that the French army had been in good shape
when it left Russia, except that the cavalry was starving to death. I
learn the Russian peasants burned their hay instead of feeding it to
the French horses and that Napoleon should have ordered more boots.
This is how so many of his soldiers died—from frozen feet.

The train rocks, and I close my eyes and try to imagine the French
horses and if any of Napoleon's soldiers gave them last rites. What are
last rites, really? I start crying. "Luke wants to be cremated," I say to
Macon. "He called me last week, before we left, and made me promise not to bury him. I told him he was crazy and that I wasn't talking
about it. I wish I were in Paris with him. Maybe we shouldn't have
come to India after all."

"We should have come to India. You have a book to write."

"Can I call him? How can I call him and find out he's all right?"

"We'll find a phone. I promise."

We get to Shimla and sleep at an old wooden bungalow made into an inn by a retired military officer and his wife. She gives us strong morning coffee like sludge with watery milk in the back garden, and it tastes so good. There's a green parakeet stock-still in a steel cage. We eat hardboiled eggs and chapati while the officer tells us about the Shimla military museum and its collection of artillery. Macon makes notes on a little pad out of respect. Then we go to the train station. Our trip feels long now. So much time away from Luke. My cramps have almost stopped, and the bleeding is mild. I want to meet Padmaja and see the poems and go home.

But there are no trains to Dharmsala. The mountain switchbacks are too steep. So Macon gets us tickets on the afternoon bus that will get us there before dawn. The bus is bright green, circa 1968, and decorated like a cupcake, with swirly pink lotus blossoms and blue elephants and curlicues all around the front window. Inside, the driver has covered the dashboard with laminated glossies of Krishna and Vishnu and Buddha like a shrine. The seats are low and narrow and covered in crinkly green plastic.

It never quiets on the bus—everyone talks and smokes and snores. I sit with my cheek against the window and stare at the brambles and the dark shape of the road. Late in the night, soldiers flag us down. Two of them climb on carrying thin automatic rifles—boys in their late teens with shaved hair under camouflage caps. They force us off the bus and make us walk to a clearing behind a concrete shed.

"Passports," one of them says to Macon. "Passports now." We fish in our packs. I try to pull the zipper open on my green passport pouch. Little surges of adrenaline spike in my stomach and travel down my arms. I finally hand the booklet to a boy soldier with doe eyes.

"America. You come from America to this place?" He doesn't open the passport. He's distracted by its beauty, maybe, and turns it over and over in his hand like it's a small animal that will soon begin to talk. Then he gives it back and shrugs decisively—done with games now.

An hour passes. Two older men from the bus are escorted to the side of the shed, where they have to stand with their arms above their heads. I can't see their faces, but their hands start to sway in the air like the men are postulating. It's as if they're deeply moved by the sound of some distant music that none of the rest of us can hear. I've read the newspaper articles this week about Kashmiri separatists floating down the Jhelum River through the Punjab to get explosives from the bigger cities. Some of the Kashmiris have been captured as far south as Delhi. Some are caught in Nepal. Many are captured in the middle.

"It's going to be okay," Macon says. The neck of his T-shirt is darker blue with sweat. "The most important thing is to not draw attention to ourselves. Let's stay calm. Soon I bet we'll be boarding the bus again."

"But not those men." I point.

"Willie, stop pointing. Don't you get it? Keep your eyes down. I won't be able to live with myself if you get hurt here, so do this for me."

Another hour passes. Two of the soldiers call us back to the bus. I follow Macon to the middle row. Three in the morning, and I can't stay awake any longer. I miss my brother. I have to meet the woman named Padmaja the day after tomorrow and persuade her to let me see her mother's poetry manuscripts. It's why we've come this far. The driver closes the door and the engine rumbles to life. I turn in my seat and watch the soldiers close in on the two men. It's a small distance between us, maybe five feet. The soldiers put handcuffs on the men.

I bang on the window with my fist. "How can we just leave them? Jesus Christ, people!"

Macon grabs my elbow and pulls me down into the seat. It happens so quickly I'm not sure it's him. "You're losing your mind," he hisses.

"Stop pulling my hair!" I try to stand but he pushes my head down again.

"I'm warning you. They'll take you away, for Christ's sake."

Passengers turn to watch us. An older man makes his way down the aisle wearing a large gray turban. He points his finger at me and places it on his lips. Then he motions to the soldiers outside and runs his finger across his neck. "They will hurt you." His English is slow and deliberate. Then he goes back to his seat.

The soldier with the doe eyes yells at the driver, who opens the door again by pushing on the black metal handle next to the steering wheel. The engine idles so loudly it's hard to hear.

"They will hurt you," Macon repeats. "If you say another thing. It will be a really stupid way to die."

The soldier goes row by row, questioning each passenger. Oh fuck. Oh God. How could he have heard what I yelled? Then there's noise outside. One of the handcuffed men runs toward the woods. The soldiers start screaming at each other. Our soldier jumps off the bus and fires a shot at the man's leg. Misses. Shoots again at the man's foot, and the man falls down but keeps crawling toward the trees.

"Oh Christ. Oh Jesus." Macon is still holding on to my waist. My whole body rings from the sound of the gun. The driver has us in second gear, then third. I turn in time to see the tallest soldier bang his rifle against the side of the fallen man's head. "Oh no." And again.

We're a quarter mile down the road. Darkness all around us. No one talks or moves. Macon and I sit with our hands on top of one another's and say nothing.

WHEN WE GET TO Dharmsala, it's five o'clock the next night. We're let off at the base of town and have to make our way north, past wooden houses built along the sides of the mountain. We're looking for a place to sleep. We haven't talked yet. I'm not sure we have words. Macon carries my pack. Most of the houses have stone courtyards and piles of firewood and a thin cow or goat for milking chained outside. The main street runs along the edge of the small mountain. We pass two Tibetan monks in long red robes and a man with a chiseled face leading a donkey on a rope. There are hardly any cars.

We find a teahouse with a sign outside that reads MOMOS AND BAGLEP. SERVE ALL DAY. FREE POCHA. ROOMS. I look inside the door, and a thin woman in a black apron waves us into her kitchen. Three Western girls sit at the table behind us, smoking little hand-rolled cigarettes. The girls look maybe twenty years old. College students on summer abroad. I could be their teacher. I take a sip of the butter tea the woman places in front of me. It's salty and hot and doesn't go down easily. "I wonder how much I'd fight for my life."

"If those men are Kashmiris in India illegally, then they will be arrested," Macon says. "But the legal system works differently at midnight in Himachal Pradesh."

"I have no idea what it would be like to risk my life for something." I look down at my plate and back at the women starting to gather their rolling papers and money together. I want to tell them about the men we left on the side of the road. I want people to know. "I think we should report the soldiers to officials in town. It's still July, isn't it? What day in July?"

"They would laugh at you at the police station. I'm sorry, but it's true."

"I don't have the capacity to imagine more violence. Maybe this is a weakness of mine. Do you think the soldier killed that man? Do you think he's dead?"

"It has been a long couple of days for you. Now you need to rest. We need to go upstairs to the room this nice woman is renting us, and we need to put you to bed."

The room is perfect—just the bed with a red Tibetan blanket and a dark wooden trunk by the door. There's a closet down the hall with a toilet that flushes and a bucket of water for washing. The woman speaks some English, and when Macon asks her about hotels, she tells us of a house for rent a quarter mile down the hill that we can see in the morning.

I dream a dreamless sleep. Then I wake up in the middle of the night with cramps again. I trace forward until I remember the men by the side of the road and I see the handcuffs and the guns, and none of it was a dream, and I can't sleep again after that.

29

Border: a boundary; an outer part or edge

The house in the woods has a square wooden table in the kitchen and a stone sink and a mattress on the floor covered in a white sheet. We rent it for three days. The back window looks out on a thicket of cinnamon trees. Years before, someone dug a small well and circled it with stones, which have begun to fall down in places. The front is a tangle of evergreen vines, but a path has been cleared a hundred yards up to the door. There are so many birds making a racket on the first morning.

I stand in the kitchen in my T-shirt and pants and watch Macon take a bucket out to the well. Dozens of insect bites itch on my thighs—small, raised bumps that I can't stop scratching.

"All the birds talk about is rain," Macon says and puts the bucket into the sink. "They are amazing." He kisses me on the lips. "How are your cramps? Do you want to rest?"

"The cramps come and go, but they're better. I'm still bleeding, but the doctor said that might go on for weeks. I can't rest. We have a date with Sarojini's daughter. I'm so excited I can't think straight."

I change into my skirt and the cleanest-looking T-shirt in my pack. Then we walk into town, toward a teahouse Padmaja gave me the name of over the phone. Little boys and girls play in the tall grass outside their houses. A woman in a burlap dress walks out of what looks like an animal stall and smiles at us and waves. I kick a stone along the road. When it falls over the side of the mountain, I start with another one. The mountains are steep, and the trees are green and lush. I want to go back to the hours when I was pregnant but didn't know it—before the bleeding started. The surprise of the miscarriage hits me again. "Wow," I say. "There was going to be a baby."

Macon pulls on my shoulder. "Let's go back to the house. This is too much. We can meet Padmaja tomorrow."

"Oh no we can't. You haven't talked to her. You don't change plans on her. I'll meet her at the café at ten or I'll never see those manuscripts. I'm okay. There was going to be a baby. I'm just thinking. It's pretty incredible."

"It will happen again when we're ready."

"You know what you're saying, don't you?"

"I'm a lawyer. I always measure my words." He kisses me on the side of the road.

"I hope she takes me seriously. Padmaja will either like me or finish her tea and never talk to me again."

"I bet on her liking you."

"I've thought about this meeting so damn much and planned what I would say to win her over—a small speech about the importance of Sarojini's work being released to a Western audience and the great opportunity to spread her poems. But now that we're here, I don't know what I'll say. I'm so nervous. I'm tired."

"Tell me what you know about her."

"She's in her seventies. When I called her from Delhi, she told me to look for an old woman with white hair in a French twist."

We get to the teahouse, and Macon puts his hands on both my shoulders. "Are you sure you don't want me to come in with you?"

"No, she asked to see me alone. Just me."

"Then I'll go for a walk and meet you back here." I feel too self-conscious to kiss him on the street, so I squeeze his hand. Then I open the door to the café and step inside the cool darkness.

"You are here," Padmaja says from a small table in the corner. The cooking fire snaps. "We will speak English, you and me. I don't speak French." I smile. "Here." She pats the red cushion on the chair next to her. "Have a seat. My mother spoke Urdu, Telugu, English, French, Bengali, and Persian. I am lucky to have the Bengali and the English and the Urdu!" She takes my hand in hers, then lets it go and reaches for the tea. On the phone she had a deep, throaty voice. In person, she's much larger than I imagined and wears an expensive pink-and-gold sari, with gold chains around her neck. "I am lucky in other ways, too," she says. "No husband anymore. He was boorish, and brought me here for diplomacy with the Tibetans. He's been gone five years. I have stayed. Sometimes I like it here. I have no children left in Himachal Pradesh. They all went back to Bengal when my husband died. But I have my mother's poems, and I have my memory, when it serves me. You want the poems, don't you? I can tell. I may let you see them. The poems are why I am here still—the library is good. The officials offered to house my mother's poetry, and they offered to house me."

"How kind."

"You are too thin. Why don't you eat more? American girls are always too thin." I smile and take a sip of my tea. "But you are smart, too." Her face is wide and wrinkled in that androgynous, handsome way that older women's faces can become. "I can tell you are smart by your face and that you are in love with that man I saw out on the road."

"You mean Macon."

"My husband did not have a kind face. He was in tea and shipped it from Darjeeling around the country. Now I find myself an old woman, talking to a girl from America. Who could have predicted this? Maybe you will take me back to America with you. Could you do that? Find room for me on your plane and take me back. It is a country I have always wanted to see."

"America has great beauty," I say. Does Padmaja really want to come to the States? "I live in France now."

"France! Ah! My mother went as far west as England. King's College London and later Girton College, Cambridge. She met famous men of her time—Arthur Symons and Edmund Gosse. It was Gosse who convinced her to stick to the great Indian themes: our rivers and temples, our inequality, our textured society. I never got over the Indian border. It is a good life here, though. The books are well taken care of at the library. There are three of them, you know."

"I do know."

"My mother and Gandhi were both sent to prison, she for almost two years. I have a memory of him talking to my mother in his court-yard with that smiling face of his, reaching for my head with his open hand. She was part of the independence movement. My mother called him Mickey Mouse. Can you imagine? She had a nickname for Gandhi." I smile. "Don't worry." She laughs out loud and throws her head back. "I am not keeping you hostage here much longer. You want to see the poems."

"I would like to, yes."

"But why? Why do you want the poems?"

"I want to see what your mother was thinking while she wrote them. Everyone in India read her poetry."

"It is a mystery, isn't it? My mother got first in the matriculation examination at the University of Madras. She was only twelve. A child prodigy. She was a mathematician. Then she wrote poems about daily life in India and began calling for women's rights. She became famous and married out of caste. No one was doing this then. She was speaking the truth, and the women listened. There is no other way for me to explain it. She was the second Indian woman to become the president of the National Congress and the first woman to become the governor of Uttar Pradesh. They have made her birthday into Women's Day here. Now come. We must go." She gets up and leans on a red lacquered cane that's been against the wall. "It is time for my nap. We will meet at the library in the morning. Nine o'clock. Do not be late."

30

Inheritance: the acquisition of a possession, condition, or trait from past generations

I'm awake before the birds the next morning. Dressed by six with a bucket of water pulled from the well for tea. Macon wakes up, and we eat the bread and cheese he got in town while I was with Padmaja. The library's a half mile toward the main street, then left up a steady hill. We get to the stone building and sit on a wooden bench outside the front door to wait.

She arrives in a silver Oldsmobile sedan. The driver gets out and opens the back door. Padmaja emerges with her cane and a flowing magenta-colored sari. "You have brought the man this time. Good. Macon, is it?" She extends her arm as she walks slowly toward the bench. He stands and meets her on the path.

"It is Macon, and you are Padmaja, the keeper of the manuscripts?"

"They are my inheritance," she says. "Under lock and key. I am deciding whether or not you get to see them."

I stand next to Macon and I smile but it's excruciating. The manuscripts are close now—right inside the library. It will be a quiet book if I get to write it. A small book. But it will have sound research and it will be thorough. I will do the poems justice. Is Padmaja really going to deny me?

"She is a fine scholar," Macon says. "She will write a good book on your mother. I would bet on this."

"I am not a betting woman. Follow me." Padmaja walks past us, into the dark library, and takes us to a small room way back with white plaster walls and wooden beams across the ceiling. "This is where we sit." She points to the oval table with a brass lamp in the middle. She hooks her cane over the back of a chair and leans over and turns the lamp on. Then she takes two steps to a painted armoire that sits against the wall. A steel padlock hangs on the metal latch, and Padmaja takes a key from a long chain around her neck. She opens the doors of the armoire, and they swing wide. The shelves are filled with cardboard boxes of papers and notebooks and bound books.

"Macon," she says. "Please take everything out and put it on the table. Then keep me company. Willie won't want to talk to us once she gets into this. So you stay." She reaches out and puts her hand on Macon's arm. He smiles at me and begins stacking boxes on the table.

My heart soars—I bet the typed manuscripts are inside there. "You are the first American to see the drafts of the poems like this. It is because of your book on the French poet Albiach. It is a good book. I did my research. The people here at the library helped me learn about you. I want you to do that for Sarojini. What you did in that first book. Do that for my mother. Do that for the Nightingale of India. Bring her out of India."

She rings a small bell on the table and a young man from somewhere in the library brings us tea. But I can't drink it. I'm too excited. The first thing I do is get out my notebook and pen. Then I stand and move as quickly as I can through the materials to see what I have. The handwritten drafts are in the flowery cursive of a young girl. There are badly typed revisions on parchment paper that look like work Sarojini did herself. Then, finally, poems in three different roughly bound books: *The Golden Threshold, The Bird of Time,* and *The Broken Wing.* These also have many handwritten notes on them in the same cursive.

I pick up the handwritten drafts first, because they're what excite me most. I haven't dared wish for many marginal notes, but there are several to a page and cross-outs and arrows and parentheses along the sides of the poems and notes she wrote to herself. Macon grins and holds up his cup of tea. "Is it all that you expected?"

I can't speak. It's been such a week. Month. Year. "She is gone from us now," Padmaja says. "We must leave her to it. She has the poems for one day to herself. You must tell me about France, Macon, and if I will like it there. I am planning to come for a long visit. I want you to take me to the top of the Eiffel Tower. My husband did not believe in travel. Why I married him I still don't know. Be careful who you marry, Macon. They can appear to be one thing on the outside and end up being a different animal underneath."

"I married the wrong woman once already, Padmaja." Macon sips his tea. I hope he doesn't delve into past lives or tell her about his divorce and other small failures. I'm trying to gain the old woman's trust.

"This woman," Padmaja says. "Will you marry her, Macon? We shall see what she is made of."

"She is a good writer, Padmaja. She will make you a book that you will want to read."

"Ah. But you did not answer my question."

"I know you are discerning enough to realize that I can't possibly address that question in the presence of the woman about whom you are speaking."

"Oh, Macon," Padmaja says. "You are old-fashioned in the end, aren't you? This may be your downfall, being too tied to the past."

"I have a son, Padmaja. I am tied to my past and to my mistakes, and I am indebted to the future."

"Children make you honest," she says. "They leave you and they don't return your phone calls and they make you see yourself in the most unfavorable lights. Your envy. Your greed. Your malice. And also the size of your heart. I think your heart is big for your son."

She looks up at me while I stand furiously making notes with my pen. "When you write the book, I want you to call yourself Willow. Not Willie. I want everyone to know that the book was written by a woman, not a man."

I stop reading at noon. Padmaja has the librarian bring in tomato sandwiches and more tea. He's an older man with white hair and bifocals, and he shakes my hand and says his name is Gobal. I've taken pages of notes by now, but there's so much to read and decipher that I'm only through the first half of the first book and I'm panicking. The acrid sweat from my armpits drips down the inside of my T-shirt.

After lunch Padmaja dozes in her chair and Macon goes outside for a walk. When it's four o'clock, I can see the librarian turning off the lights in the main room, and I try to wake her. "Padmaja." She opens her eyes and stares blankly at me for a moment.

"Willow. How is your work?" She sits up and runs her hand over her hair to smooth it.

"I need to ask you for more time. There is no way for me to finish in one day. Three books. Hundreds of notes. Because it is your mother's notes that will turn my book into something that allows the reader inside her life. The notes tell us what your mother was thinking and why she used certain words and crossed out others and omitted whole poems from the final manuscripts. I know our agreement called for one day of reading. But I didn't think there would be so much here, Padmaja. It could take weeks." I've left everything else behind in these short hours. Luke. My mother. My father. Baby Lily and Sara. Even Macon. It's just me and the poems. I'm high off of it. I only want more time.

"Yes. My mother had a strong mind. A trained mind. She was strict, and she insisted I marry my husband. He came from a wealthy family. I never met him until our wedding day. It was bad luck that brought us together. Are you sure you do not want to bring me to America? I could give lectures with you. I could help."

"Padmaja, it is a very good idea, but I teach in Paris now and I won't be going back to the United States soon. I have to ask you a favor." If I'm overstepping, she'll refuse me. I could write some version of my book now. At least I've seen the manuscripts and can explain their veracity, but there's so much more I could do with the original material.

The old woman puts her hand in the air. "I know. I know. You are going to ask me if you can take the poems."

"Copies of the poems. Only copies. I saw a machine in the office here. A copy machine." I hold my breath. The woman makes me feel about twelve years old. Maybe thirteen. Does she trust me?

"I have been thinking on it. I knew you would ask. They told me here that you would ask, and that I would have to decide. Where is Macon? Where has he gone?"

"You fell asleep and he wanted to see more of your village on foot. He has gone for a walk."

I sit down in my chair. My face is flushed. There's no ventilation in the room, and I've been working intently all day. Padmaja sucks air in between her teeth and makes a whistling sound. Then she points to the door and says, "Go. Go now. Give Gobal all the papers. Tell him I have ordered you. Tell him to begin the copying now. He has been waiting for me to decide. I will follow in a moment. I am an old woman. I am too slow. You must write a good book and bring me to America. So you go."

"Really? Oh, Padmaja. This is great news. This is going to be fantastic! Thank you. Thank you. It will take at least another full day to make the copies!" I gather up the papers in my arms and carry them into the library's office. I want to shout I'm so happy.

Macon finds us a half hour later in the library office, where I'm watching a young Tibetan clerk painstakingly copy each page of notes. I bet he won't get to the actual books until sometime tomorrow. Gobal is here too, instructing the clerk on how to position the pages on the glass of the copy machine, then stepping back to watch.

"You have moved," Macon says. I try not to grin too much.

"She has prevailed." Padmaja waves at me. "Get me a chair, Macon. I am too old to stand. Some water, too. You will come back here with Willow tomorrow and watch the work be completed."

"This is wonderful news." Macon steps into the reading room and brings a wooden chair back for her. Then he finds an empty glass on the librarian's desk near the front door and fills it with water from the faucet in the bathroom.

She drinks the water slowly. "There will be no rain today. Why does anyone spend the summer in India? I am too old to be hot like this. We must go now. Our work is done for the day."

It's hard for me to leave the photocopying. The manuscripts give me a focus. All my worry for Luke and guilt and fear for Gita have been replaced by questions about the poems. We follow Padmaja to the car. Her driver jumps out of the front seat and opens the back door of the Oldsmobile. His tin lunch canister sits on the dashboard, with a newspaper in the passenger seat next to a red pillow. Padmaja slowly climbs in the back and hands him her cane. He closes the door, and she puts her hand up to the window for a moment in a wave.

"Follow me," Macon says when she's gone. "You'll like where I'm taking you." He grabs my hand.

"You cannot believe it, Macon!" I scream when I'm sure she's out of earshot. "There are so many notes. There's so much work!"

"It's good. I knew it would be good for you to get here."

"It's almost as if I'm there in the room with Sarojini! She chose her words so carefully. Then this amazing thing happened—her poems were read by hundreds of thousands of Indians. They were a call for education. A call to marry out of caste. A call for women to leave the fields."

He walks me back down the road, toward our little house. Then we leave the road and take a dirt path into the woods. "I followed two students in here," he says. "I mean, they knew I was behind them, but I don't think they understood I had no idea where we were going." We get to a group of buildings in the woods down behind the library. "It's an ashram. I think they like visitors. I think they depend on visitors in some ways."

The compound looks like a series of rectangular boxes; each one is one story high and connected by stone paths. The buildings blend in with the trees. We're standing outside an open dining room where dozens of people sit at benches, eating. I try not to stare. "Is it okay that we're here?"

There's an Indian girl on the bench nearest to us who pours herself a cup of water. Her hair's in a braid. Is it Gita? She turns and takes us in. She doesn't smile, but she doesn't frown, either. "Are you sure we're not intruding?" I ask Macon. "I don't think we're supposed to be here."

A cowbell rings, and a man in a white tunic and white pants steps out of the dining hall. He says, "The morning session has begun. Have you come to work?" He points to the nearest fields. "Here we have beans and paddy rice. We plant and harvest as much as we can now to make it through the winter snows when the pass closes and no buses can get to the mountains."

"We're just visiting," Macon says. "We hope that's okay."

"Many people who visit us end up staying for years."

There are stone cisterns for water and chicken coops outside the dining hall, and vegetable gardens right up to the edge of the thick woods. "We won't be able to stay," I say. "We have families we need to get back to. But thank you so much."

"If you are leaving," the man says, "you should have a swim first. It's hot in India in the summer months." He points to the woods past the vegetable gardens. "Take that path on your way up to town and you will find a small lake." A lake? There? Macon can't get there fast enough.

The water is pale green and flat. Macon takes off his shorts and T-shirt and makes a shallow dive. "God, it feels good! Come in!"

"I can't," I call out. "Doctor's orders. It's too soon."

He swims back to shore and stands in the muck. His body looks thinner now. I try to imprint the shape of his shoulders in my mind while he stands there dripping. "Oh, Christ, this is me not thinking. I'm sorry, Willie. I forgot you couldn't swim yet."

"It's okay. Really. I'm just glad to be in the woods." I sit on a rock and take my shoes off and put my toes in the water.

The lake loosens my mind until I separate myself from Sarojini and India. When Luke and I camped with our father in the desert, we always talked about water: Did we have enough? Would we find more? Should we go back to the truck before we ran out? The first time we found a lake in one of the valleys, I dove in and could hear a humming sound. My father treaded water near me, and I asked him what the sound was. He smiled and said, "That's water pressure on your eardrums."

Luke floated on his back with his arms over his head next to me.

"I hear it, too. It's music." Then he kicked and glided away. "When I swim," he yelled, "I have a movie camera in my head. And the humming sound of the water is the background music."

That night we heard wolves, and Luke and I put our sleeping bags together inside the tent. I hardly slept. In the morning I checked my canteen and took a small sip. I didn't have much water left. Luke was the best at hoarding it. He gave me a swig of his. Said he didn't want me dying of thirst. He always had the most water left at the end of our trips and he always shared it with me. We've got to find a phone in Dharmsala so I can call and hear his voice.

Macon dries off by standing in a patch of sun next to the lake. Then he gets dressed and we walk to a place called the Hotel Tibet near the end of the main street. We find a table outside and order beer and lamb and potatoes. There's a plumbing shop on one side and a seamstress on the other. Metal pipes are stacked in piles outside in the dirt. Two monks in sleeveless robes carry a thick, ten-foot-long pipe. "Maybe the monastery is getting water," Macon says. "We should tell Luke that his next project should be here. Water's coming. Electricity will be next."

The potatoes are sliced and fried with onions, and the lamb is on skewers again. We eat everything. Then we follow a series of square cardboard signs with drawings of black telephones on them. The last sign is nailed to the door of an incense shop in an alley. It's been ten days since I talked to Luke. Inside, the smoke makes my eyes water. There's incense in jars on wooden shelves and in piles on a table and in baskets on the floor. Boxes of it are stacked on a desk, where a small, hunched-over man sits.

He asks for rupees and the country code for France and the city code for Paris. Then I recite Luke's phone number at Avenue Victor Hugo. The man walks inside the black booth behind him with a red nylon curtain pulled to the side. He dials Luke's number. When it rings, he motions me over with his arm.

"Luke!" I yell into the phone. "Luke, it's me. I'm here in Dharmsala. How are you feeling? Tell me. Tell me everything!"

"Where to start." He laughs. His voice is warbly and echoes. "For one thing, sister, it has taken you a serious-ass amount of time to call me. I was beginning to worry. I hate to worry. Sara is livid. She phones me every day and is getting more and more stewed because you don't call."

"There are no phones in India," I yell into the receiver and look back at Macon. He sits in the chair next to the desk, counting rupees.

"You have to know where to look."

"No, really—it's impossible to find phone lines. How do you feel, Luke?"

"I am walking the city taking Polaroids. I have so many by the time I get to the set. When are you coming home?"

"Three days. I miss you." I start to cry for no reason, and I try to wipe the tears with my shoulder. I'm not going to tell him about the miscarriage. That would be selfish. He doesn't need any more bad news. "I found the manuscripts!" I scream into the phone and laugh. "They are stupendously, amazingly wonderful!"

"Whoo-hoo! Tremendous news!"

"You sound strong. Good-bye, Luke. I love you. Don't do anything stupid while I'm away."

"Be safe," he says. "I love you and be safe."

I step out of the booth with a huge smile on my face. "He's good," I say to Macon. "He sounds really good. I'm so relieved."

"I knew he would be. God, that's great." Then Macon recites the phone number in Chantilly to the incense man, who stands and dials it. He waves Macon over just as Delphine answers. I know it's her because of the way Macon's voice changes. It's a voice I've never heard before. Even in court. Even when he's been furious at me, he hasn't had this kind of vacancy. His French is fast and defensive. Delphine has entered the incense shop. I can feel her in here with us. Macon listens with his eyes closed. She must take a breath because he tells her that he's in good health and that my research is fruitful. He asks for Pablo. Then his voice rises. He asks for Pablo again. There's a silence. He doesn't say anything for a minute or so.

Then he yells, "Helloooo! It is Papa! I am calling you from India!" His eyes open wide. "Seven hours! The flight took seven hours! I am taking photographs of everything for you! Elephants, yes! There were gigantic elephants in Jaipur. How was the beach? What was your favorite thing about the sand?" He listens. Then he says, "The sand is warm, yes. I like to lie down in it, too. Pablo, I miss you. Do you know how much I love you?" He smiles at me from the dingy phone booth. "Yes, that much. I love you that much."

We walk back to the house holding hands. Both of us still lost somewhere back in our phone calls home and our missing. We use the flashlight to undress, because mosquitoes swarm when we turn on the kerosene lamp. Then we lie in the dark on the mattress. It's too hot for clothes. "This has been a monumental day." He takes my hand. "You have found the pages you were looking for, and you've made a friend."

"I've met the daughter of a famous Indian poet. I'm not sure Padmaja would call me her friend."

"She is your ally for life. I know it. Your co-conspirator. She believes in the poems."

"I think the poems are her epistemology." I kiss him. He stayed with me when I freaked out on the bus. He didn't abandon me. "I think she loves to decipher what her mother meant with each word."

"Take any simple word," Macon says. "Like 'edifying.'" He brushes his lips along my earlobe. "You are, for example, edifying to me." Then he wraps his whole arm around me and pulls me closer. "This is good," he says into my ear. "Edifying. The word itself. Your ear."

WE TAKE SHIFTS in the library the next day watching the photocopying. It's exciting and painfully boring. Each piece of paper is placed on the glass and maneuvered just so. There's the slow whir of the machine. Then Gobal raises the top of the copier. The clerk retrieves the paper, and they start over again.

Padmaja doesn't appear until after lunch. "I have a high tea," she says. "With an adviser to the Dalai Lama. This was the work that my husband came here for. They still humor me by serving me biscuits.

You will need to buy a new piece of luggage for all this paper you are taking back to France, Willow."

"You're right, Padmaja." I haven't thought through the actual carrying of the manuscripts. But there are shops in town that sell the Tibetan rope bags.

She hands Macon a white envelope. "This is my phone number and my address. I am thinking of coming to France next June, if you are done with the book. This is the return address, here at the library, where you will mail all the materials back, along with the book. After I read it and approve it, I will come to you and we can give lectures together."

Macon takes the envelope and bows his head for a moment. "Padmaja, it has been a delight. You are a very generous woman, and we will not disappoint you. Until next June." Then he extends his arm and they stand holding hands for a minute, both of them smiling.

"I have a lot of work to do, don't I?" I say. "You two get to wait and watch. I'll be busy. Thank you, Padmaja. It's more generosity than I ever dared to hope for."

"Don't disappoint me. After I read the book and approve it, I will come to the United States and you and I will give the lectures together. Work hard. Work very hard. Nothing good has ever come from not working hard."

31

Aloo tikki: a northern Indian snack made of boiled potatoes and spices, from *aloo*, "potato," and *tikki*, "croquette"; found all over Delhi

We land in Paris at dinnertime, and Charles de Gaulle is streaming with passengers. The arrivals terminal echoes with the sounds of so many reunions. July 21 and I can't wait to see Luke. Macon kisses me good-bye in front of a line for cabs and goes to find the train that will take him to another train and Chantilly and, finally, Pablo.

Paris looks so stately out the cab window. So grand and orderly after the madness of Chandni Chowk, in old Delhi. I've got my backpack on and my white cotton skirt with blue elephants and my really greasy hair and my rope bag full of poems. Gaird meets me at the door on Avenue Victor Hugo. He smiles. "Who is breaking and entering?" Then he opens his arms wide, and we hug. "We are so glad you're home, Willie." I can tell he means it.

"Where is he? Where is the brother?"

I find Luke on the living room rug cutting bolts of gray chenille into thin strips. "You're back! And you're not wearing a sari! Gaird and I took bets on whether you'd be in one. I said yes. I thought surely you would put one on for us."

I sit down on the rug and hug him. He's still intact and the sun has been kind to his face. His hands shake when he holds the scissors. "You look great. You feel great, too?"

"It's been good. Paris gets so quiet in July. Only the American tourists are here, and I love the heat. There is nothing like dry heat to make you feel healthy."

"May I ask what you're doing?"

"Flowers. There's a girl in the movie who's meant to be making cloth flowers for hats. She wants to sell hats to help her father."

"Why the father?"

"Because he's paralyzed, of course. I didn't think you were ever coming home."

"I have the manuscripts now. I can write the book." I take the other pair of scissors and begin cutting strips with him.

"I knew you should have gone. So tell me about India. I want to hear about the desert and the temples and the food!"

I stare at him. He's alive. And vibrant and hopeful. I was grieving for him while I was gone. Letting myself feel nostalgia for him in India, and for our childhood, as if he'd already left me. This seems like treachery now. Look how determined he is to live. "You would love it there."

Gaird comes back to the living room. "The water is boiling. Who wants tea?"

"That would be lovely. I could use a cup." I follow him into the kitchen.

"He's not going to tell you how he really is," Gaird says. "He's not going to mention that his lung is acting up again and he's having some trouble breathing. He has some infection. Some yeast. Something called candidiasis. It's serious. It's spread to his esophagus. I think his whole throat hurts. Those sores on his chest? You know those sores? They are on his back now, too. It makes it hard for him to lie down at night. But he didn't want me to tell you about this. He is declining much more quickly than Picard ever thought. Sometimes I think that AZT is making him sicker."

I'd forgotten the mesmerizing singsong of Gaird's voice. All I can do is nod at the bad news. "It's peaks and valleys," he says. "That's what Picard told us last week when we saw him. But AZT isn't the drug we thought it would be. Sara is very agitated."

"So you saw Dr. Picard?" Sometimes, when I wasn't grieving for Luke in India, I almost convinced myself that he couldn't die, which masked this horrible fear that he will die.

"Dr. Picard has nothing more for us right now, Willie. He said he was out of good ideas. He wished Luke and me good luck."

I go back to the living room and look at my brother again. The virus is deceiving. He's so thin, and there's the shock of that after not seeing him for days. The skin on his face is reddish. That's the AZT. What does he want out of life? How does he want to live? I get out the silver bracelets I bought in Dharmsala—simple cuff bracelets for each of them. "They're really great." Luke puts his on.

"Will you actually wear them?" I ask. "Did I choose well?"

"We'll wear them, won't we, Gaird?"

"Thank you, Willie. It's lovely," Gaird says. "Please stay for dinner."

"The jet lag is starting to hit. I think I need to go home and pass out. Come to us for dinner tomorrow. That would be great. We'll eat on the roof and tell you our India stories."

"We'd love to," Gaird says. "We haven't been getting out much."

MACON STAYS in Chantilly with Pablo for the night, and I fall asleep on the couch in my apartment. I wake up at three in the morning and wait for the sun to rise. Paris is so much louder than the woods in Dharmsala. Car horns. Truck brakes. Airplane takeoffs. I fall asleep again around five, when the pigeons begin cooing. The sun is high when I wake up again. I walk out to Rue Monge and get a coffee and two poached eggs. Then I buy cod at the market at Gracieuse. The fish lie on beds of crushed ice, with unblinking eyes.

I talked to Rajiv last night, and he gave me my shopping list. He's going to help me cook tonight. I also buy chicken and chilies and coriander and turmeric and greens, plus three ripe mangoes. The thought of all my favorite people at the table tonight makes me smile to myself. It makes Paris feel like home—more than it ever has. I walk the streets around Boulevard St. Germain and feel a quiet happiness.

The French women in their beautiful sandals and sunglasses are out, and they remind me of my mother when she was young.

I'm the foreigner. I don't talk to anybody, and no one talks to me. But my brother and my friends are coming to dinner. I get home around noon, starving for lunch. There's African music on the stereo and I hear Macon talking in the kitchen. I poke my head in. He's putting a crêpe on a plate with the metal spatula. There's a woman there too, who reaches out her hand to grab the plate from him and laughs. Pablo's up on the counter next to the sink with a glass of orange juice in one hand. The woman has a boy's haircut and a thin face with full lips. The first thing she says when she sees me, even before hello, is "I'm leaving. I'm leaving for the Louvre right after we eat."

Macon's head is in the fridge, and he stands up. "Surprise, Willie! Pablo wanted to come for the dinner tonight!"

I can't take it in. What are they doing here? They're making tons of noise in my kitchen. What are they laughing about? It's a scene I've imagined—Macon and Delphine and Pablo cooking food together, except now they're standing in my apartment and I can't find words for it. Pablo jumps down and hugs me. I pick him up and kiss his face and cry a little, just because I'm tired and I've missed him and he's sweet. A sweet boy.

I don't want to do this—to show Delphine how much Pablo means to me. Because her eyes don't convey affection easily. She puts her hand on top of his head. "You've grown again, Pablo," I say. "How do you keep doing that? Do you feel it while you're growing?"

"I just do it." He laughs.

Macon says, "Now we eat!" He brings the crêpes to the dining table. I go along with it, because what am I going to do? But he won't sit. He brings mugs in next and pours coffee and cream. Where are we? Why is Delphine here really?

"This was all Pablo's idea," she says, looking at her plate. "He insisted. I never would have come."

"Pablo," Macon asks, "will you draw us a picture of your favorite rocket ship?" Pablo has his markers and paper out and is already deep at work on a drawing of an airplane. He nods his head.

"You have a very nice apartment, and Pablo has always liked coming here. I wanted to meet you, too," Delphine says. "I needed to meet you."

Delphine is in my home. What to say? "Pablo is a delight."

"Pablo is good enough to eat." She smiles at me for the first time. "Everyone always thinks so." Both of us watch him get up and walk to the windows behind the table.

Macon pours more coffee and goes into the kitchen. Why does he keep abandoning me at the table? "We have brownies," he calls out. "I forgot that Pablo and I made brownies this morning at the house."

"I'm so sorry that your brother is sick," Delphine says. "Macon has told me."

I don't want to go to this place with her, so I close it off. Then she can't take anything from me that I don't want to give her. She'd like to keep Macon somewhere for her own—this is her nature. She may not even be aware she's doing it. I don't think she'll ever stop trying. Not because she still loves him but because she can't let go. I can tell this about her. It's easy to read—the way possession comes so naturally to her. There's a quiet tension over this in the room, but my fatigue makes me less attached to it.

"Macon is always so happy to have Pablo here," I say. "Thank you for coming."

"This is not easy for me." She looks down at her lap. "I've worked on this." On what? I want to ask. Worked on what?

Macon's never told me how beautiful she is or how boyish. Her hair is shorter than Pablo's. "Come here," she calls out in French. "Come to me." Pablo runs to his mother and buries his head in her lap.

Macon takes my arm then and walks with me back into the kitchen. "Surprise," he says again.

"Where did they come from, and why are they here? Delphine doesn't seem very impressed by either you or me. What is happening?"

"I wanted Pablo to come to dinner."

"And Delphine?"

"She really wanted to meet you. She's getting married to Gabriel, and that has something to do with her coming here. Though I'm not sure quite what. Pablo's going to sleep over, and she's going to leave. We're going to go back out there and finish our lunch. Don't let her scare you. Really. Eat the brownies. Then she'll leave. We can do this together. We can face anything when it comes, no?" He kisses me and I let him. But my brain's fogged by Delphine. She takes so much energy from me, just by being in the apartment.

We walk out of the kitchen holding hands. Pablo devours his brownie. Then Delphine rises and moves toward the door. "It is time. I have to go back to Chantilly, and first I want to stop at the Louvre. Gabriel will be waiting for me." She's never anything but polite. She kisses Pablo's head, and he goes back to his drawing. I open the door for her. "Good-bye, Willow." She gives me an air kiss on each cheek. "Thank you, Macon, for the lunch. The brownies are not as good as they used to be, but they are still delicious."

As soon as the door closes, I laugh so loudly that it sounds like screaming. I run and flop on the couch, and Macon lies down with me and kisses my face and laughs into my hair. Pablo looks over at us from the table like we're crazy. We're safe from her. We have each other.

LUKE CALLS ME later that afternoon. "We're trying to come to dinner, but I don't know what to wear."

"Wear anything. Just come."

Pablo and Macon are building towers with Legos. I climb up to the roof and sit in the noise of the city. Then I hear Sara and Rajiv downstairs. It's the first time Sara has let Rajiv's mother stay alone with the baby, or let anyone stay with the baby. Monumental for everyone. His mother has been dying to play grandmother, pressing and pressing. I climb down the ladder and kiss them both.

"Look at your face!" Sara says. "You're emaciated! Did you eat in India? And your hair. I've never seen it so long. Was it amazing?"

"It was so good. It was intense." I think of the soldiers by the side of the road and the sound of the gun. Then the hospital in Agra and

Padmaja and her beautiful white hair. "Things happened. We'll need more time for me to explain."

When I'd tried telling Luke and Gaird about the shooting in India, I'd sounded histrionic. Or like I was only worried about what could have happened to me. Which isn't how it was. But when you're a tourist and bad things happen, you're still just a tourist. Still on the outside looking in. Maybe there's no way to explain how it felt. Maybe I don't even try.

"Your beard!" Sara yells and laughs when she sees Macon. "You look like a mountain man!"

"Well, that's fitting because we were last in the Indian mountains." Macon has the contented look he wears whenever Pablo is near. Then Sara takes Pablo's hand. They go over to the couch, where there's a small pile of picture books, and she begins reading one to him.

Rajiv and I walk into the kitchen. My Indian cookbook is open on the counter. "First I wondered if we could make tandoori chicken chaat?" He nods and smiles and closes the cookbook.

Then he says, "Now we will begin. Slice your chicken very thin."

He helps me with the spicy masala and puts extra chunks of mango in the chutney. Then we do aloo tikki with potatoes and the peas I've already boiled. He adds lots of cumin.

Sara walks in. "Aloo tikki! Let me help!"

We finish the food and bring it all up to the roof on trays to eat under the stars. Still no sign of Luke or Gaird. Pablo sits between his father and Sara. Paris stretches out as far as I can see—the dark river and the densely packed buildings under the punctuation of church spires.

Gita, I pray silently as I sit down, *if you're out there, send word. Call me.* Then I turn toward Macon and smile. She wouldn't be in Paris, would she? She's gone from this city.

"To India!" Rajiv says, and we raise our beer bottles and clink.

"What an amazing country it is," Macon says.

But where are Luke and Gaird? They're so late. Macon goes down to the kitchen to get more rice. I follow him with two empty beer bottles in my hand. I drop one, and it smashes on the floor. Slivers of glass fly everywhere. "Shit," I say. "Shit!"

"It's okay, Willie. It's only a broken bottle. It's not a big deal." Macon takes the other bottle from my hand.

"I knew Luke wouldn't come."

"I really thought he would. Maybe dinner was a bad idea."

"No, it's so nice. It's good to see them. But I need to call Luke. I'll be back up. I just want to see why he didn't make it."

I walk into the bedroom and shut the door. Luke answers on the first ring the second time I call. "I was waiting for you," I say.

"Rajiv is there, right? God, he's handsome."

"You didn't come." I close my eyes and listen to Luke's voice. He sounds completely healthy. I miss him more than I can bear, and start to cry.

"I was never coming."

For a moment, it's as if he's already left me. "You said you were figuring out what to wear." I speak slowly.

"Remember, I don't have any T cells and I might catch a cold. I've got two bathrobes on and the comforter and Gaird is making me a hot toddy and I'm still freezing. How can I come to your dinner? It's not possible. I don't think I will be going anywhere. I have a fever. It started yesterday."

"Why didn't you tell me?" Oh, God.

"You'd just gotten back from India. I swore Gaird to secrecy. It's only a fever."

"Track it." I sound like my father. "Gaird should take your temperature every four hours." I want to go see him right now. To make sure he's still my brother. A living, breathing person. I can't imagine that his death will ever become real to me, and I'm filled with guilt now for even thinking about it.

"I know. I know."

"Have you talked to Dad yet?"

"Every week."

"I mean, have you told him you don't feel well."

"I haven't put that on him, no. It's hard to figure out what to say. I was hoping maybe you could. You're good at that. Could you call him and tell him and then maybe he'll come and visit and you two can make up."

I refuse to believe things are so serious that I have to call my father. "Sleep now," I say. "I love you." I hang up and climb the ladder back to the roof and hear them all laughing.

"Tell me about Lily," Macon says to Sara. "What is she doing now?"

"She's talking." Rajiv laughs. "Didn't you know? She's one month old and looks just like Sara and she's speaking in full sentences."

"She is Rajiv's long-lost twin," Sara says. "She's terribly sweet and only sleeps two hours at a time and I'm stark raving mad."

"Worse than residency?" Macon asks. Pablo is now sitting on Macon's lap, moving one of the spoons through the air like a plane.

"I don't know what I'm meant to be doing differently." Sara shrugs. "But she doesn't sleep. She lies in the bassinet next to the bed, cooing. When she does that, I don't care how many times she wakes up. It's the shrieking that's mind-rattling. But tell us about Dharmsala! You got the poetry manuscripts, Willie! You actually stole them out of the country in your backpack?"

"Legally, Sara," I say. "Sarojini's daughter gave photocopies to me. I have a book I can write now." We do another round of toasts for the book, but I miss my brother. Rajiv tells Sara to explain how they gave baby Lily her first bath in the kitchen sink. I smile at my friends and lean back in my chair. I've missed them. But the dinner feels forced without my brother—like too much of a good thing.

I know we're each dealt different luck in our lifetimes, but Luke's got a bad hand. How is it that I can eat this meal? Or laugh at Rajiv's jokes? Is this how we try to forget? Or how we keep on living when the people we love most can't get out of bed? Sara tells us the story of Lily's bath, and I'm grateful to listen to her because I can't talk. And I was wrong. I can't eat the meal either. I feel sick. Sara knows. She gets what it means that Luke hasn't made it to dinner. Her story about Lily's bath is a small act of generosity. A tiny one. She's distracting all of us from the sad, sad fact that one of us has gone missing.

32

Drought: a long dry spell

*I*t hardly rains in Paris in August. The grass in the parks and the trees and gardens all suffer in the drought. But Luke loves it. He's a sun worshipper like my mother. He starts coming in a cab to my apartment to sit on my roof and soak up the heat. He's not working much. I love having him up there while I read through the Sarojini papers at the table. I'm taking his cues. And he and I seem to have a tacit agreement not to talk about his disease. His breathing has gotten shallower, which makes me worry about the yeast infection, and he doesn't want to eat much, but he's getting out. He's steady. The high fever he had back in July has subsided. Gaird tested negative for HIV. The disease is only more mysterious to me. They're planning a trip to Ibiza with Andreas and Tommy. Gaird says he'll cook feasts in an old house Andreas's family owns in an olive tree grove. Luke says he'll plant himself on the beach and absorb enough sun to last him through the Paris winter.

In the middle of the month Macon and I go see an ob-gyn in a gray brick hospital in the sixteenth. We want to make sure there isn't scarring from the miscarriage. The doctor is an older French woman in brown suede heels with hair in a chignon. She is gentle and self-assured and tells me everything is fine—there's nothing unusual at all about a first miscarriage, or even a second or third. She says the woman's body is just getting ready. When she walks me out to the small waiting room, she takes off her bifocals and they hang on a long, beaded chain around her neck. She turns to Macon and tells him she's certain I'll get pregnant again very soon, and he smiles boldly when she says this.

We leave her office hand in hand and walk out of the hospital—it's set on elaborate grounds with tall, clipped green hedges and finished rosebushes and a pathway through a small stand of maple trees, all of which makes me think of some old-fashioned sanatorium. Macon repeats the doctor's words: "Pregnant again very soon." Then he smiles at me, more shyly now, like he's taking in what the doctor's just said. The miscarriage is already a distant thing. I'm not ready to be pregnant—my mind's too distracted. My body's too remote. I know it isn't time yet for us to be thinking about a baby. But I squeeze his hand, and we walk through the ivy-covered gates of the hospital, back onto the one-block lane called Rue de Noisiel, not so far from Luke's apartment.

We can get to Avenue Victor Hugo on foot from here. At five in the afternoon, the summer gloaming is rich and distant from the ache of autumn. Tonight the dusk is speckled and thick—the skin of a Bosc pear or some other fruit you can hold in your hand. Luxurious even. It feels like it will always be August. Always French sandals and café tables outside. Always this reprieve.

We stop at a *boulangerie* and buy cheeses and an imported prosciutto. Then stop again, for good red wine. We bring it all to Luke and Gaird's and lay it out on their little table by the living room windows. Then the four of us eat. We don't talk about fevers or AZT. We talk about Ibiza; they leave in a week. Luke says, "There is the most incredible olive oil there to drench your bread in. And the stone patio at the house overlooks a cove with water the most spectacular shade of blue." Gaird smiles at him so warmly. It's almost as if Luke is describing Fantasy Island—but they have plane tickets. And he's strong enough to go. The sun does him such good. Restores him and warms his bones. They can't get to Ibiza soon enough.

Macon and I take the metro home from Charles de Gaulle. Tomorrow we're driving Pablo to Sara and Rajiv's to meet the baby. We'll pick him up in Chantilly, then loop back to Sara's. Then we're all going to the Bois de Boulogne for a picnic. We get off the train at Place Monge and walk home. Macon says, "Pablo's always wanted a baby sister, you know. He's made Lily drawings—a series of portraits of Sara and Rajiv and you and me as zoo animals. He says he wants the baby to know all his family."

I stare at him in the light from the streetlamp on Rue de la Clef. "He said that? He said I was part of your family?"

"Yeah, he did. Because you are." He kisses my hand. "Family is a malleable thing for a five-year-old. It's about who he trusts. Who is safe. Who he can tell really loves him."

GAIRD AND LUKE NEVER GET to Ibiza. Two days after our visit with them, there's a faculty meeting at the academy. We're all sitting in the wood-paneled conference room at the end of the second-floor hallway when Luelle knocks and leans in and hands me another note. This time, I know. This time, my heart sinks. I squint at her tiny handwriting.

i've fallen and i can't get up

No instructions or explanations. It's the ad on TV.

"Can you believe this shit?" Luke yelled when he'd first watched the ad in Montana. I was making myself drink the warm Riesling at Aunt Happy's house after we'd left Dad at the cemetery. I knew I'd crossed a line with him by yelling at him, and I wanted the wine to soften things. Luke lay on the braided rug with his glass and watched the TV. The woman in the ad fell on the floor. Then she spoke into some kind of chain around her neck that had a remote-control device, which alerted an ambulance. "Could they try any harder," Luke said, "to make a really terrible ad?" We'd both been fascinated. We stayed up and watched the ad two more times, outlasting everyone else at Aunt Happy's—even Dad, who came home and went to bed in the guest room, without talking to either one of us.

i've fallen and i can't get up

I stare at the note. I'm not calm. Some of the faculty members are new this fall. They don't know me. Or anything about my life. I'm the poetry professor to them. But I have friends in this room, too. "Polly," I say, and I lean over to her, weeping. She's in the drama department. She's someone I trust. "I've got to go." She nods understanding that this has something bad to do with my brother.

This is our agreement. If Luke falls down, he's meant to call me at school and go to the hospital. I run down the staircase and out to Rue St. Sulpice, and I jog all the way to Boulevard St. Germain before I find a cab. When I get to the ICU, there's an orderly mopping the concrete bathroom in Luke's room, wearing a face mask. An IV line is back in Luke's left hand, and an oxygen mask sits over his mouth. I back out of the room to go find someone who knows something, and I see the plastic bag on the floor attached to the catheter, the small drip of dark urine already collecting. At the nurses' station I flip through the French in my mind. It's crucial to win the nurses over.

"*Excusez-moi, madame?*" My voice comes out in a rasp.

A tall nurse with short dreadlocks stands behind a wooden counter. She's wearing baggy scrubs and has a clipboard in her hand. "What can I help you with, dear?" she says in English.

"Luke Pears," I whisper. My voice is gone. "The patient in room 212?"

Sara comes down the hall. Her maternity leave isn't over yet. "Gaird called me. I came right in. I'm so sorry." Then she leads me away by my elbow. "Luke has an intestinal blockage. It accounts for a large part of his pain. It can be really bad. It's probably the reason he fell down in his apartment. But the candidiasis is obstructing his ability to breathe. This is the infection we've been dreading. The most important thing now is to manage his pain."

Morphine allows him to sleep that whole first day. I pull a chair over to the side of the bed and watch him. The room is canary yellow this time, and the prints are close-ups of red poppies. Gaird sits in the matching chair on the other side, holding Luke's free hand. Macon comes and goes, bringing cheese and fruit and water.

I step into the hall and find the pay phone near the nurses' station. Then I dial the house in Sausalito. I've gone too long without talking to my father. Now I have no choice.

My father answers on the second ring. "I found you!" I yell into the phone. All this time, it was this easy to reach him.

"And who might this be?" He sounds more polite than I remember.

"It's me, Dad. Willie." I lower my voice. "I found you."

"I've been right here all along. Except for a few trips back and forth to the canyons. Yes, right here all year long."

"He's very sick," I say. I'm too tired, and I'm not making sense. "Luke is sick. Did you have any idea?"

"I was not aware."

"We want you to come. If you can. That is, if you want to. Luke would really like it if you could come."

"But of course I'll come. I am his father."

"Luke told me you've been calling him. But I didn't know if you realized he was sick. He's in the hospital."

My father doesn't respond. Then he says, "I just need the address of the hospital and a phone number there. That's all. I don't want you to worry. I'll be there very soon. We'll sort this out."

In the morning, Andreas tiptoes into the room with a huge bunch of long-stemmed apricot roses and a box of caramels. He stands by Luke's bed without saying a word. Luke opens his eyes and smiles. The oxygen mask is gone. "That's what we like." Andreas reaches for Luke's hand and says, "We like that smile."

"You're here," Luke says. "I haven't done my hair. It's still tangled. Can someone figure out how the bed works so I can sit up and make proper conversation?"

Gaird puts the flowers in the bathroom sink and pushes the buttons on the bed until Luke is half-sitting. "Perfect," Luke says. "Thank you. When did you get back, Andreas?" He's working hard to make the conversation go well. I want him to let it go.

"A week," Andreas says. "Which is just the right amount for Hong Kong in August." Andreas is playing along. We all are. It allows the beeping EKG machine and the IV drip and the gray linoleum floor to fade. But then Luke falls back asleep. It stuns me that he can work so hard to follow what we're saying and then be gone. The terror of how quickly he might leave us hits me, and I can't look at Gaird or Andreas, who squeezes me on the arm and leaves as quietly as he's come.

The next morning, Gaird goes downstairs to the cafeteria to eat breakfast and make calls to the studio on one of the pay phones. Luke asks for Jell-O.

"No Jell-O yet," Sara says while she reads his chart. "Let's give the intestine time." I'm so happy he wants to eat. I can't believe she won't let him. The three lesions on his chest have turned purplish now. A new one has started next to his nose.

Sara motions me to follow her out to the hall. "He's not losing his vision, Will, and that is good. We are seeing many of these cases go completely blind."

"It's Luke, Sara. He's not a case."

"He's my case. That's how I think of it. My case to solve. You need sleep. Why don't you go home?"

"You know I wouldn't ever. My father is on his way."

"Since when?"

"Since I broke down and called him yesterday."

She presses my arm. "Your father is all the more reason to rest. It's too soon to say exactly how this is going to play out. Each case is different. The candidiasis is a real problem."

"The thrush?"

"It's virulent, and it's spread to his esophagus in large colonies."

"It's bad, right?"

"It's not good. We don't know how to effectively treat it."

"But he's doing better now? Yes?"

"What seems supportable is that Luke is not going to gain back functions he's lost."

"He can talk now. And he wants to eat."

"He can take in liquids, but his liver isn't processing. His one working kidney is greatly compromised. These we see as a result of the hepatitis C." She looks at me and smiles. "I've got to go now. I've got a baby waiting to be fed at home. You rest."

I walk back into Luke's room. He sees me and says, "Today I want you to use the peacock duster when you clean." I pour him a cup of water from the plastic pitcher. "Promise me. Peacock." I pretend I haven't heard him—the drugs are making him hallucinate. "Promise me."

"Okay. Peacock." I hate any sign that he's losing his mind.

"Because peacock is much better than goose feather. Peacock is best. Right?"

"Right."

"Peacock is best?" He's looking at me but not seeing me.

"Right, peacock is best." Tears start down my face. I feel like I cry all day now. It's sort of like breathing.

"Top to bottom." He raises his voice. "I want you to clean top to bottom. That way your dust settles and you can sweep it up."

"Are you thirsty? Sara says to keep drinking. How about just one sip?" I lean over the bed and put the straw between his lips. But he falls into another deep sleep. The machines beep and send out their electrical currents, which show up as moving lines on the monitors. The nurses come and go, reading the screens. One has spiky hair, and the shorter, rounder woman hums while she checks Luke's vitals. Neither of them has told me their name. I keep getting up and closing the door to the hall whenever anybody leaves it open.

Gaird returns from breakfast and resumes his position in his chair. We sit with Luke all day, and he sleeps. But the sleep doesn't feel like a respite. It feels like he's building toward something and that things are shutting down. My brain is dry and working slowly. Macon comes back at four. He's wearing his suit because he's been in court all day. Somehow he's got more fruit with him—a plate of sliced bananas and apples wrapped in plastic from a market. What will we do with all this food? I put the plate on the shelf under the window. He stands at the foot of Luke's bed.

"How is the pain today?" he whispers.

"It's steady I think," I whisper back. "Morphine is our friend." Luke doesn't move.

Macon and I go down to the cafeteria and get trays. There's a tough-looking flank steak and some old French fries and a sad green salad. I buy all of it and hardly eat anything. "We're not eating here again," Macon stands up. "It's disgusting." We put the trays on a shelf next to a garbage pail at the end of the room. Then we hold hands and walk out to the lobby. "I have something for Luke from Pablo." He pulls a rolled-up piece of paper out of his bag. It's a red rocket ship in a blue sky blanketed with yellow stars. GET WELL LUKE is written in capitals across the side of the rocket.

"He will love it. It's so great. I'm going to ask the nurses for tape when I get back up there, to put it on the wall." Do I really believe that Luke will be able to read the card?

"Pablo wanted to come so badly. I told him Luke's sleeping. I told him hospitals are for grown-ups." Macon puts his arms around me and pulls me in.

"My dad may come any day now."

"It's good. You need reinforcements. He's your father." Then he kisses me. "Are you holding it together? Are you able to do this?"

I nod. "This is not a choice." We kiss gently again in the bright lobby, and he leaves.

I go back upstairs and lean my head into Luke's room. Gaird is standing next to the bed, talking to him. He says, "I am waiting here for you in this godforsaken chair they've given me. I am not going to move. You must come back to me." Then he bends and whispers something in Luke's ear and cries and turns his face away. I cry, too, standing in the doorway.

Thirty minutes later, Luke wakes up screaming. "Make it stop! Make it stop! For God's fucking sake, help me!" It sounds like he's being burned. I run into the hall. Everyone on the floor can hear him. "You're killing me! You're all killing me! Where are you? Where the fuck are you?" I find two nurses, and we race back. They increase the morphine drip while Luke rolls back and forth on the bed.

Gaird holds his hand. "We are fixing it. We are working on it. Just hold on. Please hold on."

I put a hand on Luke's other arm to steady him. "You left me," he says. "Don't ever leave me like that."

"I'm here," I say. "I'm always here. I had to get help. You'll be better soon. The pain is going to go away." Please, dear God, let it go away. How much can he stand? How much more? Because he can't do this kind of pain. He can't be in pain like this.

"Make it stop. Please. Make it stop." After twenty minutes or so he falls into a surface sleep—as if he's barely on top of the pain. When he wakes up, he says, "Mom? Where is Mom?" He stares at me for a second. Then he drifts away again.

DAD WALKS INTO Luke's room at seven that night. He's so familiar to me, it's as if he's brought my childhood with him. Time compresses, so it's like the last year and a half has gone by in a week. I have such regret for not calling him earlier. He looks older. I stand up. "You made it, Dad. You found us." I'm so relieved to see him, I start crying.

He wears blue jeans belted up high and a brown plaid button-down. I smile at the three pens he's clipped to his chest pocket protector. The pens and notepad have been there as far back as I remember. "Of course I made it!" he yells to us all. "My boy is in trouble, and I'm here. Simple as that." He rubs the top of his bald head with his hand. He's got blue running sneakers on and stands an inch taller than me in them. He puts his hands on my shoulders and hugs me.

"Dad's here, Luke." I can't stop the tears from slipping down my face. Luke opens his eyes. Then Dad reaches for his arm and hugs him awkwardly on the bed. Luke smiles hugely, like he's been waiting for this the whole time. They'd been closer growing up. Luke would deny this. It had to do with their obsession with compass readings and maps. Luke loved maps. Loved everything about the desert trips. I just tried to keep up out there.

Gaird stands and shakes Dad's hand. "It is very good to meet you, Mr. Pears."

"Dad. This is Gaird. Luke and Gaird live together in an apartment here in Paris."

Dad nods and holds on to Gaird's hand longer than he needs to. "Movie business, right?"

"Movies." Gaird smiles.

"Things aren't looking so good here, Dad," Luke says then.

"We'll just see about that." Dad pulls the white stool next to the bed. "Let's get a handle on your vitals." He reaches for Luke's chart, which hangs on a clipboard off the foot of the bed, and begins reading numbers out loud: "Temperature steady at ninety-nine. I'm going to watch that closely. I think that number is key. Your heart rate looks good. Blood pressure is really not too high at all."

This is how my father takes over the room. It's his way. He's done it my whole life. The two nurses stop changing Luke's saline bag and listen to him. I'm used to their masks and gloves now. "What are you people thinking?" he says to them. "Don't stand there. You have a life to save. He is my son!" He points to the bed. "It's now your job to keep him alive! I will help you all I can. There's a regimen to follow here, I'm sure. There is protocol for this kind of infection."

How can he talk to them like that? Has he lost his mind? Then he whispers to Luke in his kinder voice: "I think, all things considered, the numbers tell a pretty darn good story here."

"I've had to shave my head," Luke says. It happened yesterday. It kept getting in the way of the nurses' work. And it was falling out from the medicines or the stress, I don't know which. Tangling with the different lines and the cords, so the nurses persuaded him to shave it. It had grown down to his shoulders, and I had to leave the room while they did it. I couldn't watch. It was too sad to see him lose his hair.

"I did notice that, son." Dad finishes reading the chart to himself. Then he begins to bounce his right leg up and down. "I don't think

I've seen your hair that short since the day you were born. But you look good, son. We'll get you back on the right track here. No fever today. That is tip-top. That is A-OK. That means no infection. And no pain?"

"Morphine's a good drug," Luke says. "But you have to get me out of here, Dad. Sara and Willie are holding me hostage."

"You let me worry about that." Dad looks over at me. "I will take care of everything." Then he holds Luke's hand. "Let me tell you about my latest desert trip. I'm trying out something new. I'm using ideas of an old Christian cartographer named Cosmas, who tried to make a map of Paradise." Luke closes his eyes to listen. "I'm fooling with coordinates. Trying to see if there's anything there. You wouldn't imagine the years Cosmas spent on this. Taking measurements. Looking for clues from Scripture. I'm just poking around. But I think he might have been onto something. Not Paradise, exactly. But I'd like to write an article about the search, because the desert is always changing."

"Well." I try to be kind. Why does he spend time on this? He's a smart man. He needs to be around more people. He's too old to be alone in the desert. "You're serious about this, aren't you?"

"I am serious," he says. "I am always serious about maps."

Maps are his friends. He talks to them. Questions them. He's always on this relentless search for information. Mom was the one who got him to think before he spoke and to listen. She was always reminding him to listen. "I am thinking," he says, "of making a stone maze behind the house. I want to fill in Mother's flower beds, because it would be much easier to keep up." He talks about the kind of fieldstone he'll use for the pathway. I'm afraid I'm going to scream, I miss Mom so much.

Sara walks in then and moves the plate of fruit and sits down on the shelf by the window. It's nine o'clock at night. What is she still doing here? She needs to go home. But she's calm and patient, and walks Dad through the whole HIV diagnosis. I just watch. He never questions one word she says, which is so unlike him.

"The T cell count stands at eight tonight," she says. "A whopping eight T cells per microliter. So no coughing in here. No sniffles or you're out." She smiles.

"Thank you," Dad says when she's finished. He scribbles down a few last notes in his pad. "It's the information I was waiting for, and it's in accordance with the data I've been able to compile."

She stands up. "I leave you in good hands, Willie. Your father's got this. Why don't you all try to get some sleep."

Then she leaves me with my father. It's Gaird and me in the chairs and Dad in a second bed that one of the nice nurses rolls in. I don't know how much either of them sleeps. The chairs recline halfway. I close my eyes and see Luke and me hiking far ahead of Dad in a canyon on the day we found an oasis. It was a patch of green, with leafy trees growing on it. Luke was so excited. He had a little notebook and a pencil that he kept in a plastic baggie in his backpack, and he pulled them out and wrote down our exact location.

"Dad," he said, when our father caught up, "this fits the description of an oasis exactly! Doesn't it?"

My father was lost in thought. He often still makes people repeat themselves. Luke asked again, in a different way. Then Dad said, "Yes. There's water underneath these trees, fed by an underground stream." Luke was smiling. He'd made a discovery. Dad loved discoveries. Dad bent down and touched the ground with his hand, so Luke did that too, and they stayed like that for a minute, on the ground.

In the morning, I get a nurse to find us a tape deck, and I play Donna Summer's whole *Live* album for Luke. He loves it. When it's over, Dad reads several psalms. So there's music and preaching for hours. Macon meets Dad out in the hall by accident, and they come into the room together. "I bumped into your father getting off the elevator," Macon says.

"I was headed down the wrong hallway." This coming from a man who's always had the best sense of direction. He really is getting older.

"Are we going to get some food?" Gaird asks at noon. "It's lunch-time."

"You go," I say. "I'll stay. I'm good."

So Dad and Macon and Gaird walk down to the cafeteria, and I get to sit alone with my brother. "I'll get you home." Can he hear me? I think he squeezes my fingers, but I'm not sure.

"You promised. My head hurts. God, my head hurts."

He's talking. I lean forward. "Believe me," I say. "I've been work-ing on it, and we're taking you home tomorrow. We just had to get the kidney thing under control."

"It's about time, Willie. I thought you were going to leave me in here."

"Never." I squeeze his hand again. I can't let myself cry. The kid-ney thing isn't under control at all, but Luke's liver is the problem. Sara has already told me that his liver function is the telltale sign, and that organ is shutting down a little more every day. And the yeast. That's why things are happening so quickly: his lungs are under siege. There's a shift happening—I can't name it yet. But we've gone from trying to save his life to trying to make the end of his life bearable, which is the saddest thing of all so far. It feels like we've been in this hospital room since before time. How are we going to manage him at the apartment? How can we get him back there?

"I thought you were going to leave me here to die." Luke closes his eyes.

"Never," I whisper. He sleeps and I whisper, "Don't leave me. Don't leave me. Don't leave me."

33

Standard Body Temperature: the degree of heat that is natural to the body of a human being

Dad rides in the ambulance with Luke. Macon and Gaird and I follow behind in Gaird's car. We're taking him home. Does he know he's failing? Does he grasp it? He was so happy to get onto the stretcher in the hospital room. He smiled the whole time they lifted him up and put it in the back of the van. Gaird drives. Macon sits in the passenger seat, and I'm the woman in the back feeling a weird sense of euphoria. We're out of the hospital! We did it. Anything's possible now. He gets to go home! He gets to go home! I wipe away tears.

The shrubs outside the hospital gates have been pruned. They're a brighter green than the trees, and they look like old women with beehive hairdos. I love Paris all over again. Gaird drives so well, weaving calmly through the traffic. I love Gaird today. I love Macon! I love my father! I'm flooded with forgiveness, spilling over with gratitude for all four of these men. The sun is shining and Luke gets to live in his apartment and we can make this work. We can figure the disease out. What we need to do is buy some time.

There are two paramedics in the ambulance, and they get my brother down from the van and wheel the stretcher to the front door of the building on Avenue Victor Hugo. Then Gaird and Macon help carry him up the two flights of stairs and into the living room, where they slide him onto an electric bed I've rented from the hospital. There is a nurse with us, named Betty, and she straightens out Luke's sheets and sets up his catheter bag properly and makes sure the IV line is clear. Then Dad takes out a glass thermometer and places it under Luke's right armpit. He reads the number out loud to all of us in the room: "One hundred and one. Our challenge here, people, is to sustain a reading of ninety-nine and nothing higher. Can we all commit to that goal? Are we all on the same page?"

I'm over by the kitchen door, and I blush when he yells. But I'm so relieved again that my father's here. Who else is going to scream like a lunatic and get everyone's attention? Luke's fever spikes to 104 degrees an hour after that. He talks in his dreams. Something about Gaird in an airplane. His legs keep twitching.

"I'm falling. Falling. Watch out. Watch me. Help me." Then he says, "I am so damn thirsty." He sounds lucid. "I'm craving lemonade. Cold lemonade. Can someone get some for me, please?"

I'm sitting next to him on one of the big chairs we've pulled close to the bed. I say, "Of course." I almost don't even have to look at Macon, because he's already at the door, on his way to go find Luke some lemonade.

That night Macon falls asleep on the couch. Gaird lies down on his bed with all his clothes on. Dad stays up late to watch Luke's temperature and quarrels with Betty about the medication. He thinks Luke's getting too much morphine. Then he walks over to the cardiograph. "I don't like it. He shouldn't be presenting us with a fever." Luke's heartbeat is irregular, and Betty watches the spiking line on the machine closely. "Why are we seeing these numbers?" Dad asks. "Where is the infection that we don't know about yet?"

It's eleven. I go into the kitchen to slice more oranges. Luke shouldn't have a fever with all the drugs he's on. I'm a little bit crazed because I haven't slept. I try to be systematic about making the juice. I finish slicing the oranges and squeeze them by putting all my weight on the handle of the juicer. I've believed in the drugs. All this time, I've thought the drugs Picard gave us would buy more time, until the vaccine was available. So why this raging fever now?

Sara told me this morning that it looks like his HIV became resistant to the AZT. It's so toxic that they've taken Luke off it. I throw the used oranges into the garbage can by the sink. One misses and hits the floor. Then I throw more, aiming at the white wall under the clock. I hurl them. Some stick to the wall, and some slide down. I clench my teeth. I do that so much of the time now, this teeth clenching. Then I leave the mess and check on Luke one more time. He's asleep, so I lie down with Macon on the couch, shaking. He opens his arms and makes room for me, like a small AGA oven giving off heat.

We get up before it's light out because Dad is singing. He gets really loud on the last line: "We shall come rejoicing, bringing in the sheaves!" It's zooey. I go into the kitchen and deal with last night's orange disaster. I'm calmer. Almost removed. But the oranges remind me of this pit of sadness I'm skirting.

I bring some juice to Luke in his bed. Dad says, "It's high time I took a shower, don't you think, Luke?" There's a guest bathroom off the study, and I want my father to disappear in there for a long time so I can sit with Luke.

"I've got something for you to drink," I say after Dad leaves.

"The juice lady," he whispers and takes two sips from the straw. I put the glass on the side table and read to him from yesterday's *Herald Tribune*. Pieces on the anti-Communist protests in Poland, several articles analyzing the Tiananmen Square protests, and one criticizing President Bush for his handling of China relations. Every five minutes or so, I pause and try to feed Luke a cube of strawberry Jell-O. He says, "It's my favorite flavor, you know." I take his talking as a good sign.

Macon leaves for work. Dad announces that Luke's temperature is down to 103. Gaird goes out and gets us baguettes and salami and cheese for lunch.

Betty washes Luke's face and replaces the IV bag. Then she sits down again on the chair next to the monitor and reads her book. In the afternoon, Andreas arrives with a quiche. He leans down and hugs Luke's neck and says, "Hello, my dear friend." Luke doesn't wake up. Andreas sits and takes Luke's hand and doesn't say anything else. It's the perfect way to be around Luke right now. Because Luke doesn't want to talk. Doesn't want much TV. But he seems content. Almost childlike.

I close my eyes on the couch. I can hear Luke say "I'm so thirsty" to Andreas. He whispers it again: "Thirsty."

"I can do something about that." Andreas stands and goes into the kitchen and fills a Ziploc bag with ice from the freezer. I hear him smashing the bag against the counter to break the ice into smaller pieces. Then he sits down in the chair and slowly feeds the chips to Luke.

Macon comes back from work with more groceries. I sit up. I think I've been sleeping, and I help him unpack in the kitchen— bananas and yogurt and apples and bread for toast. It's dark outside. I think September is the most beautiful and haunting month in Paris. It's still hot out. It feels like summer, but there's a sense of so many endings.

Andreas lets go of Luke's hand and stands. We make a plan for him to come back tomorrow with Tommy. He'll call me, he says, hugging me in the living room. Then Gaird walks him to the door and they embrace, and Gaird's body shakes with sobs.

Macon warms up the quiche in the kitchen. I turn on the television in the living room, and our odd constellation of family eats and watches in the dark—Gaird and Macon and Betty and my father and me. Luke looks like he's sleeping. But when I get up for a glass of water he says, "Willie, come back and sit with me. Don't leave me alone in here. Don't leave me."

IN THE MORNING, Dad starts in on a hymn that goes, "When the roll is called up yonder." I can't take it. Gaird's out, and I go into their bedroom and lie down on the bed and cover my face with a pillow. Is it Dad's voice that's getting to me? He never used to be so loud when he and Mom sang. My mom carried the melody and Dad took the quiet harmony underneath. I can't begrudge him his faith. I still don't really understand it, but we all find strength where we can. And we need strength in this apartment. We need anything we can get but maybe not the singing.

In the desert my dad was the rule maker: "No playing in waterfalls because that's how people die in flash floods. They don't hear the rumble coming. No hiking after dark because of snakes." Once we walked four miles back to the truck to get more water, trying to outrun the darkness. We made it just as the sun set. Then Luke and I sat on the cooler and ate granola bars. Dad studied the map with his headlamp for where we'd go in the morning.

"The thing I like about maps is that they show us where we live." Luke talked while he chewed.

"Live?" I almost yelled. "We live here?"

"Of course, dingbat," Luke said. "What do you think we've been doing? We're always living. Wherever we are is where we live."

I chewed the food and tried not to cry. "I thought we lived at 46 Paso Robles, Sausalito, California. I thought we lived with Mom."

Macon finds me crying on Luke's bed. "Let me see your face."

"It started as laughing."

"What are you doing in here?" He pulls me toward him.

"Well, my brother is dying in the other room." I've said it now. This is the first time, really, to myself or to Macon. "I think it takes most of his concentration. I think he's in pain, and it's hard to lie down all the time. Also, my father is singing gospel songs. So there's a lot going on this morning." I smile at him. He pulls me onto his lap and wraps his arms around me. I haven't really seen him in days—haven't taken him in with my eyes—and he's even more handsome now because of this. But I've roped off this part of my heart a little. It's so good of Macon to be here, and I want him here. I'm sure of it. "I'm trying to keep Luke alive. But I'm planning for what's going to happen when he's dead, and it's crazy-making. Do you think I'm crazy?"

"Just go back to today," Macon says slowly. "Just worry about this hour."

My father yells from the living room, "Luke is awake! He wants to know if Macon will go to the grocery store!"

I walk into the bathroom and splash water on my face. I look older than when I got to the apartment on Saturday. There's such focus to the hours here—a sharpening. Sometimes it feels like we're centering in on something. Fixing something. It can't all be about helping Luke die, can it? Other times it's dreamlike and hot and confusing. Maybe we'll always live together like this: Dad and Macon and Gaird and me feeding Luke on the bed in the living room. I dry my hands on a towel, but my face is wet again with tears.

"I think I might be mixing things up in my mind," I tell Macon in the doorway.

"What do you mean, 'mixing things up'?"

"Sometimes I pretend Luke's better. I decide he's eaten something when I know he hasn't. I pretend for him, but I'm pretending for me. I'm having trouble with it."

"I'm glad you're talking. It's important to talk."

"Then there's the juice. Sometimes, I swear, I watch him drink it and see the juice in his throat."

"How do you see it?"

"Sticking to infected cells."

"But orange juice doesn't cure disease. You know that, right?"

"It helps." I walk toward the hall.

"It may help with hydration and vitamin deficiency."

"It helps with the immune system. I know it does."

We go into the living room, and Macon sits next to the bed. Luke says, "It's so Louis the Fourteenth in here, isn't it, Macon? But this place is all I've got, and I do love it so. Who is going to the grocery store?"

"Of course you love it." Macon reaches for Luke's hand. "It's your home."

"It's been a good home. If there's one thing that Gaird knows how to do well, it's to make a home. She's crazy about you. You know that, right?" Luke talks as if I'm not standing there. "You two are going to make some beautiful babies. I just wish I could be around to see them."

"Do you have to talk like that?" I say. "What are you saying?"

"Unless there's a drug breakthrough tomorrow, or unless you can get some of that vaccine that Dr. Picard's friends haven't invented yet, I'm not going to meet your babies. It's time to be honest about this." He tries to sit up. He's so lucid. "It's also time I took a walk. I've been in this bed so damn long. I need to get outside. Are you going to the market, Macon? I want to come with you. I want to get some pudding. Chocolate pudding."

"Luke," Macon says. "We have all the time in the world. You rest. You sleep. We'll talk when you wake up, and if you want to go then, we'll make it happen."

"Are you good for your word?" He puts his head back on the pillow. "I am feeling sort of tired right now. I'd like some barbecue chicken. Spicy. Crispy on the outside. Can I have that, please? I'm so hungry." He closes his eyes, and he's gone. Out. Sound asleep. I can't move from the bed. This part is heartbreaking. He's with us. Then he's not with us. It happens within seconds and I can't see it coming.

"Let's give him time to sleep." Macon takes my hand and pulls me into the kitchen. There are orange halves all over the counter. "Wow," he says. "That's a lot of oranges, Willie."

"You never know when you might need more fresh juice."

"I think we've got enough." He gets out a plastic garbage bag and starts sliding the oranges into it.

"Juice, you mean? Never enough." I sit at the table in the corner and make a list of what Luke's eaten in the last twenty-four hours: six bites of Jell-O, two spoons of raspberry sorbet, and half a glass of juice. I want to be able to show Sara this when she comes. "You're going to put the juicer away?"

"I'm just cleaning it," he says. But then I watch him slide it into the cupboard.

"I know what you're doing. You can put it away. But don't think I can't see you. I still have hope. If you put the juicer away, then it means you don't have any hope."

Macon stares at me. Then he takes the juicer out of the cupboard and puts it back on the counter and leaves.

Luke wakes up an hour later. Gaird is back and sitting with him.

I walk by them on my way to the couch and Luke says, "When is Mom getting here, Willie?"

"Soon," I say. I can't bear any of these parts about Mom. Sometimes I, too, think she's coming. Or that she'll send a sign. I don't mean something concrete—but something that lets us know she's here. This is what Luke needs.

I hold his hand all afternoon. He opens his eyes just as the dusk settles around the furniture. This is the scariest part of the day. This is how I'm afraid my whole life will feel after he's gone. Somewhere gray between twilight and full darkness. Crepuscular. Empty. "You have to beg Dad to stop singing." I try to laugh.

"Which one of us is lying in a hospital bed? You say something to him. I don't have the heart to. Where is he?"

My eyes fill with tears. Macon's gone to get Thai food for dinner, Betty has driven home for a few hours. She has a husband. Teenage boys she's told me about who miss her. Gaird's on the phone in the bedroom. Dad's taking a nap in the study. "He's resting. I've been waiting all week for you to make him stop."

"You've got to admit it's sort of amazing—our father singing psalms at my deathbed."

"Stop." I force a laugh again.

"But you have to give him a break, Willie. You get what you get. We got him. And you have to stop laughing, because it takes too much energy for me to laugh."

"Your fingers are cold."

"All of me is cold. I keep telling you. No one listens."

I go into the bedroom and wave to Gaird, who's lying on the bed with a notepad and pen, talking to Dr. Picard's resident about whether or not Luke can have any of the new drugs in the works now that he's been on AZT. Gaird still has hope. I grab two more fleece blankets from the closet and lay them on top of Luke. "You have three blankets now, my friend. You are very, very diva about the cold."

"Am not."

"We need to keep you warm, but you have to beg Dad to stop singing. Tell him you're not feeling well. Say the doctors think you might actually have something wrong with you—some kind of condition—and that you need rest. So could he wait on the singing?" I pull the top blanket up higher under Luke's chin and sit back down. "You have to do this for me."

"So just in case you missed something. A lot of men with symptoms like mine lose their minds, Willie. They go absolutely nuts."

"Will you not joke?"

"I bet I'll get cancer of the brain. If I do, I want you to suffocate me with a pillow." He reaches for the one under his head.

"Enough. You have to stop."

"I'm serious." He holds my wrist. "I'm so worried about you."

"Me?"

"I'm so worried about what will happen to you when I'm gone."

I can't hear this. I put my hand on his face. "Luke. Listen to me. Please. Please don't worry about me. I am good. I am fine."

He nods. "You're going to have to do something important for me."

"What are we talking about?"

"You're going to have to fight."

"Who?"

"Dad." Luke looks away.

"I always fight Dad." I can't believe he's talking so much.

"No, really. You're going to fight to keep him from burying me."

"Don't." My voice gets sharp.

"Will. Tell me you won't let him do it."

"I won't. But we don't need to go over this. Not now. Not yet."

"He wants to bury me next to Mom. He told me yesterday about the graveyard and said he would have another bench made with my name on it. It's cold in Hardin, Montana. I don't know anyone there." Tears slip down my face, and I let them fall off my chin. "So say it."

"I get it. I don't need to say it." I grab Luke's wrist.

"Please say it." Time slows down. The ephemera float away. At first this slowing down was a comfort. Now every day it feels like it slows even more, until we're almost not moving forward, almost not part of the great human march.

"I can't do this. Please don't make me." I long for the old life, where Luke used to tease me about my cowboy boots. How is it that the passage of time has changed our lives so irrevocably?

"I'm tired, Willie. I want to sleep. Say you will not let Dad bury me." He's trying to get me to face the real business of his death. The preparation. Is he asking me to let him go?

"I will not let Dad bury you." I hold my breath. It's all there. The hurt of losing him. I'm still not letting him go. "Fuck," I say to no one and to him. "Fuck, fuck, fuck." I'm crying loudly now.

"And that you will keep my ashes with you." Luke turns his head to the side and closes his eyes. "Say that you will not let Dad fly me to Hardin." I stare at Luke's hand. "Please say the ashes part," he whispers, drifting in and out. "I need to rest."

"I will keep your ashes," I whisper back. "I will keep your ashes, Luke Pears."

34

Childhood: the state or period of being a child

Sara comes to see Luke that night around seven. I'm so grateful that she's here. I meet her at the front door and hug her tightly. Then we stand in the hall together, looking at Betty and my brother in the living room. Betty is checking his vital signs and writing them down on a clipboard. "Will you make sure he's not in pain?" I ask. "He hasn't woken up now for an hour."

"You'd know if he was in pain, sweetness."

"How would we know? How do we know that Betty really understands what she's doing?"

"We know because this is a qualified nurse sent from my hospital."

"But this is not cancer, Sara. This is not juvenile diabetes, and people aren't trained. We don't know how it might turn here at the end. Do you, Sara? Do you know what he might be feeling right this very minute? He's counting on me. Can you see that? We've got to do this right."

"You'd know if he was in pain because he would cry out, and he hasn't. I can see he's sleeping peacefully. So I'll· check his morphine drip and his pulse. We've seen a lot of AIDS at the hospital, Willie. Too damn much. Every case has its own story. I'll go sit with him. And you." She fingers my hair and smooths some of the bangs that hang across my eyebrows. "You should take a shower while I'm talking to him. And I can tell you're not eating."

Sara holds Luke's hand and occasionally touches the stubble on his head. She cries sometimes. Sometimes she talks to him. A lot of the time she's quiet. After a while, I go to nap in Luke and Gaird's bed. When she's done being with him, she finds me and lies down next to me and puts her arms around me. There's nothing for us to say. I thought there would be, but really there's nothing except to be with my friend.

When she stands up, she says very quietly, "He's leaving us now, you know. It's the start of a coma, I think, Willie. Long, peaceful sleep. How lucky for him that it may end this way. I want you to try to think like that if you can. About the luck of a peaceful ending. Think about Luke. Think about making this easy for him." I nod at her and nod again and I can't really speak, but that's okay because I understand.

THAT NIGHT Gaird paces the apartment and looks for things to question Betty about—the IV drip, the occasional spikes on the EKG machine. Macon goes to sleep in the den. Dad stays up, and comes into the kitchen for a glass of water around midnight. I've run out of things to do, so I'm scouring the top of the stove. "How are the numbers?"

Dad fills his glass from the faucet. "A hundred and one degrees and holding. It's where I thought he'd be tonight. It's good it hasn't gone up. But overall, the numbers are not where I'd like. They don't tell a good story and the fever never abates, which means the body is working too hard. It feels like Luke's slipping from us, Willow." I stop scrubbing. "I want to go over things," he says. "Luke may not know anymore what he wants and doesn't want. I'd like to make some plans."

I stare at my father's bare feet. He has very small toes. I want to watch Luke sleep in the living room. It's relaxing to see his lungs fill with oxygen. "He knows what he wants," I say. "He told me yesterday."

"I know what the Lord wants for him. So let's stay calm here."

He takes a white hankie from the back pocket of his jeans and pats his forehead. "I'm trying. I don't pretend to understand my son. He's a homosexual, yes, and I don't fully understand that either, but I don't hold it against him, irrespective of what certain people think the Bible says. I'm too much of a scientist to believe all that. I just believe in forgiveness." He wipes his face with the cloth. He looks old and weak and vulnerable.

This is the first time I can imagine what it's like for him. His wife dead. His son dying. I know how much he loves Luke, and the pain of that has to be swallowing him. "I want to honor him." Dad starts to weep. "It's one of the few things we can actually do for the dying. I think it would be nice if your brother could be buried next to your mother. What is so horrible about that, Willow?" His voice rises. "What is so wrong about a son being buried next to his mother?"

Luke made me promise. But what would be so wrong about Montana? Dad is trying. He never turned his back on Luke. He's standing in his dying son's kitchen in the middle of the night, trying to figure out where to bury him. My anger at him at the cemetery last year seems so inconsequential. So small. It's another one of the things that float away. Dad was just terribly, terribly sad when Mom died. I see that now, but how can I explain that I'm sorry?

Luke forgave Gaird for leaving. Macon forgave me for lying about Gita. Gita wasn't angry with her mother or Morone for not realizing what Manju was doing to her. She taught me about this openhearted kind of love. I grab the dish towel off the fridge and dry my hands. "Dad," I say, "he doesn't want to be buried. It's just the way Luke feels about it. It doesn't have anything to do with you. He loves you. He adores you." I don't want to hurt him. He's already hurting so much. It has got to be the very worst hurt of all.

He scratches his beard and fills the glass again and drinks. Then he nods and doesn't say anything, because we don't have any more words for what this is. I walk out of the kitchen and run into Betty in the back hall, coming out of the bathroom. "He's having a good night, Willie," she says. "He's not in any pain." I smile at her and go sit down next to Luke.

This isn't how I imagined it, even though I have no fixed idea in my head because I've never gotten to this point. What I hope is that he's peaceful. Gaird sits and rubs Luke's hand and talks to him very quietly in Norwegian. Betty sits in her own chair and watches over the room. Dad comes in and stands at the head of the bed. It's one o'clock in the morning now.

I have to convince myself all over again that my mother isn't on her way. Dad looks so tired. He moves over to the couch and falls asleep. Gaird says he'll lie down for an hour in the bedroom. I stare at Luke's breathing. Then I'm in India and there's the smell of creosote. I felt so alive in that country, but so far away from my brother.

He's my history. I don't have a childhood without him. It's erased. Because he had my parents first, and they were his touchstone—his world order. Then he had me. But I had him first and then my parents. His chest moves up and down rhythmically for two hours. Then his breathing changes. Without any warning, it becomes labored and thicker. There's a rasping sound—in and out and in and out. I stand and lean as close as I can over his mouth and watch and listen. Then his arms and legs twitch under the blankets. I call to Betty. She jumps up from her sleep and checks Luke's pulse.

Each of his breaths is hard now and comes slowly. Part of me knows what's happening, and part of me is too removed. It's been such a sharp decline. Oh God, he's leaving. Our childhood's a lie now. The camping trips a lie. Because if it ends here in a hospital bed on Avenue Victor Hugo, then that's terrible. That's awful. I stand next to Betty in the dark and hold Luke's hand and I'm completely with him. Twinned to him. Then I'm separated from him and there's no way to articulate it. It's more than sadness. It's the emptiness that I've been terrified of. I feel completely dry. The EKG machine plays one long, extended high note. I look over at the nurse—the stranger I've come to trust—and I say, "Tell me. Tell me, Betty."

"You loved him. I could tell that the minute I met you. That you two were good for one another. I saw how you took care of him." She gently places Luke's arms down at his sides and stands for a minute with her head bent in prayer. Then she turns off each of the machines and walks toward the kitchen and leaves me alone with my brother.

It's happened so quickly and quietly that my father hasn't even woken up. I stand and don't say a word. It's too soon. I want more time. I have things to say, if I could just be given more time, please. Betty will come back from the phone, and Dad and Macon and Gaird will wake up. "Can you hear me?" I whisper close to Luke's ear. "I'm saying good-bye now. I'm saying it, and I know you can hear me." He's still warm—still with us partly. His face has gone slack and peaceful. His jaw is finally relaxed.

I climb up onto the bed and lie with my weight on my right hip so I don't press down on his body. My lips touch the skin on his left ear. "This is the part we didn't talk about, so you've got to help me out. Tell me you're okay." I can't stop the tears. "I'm missing you and you've only just left and you didn't tell me what to do when this part came." I close my eyes and push my face into his shoulder. "Don't leave without telling me." I cry out a little more loudly. I try to swallow the sobs by clenching my teeth, which makes my chest heave. The whole bed shakes. The grief is raw, and it comes for me.

When I open my eyes, my father takes my arm and pulls me up slowly. I sit on the edge of the bed and kiss the top of Luke's hand where the veins run. I kiss it. Then I kiss it again. Dad pulls me so I'm standing in his arms and I make a moaning sound. No words, just the sound.

Macon runs into the living room and gets me to lie down on the rug near Luke's bed. The moaning stops just as quickly as it began. Gaird walks in next, half-asleep, and cries out, and doesn't stop crying.

THE PARAMEDICS DON'T come back until after dawn. They wear purple latex gloves this time and move around the living room, packing things up. Then they wheel Luke away on a stretcher. I watch from the living room window while they put my brother in the ambulance. Two vans pull away from the curb. One carries my dead brother, and the other carries the EKG machine, the metal IV pole, three cardboard boxes of unused saline, and the hospital bed.

Luke shouldn't be alone on the way to the morgue. So I get my bag. "I'm going with him."

"No, you're not," Macon says.

"No, I'm going to follow the ambulance, because he shouldn't be in there alone. What were we thinking, letting him go by himself like that?"

"You've said good-bye, Willie. Please don't do this." He takes my arm.

"How do you know I've said good-bye? I haven't even begun to say good-bye, and please take your hand off me!" I'm yelling now. "My brother's alone with strangers driving to a morgue I don't even have the address for, and I'm following him there!"

"You don't need to go to that place!" Macon's yelling now, too. "It's not what you do now! Goddamnit! Just stop! What you do now is let me make you something to eat. Then you lie down on the couch and you rest."

"Then what? And then what?" I can't stop myself. It's the part after this that terrifies me.

"Then I will still be right here."

By now the vans are gone. I go and stare at the street for a minute. "Okay. You've made me miss them. Okay," I whisper. "You win. But I still want to go out. I haven't been outside in days."

"I'll come with."

"I'm just getting flowers. I'll just have a quick walk alone. Please."

"Promise?" He looks at me. "Promise I can trust you."

"It's fine." I stare back at him. I walk to the flower market on Rue St. Didier and ask for calla lilies. I go back to the apartment and cut the stems under the faucet and place them in a glass vase on the mantel. I call Luelle at the academy and explain that Luke's dead and that I won't be coming in to teach next week or the week after or maybe ever. I'm scarily efficient. I call Sara next. She answers right away.

"Luke's gone." I don't cry. My voice is flat. "He's gone. He died in his sleep. I'm so glad you got to say good-bye. I'm so glad you came yesterday."

"Oh, Willie, he was such a good brother. Such a good friend. Oh Jesus, I'm so damn pissed off at this disease. Is Macon there?"

"He is. He's right in the kitchen, cooking."

"Do you want me to come over? Lily and I could come over right now and be with you."

"I'm okay. I'll call you soon. I just wanted you to know. I couldn't live with the idea that Luke was dead and you didn't know."

I put the phone down. I'm not okay. But the whole time I'm floating somewhere above my body, and none of it's real. Macon has scheduled the cremation for Friday. At any moment Dad might sneak a call to the Paris morgue and change the instructions, so I guard the phones. I'm in the sadness entirely. Then I'm observing it from somewhere above and it's crazy-making. To be in it is better than to be observing it, I decide. My mind can't slow down. Can't help circling and circling. I know this feeling of losing Luke—really losing him—is just settling in now deep in my bones and in my bloodstream and in the web of veins around my heart and that it will get worse before it ever gets better and I observe this cliché and see it for what it is—a sickening thing. Worse before it gets better. I'm observing again. Better to be feeling. But I can't control my mind like that. It's much stronger than me today. Playing tricks.

Dad comes out of the den before lunchtime, looking like he's been crying. "Do you want lunch, Dad? You should really eat something. Macon's making chicken soup. It's important that you eat. Why don't you have something with us?"

"I'm fine. I had toast. I'm not hungry. I think I'll go to church. Then on to the airport. I have a flight home tonight."

"That soon? You're leaving? I thought we'd have more time." I mean this but I'm also the tiniest bit relieved. Or maybe even more relieved than that. Maybe I'm glad he's going, because Dad requires an effort. Too much. I'm not capable. And I wish I could reach him. I wish we could prop each other up, but that's not our history. Maybe we're too much alike in ways I never knew before. Maybe we each need to be alone.

"There's nothing left for me to do here right now. I'd like to go home. I want to be in the house. I want to be around your mother's things."

I stand up from the couch and hug him. It's a long hug, and he's crying quietly—an old man crying in the hall by his dead son's front door. Then I cry, too. He says, "Say good-bye to Macon and Gaird for me. I've never done good-byes. I'll call you when I land."

"You never call, Dad," I laugh. "I'll call you. How about that? I'll call you and see how you're doing."

"That would be fine. That would be good."

Then he leaves, and I go back to the couch and I don't get up the rest of the day, except to pee. I don't want to eat, either. I'm not hungry, no matter how many times Macon tries to serve the soup. Down on the street, a mother uses her arm to herd her two daughters into the back of a waiting car. My mother could have made Luke better. She would have known things to say to him. She would have known what to do, and he would have lived longer.

Gaird comes home. He's been with Andreas and Tommy all day. Then he takes a nap in his bedroom. When he wakes up, he walks into the living room and embraces me on the couch. He says his friend Clarisse—the one with the stiletto heels at Andreas's party—is cooking dinner for all of them. I nod from the couch and say, "That's good. That's nice." But inside I'm thinking, *How could you leave us? Leave the apartment? How could you be with anyone else but Luke and me and Dad?* And still another part of me is thinking of how much I don't want Gaird to stay. And how relieved I am that he's going. I don't want to talk to him. I just want this unspoken thing. This shared grief. Then he's gone and I'm alone and it's better.

Macon finally doesn't ask me about the soup; he just brings two bowls into the living room, and we eat on the couch. "We shouldn't sleep here," he says. "I think it would be better if we went home. It's been a long time since you were in your own bed."

I nod. When I finish the soup, I stand and get my coat from Luke's bedroom. "Let's go home. I want my mother."

Macon turns out the lights. "I know you do." He takes my arm, and we walk down the hall.

"You didn't know my mother, did you?" We're out on the sidewalk, Luke's sidewalk, and I'm confused. It's such a warm September night. The air is soft and sensual, even, and bitter with all this sadness.

"We can take a taxi." He leans into the street to hail a cab.

"I remember now. You never met my mother. She died first."

35

Homecoming: a return to one's home; an arrival

y mother took to her bed when she missed my dad. I've
always thought that's what you do when you're sad. So I
go to bed for most of September. I grieve for Luke every day. Sometimes I'm still so surprised he's gone missing that I want to get up and
look for him on the street or over at his apartment. Where is he? It's
almost been my undoing—this need to find him. My grief is private.
It's not something I can fully describe to Macon, and in a way that
makes it scarier. It's a leveler. My brother's dead, and I'm not.

I like to be in bed because I'm lower to the ground and somehow
this makes me feel closer to Luke. I keep the fan on and read on top
of the sheets. Sometimes I try to smoke in Luke's honor, even though
I hate the taste of cigarettes. Macon wants me to go to my office at the
academy and teach and work on the Sarojini, but nothing has made
me get up yet. The academy was my old life, where I read small notes
from Luelle on bits of scrap paper that told me my brother was dying.

Will I drive Macon away for good? Sara calls every day and asks
me if I'm angry. She thinks anger will help. She wants me to punch
something. A pillow or a wall. I can get angry at politicians who've
slowed down the research and doctors who may be in over their heads.
But my anger doesn't last, because I'm really just sad. A long sadness
has moved in, and it doesn't surprise me except how pervasive it is. His

dying is this physical, visceral thing to me now. A long O of sadness. I used to think about getting sick when he was sick, but now I seem to be really sick. Feverish. Sweaty. I have the dream that we're climbing the rock face together again, except this time it's Luke who's falling. He can't hold on. And I'm not asleep dreaming the dream. I'm wide awake.

Did I say "I love you" enough to my brother? That's what makes me crazy—all the looking back. Where is he now? I want to know much more about his dying. Some days I honestly think he will appear, and I let the rest of the world go. I don't feel indebted to anyone, and on these days I retain only the thinnest connection to Macon and Sara. I can't reattach the different parts of my life. My mother. My father. My brother.

Then it's October. Macon cooks eggplant in the kitchen for dinner one night. He's made so much food for us this fall it's like we run a small restaurant. "Willie," he says, bringing the plates to the table, "I went to the center on Rue de Metz today." I'm on the couch reading *Anna Karenina*. I stop when I hear him say the word "Metz." He says, "I think it might be time for you to go around there again. I think you should call Sophie."

"You didn't have to do that. You didn't have to beg to Sophie."

"I didn't do anything. It's my job to go there. She asked where you were. I told her about Luke."

"Sophie isn't talking to me. Besides, people mourn for entire years. They wear black and they don't leave the house. Luke hasn't even been dead a month. I thought it would be better after he died."

"It will get better."

"Sometimes it feels like I'm completely alone. Where is Pablo? It would be so nice to talk to him. We could all go to the playground in the Tuileries. We could go look at cheetahs at the zoo. Let's do that tomorrow—let's go back there."

"Pablo is in school." Macon takes my hand. "You could get dressed tomorrow. That might feel good. That might be a start. To get out of bed and get dressed."

It takes two more weeks. Maybe I go a little crazy. I fixate on things. I have cycles of repetitive thinking. It's almost like when the words used to appear. My mind plays tricks. I can't get Gita out of my head. I see her fully. I miss her like family. She's walking toward me sometimes in my head while I try to sleep.

Then one day I get dressed. I don't know why. I just do. I knew Luke better than anyone else in my life. Getting out of bed isn't going to change that. It just changes the shape of the grief. I call Sophie at the asylum center and hang up when the phone starts ringing. I'm afraid of what she's going to say. I dial her again. It's Tuesday morning, and she answers on the third ring. I don't hang up this time.

I lean against my kitchen counter with my eyes closed. "Sophie, it's Willie."

"Willie," she says flatly. "It's a busy morning here. How are you? I'm not sure I have time to be talking."

"I'm calling to tell you I'm sorry. So very, very sorry."

"Oh, you caused me some trouble. I had the OFPRA people here every day for weeks. They checked everything. All the sign-in sheets and the surveillance footage, and we had so many meetings you don't even know, about protocol and training and how to hire responsible volunteers. Of which I thought you were. Lord above, I really did. But this has also been my fault. My education. Macon told me about your brother. I have been praying for you."

"Gita was the first person who ever asked me to help her like that. I wasn't thinking about anything when I let her go. I wasn't trying to deceive you."

"I know about this. You got swept away on emotion, and there's enough emotion for us all in here to drown. You've got to stay the teacher. Not the friend. She won't be the last girl to ask you for help. Oh, the headaches you caused me."

"I hope you can forgive me someday."

"You should be asking God for forgiveness. You should be asking

Gita's mother. Because that woman must be worried sick about her daughter. You turned everything on its head."

"I think about Gita every day."

"By the grace of God, we hope she's okay. We hope all the girls here are okay."

"How is Precy? Is Precy still there?"

"Gone. Back to Monrovia. Oh, it was a hard day. Esther is here. She is the only one left from when you started teaching. She is the only one they can't find any family for."

"Is she speaking any louder?"

"She whispers. She needs you to come back and get her to tell some more of her stories. She spends too much time in her head. There's more pain in there than a girl should have to live with. So why don't you do that? Why don't you come back and teach a class for Esther."

"You would have me back there?"

"There is no law I am aware of that says volunteers can't be rehabilitated. You will be on probation. Do you think you'd be able to handle it again? Can you find a way to be just their teacher?"

"I can do that. I can get your trust back." I'm so grateful to her for giving me a second chance.

"God gives and he takes away and that is in the past now. Esther will be so happy to see you."

I WALK TO the metro at Place Monge on Thursday and get on the train and take it to the St. Denis stop. I make it to Rue de Metz and stand outside the orange door and wait. This has been my orbit—all winter and spring and the route is engrained in me. I can't stop myself from ringing the buzzer. Sophie opens the door. "Dear God, child, get in here. You cannot stand outside here and cry." I didn't even realize I was crying. The tears just come sometimes.

She pulls me inside and puts her arms around me in the hall, and I can't speak now because I'm crying so hard. I'm so happy to be with her. All the time that Gita's been gone, Sophie's been the person I wanted to cry with. She's the one who understands. She opens the door to her office. I sit on the stool. It's a small homecoming. She hands me the box of tissues and laughs so loudly. "Girl, you are going to make me cry."

"I'm crying because it's good to be here. You're kind to have me back. Have you lost people in your life, Sophie?"

"I lost people in Egypt before we got to France. Uncles. Cousins. My grandparents. We kept vigils. It was God's work—the taking of them. They are all busy in heaven."

"My brother died, and I tell you, some days I can't figure out how I let it happen. I was right there with him."

"God took your brother from you, but you cannot sit here in my office and pretend to yourself that you didn't do everything you could to save him. You would be lying to yourself, and you know how I feel about lies."

"But I did that, too. I lied to you."

"No more. We've covered it. You made a mistake. This is forgiveness."

"I can't get Gita out of my mind."

"You need to let her go now, too."

"I think maybe she's in Lyon. Maybe Toulouse. Or Rennes. I keep waiting for a sign. I've never stopped thinking she might contact me."

"You sent her off with a good boy. I want you to stop worrying over her now. Do you hear me? We have other girls inside here. Many of them."

I'M IN MY BED again when Sara calls. "What's the news?" Every day she asks me the same thing, and every day I'm grateful for it.

"The news is that it's colder outside than I thought and I forgot my sweater when I went to Rue de Metz and I'll start teaching there again next week."

"This means you've gotten out of the apartment! This means you've taken a shower! This is big. This is the first real news we've had in months!" The baby cries in the background.

"Which means you don't need to call so much, because I am now a professional grown-up."

"I like to call you. I like to talk to you. It's four o'clock and I love you, and the hope is that Rajiv will work from home the rest of the day and take the baby so I can meet you for a run in two hours. I need you to babysit for me on Saturday night. I need you and Macon to come, because I want to go on a date with my husband. I haven't talked to him since the baby was born."

I put my running shoes on while I listen to her. I haven't gone for a run since way before Luke died. I say, "I'm leaving for the river now because I have to stay far, far away from my bed. I'll meet you there."

On my way to the Seine I see a tall man with long brown hair walk out of an apartment building on Rue St. Michel, and I run toward him, sure that it's Luke. It isn't possible that my brother could be living in a single-family home near the intersection of Rue des Écoles. But it also isn't possible that he's gone from the earth. I want to turn around and go home. I want to go back to bed. Where are my brother's hands? And his eyes and hair? But I make it to the river. I don't wait for Sara. I can't. I run alone and it feels okay and I don't stop.

I call my father that night when I get home. He picks up on the second ring. "Jack Pears here."

"Dad, it's me. Willie."

"Well, is it now? I'll be damned."

"Dad, where have you been? How are you? I've been trying and trying the phone for days."

"Where have I been? Well, that's a funny question for a woman who never calls."

"It's good that you answered. I was beginning to worry."

"Well, it's timely, because I just returned from a walkabout. I was out near the Nevada border."

He isn't going to ask me how I've been. Does this make him a bad person? There's silence on the phone. "I wanted to let you know I was okay."

"Good, good." My father coughs. "I was just getting ready for a zucchini casserole. Your mother's gardens have gone hog wild. Did I tell you about the maze I've made out there?"

"You didn't, Dad."

"Well, it's big. Enormous changes. You'll have to come and see. I think your mother would really approve."

"You said you were thinking about some stones or something." I close my eyes. He's going to talk about the stones and act like we do this all the time—call each other on Thursday nights to check in before bed. But he's asking me to listen. I can do that.

"Well, I ripped up most of the flower beds. It was a hard decision—all the azaleas and phlox and the lilies and irises. But it was time, and now it's much easier to walk out there, and I think, frankly, the vegetables get more sun. Everything was too crowded."

"That's good, Dad. That sounds fine." It's heartbreaking to hear him try to go on without Luke. And brave, I decide. He's brave. Because he's a passionate man, and holding in such a great sadness alone can unhinge your mind. He's tending the sadness. Tending it. But privately. I know how private he is. How much he lives in his own head. And how stubborn. The tears start down my cheeks for how old he is now and how much he's working on the gardens and trying to change them into something new. Something my mother would love. More vegetables.

"The zucchinis are certainly happy. Everyone in one piece there?"

"Yes, I think so." I stare down at my feet. "Well, I can only speak for me."

"It's good that you called," he says. "You should have called sooner."

But I did call. I tried several times. He never answers the phone. It's hard to win with him. "I'm glad for that then. That's all I wanted to do—call and tell you I'm going to be okay."

He's the parent. I'm the child. He needs to do the things that parents do. My mother used to call me "lovey" and make me tuna fish sandwiches, and she also used to take to her bed. We grew up together in a way, my mother and me, and I can forgive her for that, too.

"Of course you're going to be okay." Dad laughs. "You're a force, you know. Always much stronger than you think. Paris is your place now, isn't it? You'll stay there, even now that Luke's gone?"

"I think it is, Dad. Macon's here. And Sara and Rajiv and the baby."

"Then really make it your place. Know it. Like the back of your hand. All the coordinates. All the side streets. Never feel like you couldn't find your way home. It may be a life's worth of work. And don't forget your brother's birthday next month."

"Dad, I would never do that." I feel sadness for both of us then. But I've got the tiniest bit of distance on my grief. People are allowed to fall apart sometimes. People get damaged, and they're allowed to go to bed. Then they get up. It doesn't mean they stop grieving. They just get up. "Dad, call me before you go on another walkabout alone."

"Will do. Will do," he says. "All right then."

On Saturday night Macon and I take the train to Sara and Rajiv's to babysit. I don't want to be out after dark. It feels like too much—the walk to the metro station and the cold wind. I'm nervous on the street. Tense. "Let's just go home," I say in the station. "Can we do that? Sara won't really mind, will she?"

"Sara will become homicidal if we don't go. I was the one who talked to her last night. She's counting on this."

We take the No. 10 and switch to the No. 8 and get off at the Lourmel stop. Then we walk to Rue Lecourbe in the fading light. Rajiv meets us at the door with Lily in his arms. It's the greatest thing to see the baby. She's almost four months old and holds her head up and stares right at me with her beautiful moon face and chubby little feet, and I take her in my arms and laugh.

Sara walks out of the bedroom with a brown clip in her mouth. She sticks it in her hair and says, "The nannies are here!"

"Are you actually going to leave us?" I rock the baby in my arms in the kitchen. "You're really going to trust us? I don't think I've baby-sat in maybe fifteen years."

"Well, here is the name of the restaurant." Sara shows me a notepad by the phone on the counter. "And here is the phone number. You'll be fantastic! I'm going to have dinner with my husband. I might not come home for weeks because that baby girl right there never sleeps."

I know what Sara's doing. She's working hard to make this feel normal. We're all finding our way without Luke—adjusting and searching for ways to cover our gaping loss. Because we have to live without him. We can't just stop. And sometimes, like tonight, it's better not to name the loss. I can see that now.

"We would be very happy to move in here and take over for you," Macon says, looking at the baby. "She is lovely, Sara."

"Just wait until you hear her scream." Rajiv smiles. "If she doesn't get her milk, she gets very mad, and she really doesn't like the bottle, so I wish you luck."

They leave, and I stand in the kitchen with the baby asleep in my arms, and I don't speak. I don't want to wake her. I smile at Macon. I see that I'm going to live and that Luke has died. If I begin to talk about it, I'll ruin it. But I see it. I've lost my brother, but he hasn't blurred like I'd expected. Certain things, like his long hair and his generosity, have taken shape in my mind. I don't have to hold on to him so tightly. This is how his death is going to become less frightening to me.

36

Courage: moral strength to withstand danger or fear

I go back to the academy on Monday. The woman they've had filling in for me has gotten through Albiach and is halfway through Anaïs Nin. It's good to be on my feet, circling the classroom. Then I spend three hours in my office, sorting through the Sarojini papers. It will take months. That's okay. Sarojini was such a fighter. I try to imagine the Indian prison she lived in for almost two years. Then I read her poem about "high dreams" again and smile. How could I have inflicted it on the girls at the asylum center the way I did? It's hard for even me to understand the language. Or what Sarojini really means with these dreams. Maybe one high dream is her faith. Maybe another is her courage. My book will be about sorting all of this out.

Then it's Thursday, and I wait on the stoop at Rue de Metz. Someone has added to the wall of graffiti. There's an orange bird of peace there now. At least, I think it's a dove. And doves mean peace. And there's an electric-blue fish, and this feels right, too. The wall looks perfect. Truffaut buzzes me in. I walk into the common room and put my bag down on the floor. I get out the mithai I've brought and unwrap the plastic and put the sweets down on the table. Then I wait for the new girls.

Sophie comes and sits with me. I'm very nervous. She says, "The girls are always changing faces. You'll see these girls need your help as much as Gita did. As much as Moona did or Rateeka or Precy or Esther."

Here's what I think happened to Gita. She and Kirkit left Paris that day as planned. It would have been a scandal for them to be traveling alone like that in India—an unmarried girl with an older, single man. But they were in France, and they could flout Indian customs. They went to Kirkit's aunt's apartment. Then south down through the working-class neighborhoods where the new immigrants live. I'm betting Kirkit's aunt had other friends in France—people she knew in the central cities. I can see the couple there: both of them working at a restaurant not unlike Ganges. Kirkit is the cook. Gita helps people find their tables. She would be good at running a dining room.

Gita showed me how to risk everything. She got me to open my heart. And I'm trying to keep it open now that Luke's gone. It's my heart, after all. It's mine.

Seven girls come to the workshop that night, including Esther. She smiles shyly at me when she walks in, and I go to her by the door and embrace her. It's so good to see her again. There's a flood of memories—of the first class we had in this very room in January. Of the day Gita said she was my friend. The maps I'd spread out on the floor, and how each of the girls traced her own geography. Where are those girls now?

Esther sits down on the couch, and Sophie asks all of them to go around the circle and say their names. Then I stand and say, "Hello, my name is Willow, but you can call me Willie. Everyone always calls me Willie."

The girls are from Algeria and Bangladesh and India and Liberia. Macon told me that the courts are busier than they've ever been this fall. None of the girls look at me. I know about their conspiracy against the teacher. But they've shown up. That's all I ask of them on the first night.

"I'd like to talk about the word 'courage,'" I say. "You can use it in your stories for the courts. I think all of you show that you have courage by coming to this class tonight." I hand out the pencils and the notebooks with snowflakes. "I'd like to start by doing some drawing."

Sophie stands in the doorway, smiling and shaking her head. " 'Courage,' " she says to all of us. "It's a good word."

Gita understood the word, and she also understood hope. To walk away like she did was to have both, maybe. Luke had it too. He didn't seem scared in the end by what was happening to him. Even when Gaird and my father and I were talking about Luke's death at the apartment, I don't think we believed it would happen. This may seem surprising, but there was so much I didn't understand about the disease. After he died, I thought I might die. It sounds dramatic, but it was simple.

He was the person who could make me laugh more than anyone I've known. My beloved. He was family. And family can be everything. The girls open their notebooks, and a sob rises in my chest. Maybe I'm not ready to be here yet. I got to say good-bye to Luke and to Gita. How amazing is that? They would expect things of me tonight. They would want me to be strong and to also have hope and to be damn funny. The girls and I have three hours together. It's time to tell some stories.

Acknowledgments

First thanks go to my editor, Carole Baron, for whom my gratitude is unending. She understood this story before I really did. I'm indebted to her genius for knowing what to ask for and when. And to the way she embraces life. It has been one of my greatest gifts to get to work with her.

Thanks also to Ruthie Reisner at Knopf for her smart, nuanced edits and all her help. I'm also very grateful to Erica Hinsley, Bette Alexander, and Bonnie Thompson (Bonnie of extraordinary copy-editing talents) and to Maria Carella and Kelly Blair.

My agent, Stephanie Cabot, has been the biggest supporter of this novel from the start, and her readings have enriched the story in so many ways. I'm deeply thankful.

Thanks also to my friends and readers Sara Corbett, Caitlin Gutheil, Anja Hanson, Lily King, and Debra Spark for their wise input and for moving the book toward where it needed to go.

Next, to my father and mother, the most incredibly supportive parents. To John Conley for his wisdom and to Erin Conley for her sisterhood.

Thanks lastly to Winky Lewis, Katie Longstreth, and Lou Honore for their friendship during the making of this book.

The novel is for my kind husband, Tony. And to my boys, Thorne and Aidan.

In memory of Keith Taylor.

A Note About the Author

Susan Conley grew up in Maine. Her first book, *The Foremost Good Fortune,* was a finalist for the Goodreads Choice Award and won the Maine Literary Award for memoir. Her work has appeared in *The New York Times Magazine, The Paris Review, The Huffington Post, The Daily Beast, Ploughshares, Harvard Review, North American Review,* and elsewhere. She's received fellowships from the MacDowell Colony, the Bread Loaf Writers' Conference, and the Massachusetts Arts Council. She teaches at the University of Southern Maine's Stonecoast MFA Program and is the Jack Kerouac Visiting Writer at the University of Massachusetts at Lowell. She's also the cofounder of the Telling Room, a nonprofit creative writing lab in Portland, Maine, where she lives with her husband and two boys.

A Note on the Type

This book was set in Granjon, a type named in compliment to Robert
Granjon, a type cutter and printer active in Antwerp, Lyon, Rome,
and Paris from 1523 to 1590. Granjon, the boldest and most original
designer of his time, was one of the first to practice the trade of
typefounder apart from that of printer.

Linotype Granjon was designed by George W. Jones, who based
his drawings on a face used by Claude Garamond (ca. 1480–1561) in his
beautiful French books. Granjon more closely resembles Garamond's
own type than do any of the various modern faces that bear his name.

Composed by Digital Composition, Berryville, Virginia

Printed and bound by Berryville Graphics, Berryville, Virginia

Designed by Maria Carella